MEXICAN HIGH

A NOVEL

Liza Monroy

SPIEGEL & GRAU

NEW YORK

2008

PUBLISHED BY SPIEGEL & GRAU

Copyright © 2008 by Liza Monroy

All Rights Reserved

Published in the United States by Spiegel & Grau,
an imprint of The Doubleday Publishing Group,
a division of Random House, Inc., New York.
www.spiegelandgrau.com

SPIEGEL & GRAU and its logo are trademarks of Random House, Inc.

Book design by Caroline Cunningham
Photograph on pp. x–xi © Herb Lingl/aerialarchives.com

Library of Congress Cataloging-in-Publication Data
Monroy, Liza.
  Mexican high / Liza Monroy.—1st ed.
    p. cm.
   1. Teenage girls—Fiction. 2. High school students—Fiction. 3. Americans—Mexico—
Fiction. 4. Mexico City (Mexico)—Fiction. I. Title.

PS3613.O5377M49 2008
813'.6—dc22

                                   2007032219

ISBN 978-0-385-52359-2

PRINTED IN THE UNITED STATES OF AMERICA

10 9 8 7 6 5 4 3 2 1

First Edition

to my mother and Alex,

who gave me the greatest gifts

AUTHOR'S NOTE

This is a work of fiction marginally inspired by actual places and the lifestyles that accompany them. The International High School in the novel resembles the one I attended but this is not my story. It has sprung from imagination and possibility alone. Any resemblance to politicians, psychics, drug traffickers, rich kids, street kids, fathers, friends, enemies, ex-lovers, or myself—alive, assassinated, comatose, or dead—is purely coincidental.

Given the history of virgin births on both sides of the dualistic culture of Mexico, the man who has sex with the mother of his children symbolically violates the virgin; better to have sex with another woman, because it is possible then to enjoy the act without shame.

—Earl Shorris, *The Life and Times of Mexico*

I'd never been to Mexico City before—it was crazy there.

—Mickey Rourke

PART I

Summer, Fall

The Big Move

I'll never forgive my mother for naming me Milagro.

"Milagro!" she would yell. "Come down to dinner," "Do your homework," "Put that book down and get ready for the ambassador's dinner." I always said I'd do whatever she asked if she would only call me Mila or, even better, Jenny, which wasn't my name at all. At least Mila sounded like an actual girl's name, but my mother, Maggie (not short for Margaret, so I couldn't retaliate), wouldn't listen. She may have been a successful diplomat, but she was never one for compromise. Her stance on moving away right before my senior year of high school would prove no different. She wouldn't even consider letting me stay behind in Washington, D.C., where we'd lived for four years, the longest I'd ever stayed in one place.

I may have hated the name Milagro, but I knew why my mother chose it. After getting her degree in foreign languages at Berkeley in the early seventies, she moved back to L.A. to live with her parents. One month later, after thirty years of marriage, her cardiologist father left her mother for a Thai waitress just a year older than my mother, who was twenty-three at the time. He never apologized or explained, and my grandmother allowed no one to bring it up.

My mother dealt with her family's derailment in the only way she knew how: by taking off. She sold her car, quit her job at the farmers' market, and climbed onto a bus from Los Angeles to Tijuana. She had studied Spanish since high school, and by the time she'd drifted farther south to Mayan territory, she was fluent. She rented a room by the beach in Playa del Carmen, a town on the Mayan Riviera where expatriate types flocked for sun, beautiful beaches, and bohemian lifestyles. To earn enough money to support what soon became a traveling habit, she apprenticed with a jeweler and was soon making her own necklaces, earrings, bracelets, and rings, using unique Mexican charms called *milagros,* the Spanish word for miracles and surprises. The little bronze and silver eyes, crosses, hearts, fish, and houses were said to bring luck for whatever they represented. An arm stood for strength, a leg for travel. The mule brought fortune in work. Tiny kneeling saints answered prayers.

The *milagros* might have been responsible for my entire existence: Maggie was supposed to be infertile, having been given a diagnosis of premature ovarian failure as a teenager. So the biggest miracle-and-surprise was when she found out that she was constantly vomiting not from untreated Mexican vegetables or bad tap water but from pregnancy. When she told her best friend, Estela, a local Mayan girl with a thick black braid whose father was the town shaman, Estela pointed straight to my mother's *milagro* necklace. Since discovering the charms, my mother always wore a string of her favorites around her neck.

"Isn't this something you wanted?" Estela asked, seeming confused.

"Why would you say that?" Maggie said.

"You're wearing the hen, a sign of fertility, right here. And this one"—Estela took a tiny silver child between her thumb and forefinger—"means the wearer asks the saints for a baby girl."

"But it's physically impossible for me to get pregnant," Maggie said. "I've known for years."

"*Milagros*," said her friend, "work to bring about miracles. What did you think they were for?"

"Estela, what I *think* is that the doctor in America was wrong."

"You gringas," said Estela, smiling and shaking her head. I imagine she paused for a moment before the obvious question dawned on her. "*Magita!* Who is the father?"

The randomness of my conception always made me wonder if maybe Maggie, with her wild, free spirit, long flowing hair, and complete self-obsession, perhaps wasn't built for motherhood in the first place—and I'm not talking ovaries. Half globe-wandering hippie, half glamour girl, she was upper-middle-class L.A. breeding meets nomadic adventuress, with a romantic ideal of what a jet-set life might be. But for some reason that I suspect had to do with not being a statuesque, leggy blonde, international playboys weren't exactly inviting her to coast the French Riviera on their private yachts.

Maggie sold the *milagros* on the beach until right before I was born. Then she went back to her mother's house in West L.A., where the streets were all named after rural states: Montana, Nebraska, Iowa. She was only twenty-five. Three months later, she took an administrative job at the Mexican consulate, and sold my grandmother's prized Brandywine heirloom tomatoes at the farmers' market on weekends. One day at work, she heard that U.S. Foreign Service recruiting officers were coming through town looking to hire more women. She decided to take the exam that could grant her entrance into a whirlwind life in far-off places on diplomatic assignments. She passed, and a few months later we left L.A. for good. I was barely two years old.

My life became a blur of ever-changing cultures after that. My mother's job made us country-hoppers, gypsy vagabonds who came and went with the wind. When I landed in D.C. after Shanghai,

Guadalajara, Bolivia, Rome, Oslo, and Prague (in that order), I decided I'd make more sense as a person if I had an accent, but there was nothing I could do about that—I spoke perfectly American-sounding English.

As for my father, I'd never met him, but my mother admitted that he was Mexican, married, and that she'd had an unexpected one-night stand with him that summer in Playa del Carmen. She wouldn't tell me his name, or anything else about him; she even said she invented my last name, Márquez, simply because she liked the way it sounded.

"Milagro Epstein didn't sound good," she'd said. Maggie was all about keeping everything as harmonious as possible, even when that was impossible.

Still, I must have resembled the man, whoever he was. My mother had olive-toned skin and eyes so dark you could barely tell the iris from the pupil. She was the one who looked Mexican, not I. I had green eyes, a color people often mistook for the effects of colored contact lenses. My hair was naturally dark blond, lighter in the summer. Everyone always seemed surprised when I introduced myself as Mila Márquez.

"You're really Hispanic? You have that all-American girl-next-door look," said my best friend, Nora, a petite but enviably curvy half-French, half-African girl. We became close our freshman year in D.C., when Nora had the locker right next to mine at our Georgetown high school, which was mostly made up of international students. Her father was the Kenyan ambassador.

"It's true," I said, clasping my lock shut and spinning the dial. "I must be the only blond Mexican ever." Only when we arrived in Mexico City, four months before my seventeenth birthday, did I find out that I was but one of a million light-haired, pale-skinned Mexican girls, and they all seemed to go to ISM, the International School of Mexico.

~   ~   ~

The week after I took my SATs, everything changed. I'd spent the afternoon at Nora's house in Bethesda. We were working on a science project, making model DNA strands out of toothpicks and little balls of colorful Play-Doh.

"Isn't it amazing how it all comes down to DNA?" I mused, making a bright-blue clay ball between my palms. "Your fingernail shape, your eye color . . . probably your entire personality."

"It even predetermines if you're gonna get cancer, right?" Nora said.

"How's your mom doing?"

"Well, since DNA is so unique, she can't find a wig that's her exact hair color. Did I tell you she dyes her wigs to get them as close to right as she can?"

"She does?"

"Yeah, with those little boxes from the grocery store. Wanna see?"

"Sure."

We ran up to the bathroom. I held the box of Nice 'n Easy Blue Black up to my face in the mirror.

"I bet my eyes would really pop if my hair was this color."

"Dare you to try it," said Nora.

Being a straight-A student was a simple cover for the troublemaking streak in me. I was never one to pass on a dare.

"You have beautiful light hair!" my mother shouted when I got home that night. "How could you ruin it like this? We'll be in Mexico City before it will even have a chance to grow out, and they just *love* blondes in Mexico."

"What do you mean, *Mexico City*?" It was the first I'd heard about the move.

"This wasn't quite how I'd planned to tell you." She shook her head, slowly, deliberately, from side to side. "But now you won't stand out."

Stand out. So typical, I thought, remembering the time she'd made me pose in a leotard in the snow when I was four in hopes of molding me into a department-store-catalog supermodel. ("Just a second longer! Just one more shot!") She was like a stage mother, except I wasn't an aspiring actress.

"How long were you going to wait to tell me if I hadn't dyed my hair?"

"I was going to mention it, Milagro."

"Mom. Mila. Please."

"But you're lucky to have such a beautiful name. No one else has that name."

"Because they were born to normal people." It was a dialogue we repeated over and over. "Can't I stay here? I'll live with Nora and her parents. I'm newspaper editor next year. And I'm supposed to be cheerleading captain!"

I wanted to graduate with my friends. I was close to people for the first time in my life, having finally been able to stick around one place long enough to form real relationships. Knowing that I wasn't going to move again after a year or two had made me actually try.

"You'll develop new interests in Mexico," said Maggie, having no idea how accurately she was predicting the future with those words, or how far those new interests would be from what she intended. "Besides, you know it would be too much of a strain on Nora's family, with her mother's situation right now."

She pulled off her navy pumps, undid her chignon with one swift pull, shook her hair out like one of those unnaturally happy shampoo models, and walked toward the kitchen to put water on to boil for Spaghetti Wednesday.

"We need to get you a new wardrobe!" she shouted from the other room. "All the Mexican kids will be wearing tropical colors."

I looked down at my black jeans and hooded dark-gray sweater.

"No way am I dressing like the Tropicana lady," I shouted after her.

"Then you won't fit in, and you'll be sorry," came the singsong voice from the kitchen.

After the movers came to take our furniture to Mexico at the end of the school year, we slept on mattresses on the floor of our apartment. I noticed the sound of my voice echoing when I was on the phone, and recognized this empty sound as a precursor to a vacant space formerly known as home. It meant that something was coming to an end.

The morning we lifted off toward our new life in Mexico City, I gazed out over the shrinking toy cars and houses, my mind drifting back to the events that had brought me here, to Mexicana Flight 865, climbing to cruising altitude at five hundred miles per hour, my mother's face hidden behind her newspaper, me with my journal and pen in hand.

"Milagro," said my mother, snapping me out of my thoughts. "Turn that Walkman off. We're starting our descent."

Dr. Dre halted mid-"muthafucka" and the sound of the jet engine roared in my ears. I took a sip of bottled water. No tap water for the next year, I thought. Maybe tap water was one of those simple, ordinary things that I would miss, one of those details you notice only once they're gone. Or maybe it was only the kind of thought that would cross my mind at a rapidly decreasing altitude when my ears were popping and I was hoping we didn't crash into the huge volcano below us. I noticed the flashing lights on top, warning signals to wayward aircraft. Houses crept up the volcano's surface, then stopped suddenly in an exact line as though there were an ordinance not to build anything above it. From up in the sky, Mexico City looked nothing like D.C., or anyplace else I'd ever seen. I knew that my mental layout of D.C. city streets, movie theaters, favorite coffee houses, and museums would soon be replaced by a new map. Ten thousand feet below lay a city that would gradually become familiar, whose streets I would eventually learn to navigate. I've always thought cities resembled people, with limbs and arteries, voices and personalities. Maybe it was a side effect of moving around so much, but I always knew that nothing influences a person more than the place she calls home.

I studied the faces of the other passengers, mostly Mexicans headed home from visiting the American capital. Below me were people who would eventually become friends, though for now they were as unfamiliar as the maze of streets, cars, and houses stretching for endless miles below. I had no idea who or what awaited me beneath the blanket of smog, and thought of my father—the stranger—walking the earth somewhere down there.

The week before we left, my mother had sat me down and finally told me the truth about him. She used to claim that she had no idea who the man was, that he could have been any of a number of people she'd been casually seeing. This was, after all, back when she was partying with the same intensity she now poured into her career. It was the late seventies, and the woman who would become my mother was drinking, dating, and basking in her freedom. I had always suspected that she was lying about the father story, though. I had a knack for being able to tell when someone was hiding something, maybe because I was good at doing it myself. So I wasn't completely surprised when she explained that she did know, after all, and that as much of a burden as it was to carry this secret, she couldn't reveal his identity, so I shouldn't even ask.

"I'm only telling you this because I want to be clear that you're not going to get it out of me. I don't want you to get any ideas that since you'll be in Mexico you might try to track him down," she said. "I wanted to get that thought out of your head before you even mentioned it."

"*Why* can't I?" I insisted. Of course the thought had already occurred to me.

"Because," she said, her tone matter-of-fact. "He's a public figure, and that was part of our agreement in negotiating the amount of money he gave us."

"You took his big check, and I can't even know his name?"

"It was cash," she said. "Now, come help me bubble-wrap my headboard."

My mother told me that the man had wanted to help with the cost of raising me, but also to keep her quiet, or to make sure she—and I—would go away. Counter to her intention, Maggie's revelation that he was a prominent figure made me all the more curious to uncover his identity. But in the largest city in the world it seemed impossible, anyway.

I pushed the seat-back button and jerked upright. The plane taxied over the sprawling dust bowl, still waiting for clearance to land. In Mexico City, there was heavy traffic even in the air. Smog and population stretched as far as I could see from thousands of feet above the earth. It looked as if a rolling pin had been taken to the city, expanding it in every direction.

"What's the volcano called again?" I asked my mother.

"Popocatépetl. It's still active," she said. "But it's dormant, at least for now."

"Comforting thought, Mom."

"Oh, you're only nervous about starting in a new school," she said, absentmindedly flipping through the in-flight magazine. "Don't worry, okay? My new boss's daughter is a senior, too. She'll take you around the first few days."

I wasn't really nervous, or at least that's what I told myself at the time. I decided I would breeze through this last year of high school and get on with my life in college, which I'd gotten excited about only after opening the envelope with my SAT scores and being pleasantly surprised by the numbers. I had always been focused on school, for lack of anything else to concentrate on. When I was "the new kid," a pretty perpetual state throughout my childhood, sometimes it was all I had. I wasn't going to care about whether I connected with anyone at ISM or not. Still, I didn't mind the thought of being introduced to a potential friend.

I looked out the window again just in time to see us coast over a tangle of huge, crisscrossing highways. We touched down with a bump, then skidded to a halt on the runway. People on the plane burst into applause, as if they expected the pilot and the flight attendants to come out holding hands and take a bow. *"Pasajeros y pasajeras, bienvenidos a la Ciudad de México,"* the pilot announced. *Ding.* Seat-belt sign off.

Maggie leaped out of her seat. "Quick, grab our bag from the over-head and let's squeeze out in front of all these people." I smiled to myself as I reached for the latch above. Whether in her career or a line to deplane, my mother always pushed to get ahead.

An Embassy driver holding up an EPSTEIN placard waited for us at baggage claim to take us to our temporary apartment near the Zona Rosa. We drove along the Circuito Interior artery, which was jammed with traffic; dividers in the road were a shade of yellow browned by exhaust and pollution, and the sky was a flat, hazy gray. The driver told me it was a red-flag day.

"What does that mean?" I asked.

"The *contaminación* is *muy alta* today, señorita," he said, lifting his right hand from the steering wheel to gesture toward the sky. "Stay indoors if you can."

The car rumbled forward. I scanned the gray buildings, the slab of traffic in the downtown business neighborhood along Reforma, Mexico City's famous large avenue. The scene was chaotic: street vendors milled about, men peddled bicycles trailing carts of colorful juices for sale, water-delivery trucks packed full of multigallon bottles idled near the curb blocking traffic, buses emitted black exhaust into the atmosphere. What is this place? I thought, nestling into the leather seat and closing my eyes.

"Hurry up, Milagro," Maggie chirped. "We're home!"

"What?" We were still in the same jam-packed zone of hotels, high-rise offices, and dreary brown-stained buildings.

"Come help me unload," said Maggie as she grabbed a suitcase the driver passed to her from the town car's trunk.

"So this is it?" I squinted up at the dingy apartment tower.

"Don't worry," she said. "Our permanent house is in Lomas. It means The Heights—doesn't that sound fancy? It'll be ready in time for your birthday."

"But that's three whole months away."

"We're right near the Zona Rosa. There are lots of shops, even a Mc-Donald's. You can walk around there as long as you're careful."

"Is it dangerous?" I asked, dragging my rolling suitcase behind me.

"Not if you blend in."

"I thought you wanted me to stand out," I said, just to get on her nerves.

She held open the building's main door so that I could walk through.

"You'll get used to it here the way you did everyplace else," she said, following me in.

"Why do you always have to be so optimistic?" I snapped.

The apartment had carpeting that was the same color as the smog, and government furniture, which looked as if it belonged in an office under fluorescent lighting, not in our living room. Maggie was unfazed by the décor. That night, after a trip to a nearby grocery store, she stood in the small yellow-tiled kitchen smashing avocados into a bowl, alternately squirting a lime and stirring in diced onions and tomatoes. Spaghetti Wednesdays were a thing of the past. Now it was Taco Tuesdays. My mother loved to adopt local customs wherever we lived, whether in the cuisine department or dating native men, and Mexico would prove no different.

She put dinner on the table, but I couldn't eat. I moved the shredded chicken taco filling around on my plate with a fork.

"What's wrong?" Maggie asked.

"I wish I knew even one person in this city," I said. A tear rolled down my cheek and fell straight into the bowl of guacamole. Maggie pulled the bowl toward her and slapped an onion-flecked green blob on a tortilla cupped in her free hand.

"Since you have a month before school starts, why don't I arrange for you to work at the Embassy? You'll meet people that way." She leaned across the narrow dining table and kissed me on the cheek. "I'm very proud of you, Milagro."

~   ~   ~

I've always kept diaries. They were the one thing I could count on, besides plane rides, to remember the details of my past. When you moved around a lot, there wasn't anyone to turn around to and say, "Remember that time a few years back when . . . ," the shared memories that I had come to view as the foundation of any human relationship. My journals took the place of that specific friend, the one who helps you see yourself more clearly than you possibly could. Maggie used to think I was hypergraphic, that I wrote to the point that it was some sort of compulsive problem. I also collected random objects. Nothing traditionally "collectible," like stamps, coins, or butterflies, but familiar objects to trigger memories: plane tickets, train tickets, restaurant matchbooks, magazines, and newspaper articles. I piled them in desk drawers, stuck them in purses. There was only so much for me to hold on to. When you lived the kind of life we did, "we" being the children of the Foreign Service, international business, and the other sorts of jobs nomadic families traveled for, you would go to a new place and reinvent yourself. It was always out with the old. Nobody ever kept in touch. Maybe you said you'd write, and maybe you did once or twice, but it was impossible to remain close. Out of sight, out of mind. I thought of Nora's infectious giggle and acute observations and hoped it would be different with her. That first night, as I lay on my bed, the unfamiliar sounds of the city six stories below, I wrote my first letter from Mexico.

July 30

Dear Nora,

Mexico City's huge and polluted, and there's a weird haze of gray in the sky even though you can tell that, behind it, it's clear and blue. I wish I didn't have to start from zero our senior year, in a new place where I don't know anyone or even speak the language. You remember how it is. Even though I've done it before, I was just a kid then and it's different now. I really hope we'll keep in touch. I miss you tons already. It hasn't sunk in that I'm not going to be graduating with you, Karim, Rob, and everyone else. I miss Karim so much. It's as though my life is there with you guys, going on without me, and I'm here, suddenly living someone else's life, or like this is a dream and I'm going to wake up, relieved, in my own bed. My mother says I'll get used to it here, as I did everywhere else, but something tells me this place is different. Or maybe I'm just different now. Isn't that all our environment is, after all? A reflection of who we are? Or are we reflections of our environment? In the detached, impersonal surroundings of cities, it seems like people are detached and impersonal, too.

Well, time for sleep, if I can. Say hi to your dad and mom. I hope your mom is still feeling better every day and that the rest of your summer vacation was great. I hope you had an amazing time on your Kenya trip!

Love always,
Mila

My energy was drained from the flight. I couldn't think of anything else to say to Nora, and it crossed my mind that for the rest of the year my best friend would be delivered in the form of ink on paper. I sealed the letter, addressed it, and put it on my nightstand, making a mental note to give it to my mother to mail from the Embassy. That's how it always worked from abroad: we sent everything out with domestic postage and it went in some special military overnight pouch. Foreign Service life had so many intricacies, even when it came to something as mundane as the mail.

The summer of 1993 was almost over. Come September, I would begin my final year of high school in a city of twenty-five million people where I knew only one: my mother.

TWO

Visa Barn

Summer brings the rainy season to Mexico City. It poured the entire month of August. The weather is counterintuitive, thunder clouds rolling in after the hazy warmth of afternoon, when the sun beats down through perpetual smog, the thin air at the city's 7,400-foot elevation feeling even lighter. Then the sky darkens with clouds and the storms arrive, bringing pounding, monsoon-style rain. There were only two seasons: wet and dry. The climate, at that altitude, was far from sultry. Tropical colors were nowhere to be seen; people dressed in palettes as dark and earthy as the city itself.

Maggie arranged for me to work in the visa section of the Embassy, called the visa barn because of its shape, though inside it felt more like a greenhouse. I'd ride in to work with her every morning, through our neighborhood, Colonia Cuauhtémoc, where the streets were named for rivers: Rio Nilo, Rio Ganges, Rio Niagara. My mother's new title was Chief of Citizen Services, which sounded really important but basically meant that she helped crazy Americans who got into trouble in Mexico City, or tourists who were robbed or kidnapped. There was plenty of that sort of work to do here. My job was simpler, wheeling carts of passports back and forth, but I had no idea quite what I was in for.

On my first day, I got my picture taken for my Embassy ID. The receptionist in the photo-ID department laminated my badge and handed it over.

"Wait here," she said, looking at her computer screen. "Dave Johnston is coming by to take you down to the visa section."

I didn't expect Dave to be close to my age, but he was a summer temp, too. He looked about eighteen and was tall and built like a football captain, with floppy blond hair that spilled over his eyebrows and into the bluest pair of eyes I'd ever seen. His head was covered by a blue Dallas Cowboys hat. It looked funny with his baggy pin-striped suit. Still, he never took it off.

"Hi, I'm Mila," I said. I smiled and made eye contact as I'd read in a *Seventeen* article on how to flirt. It worked—his lips parted and I saw two rows of straight, white, post-braces teeth. He looked at my shoes. He seemed a little shy in spite of his homecoming-king looks.

"Dave," he offered. "Welcome to Mexico."

"Thanks. Have you lived here a long time?"

"Not too much longer than you. I've been working in the visa barn for almost three months, thanks to my parents." He glanced around to make sure no one was in earshot. "It sucks."

"Really? Why?"

Dave's eyes rolled skyward. "You'll see."

We walked across the Embassy compound toward the visa section, which was right next to the street, since so many hordes of people had to come in from the outside.

"Have you moved around a lot?" I asked.

"My parents got transferred here from Manila, in the Philippines, but I grew up in Dallas, mostly." He pointed at the hat, and I nodded.

"I was in D.C. the past four years. I think I might hate it here."

"It'll get better. You have to remember that those shithole apartments on Reforma are only temporary."

"How long did you have to stay there?"

"Still am. Seventh floor. The side of the building facing the front."

Though Dave seemed to hate the apartments as much as I did, I felt a rush of excitement that the cute boy was now the cute neighbor.

"I'm on the sixth. Same side."

"So I'm right on top of you," he said, and smiled again. I felt my face flush.

"I think maybe I'm down on Mexico City mostly because I haven't met anyone yet," I said, brushing my hair out of my eyes.

"You've met me."

I practically floated the rest of the way across the grounds, until Dave was holding open the visa-barn office door.

"Come on," he said. "I'll show you how a thing or two works."

Inside the barn, one overworked fan propelled air onto the sweaty masses. They were already flustered with impatience, because the visas weren't given out in any particular order. Applicants who arrived at six in the morning didn't necessarily get processed before those who got there at noon.

It was the strangest summer job ever. I'd scooped ice cream, delivered pizzas, and torn movie tickets. Here, I had to physically make the visas, from entering applicant information into the system to printing and laminating them. When the plastic cooled and the visas were done and ready, like cookies on a sheet coming out of the oven, I cut them individually and slipped the glossy cards one by one back into the passports. I didn't have to alphabetize them—order wasn't required— but I did it anyway. It was a semblance of reason that I could bring to my job, a little organized touch in the chaos. Then I rolled a big metal cart out into the main barn area and distributed the passports back to the public.

The job might have been easy if it weren't for the visa screamers.

"*Señorita!*" they would yell. "*Donde está mi pasaporte?*" "Where is my passport?"

"No es mi culpa," I'd yell back, putting my *Introduction to Spanish* knowledge to use as best I could. *"No puedo hacer nada!"* "It's not my fault. I can't do anything!" I understood why they were angry. It was a level of disorganization that turned me off from bureaucracy for the rest of my life, and years later I blamed my distaste for office work on this experience.

The applicants lined up at five or six in the morning and by the time the Embassy opened the line extended around the block. There were rows of benches for the lucky early ones to sit on, and some enterprising applicants brought lawn chairs to rent out.

Many were desperate. One woman handed in an application for a tourist visa for six months. As with every form, it had her passport-size photo stapled to the top left-hand corner. As I processed the data into the computer system, I couldn't help noticing the only thing she'd written in the "Reasons for visit" box.

"What do you plan to do in the United States besides go to Disneyland?" the junior officer asked.

The woman's expression was blank. *"Pues, nada."* "Well, nothing."

"You're telling me you're staying at Disneyland for *six months*?" he said. "Denied."

"Pero solamente quiero visitar a Mickey" was all she said before starting to cry and being escorted away by security. Like many of the fabricated stories, hers didn't add up. When I told my mother about it that night, she explained that "going to Disneyland" was a classic story, that maybe the woman really *was* going there but she wouldn't be riding It's a Small World or eating cotton candy with her kids. She would be looking for work cleaning hotel rooms or busing tables.

It didn't take me long to see that far more people were turned away than granted access. Most of the applicants couldn't prove sufficient financial ties to their country. "What will stop you from staying in the United States?" was the starting-off point for every interview. The visa officers were junior Foreign Service workers on their first tour of duty. Often, they seemed even more disillusioned than the applicants.

"How's the barn treating you?" asked Maggie as we sat in standstill traffic on Reforma. Every day it was the same question.

"I hate it, Mom," I said. "It's depressing. I hate seeing people get denied the chance for a better life, even if they are trying to get to it illegally."

"Milagro, people can't just flock into the U.S. because their own country doesn't provide them with opportunities."

"It's hypocritical. America was founded on 'Give me your tired, your poor.' "

"That changed."

My mother saw in black and white. She was uncomfortable with gray areas and always tried to tie up every conversation with a string and a bow, or with a stamp of approval like the paperwork she dealt with all day. Done deals were good, ambiguity bad. Maybe that was one of the reasons she was so effective in her career, but it made me feel trapped. I got quiet and looked out into the windows of the other cars around us, wondering about the lives of the people whooshing around the city inside those steel sardine cans.

"What are you up to after work today?" Dave asked on Friday, as we rolled our carts next to each other out of the back office, toward the podium.

"Getting dinner with you?" I offered with a wide-eyed blink, surprising myself with my boldness. I usually felt shy around boys, however confident I pretended to be. But nobody knew me here, so it was a chance to reinvent myself. People made character judgments so fast that the window would be open for only so long.

We went to the Zona Rosa and got take-out burgers and greasy fries, then sat up on the roof of our building. I could see a helicopter landing pad on a hotel in the distance, one of the tallest structures around. Dave lit a Marlboro Light and held out the pack to me.

"Want one?"

I shook my head. "I don't smoke," I said, biting a fry in half and chucking the other half at a pigeon that had alighted on the ledge. "What section of the Embassy do your parents work in?"

"They're on the fifth floor."

I knew then not to ask any more questions about what Dave's parents did. The fifth floor was different from the others. The first four floors were open offices, people running around in a frenzy preparing visa papers, helping Americans in trouble, and talking on the phone with the Mexican authorities. The fifth floor wasn't like that at all, which I discovered one cloudy afternoon when I couldn't stand the visa barn anymore and decided to do some exploring inside the main building. I pressed five in the elevator, hoping to discover a way to get onto the roof and catch a good view of the Ángel de la Independencia— the huge twenty-four-carat-gold angel in the *glorieta*, a traffic island in the middle of Avenida Paseo de la Reforma. Instead, the elevator doors slid open into an empty hallway silent as a catacomb. On either side of the hallway were doors you needed a code to open, a code that I later found out changed every few minutes. No one who didn't work on the floor could enter. Even then, there was a machine that scanned the dark-suited men and occasional women down to their eyeballs. The area was home to the CIA, the FBI, and the DEA. I dubbed it the secret-acronym floor. So Dave's parents were spies.

"Hey, Mila," he said, exhaling a stream of smoke. "I want to ask you something."

"Shoot."

"Are you still a virgin?"

"Why, do I seem like one?"

I felt my cheeks burn and didn't wait for him to answer. "I had a serious boyfriend, Karim, in D.C. We had very elaborate plans for senior prom, and it was going to be so romantic and everything."

"Why didn't you do it before you left?"

"I thought about it, but I wanted it to be special, as cliché girl talk as it sounds. It was important to us. But it would only have made it harder to leave him, so we broke up instead." I stared into the distance, trying to pinpoint where the city ended, an impossible task.

"After all that waiting?" said Dave. "Seems pointless. I was thirteen."

"And you're what, all of seventeen now?"

"Eighteen. Legal drinking age in Mexico. Not that it matters. But you don't want to get it over with?"

"I'm not really in a rush. I'd think about it if it was the right guy."

"We'll probably get to spend a lot of afternoons alone together, if you're"—he paused and leaned closer to me—"ever interested."

I laughed nervously. Maybe, I thought, as he leaned into our first kiss. He was slow, intense, as though he were concentrating on every move of his mouth. I couldn't tell him the real reason I was a late bloomer at sixteen and a half. Since I'd been a little kid, I'd been hearing Maggie through the bedroom walls of our houses, with different men. She was so loud, I always wondered if it was pain that made her cry out so wildly. It made me queasy, and that was the feeling I came to associate with sex, though I was trying to get over it.

I opened my eyes. The sun was setting through the smog, behind a black skyscraper with a helicopter landing pad on top. Every sunset in Mexico City looked apocalyptic. Dave was experienced, I could tell. I slowly let down my guard, hoping that we would fall really fast for each other, that I could start the year off with a boyfriend. At least then I'd have one necessary element of high school in place, and the others— friends, popularity, grades—would follow.

An hour later, I went downstairs, still tingling in the spot between my legs where he'd touched me. It felt new, even all right. The sun had descended in the orange haze over the skyscrapers along Reforma, and my mother was chopping onions in the kitchen for yet another Mexican meal.

"Look what I learned how to do just now," she said, holding out a platter of tortillas that I imagined she rolled with her usual focused intensity.

You're not the only one who learned something new today, I thought as I walked down the hallway to my room.

~   ~   ~

Orientation at ISM was the next morning, so I had the day off from the visa barn. Sisley, my mom's boss's daughter, was picking me up to take me to the school. She'd been going there since seventh grade. I was excited to make a friend who'd introduce me around. Still, I lay in bed that night unable to sleep. A periodic shrill, high-pitched whistle echoed incessantly through the street below. It started out a low groan and escalated to a shriek: *Brrrrr-rrr-eeeeee-eeeeeeeeeeet,* over and over. I opened the window and looked down, craning my neck to see a man pushing a little cart with some sort of steam whistle on it, but I couldn't figure out what he was doing.

I'd never seen ISM other than in the fancy brochure, with its pictures of a lavish campus complete with a huge pool, and kids every color of the rainbow smiling with their arms around each other's shoulders. Maggie presented me with two options soon after telling me about the move: the International School of Mexico City or the Gates Institute, a British school that offered the intense European international baccalaureate program I'd been following at my D.C. school, which had tons of students from other countries. The ISM brochure said its three thousand students were 85 percent Mexican, 10 percent American, and 5 percent Other. That didn't sound very international to me, but the Gates Institute had a half day of classes on Saturday, and no way was I doing that. I was angry about the move and wanted to have a little fun for a change.

"I'll go to this International School," I told Maggie, sliding the colorful catalog across the kitchen table.

"Are you sure?" she said. "What if at the last minute you want to go to college in Europe?"

She was all about options, options, options. "Look, I decided, okay?"

I didn't want to talk about it anymore at the time, because I was still in the phase of pretending that we weren't really going. But if I had to go to school in Mexico I might as well go to one where most of the kids were Mexican. They'd probably be more welcoming than Gates, which sounded snobbish to me.

"You're lucky you can go to this school," Maggie said. "Just look at the price tag!"

I'd skipped the tuition section because we didn't have to worry about things like that. The U.S. government paid for my school—one of the many perks of Maggie's job. All she had to pay out of pocket was our phone bill and food. Everything else was taken care of by tax money. I flipped back to the page and my eyes widened: Forty thousand U.S. dollars per year.

"Better be one hell of a high school," I said.

"Don't say 'hell,'" said my mother, still flipping through brochures. "Hey, here's a French academy. Want to learn French?"

The doorbell rang promptly at nine. I opened the door in my new, tight jeans, white button-down blouse with embroidered flowers, and brown suede Keds, an outfit I thought was school-girly and just sexy enough with the top two buttons undone. I felt put-together and ready. Until I saw Sisley, in a burgundy velvet jacket, lipstick and hair to match, hip-hugging jeans with holes, and big steel-toed combat boots that were so worn at the toe that the metal showed through. She looked much older and more sophisticated than me. I'd seen her father, my mother's boss in the Citizen Services Department, and he was five-two, going bald, and wore thick glasses. Sisley looked more like a girl who played bass in her boyfriend's punk band than someone who played flute in the ISM Philharmonic. She sort of sneered when she saw me, and looked me up and down. I knew she was thinking I was too ordinary to be seen with her. Her pouty dark-purple lips finally parted.

"Hey," she said. "Let's go."

Without waiting for an answer, she spun around, flung her burgundy hair over her shoulder, and walked to the elevator. She jammed her finger repeatedly on the button.

"That won't make it come any faster," I said.

"Whatever. I just want to get to the school thing and see my friends."

"What do you guys do at orientation?"

"It's volunteering, you know, hanging signs and helping the new kids find their way around. Really, we just like checking them out ahead of time. Sometimes cool people move here and other years . . . well." She eyed me again. "Let's go."

Great, I thought. She hates me. I needed this to go well. I wanted the stunning, artsy Sisley to be my first girlfriend, or, even better, I wanted to *be* her, save me the trouble of acclimating, plus I'd have an edgier look and buoyant C-cups. I didn't care that waifs had ruled the runways and Calvin Klein ads that year; I hated my boyishly skinny body and the fact that I had the option of whether or not to wear a bra. Sisley was the epitome of alterna-chic, that look that was so popular in the early nineties it even trickled all the way down south of the border.

We got into her gray Chrysler and rode up Reforma for ten minutes without speaking.

"Do you have a boyfriend?" I asked, trying to break the silence.

"Yeah, for a couple years," she said. "His name's Tyler."

"Does he go to our school, too?" I hated my obvious attempts at conversation, but I couldn't stand to go the whole way without talking.

"He's older than we are, but he dropped out. He's not into school. He's more, like, philosophical and self-taught. He reads about Che Guevara all day and stuff, writes manifestos for the revolution, and plays guitar."

"Um, what kind of revolution?"

"I'm not really mainstream," she quipped, ignoring my question. For the rest of the ride, Sisley sang along to loud music with indecipherable lyrics that I later learned was a new band called Nirvana, so popular that they practically put Sisley exactly in the place she was most afraid of: commonness.

The Tacubaya neighborhood was as poverty-stricken as most of el D.F.—el Distrito Federal—as locals called Mexico City.

"Well, here we are," said Sisley, as she rounded the corner of a tall gated complex. "Good old ISM."

"This is it? It looks like a maximum-security prison."

The school was a fortress. High, peach-colored concrete walls provided a pastel illusion of pleasantry, a distraction from the fact that they were topped with barbed wire to shield the campus from the dangerous neighborhood outside. Even the run-down houses a few blocks away had their own version of security: amber-and-green glass from broken beer bottles implanted atop their walls, protruding like jagged teeth from cement gums.

Sisley parked near the entrance and we passed through a guarded gate, where we had to show our picture IDs and sign a form.

"You can't leave campus during the day," said Sisley. "Unless, of course"—she nudged her shoulder in the guard's direction—"you give him a *mordida*."

Mordida? I searched my limited Spanish vocabulary. Didn't that mean . . . ? "You bite him?" I asked, recalling the word's translation. Sisley rolled her eyes.

"Well, literally it means 'little bite.' You don't, like, physically sink your teeth in. It's more of a metaphor, see, you *pay* him. Money is, like, magic here. You'll learn."

Sisley waved to a girl with a shaved head and some boys in leather jackets and flannel shirts. "Have fun," she said to me, and I thought I saw her sneer again. She pulled a pack of cigarettes out of her back pocket, took one out, lit it, and went to join her friends, who resembled budding rock stars, with their wallet chains, piercings, and tattoos. I looked down at my tight, waist-high jeans and tucked-in blouse. I was going to have to do something about my wardrobe. If I could make friends with Sisley, maybe I could get her to take me shopping. I was just thankful I hadn't taken Maggie's life-ending advice about tropical colors.

I followed the signs to the auditorium and settled into an uncomfortable, hard, blue fold-down chair for the orientation talk. I looked around for Dave but didn't see him. Principal Perez, a stout, stern orange-haired woman, and Vice Principal Horney, a gray-haired Brit with a most unfortunate name for a high-school administrator ("Hoah-neigh," he pronounced it), stood onstage behind a podium. They lectured for an hour about after-school programs and all the clubs and sports ISM offered: the Community Service Leadership Team, Model United Nations, the Italian Club, water polo. We new students were promised a fantastic education and a culturally broadening experience.

"It's also worth noting," Mr. Horney said, "that here at ISM we have earthquake drills as a standard once-a-month procedure. We're always at great risk for an earthquake here in Mexico City." As Mr. Horney launched into the plans for renovating the computer lab, I got to thinking that if my life weren't on shaky enough ground already, at least I was sitting right on top of a massive fault line.

Afterward, we were ushered downstairs and outside to the *palapa*, a gigantic straw umbrella, to sit at benches, eat tacos and rolled-up fried tortillas called flautas, with sauces far spicier than we were used to, and mingle. I spotted a good-looking blond boy I'd seen in the auditorium and sat beside him, putting my plastic plate of food and sauce down next to his.

"This sauce is out of control," he said. "Stay away from the green stuff, unless you want to expel something the same color out the other end."

"I think I just lost my appetite."

"Sorry about that," he said. "I'm Ken."

"Mila."

We nervously nibbled the edges of our food.

"Are your parents at the Embassy?" I asked Ken, looking for common ground.

"Nope. Missionaries."

"Missionaries?"

"We're Mormons. Huge community down here in Mexico. My family just moved from Ogden, Utah."

"Wow, really? Do you like Mexico?"

"It's so different," he said. "I haven't quite gotten a handle on it yet."

"I know. I don't usually get overwhelmed by things, but this city redefines the concept of enormous."

"Totally." He smiled. "And it's so not what I expected. Some of my friends back home were, like, 'So, Ken, will you ride to school on a burro?' "

We both laughed.

"They'll have to come visit you," I said. "Then they'll see about burros."

"There are probably more donkeys in Utah than in this town," he said, making me laugh again. Then we came to the inevitable awkward pause in the conversation, which I quelled in my usual way, by pretending that I urgently had to be someplace else.

"Is it two o'clock yet?" I asked.

"Five till."

"I'm supposed to meet my friend for a ride home," I said. "It was nice meeting you."

"Good luck, Mila. See you around."

Ken stood when I did, threw the rest of his lunch in the garbage, and went to join a table full of similar-looking blond kids, presumably also Mormons from Ogden, Utah.

I found Sisley outside the gates, smoking and talking with her friends, who laughed a lot at their private jokes. I sat along the concrete ledge at the base of the tall fence that would contain me within ISM's walls from seven to three, Monday through Friday.

"Do you want a cigarette?" a guy who looked like a teenage Keanu Reeves asked. He had a pierced eyebrow and wore a silver-studded black leather jacket.

"I don't— I mean, sure, I could really use a cigarette right now," I said, trying out the phrase and smiling at the boy. One thing I'd noticed was that, like a sort of "Fuck you" to the pollution, everyone in Mexico City seemed to smoke. *It's all about blending in with the culture,* my mother's voice echoed in my head as I reached for the Marlboro Light. I knew she didn't mean smoking, but I didn't care. From moving around so much, I'd learned that I had to do whatever it took to slip into my surroundings unnoticed. And my surroundings here felt dangerous. The ISM students dressed and acted older, and everything seemed huge and intimidating.

The dark-haired boy bent toward me, flipped open a silver Zippo with a skull insignia, and lit my cigarette. I gulped blue smoke and stifled a cough. A gray puff came out my nose and I glanced over to make sure no one was noticing that this was the first cigarette of my life. But they were back to being absorbed in conversations about the great parties they'd gone to over the summer and people I didn't know whom they couldn't wait to see again. I'll get this right, I thought, taking another, smaller puff and trying to enjoy the taste of toasted chemicals in my mouth.

"I've gotta go, guys," Sisley finally said. "Mila has to get home."

I stood up and stubbed out my cigarette underfoot. "Bye," I said to the group, offering a wave and worrying that I stuck out, not a chameleon but a gecko on a glass window.

"See ya," said the guy who'd given me the cigarette. He hadn't told me his name, and I'd felt too shy in front of the group to ask. I wished I could evaporate into the smog.

"That was Kai," Sisley said as we walked toward the car. "Kaiosaki. Isn't he cute? He's half Japanese, half Mexican. Good DNA."

"I want a jacket like his. He's adorable."

"Unfortunately for us girls, he also happens to be gay."

"Really?" I didn't know anyone out of the closet at my old school.

"Yeah, he gets a ton of shit because Mexico is so homophobic. It's the Latino machismo thing. You could have told him you didn't smoke, you know."

"Sometimes I do."

Sisley gave me a skeptical glance.

"So, what do you think of the lovely ISM?" she asked. I ignored her sarcasm. I desperately wanted to love my new home. She unlocked the car doors and we got in.

"It seems all right. I think I just have to adjust."

"You will," she said, her voice muffled from holding the cigarette she was lighting between her lips. She exhaled, and for the first time that day I saw her smile, just a slight upturn. "It takes some people a little more time to find their place."

Her comment stung, but I pretended it didn't faze me.

"Have you gone to an international high school before?" she continued.

"My school in D.C. was pretty international."

"No, I mean a real one, abroad."

"I haven't lived overseas since the eighth grade."

"Then there's two things you should remember," said Sisley in her best authoritarian tone. "Everyone's rich, and no one has parents."

"What do you mean?"

"Everything's cheap here, including labor. The people at our school have drivers and maids and all kinds of stuff you'd never imagine. The important people's kids even have bodyguards who sit outside all day and wait for them."

Sisley threw the car in gear and barreled out of the parking lot's high steel gates.

"And their parents," she continued, "are totally self-involved. They have so much money, they shower their offspring with stuff—whatever they ask for. They *always* travel—for work, pleasure, or some combination of the two—and the kids stay home with the maids, go to school, and party like crazy at the bars and *antros*. That's Spanish for 'clubs.' "

"That sounds pretty cool," I said, trying to be nonchalant. Sisley changed lanes without signaling, dodging squat little microbuses called *peseros* and the ubiquitous green-and-yellow VW bug taxis.

"If you're into nightlife, which, no offense, you don't look like you are, it's fucking amazing."

"Where's a good place to shop for new clothes around here?" I asked.

"Like what kind?" She eyed my outfit again.

"The kind that wouldn't make you think what you just said."

"I only go to the vintage stores in La Condesa, but don't even think about going all copycat on me."

"Wouldn't dream of it," I said. "Thanks for the tip."

On the ride down bustling Reforma, I noticed that all around the city, walls were painted green, white, and red, the word COLOSIO in big black letters in the center.

"What does that mean?" I asked, pointing to the signs. Sisley sneered again and said the elections were coming up, that Colosio was the favored candidate, basically a shoo-in. She told me he was a member of the PRI, the Institutional Revolutionary Party, which had ruled over what had been called "the perfect dictatorship" of Mexico for almost seventy years. Colosio was at least an honest politician, she explained. He opposed his party's corruption and the government's alliance with drug cartels. I guessed Sisley's Che Guevara revolutionary dropout boyfriend had something to do with her eloquence on the subject of Mexican politics.

I got back to the apartment and wrote in my diary until I heard Maggie's key turn in the lock. I stashed the notebook under my mattress and went to meet her in the living room.

"How was orientation?" she asked, dropping her briefcase and the mail on the dining-room table.

"I need to go to La Condesa before school starts."

"Why?" she asked.

"My wardrobe doesn't seem to be appropriate."

"What did I tell you? You should have listened to me."

"I'm not talking tropical colors, Mom. No one wears them. Not even close."

"Well, you'll have to show me what they *are* wearing, then." She waved a hand dismissively and went into the kitchen. "Hey, I found out what that whistling sound is. I asked a Mexican lady at work today."

"Whatever it is, it's been keeping me up all night."

"It's a guy selling sweet potatoes," she said triumphantly. "Apparently they're pretty common."

"Potatoes? Why does it whistle like that?"

"It's the steam. The noise attracts customers."

"At least now we know we can get a potato at midnight," I said, plopping down on the ugly gray couch.

"I hope he doesn't keep you awake again tonight," said Maggie. She sat down beside me, put her arm around me, and jiggled my shoulder in that way mothers do when they are trying to pep you up. "Cheer up, Milagro," she said. "It's your last week of visas before school starts. This is the beginning of a whole new life for us."

"Yeah," I said. "I guess so."

"I'm so glad you're excited. Oh, you got a letter today," she said, plucking one of the envelopes from the table. I snatched it up, recognizing Nora's loopy handwriting in her favorite pink pen. I smiled, thinking of Nora sitting at her desk, writing it, the hot-pink feathers on top of the pen jiggling wildly as she scrawled. I ran to my room with the letter and closed the door.

August 20

Dear Mila,

Thank you for your letter! I miss you so much. The trip to Kenya was great as usual. We got back yesterday. Mom's doing well—the doctors say she's really in remission! I hope you won't be upset, but they made me cheerleading captain since you moved away. And I have more big news: Rob and I had sex. . . . It was really, really everything I ever hoped for. He took me out on a date, to a really nice dinner and everything. They even served us red wine—can you believe that! The restaurant was so superfancy, I guess they just assumed we were Georgetown students. Next year we will be! I'm also applying to Princeton, Columbia, BU, and Tufts. How about you? Can you come visit for Thanksgiving? And guess what?! My dad said I can visit you in Mexico sometime, too. Write back and tell me all about it. Do you have a boyfriend yet?

    Love you, too!

Nora

I'd never realized she was such an exclamation-point fanatic. Funny how people can come across completely different in letters. It sounded like Nora was moving on without me, busy with cheerleading and losing her virginity to Rob. I missed Karim, regretting that I didn't just do it when we were still together, and I wondered whether I'd meet anyone I liked enough in Mexico. I folded the letter and put it away. I'd write Nora back later, once I had good news to share and maybe a "yes" to that boyfriend question. I hoped we would keep in touch and that she'd really come visit. Old friends always said that when you moved away, usually right before they disappeared.

I caught Dave staring at me through the glass wall between the barn and the back office, where he laminated visas as I called out names and handed back passports. We were in that limbo state between friends who kissed and dating. A black-mustached man in a plaid shirt and a cowboy hat tapped me on the shoulder, bringing me back to the job at hand. "I've been waiting since seven in the morning," he said in Spanish. I looked at the clock: 3:29 P.M.

    "*Disculpe,* there's nothing I can do," I replied as I turned back to the microphone and called other, lucky visa recipients up to the podium. "Juan Rivera . . . Maria Hidalgo . . . Lucinda Cruz . . ."

The cart squeaked on its wheels as I pushed it back to the office to collect more trays of passports from Dave.

"Want to have a drink after work in the Zona Rosa?" he said. "We can hang outside in the beer garden."

"I'd love to," I said, "but I don't turn eighteen for another year and three months."

"You're young for a senior."

"My birthday's in November. You're either a year older or younger than everyone when that happens. My mom went for me being younger, of course. 'Push to get ahead,' that's her motto."

"No one cares here, anyway. They don't card. The saying goes that if you're tall enough to see over the bar, then you're old enough to drink."

It always stayed light until eight in Mexico City. We crossed Reforma, passed the Ángel de la Independencia, and then diverted into the supremely touristy Zona Rosa. It translated to the Pink Zone, which at first I thought was because the area was popular with gay people, but then I found out that most of the buildings in this part of town actually used to be pink. Dave and I walked through the streets, which were all named for European cities: Londres, Hamburgo, Florencia. The Zona Rosa was the only place in the city I'd seen that was built, logically, in a perfect grid. There was the chain music shop called Mixup, with its trademark industrial-steel sign, Burger King and McDonald's alongside traditional taquerias, and American-import shops like Guess? and Levi's. The pretty architecture was Spanish Colonial, according to the Mexico City guide I'd bought at the Embassy gift shop. The houses around here were called *casas porfirianas,* because back when Porfirio Díaz was a dictator and lived in the gigantic Chapultepec Castle, perched up on a steep cliff, the Zona Rosa was a major residential area. Today it was basically all commercial, touristed, and chaotic. There were some tree-lined streets with little cafés and bars, and Dave led me through a restaurant that opened into a back garden. We sat in plastic white chairs at a plastic white table underneath a Corona umbrella, and Dave asked the *mesero* for two *cervezas.*

"*Claro, joven,*" he said, and walked away. Dave leaned in toward me.

"So these twins who are seniors at ISM are having a welcome-back party at their house on Saturday. Do you want to go with me?" he asked.

"How do you know them?" I asked.

"My dad was in some secret society at Yale with their dad, George Rothman," he said. "Mr. Rothman's president of the Globe Bank, and he's been working here for a few years. We went to their house for dinner last night. Man, you should see this place."

"If their dad's president of the Globe Bank, it *must* be nice. Where do they live?"

"Lomas de Chapultepec, straight up Reforma to the north."

"That's the neighborhood my mother and I are moving to the weekend of my birthday. Getting out of the Embassy building will be the best present ever."

"Ours is going to be someplace called Herradura," he said. "I guess it's pretty far away, almost an hour's commute."

"Those fifth-floor people and their privacy."

"Shut up," he joked. "Anyway, it won't be ready for a while. Family that's in there now isn't getting transferred for another six months."

The waiter brought our Coronas and we pushed the limes in.

"So will you come to Nina and Naldo's little *fiesta* with me or not?" He pronounced the word in three exaggerated syllables, so it came out *feee-yes-taah*.

"Your accent is cute," I said, batting my eyes flirtatiously and hoping he couldn't tell that it was calculated. "Sure, I'll go. I'll probably have to be home by midnight or something, though."

"Don't worry about it," Dave said. "Their parents are away. We can stay all night. Just say you're sleeping at a friend's house."

"What do you think of this one?" My mother was pointing at a painting of a woman with a basket of calla lilies, possibly the worst Diego Rivera rip-off I'd ever seen.

"I don't know," I said. "A little clichéd."

It was bright and still way too early on Saturday morning to be hunting for typical Mexican décor for our future house. Earlier that morning, I had been dreaming of earthquakes. The quake gathered force, ripping apart the concrete of the city and jarring me awake. Maggie was sitting next to me on my bed, shaking me by the shoulders. I was a deep sleeper and turned over, squeezing my eyes shut and pulling the pillow over my head.

"Bazaar del Sábado!" she'd cheered. "We have to get an early start before things get picked over." It was the agreement we'd made: first, Bazaar del Sábado, then, if I was helpful with the paintings, shopping in La Condesa. So there I was, in the outdoor art market in the San Angel district, where typical Mexican crafts and decorative trinkets were sold, mainly to tourists, for *muchísimos pesos más* than they were worth.

"Milagro, this is *Mexico!*" said Maggie, opening her arms as if to wrap them around the plaza. "The colors, the crafts, the mariachi . . ." She got this elsewhere look in her eyes and I wondered whether when she was in her twenties in Playa del Carmen, making jewelry and sleeping with a married guy, she cared about colors, crafts, and mariachi.

"How can you say that?" I said. "This is like a show. It's a carnival, or a circus."

"Be respectful, Milagro. It's also the livelihood of all these people."

"You think any of this would be here if it weren't for *tourists?*"

"We're not tourists," she said.

I cocked my left eyebrow at her, the only one I could arch voluntarily.

"What?" She looked at me accusingly. "Tourism fuels the economy!"

"All I'm saying is it's sad that it has to." I changed the subject so our discussion wouldn't escalate into an argument, which seemed to happen every time we talked these days. I wasn't proud of it, but avoidance was one of my primary tactics. Confrontation always made me feel like a five-year-old caught with her hands in finger paint, standing in front of a wet red, yellow, and green splotched wall.

"I'm going to a sleepover tonight," I said.

"You mean *may I* go to a sleepover tonight. How is that possible when you haven't made any friends yet?"

"I met this girl, Nina," I said, almost forgetting her name. "She goes to ISM. She's a senior, too. She's from Argentina, apparently."

"Apparently?"

"I mean she is. From Argentina," I said, trying to hide the fact that I hadn't actually seen Nina in person yet.

"Where did you meet this Nina?"

"Dave introduced me to her, at lunch during work," I lied. "Her father is head of the Globe Bank and met Dave's father at Yale."

As I suspected would happen, Maggie's entire demeanor changed when she heard that I was associating with someone from an "important" family.

"Oh, wonderful!" she said. "And do I need to ask if her parents will be home?"

"Of course they will." I smiled and put an arm around my mother's shoulder. We were exactly the same height now.

"Be sure you get picked up and dropped off. I don't want you going around the city by yourself, at least not for a while."

"I'm perfectly capable of getting around, Mom."

"Milagro—"

"All right, okay. I'll get rides."

She looked satisfied and went back to the papier-mâché toucan statuettes she'd been eyeing. "What do you think of hanging some of these from the kitchen ceiling?"

"Um, yeah, they're . . . great. They're beautiful, Mom," I said, picturing getting ready for the party in the snap-front plaid shirt, burgundy leather jacket, broken-in 401s, and black nail polish I was imagining finding in La Condesa.

Nina came down to the gate when we buzzed, all cascades of long dark hair and floral perfume. She was gorgeous, tall and long-legged in her

high-heeled snakeskin pointy boots and tight Versace jeans, her features as delicate as a model's. I could tell right away that she was one of those free-spirited girls who could fit in anywhere and get away with saying or doing pretty much anything.

"Hey, sexy," she said to Dave, planting the customary kiss on his cheek. "Good to see you again, my friend." Then she kissed my cheek. Her breath smelled of lemons and tequila. "Nice to meet you, Mila. Love the jacket."

I, too, loved the new burgundy leather belted jacket that I'd found at a funky thrift shop. The shopping expedition had worked; I had the beginnings of a new look that was more in line with Sisley's alternative style than with my old preppy gear.

"Thanks," I said. "And thanks for inviting me." Pearl Jam blasted out of the two-story mansion. I scanned the crowded room behind her.

"Half the school is here," she said. "I'm totally surprised, since no one does these parents-away house parties like in the States. We usually go to clubs and bars, so I guess it's a nice change to stay home on a Saturday night."

If this was "staying home," I couldn't wait to see what going out in Mexico City was like. There was a static freedom here that seemed to pulse through the atmosphere. I could feel its pull. Nina clasped my hand and we weaved through the crowd toward the bar.

"Where'd your parents go?" I asked, raising my voice above the music.

"Globe Bank conference in Buenos Aires. It's my dad's business trip, but of course my mother simply *had* to go along," she said, affecting a socialite's inflection and smiling. I liked her already.

"What about you and your brother? They just leave you here alone?" I still wasn't sure that Sisley hadn't been exaggerating what she told me about everyone being rich and virtually parentless.

"You really *are* new, aren't you?" Nina teased, her concentration all on slicing the limes she'd lined up on the kitchen counter. "My brother and I aren't unusual. The 'rents are wrapped up in their own shit. Dad's got his high-powered bank job, and Mom loves the fuckin' spa—in

Tokyo. They figure Concepción and Rodrigo are always around. My brother and I had to pay those two a little extra *not* to show up for work this week."

Nina talked fast, stray wisps of dark hair falling on the cutting board, their ends mingling with the lime juice.

"Concepción?"

Her huge eyes darted up from the cutting board. She pushed her hair out of her face with her forearm, licked lime off her fingers. "Our maid. Rodrigo's the driver."

"What kind of name is Concepción?"

She shrugged. "A pretty normal one for here. It has to do with, like, extreme Catholicism, obviously."

Maybe Milagro wasn't that weird after all, I thought, for the first time ever.

"Where are you from?" Nina asked, pouring us two amber shots from a bottle labeled Herradura. I'd never drunk tequila before and wondered if it would taste as repulsive as it smelled, like acetone.

"Tough question," I said. "I was in Shanghai when I was really little, but the first place I remember living in is Guadalajara. Then we spent two years in Bolivia, two in Rome, one in Oslo, then Prague, Washington, D.C., and now here. . . ."

"My dad's from D.C. We lived there for a while, too. Trust me, you'll have *way* more fun here. It's crazy." She handed me a shot glass and held hers up to her lips. "Ready?"

I smiled and nodded.

"Arriba, abajo, al centro y adentro!" she shouted, waving the tequila shot around before throwing it back. I followed with mine and almost gagged, the burn in my throat and nose was so intense. I grabbed a slice of lime from the counter and sucked it hard. I should've eaten dinner, I thought.

"You don't look American at all," I said when I recovered, a bit light-headed now, and fuzzy.

"My mom's from Buenos Aires. I consider myself Argentine. Trust me, you don't want to say you're from the States at school."

"Why not?" I asked, but she'd turned around and was screaming and hugging a pixieish brown-haired girl who'd come up behind her. I poured myself another shot of tequila and downed it fast. It wasn't so bad. I threw back another, and wavered back out into the swarm of people to look for Dave. He was standing in a big group of guys, next to a boy who was a male version of Nina, tall with blue streaks in his dark hair. Her twin brother, Naldo.

"There you are!" Nina grabbed my hand. "Come on, I'll introduce you to my brother. He's a total skate punk, but really into school and water polo these days."

The guys wanted to play drinking games, so we lined up more shots on the coffee table. I was extroverted and rambunctious, thanks to the alcohol, and loving everyone I met. By the time I realized that a ninety-five-pound girl probably shouldn't do five shots on an empty stomach, the living room was spinning and I couldn't remember what Nina said the moment the words came out of her mouth. I went to the kitchen, crouched below the marble-topped island, and ate four slices of bread I got from the fridge. Then I found the twins' parents' room and collapsed on the bed. I felt like I was on a boat, rocking on the ocean, and thought it was the effect of the tequila until I realized that I was actually lying on a water bed.

When I opened my eyes, there was a silhouette standing over me.

"Are you all right?"

"Dave?" I said.

"Yeah, it's me," he said, moving out of the light and lying down beside me. We kissed a little, then he got back up, switched off the light, and closed the door. In the darkness, I noticed a full moon shining through a skylight in the ceiling.

"Can you ever see the stars in Mexico City?" I asked.

"No," he said. "Too smoggy."

The moonlight cast an eerie midnight-blue glow over the room, like a scene from an old spy movie—a film noir. I titled it in my head: *Son of the Fifth Floor.* I may have giggled out loud, though I don't remember.

"Are you drunk?" he teased, tickling my rib cage.

"No! Okay, maybe a little. Just a little."

We started kissing again, deeper this time. I could almost feel my-self falling for him. I loved almost everything about him: how easy-going he was, the way his hair flopped into his eyes when he took off his baseball cap, the slight mystery of what was ever really going on in-side his head. There was nothing in the room but shadows. He sat up on top of me, legs bent behind him as if he were kneeling.

"It's perfect right now," he said. "Just you, me, and this water bed. I even brought protection."

"How could you be so presumptuous? I already told you, I'm not ready."

"Yes, you are," he said, as though I'd argued that my hair wasn't black or said it was snowing outside. He ran his hands down my arms to my wrists and kissed me harder. I tried to wriggle out from under him, but he was too strong and I was unsteady with drunkenness. He held my arms firmly above my head and pressed my legs down with his. I heard the sounds of zippers being unzipped, felt the tugging of my jeans and underwear, the tearing of wrappers with teeth, the un-natural scent of latex. His breath smelled of alcohol and he pressed his way inside, fighting back as I struggled, kicking and trying to yell, but the music was too loud for anyone to hear and I knew he'd locked the door, anyway. "Get off," I tried to say, but the words came out muffled. I was a piece of wood and he was a hammer with a nail, breaking through. After a while, I gave up resisting and waited for the pain to subside, and it did. I got wet; my body was rebelling against me, echo-ing Dave's words: *That's right, relax, just enjoy this.* There was no way to undo it now. I fixated on a dark splotch on the ceiling. Was it a stain? A *cucaracha*? My mind began to drift and I clamped my eyes shut, willing myself out of my physical presence, to fall asleep, to be anywhere but here. I silently recited lyrics to that children's song about a pot-smoking cockroach: *Ya no puede caminar . . . porque no tiene, porque le falta, marijuana que fumar.* I'd read somewhere that it dated back to the Mexican Revolution, maybe earlier. A soldier's song. A sarcastic hymn, a bizarre image, a joke. His breath was hot. I opened my eyes. Shadows danced across the ceiling. His nose in profile resembled an Alpine ski slope, and he smelled like aftershave mixed with sweat. His skin was damp, slick as oil. I imagined pushing his body into a giant deep fryer, listening to him scream and begging me to help as I watched his body burn away to nonexistence.

"Dave?" I said. It came out in two syllables, with my body moving above the undulating water. The sheet had slipped off and I felt the cold plastic slapping against my back, his warm body against my front. I was being torn apart, split open, suspended in limbo, filled with something. I looked down and saw him sliding in and out, an alien sight, like watching something that was happening to somebody else.

"You like that?" he said, over and over, so that it came out as *Youlikethatyoulikethatyoulikethat?*, until the words didn't sound like words anymore but became a perpetual drone in the background. I was a lost raft on a water-bed sea, caught in a storm, waves smacking its sides until it sprang a leak that couldn't be plugged. It was too dark to see color, but I wondered if the slippery wetness inside my thighs would be red. He groaned and then, as suddenly as he was in, he was out. The dim glow of the moon leaked in through the skylight. It was over, but I knew right then that the aftermath would be worse.

"You didn't come, did you?" Dave asked.

"What?" I couldn't believe he'd asked that. "Are you insane?" Tears welled up in my eyes, a familiar lump in my throat that meant my defenses were crumbling.

"Never mind, get dressed," he said. "I'm going back out to the party."

"Please, wait . . ." I blurted through sobs, but the door opened, a stream of light and ambient party noise passed through the room, and then the door clicked shut. So what were Dave and I now? I thought. How could he do this to me? Had I somehow given him the idea that it was okay?

I gathered the sheets around my body, tight like a papoose, and lay with my eyes closed. Eventually I must have passed out, because I woke up to beams of sunlight pouring between the blinds and the skylight, illuminating tiny dust particles on the other side of the room. I sat up, still naked in the water bed. "Everything will be back to normal soon," I told myself, fully aware that it wouldn't be. Small bruises peppered my thighs, and a few spots of blood dotted the mattress. Since it was a rubbery water bed, I just scratched the marks away with my finger-nails. I had to get rid of the evidence.

I dressed, stepped over sleeping bodies in the living room, and left the house, running until I reached the gate. Outside, I flagged down a *pesero*, a small green-and-gray microbus that cost a peso. *Peseros* had no official stops, and you could tell where they were going only if you knew the meaning of "Ruta 2" or "Ruta 4," painted inside a tiny trian-gle on the side. The other people on the squat bus eyed me, seemingly wondering what a girl like me was doing there. My sense of direction was acute, thanks to years of having to adapt to new cities, but I sur-prised myself by not getting lost, considering Mexico City's size. I got off near the Zona Rosa and started walking. I needed to do something mundane to make myself feel regular again, so I stopped at Mixup to buy a Discman to replace my Walkman, and a CD, one I'd seen on the floor of Sisley's car, Radiohead. I needed to hear that one song. It was always on the radio, and it would soothe me. "What the hell am I doing here?" the singer sang.

I paid the cashier and left the store. Buying something was such a simple, everyday act. I could never deal with anger by cutting myself, or not eating. Shopping was my tension relief of choice, spending money that I was supposed to use on practical things like lunch or a taxi on some little luxury instead. It made me feel that I was back in con-trol. I walked the rest of the way home, trying to block the image of Dave's face from flashing through my mind.

"Hi," Maggie said when I walked through the door. She put the Sun-day newspaper down on her lap. "Did you have a nice time at the sleep-over?"

"It was great," I said. "Really fun."

"How did you get home?"

"Nina's mom."

"She should have come up to say hello."

"She was running late. Spa appointment or something." I knew this was exactly the kind of thing Mrs. Rothman would be rushing off to do.

I went straight into the shower, and then shut myself in my room. I lay on the bed with one white oversized towel wrapped around my body and another on my head, twisted into a turban to absorb the water from my hair. I put a headphone in each ear to listen to my *Pablo Honey* CD on the Discman. Thom Yorke's ethereal voice calmed me, the songs transporting me away from my anxiety. I closed my eyes. When I opened them again, my mother was standing in the doorway.

"I want to take you out to celebrate," she said.

"Celebrate what?"

"You made sixteen hundred dollars at the visa barn. You can't put it *all* in savings." She smiled.

We went shopping at the Guess? store in the Zona Rosa, and then she took me out to a fancy fondue restaurant in Polanco, the Beverly Hills of Mexico City, of which Avenida Presidente Masaryk was the equivalent of Rodeo Drive.

"Aren't you excited for your first day tomorrow?" she asked as we strolled through Masaryk's strip of sidewalk cafés at dusk. I wished she would stop constantly asking if I was excited about stuff, especially since I wasn't feeling much of anything other than a desire to escape, to travel either far forward or backward to a place where it hadn't happened, or where enough time had passed to make it less immediate, less raw, or at least to erase the fading bruises on my legs. I went through the motions, the images from the night before growing fuzzier now, a film sliding out of focus.

I lay in bed that night, frozen and crying soundlessly. Tiny tremors shot through my body. My mother was fast asleep; I could hear her snoring like a truck downshifting on the highway. Through the window, I saw the infinite stream of cars going by and the people by the taco stand and the man playing guitar on the corner. I got up and washed my face in the darkness of the bathroom, splashing the cold water on my puffy eyes, then slipped out of the apartment and down the street. It was half past midnight, but traffic was still as heavy as it was during rush hour. Nothing slowed here. The deep-purple sky was bright with city lights. There were no stars. I walked into a *tiendita*, a little store that sold candy, soda, magazines, and bootleg cassette tapes.

"*Cigarro, por favor,*" I said to the vendor, giving my still embarrassing Spanish a whirl.

"*Que tipo?*" What kind, he asked, producing a giant tin full of loose cigarettes. Unbeknownst to me at the time, I had asked for just one cigarette, and it turned out they were commonly sold that way, under the table. I later learned that many people couldn't afford the price of an entire pack, which was the equivalent of two dollars that year.

I peered into the tin. How convenient that I wouldn't have to buy twenty smokes when I wasn't feeling entirely committed to this new habit. "Marlboro Light?" It was Sisley's brand, and now mine, too.

The man plucked a cigarette from the center. I grabbed a pack of Chiclets, held it up for him to see, and paid. Back at the apartment, I went out on the balcony, quietly slid the door shut behind me, crouched down, and lit my cigarette. I smoked until my throat felt used to the burn, irritation replaced by a new, adult-feeling pleasure, like what would happen with sex the next time, I hoped. I exhaled a long gray stream, my contribution to the already exhaust-filled air.

I stubbed out the butt and tossed it over the balcony, then eased back into the apartment. The nicotine only amped me up, so I turned on my reading light and grabbed some stationery and a pen.

August 23

Dear Nora,

I can't wait until you visit. I'm going crazy waiting for school to start. And speaking of crazy, there seems to be an insane amount of freedom here—we could go into a bar and no one would ask for ID.

No one even cares here. It's weird, like being completely on your own. My mother is clueless, as usual. I went to my first Mexico City party the other night. These twins who are seniors at my new school threw it because their parents were away. Nina is my newest friend, and her brother Naldo is friends with my boyfriend, Dave. Dave and I totally planned it so we could have sex. So that makes two of us! How was it with Rob? Honestly, Dave was kind of aggressive. But at least that's over with. The first time's always the worst, right? Well, except in your case. Your night sounds like it couldn't have gone any better. Call me if you can sometime: 011–52–55–5241–2600. There are so many people in Mexico City that the phone numbers need an extra digit.

Besos (kisses),

Mila

Before I could change my mind and tear the letter to shreds, I folded the envelope, licked it shut, and wrote Nora's address on the front in big block letters. It felt oddly therapeutic to recast what happened with Dave as my choice, to put the words down as fiction on paper.

I still couldn't sleep, so I sat outside on the balcony, feeling bewildered that I was really here in Mexico City: the oldest metropolis in the Western Hemisphere, the busiest city in the world, the easiest place to feel alone.

THREE

Cruising Altitude

Space does not separate people so much as culture.

—Mexican saying

The morning news always had a story about how the peso was devaluating. It had been three to the dollar earlier in the summer, and now, on my first day of school, it was hovering around twelve. In the past month, the poverty level had risen, the crime rate had skyrocketed, and a substantial portion of the already small Mexican middle class had nearly been destroyed. The streets became more dangerous almost immediately. Tourists were robbed by cabdrivers. The typical scenario involved them being driven somewhere, tied up, and all their money and credit cards stolen. Swiped U.S. passports went to counterfeiters. Then the victims were left along some shady side of the Toluca highway, where anything could happen. It was my mother's job to help them, and any Americans who ran into other kinds of trouble in Mexico. I had no idea there were so many possibilities: kidnappings, suicides off the balconies of five-star hotels, abusive behavior by macho husbands toward their rotund blond American wives in dusty villages, the theft of private jets out of Texas by Mexican drug runners.

The bright-yellow ISM bus picked me up the morning of my first day of school, a sign that read COLEGIO INTERNACIONAL NO 11 in the front window. I sat in the back and wrote in my journal. A novelty car horn played the theme song from *The Godfather,* and an old woman shrouded in black begged car to car for change at a stoplight.

There was a carnival at the intersection of Reforma and Esplanada, as if an invisible curtain had risen when the light turned red. A man walked up and down between lanes with individually wrapped bags of cotton candy, as another elderly woman in a black dress, her gray hair loosely draped by a shawl, sold *"chicles, un peso"*—gum for one peso. A fire-breather rinsed his mouth with gasoline and blew on his torch, projecting a stream of flames up into the air. A little boy with a black smudge on his face ran out into the middle of the street, wearing a clown costume with two inflated balloons on his bottom, held in place by elastic-waisted pants. In front of the row of cars on Reforma, he danced and shook. The balloons jiggled, creating the illusion that his derrière was twice the size of his head. Two other boys cartwheeled into the street, and the three of them crouched and jumped on one anothers' backs. They stood, the biggest kid on the bottom smiling, though his trembling legs betrayed the weight on his shoulders. The balloon boys leaped to the ground, bowed, and ran between cars, collecting whatever spare change drivers handed out. I watched them from behind the glass, wishing I could drop my lunch money into their plastic cup, but the school-bus windows didn't open. The light turned green. The boys scattered to the curb, and we rolled forward into another smoggy day.

In the hall between third-period calculus and fourth-period Mexican history, a girl said something to me in Spanish that I didn't understand.

"I'm sorry," I said. "My Spanish isn't that good. Yet."

I smiled and waited for her to ask the question in English. Instead, she shrugged, turned, and walked away, the Prada decal on her backpack receding with her every step. It was my first encounter with the icy treatment of the "outsider" kids by the Mexican élite: jet-setting, label-clad teenage socialites whose parents were all part of the small power circle that governed Mexico.

I ran into Sisley in the hall after the bell rang for lunch.

"How's it going?" she asked, looking around for her friends.

"This girl talked to me in Spanish, and when I didn't speak it back she totally snubbed me," I said.

"Was she a *fresa*?"

"A what-a?"

Sisley nodded, a knowing look in her eye.

"They're called fresas. Literally, it means strawberry. It's sort of like preppy, except they're far more chic. They wear, like, Gucci, Miucci, Pucci, Prada, and Fuck Yucci—you know, that cutting-edge Japanese brand." Sisley winked, laughing at her own joke. "There's even a 'Most Fresa' category in the yearbook. Except the yearbook's in English, so they call it 'Best Strawberry'—how retarded is *that*?"

"Why strawberries, anyway?" I asked.

"Think about it. What's the fruity-tooty-est of all fruits? Not apples or bananas."

"I'm partial to kiwis."

"That's already taken by Australians," she said.

"You mean New Zealanders. So why wouldn't that fresa talk to me in English?"

"Because they're, like, totally nationalistic," said Sisley. "Which is funny, considering they're rich and white and they repress the *real* Mexicans, the ones whose ancestors were actually born here. Tyler gets really pissed off about that. He's always ranting about it." She smiled in that familiar way of girls who pretend to complain about their boyfriends but are really just showing off the fact that they have one and you don't.

"So fresas are of European descent?"

"Exactly. They're Eurotrash with Mexican passports, only their passports don't hold them back like they would if they didn't have so much cash. And don't even think about trying to hang with them unless you speak Spanish without a trace of a gringa accent. They're very snobby that way."

It was as if a camera had pulled back to reveal a crowd of background actors whose costumes I hadn't noticed until then. Now I saw it. The fresas wore designer clothing and Italian leather shoes with, for the girls, very high heels. As I went from class to class, I now noticed them in the halls, standing in their cliques and sitting in front of the pool during lunch, gossiping and looking perfect. (Beatriz, a girl in my grade, went on vacation with a big nose and came back with a button. She subsequently won the "Best-Looking" category in the yearbook.) What shocked me was that, as an American coming to Mexico, I turned out to be one of the "underprivileged" in my school. I thought of my mother, the adventurer, with her lectures on the importance of blending in with the culture whenever we moved somewhere new. Or, at least, her version of the culture. Her Mexico—an idyllic land of tropical colors, upbeat mariachi music, and mole sauce—was one giant Bazaar Sábado. She had no idea about this, not yet.

When the bell signaled the end of the day, I went back to my fourth-period classroom to sign up to write for the *ISM Observer*. Like the yearbook, it was written in English. Jonathan Payne, the British Mexican-history teacher, who was in charge of the tiny basement newsroom I'd seen on my orientation tour, was sitting at his desk marking up papers. Mr. Payne was some kind of poet and had even published a few books about Mexican politics, which he covered for years as a reporter for an English-language newspaper before quitting to teach. He was in his forties, handsome in a rugged-journalist way, with a mop of dark hair that curled at the ends. So far, his Mexican history was my favorite class. When he mentioned that he ran the school newspaper, too, I was sold on joining.

"What do you want to write about for your first article?" he asked.

"I'm going to sign up for the class trip to Angahuan. I could do a story about that."

"Great. Do some research and tell me what you're planning by Friday."

Angahuan was in the state of Michoacán, about five hours west of Mexico City on the *carretera* (highway). For the class trip, which was two weeks away, we would examine the town that had been destroyed by the volcano Paricutin when it erupted in 1944. Since then, Paricutin had come back to life, a phoenix risen from the ashes, new and stronger, the start of a fresh cycle. That first day of class, we'd learned about the Aztecs. They believed that time wasn't linear, with a beginning and an end, but cyclical—like the planets revolving around the sun. According to them, the whole universe was structured in circles, and that's why their Stone of the Sun was round. The face in the middle was sticking out its tongue as if to mock how powerless people are over time—and over most other things, for that matter. The world, they believed, had been created and destroyed four times by the gods; they lived in the fifth sun, and the end was near, again. When Cortés arrived, it had all but ended. I wrote down the word Mr. Payne scribbled on the blackboard, a word that encompassed the mingling of the Old World with the New:

> Syncretism—the reconciliation or fusion of differing systems of belief, as in philosophy or religion, especially when success is partial or the result is heterogeneous.

People the Aztecs originally thought were gods ended up destroying them.

My mother was crying hysterically at the dining table on Tuesday, the second morning of the school year.

"What's wrong?" I asked. It was only seven. I was afraid that something had happened to my grandmother in L.A.

Maggie looked up at me, crying harder. "How could you have sex with that boy from upstairs! You barely even know him."

"What? What are you talking about?" I yelled, immediately defensive.

"You lied to me! You said you were going to a sleepover!" she screamed back.

Then I saw it: my letter to Nora, unfolded in her lap.

"What are you doing with that?" I asked, my voice growing soft. "I gave it to you to mail, not to read!"

"I knew something was wrong when you got home from that party, Milagro. A mother can tell."

I imagined her huddled over the sink steaming open the envelope I'd so carefully addressed and sealed.

"I didn't lie to you. I lied to Nora."

"Why would I ever believe that?" she demanded.

"You say you want the truth, but you can't deal with it."

I grabbed my bag and ran out of the apartment.

"Why would you lie to your best friend?" my mother yelled as the door slammed shut behind me. I didn't know how to answer her question.

I'd kept my distance from Dave ever since the party, but as I ran up to the open doors of the bus I fell in line behind him, panting from the run.

"You almost missed the bus," he said, as we filed in.

"There was a little problem at my house this morning."

"What happened?"

"My mother knows we . . . she read a letter I wrote to a friend."

"Well, what did you write?" he asked, suddenly nervous.

"Fuck you," I said, walking past him as he sat down. I took a seat in the back of the bus, turning the volume on my Discman way up. The Stone Temple Pilots song "Plush" blasted into my ears as the indifferent city flew by. Chapultepec graveyard, Observatorio, Bon-dojito.

"You didn't tell your mother anything, did you?" Dave asked as we got off the bus in the school parking lot. "You didn't write it in that let-ter, right?"

"She wouldn't believe me, anyway." We both exited the front gate and walked over to where the smokers stood in their clusters, the fre-sas in their Armani jeans, the alternative international crowd, and the Americans in baseball hats.

"What's up, guys?" said Naldo when we got to the American and the Americanized-international spot farther up from the fresas.

"Get this," said Dave. "Mila's mother read some letter and found out that she and I had crazy sex at your party."

My eyes widened in disbelief.

"Sorry that went down, Mila," said Naldo.

Suddenly I understood. Dave was starting something preemptive, protecting himself. If I told people what happened now, they would think I made the story up to take revenge on him for spreading rumors about me.

"What did the sex diary say?" asked an American boy named Joey, who'd overheard.

"It said none of your business, okay?" I snapped.

"Chill out, girl," he said. "It's *your* boyfriend who's saying it."

"It said 'Dave is a sex god and I'm his slut slave,'" Dave said, as some other guys gathered around to see what was going on. Dave pointed at me. "She begged me to fuck her. Then she wrote about it and her mother read the headlines. Maybe she'll write about it for the newspa-per. What do you think, Mila, will we read about it in the *Observer*?"

I felt my face getting hot and red. "Maybe you will," I said. "But it will be *my* story." I left the group of guys chuckling behind me. I didn't believe in the word *slut*. I thought it was ugly, that girls should be free to do what they pleased—or what pleased them—without judgment. But I'd been a virgin until the other night, and the circumstances made this new label even more of a slap in the face. I knew Dave was afraid I would say something, but I never would. I didn't want to draw any more attention to myself than he already had.

I was sitting by myself under the palapa at lunch, unwrapping a ham-and-cheese sandwich, when Dave came over to me with Joey and a few other American boys he'd befriended, boys who made no effort to understand the culture they were living in and acted as if they were still in Iowa or Georgia, or wherever they'd come from.

"What are you doing over here all alone? Haven't made any friends yet?"

"Go away, Dave."

"Will you give me a blow job?" said Joey. The other guys snickered. I hated them and their backwards baseball caps and boxers that stuck out over their jeans, their stupid dimples and greasy foreheads. No wonder the fresas thought Americans were low-class, if this was what they were seeing as a cross-section. I'd wanted a friend or a boyfriend so badly that I'd fallen right in with Dave without seeing who he really was. The signs were there—he'd never wanted to converse too deeply, and he'd offered to relieve me of my virginity even before our first kiss. The mysteriousness that had attracted me to him in the first place now seemed like denseness. How had I failed to notice what seemed so obvious in retrospect?

"This is all going to come back around on you," I told him, looking him straight in the eyes. "Ever hear of karma?" I stood up, packed up my sandwich, and walked away, toward the soccer field, where some fresa guys were kicking a ball around.

"That's right, walk away and hide, little whore," Dave yelled after me. After a second round of laughter from the group behind me, I couldn't help what I did next. I spun around and pitched my sandwich at Dave, throwing it harder than I'd ever thrown anything, as if all my rage were absorbed by that stupid white bread, mustard, and ham. It hit him squarely in the chest, a huge mustard splotch staining the front of his white T-shirt. He looked down at himself, then shot me an icy glare. He stood really tall, stuck his neck out, and strode toward me. I froze, afraid he was going to hit me.

"You're the one who's going to be sorry, Mila," he sputtered, his breath low, tiny drops of saliva hitting my neck as the words came out. Then he walked the other way, leaving his friends gaping.

Dave went right to work making good on his promise. People whose names I didn't know suddenly knew mine. The girl who slept with Dave and all his friends at a party. A lesbian prostitute who was into gang bangs and bestiality. An aspiring porn star, a drunken lush. It was like a vulgar game of telephone, and it was amazing what people would believe just to have something to talk about. Guys stared me down in the hall, and girls avoided me, turning to their lockers and whispering when I passed by. I knew from three years of high school that first impressions were hard to change, whether you lived in Mexico or Milwaukee. But ISM was big enough, its world made up of so many little, self-contained universes, that it had to be possible. They weren't cells with permeable membranes, though, and I knew it wasn't going to be easy finding a way in.

The next day at lunch, I walked around the ISM campus feeling claustrophobic inside the barbed-wire-topped walls. School felt like a maximum-security prison, with the guards at the gate and the fresas' bodyguards waiting outside all day by their black town cars, Mercedes, and giant SUVs. Down by the elementary school, there was a little hill with a ditch below it. I headed over to hide out and write in my journal until the bell rang. But when I got closer I heard voices. I looked over the ledge and saw Nina and Naldo with Sisley and Kai.

"I thought you were Mr. Horney," said Kai when he saw me.

"Do I look like a bald Englishman?" I hopped down into the ditch where they were smoking.

"I'm Kai, by the way," he said.

"Mila."

"I know who you are."

"It takes much longer to put out a fire than it does to spread it, doesn't it?" I snapped.

"That's not even what I meant," said Kai. "We sort of met on orientation day, though you didn't introduce yourself. I gave you a cigarette, remember?"

"What's up with all those things Dave said, anyway?" asked Naldo, running a hand through his blue-streaked hair.

"*Nothing,*" interjected Nina before I could open my mouth. "Dave's an asshole. We're not speaking to him anymore, okay, little brother?" Nina called Naldo "little brother," though technically he was only two minutes younger.

"Can I have one of those?" I pointed to the pack of smokes he was holding. "Thanks," I said, lighting the cigarette he passed me. Then a shadow fell over us, blocking the sun. I looked up and blew smoke straight into Mr. Horney's face.

"Hello—Miss Márquez, isn't it?" he asked. He knew, of course; he was famous for making a point of meeting all the new students and remembering their names. "All of you"—he waved his finger around in a circle, like a magician conjuring something up—"come with me."

He walked us to the office and gave us a day's suspension for smoking on campus. Everyone saw Mr. Horney taking us in, a wrinkled goose leading naughty ducklings all in a row. I felt Dave's eyes on me. He looked so satisfied.

Mr. Horney kept me in his office after the others left. "Do not hang out with this crowd," he said. "These are not the people you want to make friends with. They are our blacklisted students and we watch them carefully. I won't suspend you, since you're new and I assume you don't know all the rules yet. I won't call your parents—this time. But I'll be keeping an eye on you."

"Yes, sir," I said.

"We have a firm regulation against smoking on campus," he said. "Now get to class."

Kai walked me upstairs to our sixth-period chemistry class. "What's the blacklist?" I asked.

"Horney pulled that on you? He writes down who all the trouble-makers are. It has about fifty names, we think, ranked according to how bad he thinks we've been."

"I guess I'm on it now," I said. "You have no idea how ironic that is." I thought about Washington, D.C.: cheerleading, getting an A in AP World History, doing schoolwork on a Saturday night, even if it was in Nora's room while sipping the warm beers she'd stolen from the kitchen cabinet.

"Don't worry, it's a badge of honor," said Kai. "I think I was on it from the moment Horney laid eyes on me. I scare him. Takes one to know one, you know?" He winked.

I tried to laugh, but looked down at the linoleum floor instead as warm tears blurred my vision.

"Hey, it's just detention. Nothing worth crying over." Kai put his arm around my shoulder.

"It's not that, Kai."

"Those rumors?" He looked at me and knew. "They'll blow over. Three thousand kids go to this school. A few weeks and you're in the clear. Try to see him as a loser with nothing else to do."

Along the hallway of the science wing, jars of formaldehyde-preserved baby animals—pigs, mice, and even a kitten—were dis-played. The worst was a hamster that was split open down the belly from head to tail, its insides exposed.

"That's how I feel right now," I said, pointing at the hamster. "Vio-lated and on display."

"You're still better off than he is," said Kai. I wasn't sure whether he meant Dave or the gutted hamster. "Give me your phone number. We'll give you a proper introduction to the city, a night on the town."

I hoped he wasn't asking because he felt sorry for me.

"I do need to get out," I said, wiping my face with the back of my sleeve and trying to smile as I wrote the number in Kai's notebook. "So don't forget to call, okay?"

The jarring second bell sent us scurrying to our desks. Kai slid into the one directly behind me. I noticed a fresa guy sitting a few rows toward the front, in a crisp white button-down shirt, jeans, and new motorcycle boots. He caught my eye and smiled. I immediately looked down at my textbook, a picture of a pink Bunsen burner on its cover.

"Amador, Manuel," said Mr. Suarez, starting the roll call.

"Here," said the fresa.

"Atsuhiko, Kaiosaki."

"I go by Kai."

He ran down the alphabetical list. I was mortified when he called out "Márquez, Milagro."

"It's Mila," I said.

"Okay, Mila," said Mr. Suarez, making a note in his attendance book. If only my mother were so easy.

"I assumed your name was Camila," Kai whispered, leaning forward. I just blushed and shrugged. "Milagro is way cooler," he said.

I thought I was going to get a lecture that evening for sure, but my mother came home from work whistling and didn't mention the morning's incident. It was just like her to explode and then pretend that nothing had happened, that everyone was happy and everything was fine.

"Guess what?" she said. "Our house is ready early. We're moving in this weekend."

I jumped up off the couch when I heard the news. "Thank God. I'm suffocating in this apartment." And the sooner our house was ready the sooner I would be farther away from Dave—from watching the back of his baseball cap on the bus in the mornings, from staying inside all afternoon for fear of running into him in the building's halls.

I came back to the apartment after school every day, spread my homework out across the coffee table, and played the Blind Melon song "No Rain" over and over. I would stare out the balcony window—the balcony no one ever wanted to go out on because it looked out over Reforma and smelled like toxic gas—at the Days Inn sign. Each day, I'd stare at the sign until my vision blurred. Days Inn. Days Inn Jail. Days

Inn Hell. Days Inn Between. I became obsessed with the passing of time. Every afternoon, I looked up at the sign all over again, in between calculus and AP-lit homework. It was just a sign, a yellow sun rising above big white block letters on a black background. But every day that I looked up at it, it reminded me that another day had passed. And with each day that passed I was one day closer to going home, wherever that might turn out to be.

The moving van the Embassy hired showed up first thing Saturday morning. Men in brown jumpsuits carried our boxes downstairs. Our bubble-wrapped furniture, shipped from D.C., was already in the back of the truck. The government had this moving business down to clockwork, maybe the one efficient thing in the bureaucratic swarm of the Foreign Service.

We pulled up outside our new house on Calle Monte Athos in the beat-up old Volkswagen Golf my mom had bought for cheap and had newly christened with diplomatic (aka "get out of jail free") license plates. A high black gate opened inward on a long driveway with yard on either side, full of bougainvillea and birds-of-paradise. Two palm trees stood close enough together to string up a hammock. The house was white, with thick stone walls and a paint texture that made it appear to be melting, like a three-dimensional, monochromatic Jackson Pollock painting with a flat roof. Huge windows with black windowpanes completed the structure, which was oddly beautiful. Maggie's enormous master bedroom stood at the top of the stairs. I had two smaller rooms to choose from—one right across from my mother, the other down a bowling-alley hallway on the other side of the house. It was an easy decision. I wanted to get as far away from her as I possibly could. I'd spent my allowance that week stocking up on booklets of international stamps so she'd never be able to open a letter I wrote to Nora again.

Lomas de Chapultepec was spectacular. It was known as *the* premier residential area in el D.F. and was quiet, and almost green sometimes, against the gray of concrete and sky. All the houses were huge and enclosed behind tall gates. There were *glorietas* in the middle of the streets, with palm trees, flowers, and greenery. All the streets in Lomas were named for mountains: Monte Everest, Himalaya, Monte Blanco, Alpes, Tarahumara.

"How much do you think a house like this costs?" I asked as we adjusted some of the paintings from Bazaar del Sábado on the hallway walls.

"At least seven hundred thousand dollars," my mother said. "Maybe eight or nine."

"Holy crap." Ours was the smallest house on the block.

My mother stood back to admire her fake Diego Rivera. "I'm going to paint this house Mexican," she said.

"What?" I asked.

"The walls are so white. Let's go to the hardware store. We'll make them more appropriate, beautiful bright pinks and oranges. Maybe a vivid royal blue for the kitchen."

"Mom! I doubt any Mexicans really do that."

"That's because you've never been to the Casa Azul, where Frida Kahlo lived," she said, grabbing the imitation Diego off the wall.

"Right, but that's for show," I said. But she was humming a tune, taking the paintings down again, already imagining the brightly painted walls.

That night I was supposed to go with my mother to the Ballet Folklórico, a traditional Mexican folk-dancing show, but Kai called and invited me out to La Onda, a trendy taqueria across Reforma, with the lunchtime smokers. I sat down next to Maggie on our oversized off-white couch, which was now in the giant living room, with its huge bay windows that opened out over our garden.

"I can't go with you tonight. I got invited to the movies."

"With that Dave boy?"

"No, Mom, not with 'that Dave boy.' "

My mother put the Mexico guidebook she was reading down on the coffee table and leaned toward me. I instinctively inched away.

"He won't ask you out anymore since you slept with him, am I right?" she said.

"What? No!" I yelled. "You'll never understand."

She softened. "I forget sometimes how difficult this moving around is for you. I'm sure you only wanted to feel close to someone. I only want you to avoid the mistakes that I made."

"What mistakes, Mom?"

"Nothing, never mind."

"No, *what mistakes*, Mom?"

"Like getting pregnant so young, having to give up the life you're leading to take care of someone. I never want you to have to give up all the adventures and travels ahead of you."

I got that hollow feeling in my chest. Though I may have been an accident, she'd always said I was her miracle. But when she was feeling overwhelmed she acted as though I'd come along and ruined everything.

"Then maybe you should have named me Mistake-o," I said. "And maybe leading some faux-glamorous life isn't what I want, have you ever thought of that?"

"Don't go taking this the wrong way," she said, picking her book up off the coffee table. "Believe me, I don't know what I would do without you. I'm only trying to make sure you get the chance at a life I never had."

"By reading my letters, going through my stuff, saying you'd rather have some life of freedom than take care of me?"

"Look at you," she said. "If I had your face and your upbringing, I'd just be grateful the world was going to be all mine."

"Is that all it takes?" I demanded.

"If you stay away from alcohol and the wrong men, yes."

She opened her book where she'd left off and started reading, which meant that the conversation was over. I ran up the stairs to my room, trying to swallow the lump in my throat. I knew my mother didn't mean half the things she said, but when it came to us her words and her intentions didn't always align.

~ ~ ~

Nina came to pick me up for the night out with Rodrigo, her driver. My mother whispered her instant dislike when Nina came inside to use the bathroom.

"There's something off about her, I can tell," she said.

"She's the best friend I have here," I argued. "And there's nothing you can do about that." Did Nina's wild energy hit a little too close to home for her? I wondered.

"All I'm saying is that you should be friends with some of the Mexican kids instead," my mother said in a hushed tone.

"You think the fresas are so perfect," I said. "You don't know the half of it."

One of the president's sons was rumored to do so much coke on the weekends that he regularly got into fistfights at *antros*—the clubs—and punched holes through walls. Still, I secretly wouldn't have minded getting to know him better, or even Guillermo—Memo for short—the son of some big honcho in the PRI. Memo was big and bulky, with a mop of blond curls, a voice like a dragon, and perpetually half-shut eyes, but somehow he pulled off an appealing charm. The fresas had private jets, drivers, and as many trips to their parents' houses in Valle de Bravo, Ixtapa, and Acapulco as they could handle. I secretly wanted in, but I would never admit it to my mother. They *were* off-putting. Their parents controlled the government, business, industry. It was as if all their money, designer clothes, important family members, fancy cars, and bodyguards made them superior, which wasn't exactly surprising. I thought about writing some kind of exposé about their mysterious clique, but I'd have to break in first. Now that I was getting more comfortable with Spanish, I knew I could figure out how to do it; it would just take time. I imagined I could have been one of them if things had turned out differently with my father. I was more connected to the fresas by DNA than any of them knew.

"Mila, I'm ready," Nina called out from down the hall.

"See you later, Mom," I said.

"Please be careful, Milagro."

"Ugh," I said, and walked out.

"What's up with the half-orange bathroom wall in there?" Nina asked.

"My mother's idea of Mexico," I said. "And she's just getting started."

We were all meeting at Sisley's dropout boyfriend's house on Schiller Street first, in Polanco, an upscale area where the streets were named for philosophers and political figures: Masaryk, Galileo, Socrates. Tyler had gone to ISM for a year after his family moved to Mexico City, and met Sisley and Kai there. But he dropped out after his junior year and now stayed in his room all day, painting and playing guitar. He somehow got his parents to let him do whatever he wanted. They never asked him where he was going or what time he'd be back.

"How'd he manage that?" I asked Nina after she explained the group's history.

"His parents are Mormons," she said. I thought of that boy Ken from orientation. Huge community down here. "He used to be one, too. I guess they've disowned him."

I knew it was dysfunctional, but it also seemed kind of romantic.

"And you want to hear the craziest thing?" Nina was saying.

"Tell," I said.

"At one of Tyler's parties last year, some guy was so high on acid that he flipped out, took off his clothes, and ran out into the street."

"Holy crap."

"But that's not the crazy part. He ran straight to Chapultepec Park, into the forest over there, which made him freak even more. He ran and ran until he got to a big wall, and he scaled it, one of those super-human feats of strength that you hear about happening to tripping people sometimes. Anyway, he jumps over and falls straight into the hyena pit at Chapultepec Zoo."

My eyes widened. "You knew him?" I asked.

"Not exactly." Nina shrugged. "But Kai swears it happened. He was at the party."

~ ~ ~

Tyler's house was huge, his room up a flight of stairs all on its own. It opened out onto the roof, a giant deck overlooking the Canadian Embassy. He was tall and angular, with large features and huge blue eyes. He didn't talk much, but he almost didn't have to. His silence came off as mysterious. I thought of Dave and warned myself not to rush to judgment. Tyler reminded me of Kurt Cobain, now that I knew what Nirvana was. I had even stashed my Boyz II Men CD in the back of my closet in favor of the angst-ridden new sound. I loved the grinding guitars, the wailing voices and dark lyrics; they may have been from Seattle, but they provided the perfect soundtrack for Mexico City.

We went outside on the roof to smoke. Kai passed me a filterless cigarette and held out the match he'd struck to light it.

"Is this a clove?" I asked, taking a drag of sticky-sweet smoke.

"Very funny," he said, mock-pushing me on the shoulder.

"What's funny?"

"You really don't know?"

"Know what?"

Kai didn't answer me. Instead, he turned to the group. "Guys, Mila doesn't know she's smoking"—he lowered his voice for dramatic effect—"weed."

"This is pot?" I felt idiotic. I'd never seen or smelled it before.

"Maybe Horney was wrong to try and blacklist you," said Kai.

"Maybe you've just been a bad influence," I joked.

"Someone had to do the job," Kai said, teasing me back.

After the past few weeks, I'd do anything to get out of my head, and a mental escape sounded perfect. I took another pull, inhaling so deeply that I coughed.

By the time we got to La Onda, a small, brightly lit casual taco place, there was a gaping void where my stomach used to be. The crowd in the cavelike room was a mix of fresas and more typical Mexicans. This was one of the few restaurants where the castelike system of separation vanished and both groups could be seen in the same room, eating the same traditional food.

We ordered plate upon plate of *tacos al pastor,* pork sliced off a spit and topped with spices, pineapple, and onions. The *mesero* brought over an array of colorful sauces made from different types of chilies. I'd never tasted anything so delicious. I ate five or six of them, washed down with gulps from Jarritos, brightly colored fruit-flavored soda.

"This is why we get so high before coming here," said Nina.

"Yeah, I understand. There are so many intricate layers of flavor to this taco," I said. "It's totally intense."

Everybody laughed, but it wasn't mean like the mocking laughter of Dave and his friends. We were having a great time. For the first time since coming to Mexico City, I felt uninhibited and happy.

"A little different from what you're used to, isn't it?" said Tyler.

"How'd you know?" I asked coyly.

"I can just tell," he said. Sisley shot me what I thought was a dirty look, but I brushed it off, figuring I was a little paranoid from the pot. And she'd never really warmed to me, anyway.

"*Después de un buen taco, un buen tabaco,*" said Kai, leaning back in his chair and lighting a cigarette. "After a good taco, a good smoke. It's a saying around here."

"And *café de olla!*" Nina shouted. The *mesero* overheard and brought steaming coffee in clay mugs for everyone at the table. I took a sip.

"This is amazing," I said. "What's in it?"

"I make it all the time," said Kai. "You have to use these earthen-ware pots for the flavor. It's got aniseeds, cinnamon, and *piloncillo,* a specific type of brown sugar."

"You have to give me the recipe."

"Come over one day, we'll make it together," he said.

Later, in Kai's car, we passed another joint around when we left La Onda to go dancing at a New Wave club built to resemble a cave, with faux-rock walls. The flashing colored lights made me feel even higher as I sang along to the Depeche Mode song "Enjoy the Silence."

I barely cared that it was four in the morning when I got home. I tried to sneak in without my mother noticing, but she ran outside as soon as the gate creaked open.

"Where have you been?" she demanded.

"I told you, we went out to eat, then dancing." I walked past her and into the house.

"It's four in the goddamn morning!" she yelled, following me up the stairs.

I turned around on the landing. We were face-to-face. "You always say to blend with the culture! I'm blending with the culture."

"Don't tell me what I say. I mean the real Mexican culture, not partying like an alcoholic. Go to bed."

"Alcoholics don't party! They're desperate!" I shouted. She spun around wordlessly, her red bathrobe swinging with her steps, and shut her bedroom door. We rarely mentioned my mother's drinking problem these days—she'd been sober since I was nine—and I knew she was doing the best she could, the best she knew how. I'd never used it against her in an argument before. I barely slept at all during what was left of the night.

The next morning, Saturday, my mother came into my room, pulled up the shades, and told me in her singsong voice to get up and get dressed.

"We're going to Rosa's for lunch today, to meet her family and get to know her a little better before she starts working next week," she chirped, way too enthusiastically for nine on a weekend morning.

I rubbed the sleep from my eyes and sat up in bed, exhausted, with the dry mouth and throbbing head of my first hangover. Rosa was our new housekeeper. Another fact of Mexico City life was that every house in the neighborhood had adjacent, smaller living quarters. But my mother thought a live-in maid would be uncomfortable and ridiculous for just the two of us, and for once I agreed with her about something.

Rosa was hired to come over three days a week—to cook, clean, and take care of anything I needed on those nights that my mother worked late.

We drove two hours to her town, which wasn't far outside el D.F., given that it was, at the time, the world's largest city, but road access was terrible. Her family lived in a cement house whose dirt floors were covered with handwoven rugs. Between these dirt floors and the mansions where the fresas lived was a vast gulf of nothing. There was barely any middle class, and it was shrinking.

I was doing a jig after the car ride, so my mother and I went to find the bathroom, which turned out to be a drainlike hole in the backyard that she helped me squat over. I played makeshift soccer with Rosa's two little cousins in the dusty yard as goats and chickens scurried about, until her mother and brother came outside. I watched, puzzled at first, as they lunged after a chicken.

"Van a matar la gallina!" one of the boys screamed. I understood enough to know that I was looking at my lunch flapping desperately around the yard. It occurred to me then that in Spanish certain edible animals had one name alive and another, "food" name: *Gallina* = live chicken; *pollo* = dead chicken. *Pez* = swimming in the stream; *pescado* = fried up and served on a plate. It was an interesting distinction.

Rosa's mother grabbed the chicken by its neck and waved it around above her body until the head snapped off, the carcass running aimlessly in circles. My mother made me hold the chicken's head and snapped a photo in which my nose is crinkled in revulsion. I felt discernibly guilty for enjoying the resulting tacos.

The family talked and laughed around the table, their eyes warm and welcoming. Rosa taught me to make tortillas, her hands guiding mine as we worked. They treated us as if we were related. In many cases, women like Rosa were integrated into the upper-class families they worked for. They were around more than the parents and formed close bonds with the kids. Other domestic workers resented the wealthy, stealing their jewelry and feeding their babies dry cereal. When Nina's family eventually left Mexico for New York City, where

George Rothman was to head a division at an investment bank, they took Concepción with them; my mother helped expedite her paperwork. While in New York, Concepción joined a group of Jehovah's Witnesses and disappeared one night three months later, along with all her possessions, only to resurface with a lawsuit that cost Mr. Rothman twenty thousand dollars.

Rosa didn't seem to have an agenda. When she came over, we made quesadillas and baked cakes together when I got home from school. In her early twenties, Rosa wasn't much older than I, just in a completely different place in life. She didn't want to clean houses forever; she wanted to become a hairdresser and beautician and open her own salon in her hometown. She went to beauty school and pierced my ears slowly with a needle and ice as I lay on the couch with my head in her lap. My mom let her practice hairstyling in our house so often that the living room reeked of ammonia from the hair dye she used on her volunteer clients. When my light roots started to show, I persuaded her to redo the black even though my mother had made me promise to let my hair return to its natural shade of blond.

Maggie also hired Rosa's neighbor as our gardener, since the grounds required too much maintenance for us to handle on our own. Señor Flores came over on Wednesdays to cut the grass and tend the bougainvillea and the rosebushes. He was about five-two and ancient, his face deeply grooved, the consequence of years spent gardening in the sun. He carried old, rusty shears that were almost as big as he was. Señor Flores was always in a good mood, singing as he worked, or blasting Ranchera music from his tiny cassette player.

"*Hola, niña!*" he would call to me in his raspy voice from the lawn when I came home from school and walked up the driveway from the gate. I'd look over and there he was, in his overalls and undershirt, waving, his forehead glistening in the sun. The day Señor Flores's tape player finally gave out, he took to singing that old familiar song, but with verses I never knew existed: "*Ya murió la cucaracha, ya la llevan a enterrar . . . Entre cuatro zopilotes, y un ratón de sacristán.* ("The cockroach just died, and they carried him off to bury him/Among four buz-

zards, and the sexton's mouse.") The song always took me right back to
the bad night I was still trying to gain distance from.

Everything that happened with Nina and me started with the rides to
school. My house in Lomas was only two blocks from Nina and Naldo's.
Rodrigo always pulled the Escalade out of their driveway at seven on
the dot, turned down Esplanada, and went in the other direction from
the school bus, the shortest route to school. I was standing there as
usual one morning, eyes peeled for the bus, when Nina spotted me
from the corner. The Escalade came to a stop on the curb beside me
and a tinted back window rolled down.

"Get in!" she called, and I obliged.

"You must be the only senior who rides the bus," she said, as I settled into the leather seat.

"My mother thinks it's too dangerous for me to drive here. I just got
my license before we moved."

"Why don't you have a driver?" asked Nina. I cracked the automatic
window and morning traffic sounds filled the SUV as we sped down the
main road connecting Lomas to Tacubaya.

"The Embassy doesn't pay for it," I said. "And of course my mother
thinks it's unnecessary. She says no regular person in the States has a
driver, so we don't need one, either."

"Doesn't she get that this is *not* the States?" Nina said. I chose to ignore her patronizing tone. "Then I absolutely insist that Rodrigo and I
pick you up every morning. *Está bien, Rodrigo?*" she said to the driver.

"*Claro que sí, Señorita Nina,*" said Rodrigo, a bearlike man with a
goatee and an easy smile.

"Where's Naldo?" I asked.

"The responsible twin has water-polo practice at six every freakin'
morning," Nina quipped. "It's just you and me, gorgeous."

Drama queen though she was, Nina's exaggerated ways always
amused me. The rides became daily bonding sessions, and soon I was
referring to Nina as my best girlfriend in Mexico City, and she would

say the same. I would sit outside the black gate at my house until I saw the SUV pull around and come to a halt in front of me.

"Hey, baby." She always yelled this as she rolled down the window, pursing her lips in a mock kiss, like a model in *Mirabella*.

"Hi, beautiful," I'd call back, pulling the back door open as I slid in beside her and kissed her on the cheek. The air was always hazy, the sky pale, with the perpetual morning mist hanging over the neighborhood.

Nina had Rodrigo give me rides home after school, too, but instead of dropping me off we usually spent the afternoons together. My mother never got home until around eight, and Nina's father arrived home even later, if he was in town at all. The twins' mother, Sonia, was usually nowhere to be found. Born to a working-class Buenos Aires family, she'd become a socialite through her marriage to the international businessman. Sonia shopped for a living, ran on a treadmill at the gym, and had her hair done by Luca of Luca Paolo, a fancy salon across Palmas, for evening charity benefits. I crossed paths with her in the kitchen one evening when Nina invited me to stay for dinner. The first thing I noticed about Sonia was that she was the exact opposite of my mother, tall and birdlike skinny and either a quiet introvert or a cold snob. I couldn't quite tell. She always seemed to mind her business and not tell Nina or Naldo what to do.

One sunny and oddly clear Thursday in mid-September, Nina and I smoked a joint on her roof and went for a walk around the neighborhood, stopping outside a gated mansion to lean against a potted plant and share a cigarette. The grounds were surrounded by a giant wall with an electric fence on top and strategically placed surveillance cameras. Bodyguards lingered around the front.

"When will I ever get to know the enigmatic Mr. and Mrs. Rothman?" I asked. I had barely laid eyes on Nina's parents. When they were around, they were usually getting ready to leave.

"Probably at my wedding," she joked, taking a drag of the Marlboro Light and passing it back to me. "My father was hardly ever home the entire time he was moving us between Buenos Aires, Paris, and Washington. Now he spends so much time in Japan, I'm surprised we didn't move *there*. Half my Prada bag collection was presents from Tokyo."

George Rothman showered his daughter with a large allowance, designer clothes, shoes, and purses that he picked up on business trips, pink leather jackets that were all the rage in Rio, and anything she asked for to complement the gifts. I'd heard her on the phone with him ("Daddy, please bring back the Cartier earrings that go with the necklace. It's supposed to be a *set*"). Daddy always obliged.

"My brother and I are total opposites," Nina continued. "You'd never guess we shared the same womb. He's obsessed with his water-polo matches and making a 4.0 average."

"Does he have a girlfriend?" I asked, twirling a strand of my hair around an index finger.

"I hope you're not asking because you're interested."

"Oh gosh, no. Just making conversation." I did think Naldo was cute, but I was interested in becoming Nina's friend, not her brother's girlfriend.

"Good, because he says he's starting to think he's bisexual. Totally gross."

"I don't think it's gross." I shrugged. "Do you want any more of this?" The cigarette was almost down to the filter. Nina shook her head no. I took a long last drag and crushed the butt underfoot. The neighborhood was almost silent. I even heard the sound of birds, and the wind rustling in the palm tree of the *glorieta* down the block. We were coming down off the weed, but my senses still felt heightened.

"I've been meaning to tell you how glad I am you moved here," Nina said, lowering her voice even though no one else was around. "I love our friends, but I feel like you and I really *connect*, you know?"

"Me, too," I said. "Thanks for sticking up for me about Dave that time in the ditch. You don't just follow the hordes."

"Baby, I'm the shepherd," she said. "That dickhead should be banished for talking about you like that, and I'll make it my personal business to see that he never does again."

"I've always believed that what goes around comes around," I said.

"I've never felt so compelled to take revenge on someone, though. He raped me at your party, you know."

It was the first time I'd told anyone, and it spilled out before I had time to think. The secret had been suffocating me. Still, I felt dirty saying it.

"What the fuck, Mila?" she yelled. "Why didn't you say anything before?"

"It's too late," I said. "It would be my word against his, and he's positioned himself pretty well to make it look like I'd be trying to take revenge for those rumors he spread."

Nina reached over and squeezed my shoulder. "He'll get his," she said. But we avoided each other's gaze, looking, instead, across the street at a gardener mowing the grass outside some rich person's gate.

"Not that it would make you feel any better, but something worse happened to this girl I used to be friends with last year," said Nina. "She moved to the States right afterward. To a mental hospital. I mean, she was neurotic to begin with, but this pushed her over the edge."

"What?"

"Spring break last year, I went to Acapulco with Beatriz, Tomás, and Catalina."

"The fresas?"

"Yeah, I used to be really close with them. We stayed at this famous pink-and-white hotel that rents what else but pink-and-white jeeps to guests. They're pretty obvious targets for crime, which there's tons of in Acapulco. Our other friend Gabi was driving hers back from Baby'O, the superfresa club we all went to, and she got held up by a group of men. They sprayed mace at her, drove her somewhere, stole all her money and jewelry, and, you know."

"*All* of them?"

"Yeah. Some fresa guy from the club was in the car with her, too. I guess they were going to hook up. They beat the shit out of him. Someone found him lying on the sidewalk and rushed him to the hospital."

"Jesus."

"I told you, crazy things happen here. Usually the good kind of crazy, but when it's the bad kind it can get really, really ugly. Everything's just way more extreme."

Suddenly the gate to the driveway we were standing in front of creaked and inched open. A black SUV pulled in from the street and the dark-tinted driver's window rolled down. It was Manuel, a fresa from my chemistry class. Apparently, this was his house.

"Hey, Nina," he said. "And Mila, right?" My name must have sunk in from his hearing it over and over during roll call. I wondered if Nina had stopped in this particular spot on purpose.

"Hi, Manuel," she said.

"I'll be right back," said Manuel, pulling the car into the gate.

"Why is he coming back?" I asked.

"To hang out," said Nina with a shrug.

"No way," I said.

"Why not? I was thinking about buzzing upstairs to see if he was home. You didn't know this was his house?"

"How would I?"

Nina was the only person I knew who could permeate the membrane between the fresas and the rest of us. She had the designer wardrobe and the money, and she spoke Spanish flawlessly even though she'd lived most of her life in the States, because her mother was Argentine. But she was also heavily into pot and told me about the acid trips she sometimes took with Sisley and Tyler, a decidedly unfresa thing to do. "I'm experimental," she would say. "I can't confine myself to just one thing." I thought it depended on which of her moods she was in. I'd noticed that when Nina wasn't hyperactive and highly social she seemed a bit morose and depressed. Sometimes she oscillated between one and the other like an out-of-control metronome.

Manuel Amador was one of the most popular fresas in the senior class. His father was Mexico's top plastic surgeon and a major art collector. His mother owned a gallery in La Condesa, a funky, artsy district that was Mexico City's version of SoHo. I knew Manuel dated Cristina, the blue-eyed, honey-haired prettiest girl in school, though

I also found out that she'd recently dumped him to go out with the president's son.

Nina was about to say something when Manuel came back. "What are you girls doing?" he asked, twirling his car keys around his left index finger.

"Just taking a walk," I said.

"A walk?" he asked, as though I'd said we'd been streaking down Reforma.

Fresas didn't understand the concept of walks. They were always hidden away behind the tinted windows of fancy cars, and in bars, cafés, restaurants, exclusive clubs, and shops. But never outside. It might have been dangerous for them, with kidnappings and holdups on the rise, but I didn't have expensive watches or Gucci purses. I suddenly felt incredibly self-conscious about the way I looked. I was wearing an old silk floor-length black skirt inherited from Maggie's Playa del Carmen hippie days, one of two things that had lasted from then; I was the other one. My shirt was a tight white Pixies tank I'd borrowed from Kai's locker one afternoon when I forgot to bring a change of clothes for PE. The ensemble was bottomed off by my recently purchased knee-high Doc Marten boots. Now I wished I'd bought platform heels like Nina's instead.

"Do you know you have snails crawling up your skirt?" Manuel said to me.

"What?"

"Look. On your skirt. *Caracoles*—snails."

I looked down and saw three giant snails making their way up the black silk, leaving three shiny rainbow roads of slime inching toward my belly button.

"That's so weird," I said, pulling them off and placing them back in the potted plant. "Thanks." I kneeled down to scratch some dried slime off the skirt.

"Let's go, Mila!" Nina called from the driveway. I realized that I'd been crouching alone out on the sidewalk.

Manuel's family's mansion was labyrinthine, with rooms upon

rooms in every direction. A Picasso hung above the staircase in the entryway. He noticed me eyeing the painting.

"I collect them," he said. "My dad got me that one for a birthday present. Come upstairs, I'll show you the others."

"*You* collect them, or your dad?" I asked, not believing that a high-school boy would be that into art, and be able to afford it.

"Me, why?" he said, in the tone of someone who had just been asked if he spoke Mexican.

"I think it's impressive, that's all," I said.

"My dad prefers Renoir."

"Manuel's mother is one of the most important art dealers in Mexico City," Nina said.

"She only runs a little gallery," he said, his face flushing pink. Cute *and* humble, I thought, before mentally chiding myself for even thinking that way about someone who was so clearly out of my league.

We sat on black leather couches in one of his living rooms. A row of Picassos lined the wall, and I walked up to them one by one, as I would in a museum. His housekeeper brought us Coronas and *taquitos de pollo.* Nina flirted with Manuel relentlessly: leaning in, winking, flattering him a lot. I wondered if her mother had turned on a similar charm to get her father interested. Sonia had nabbed the rich businessman while he was on an extended work trip in Buenos Aires. Maybe our parents' habits were somehow ingrained in us all, though I hoped not, because that would mean I was fucked. I took in the last of the paintings and sank into the couch next to Nina, the leather squeaking as I settled in.

"Do you also live around here?" Manuel asked me.

"I'm around the corner, on Monte Athos," I said.

"That's different. Most of the Americans' houses are really far out in Bosques or Herradura," he said. I cringed when he said the name of Dave's neighborhood.

"Thankfully," I said.

"Why?" Manuel asked. Nina shot me a knowing look but shook her head quickly back and forth, warning me not to mention Dave.

"My mother likes us to blend with the culture," I said, improvising. "And I'm Mexican, also . . . I mean, my father was Mexican, so I'm not completely American. I lived in Guadalajara when I was little. I originally learned Spanish there, then I forgot almost all of it. But now that I'm here I plan on picking up the language again really quickly," I added, realizing that I was rambling.

"I wish I'd known that before." He smiled. "You seemed like a gringa so we just assumed."

The upper-class Mexicans thought *los gringos* had no culture or identity; that Americans, even internationalized Americans, were provincial and didn't care about anything outside their own world. But being on the opposite side of the prejudice coin threw me off every day. It was funny, considering that we American kids were nowhere near as glamorous as the ridiculously wealthy, put-together fresas, who looked and acted like classy movie starlets from another era. I wondered if the resentment had been passed down through the ages, from the days of the Niños Héroes, who were young boys, soldiers in the Mexican-American War who were said to have wrapped themselves in Mexican flags atop Chapultepec Castle and plummeted off the ledge to brutal deaths rather than surrender to the U.S. army.

"Didn't the word *gringo* come from some kind of song?" I asked.

"Most people think it comes from the Mexican-American War," Manuel explained. "From a song that American soldiers used to sing. But that's a myth. Really, it's just a variation of *Griego,* which means "Greek"—you know, like 'It's all Greek to me,' because they were so foreign."

"You know a lot about history?" I asked.

"Only as a side effect of art history," he said. "I'm secretly a painter."

"Secretly?"

"I'm being forced into studying engineering or medicine next year." Manuel took a sip of his beer. "So, your mother is in the Foreign Service? Where did you grow up?" he asked, changing the subject.

"It's a long story. I went to second and third grade in Guadalajara.

When I was in seventh grade we lived in Prague, though what I remember most was drinking hot *čokoládový*—that's chocolate—when it was cold," I said, trying to impress him by tossing in a Czech word. I'd learned the language of whichever country I lived in, but promptly fell out of practice and lost it when we moved and I had to focus on picking up a new one. "Then, when I was thirteen, my mother transferred to a position at State Department headquarters in Washington, D.C., and I lived in the U.S. for the first time."

"That's quite a life," said Manuel. "Very cosmopolitan."

"Yeah, right. Not compared to yours."

"Mila," said Nina, who had been quiet for a while. "We have to get going."

"We do?" I said.

"Why so soon?" asked Manuel. But she was already standing, putting on her jacket and heading for the door.

"Um, she's leaving, so . . ." I said to him, pointing to the doorway Nina had disappeared through.

"Give me your phone number. You should come to my house in Valle for the weekend sometime. Tell Nina, too," he said. I scrawled the number on a napkin and left it on the coffee table. What a useless gesture that was, I thought. He'll never, not in a thousand years, pick it up and dial.

"I think he was interested in you," Nina said as we walked down Esplanada, passing the gated mansions and palm-treed *glorietas* on our way back to her house.

"I don't think so. I'm no Cristina. Besides, you were the one flirting with him."

"He didn't even notice. I had such a crush on him last year."

"He's nicer than I thought he'd be," I offered. "And cute. I love dark-haired, blue-eyed boys."

"Don't bother getting interested," Nina snapped. "He probably heard all those rumors Dave spread and wants to get in your pants. Remember, guys only care about getting laid."

"Manuel doesn't seem that way."

"Well, don't expect to be an exception. I guess I'll talk to you later." She turned and walked away, leaving me alone on the corner of Monte Athos. I guessed I wasn't going to her house that afternoon. I couldn't believe she was mad because Manuel and I had hit it off. But I booked an extra session with my Spanish tutor for the following week just in case.

The next morning, the Escalade didn't turn up my street. I saw it go straight on Esplanada and disappear around the block. I rode the bus and went looking for Nina as soon as I got to school. I found her already walking over to the field to smoke without me.

"What's wrong?" I asked. "Why didn't you pick me up?"

"Nothing. Rodrigo took a sick day," she said, fumbling distractedly in her purse. "My dad dropped me off on the way to work and we were in a rush." Her eyes flicked over to the left and I knew she was lying. Nina was too used to getting everything she wanted, from designer bags to boys, and I guessed that not being able to date Manuel last year must have made her resentful that he'd talked mostly with me at his house.

"He didn't even say hello to me in chem class this morning, Nina."

"Whatever," she said dismissively. "I don't care if you like him."

"He's just some fresa. You're making a big deal out of nothing."

Nina turned and walked away. I decided not to react to her petty behavior and went to smoke on the soccer field with Sisley instead. I found her behind a tree at the end of the field. She was unusually quiet, distracted and chain-smoking.

"What's the matter?" I asked. My question was like the last drop that makes a leaky pipe burst. Sisley's eyes welled with tears, then she burst into sobs.

"What happened?" I put my hand on her back, but she shook it off.

"My father's getting transferred!" she cried. "To Kenya! In fucking *Africa*. We're moving right before winter break. I can't believe I have to leave Tyler. Why did my stupid-ass dad have to go and get promoted *senior fucking year*?"

My first thought: Maggie would soon be lobbying for a promotion, which would mean a lot of late nights at the office for her, take-out Chinese or sushi from Tai Itto—the swanky Japanese restaurant on the corner of Monte Athos—for me. I felt sorry for Sisley, because I knew all too well what she was going through. Things always shifted unexpectedly in a Foreign Service child's life. You could be in Mexico one day, Africa the next, and you never knew what was coming, or when. Sometimes I felt like Maggie's Raggedy Ann doll, different pieces of fabric patched together and dragged around the world. I knew it was far from a terrible life, that it had opened me up to all kinds of experiences I might otherwise never have had. But I was also constantly having to abandon ship, leaving my life and my friends behind when everything finally hit that particular rhythm of actually being predictable. Predictability as elusive—that was my favorite contradiction, and I knew it all too well.

"One of my best friends from D.C. is half Kenyan," I told Sisley. "She still knows some people our age there."

"Do you have a Tylenol?" she asked, ignoring what I'd said. "I'm getting a huge headache."

"It's the stress. I'm so sorry you're going through this. Let me see if I have one." I dumped the contents of my bag out on the ground, scattering collected clutter and memorabilia on the grass.

"Don't you ever clean out your purse?" Sisley asked.

"Nope," I said, plucking a two-pack of Advil from between a postcard of Istanbul and a matchbook from Dublin and handing it to her.

At the end of September, ISM hosted a college fair. Hundreds of universities from the U.S. and Mexico piled into rows and rows of tables in the high-school gym and on the elementary-school field. The administration held the event every year in order to help students make informed decisions about colleges in the States that they might not have a chance to visit before matriculation. To round things out, Mexican universities were invited, too.

Kids from South Hill came to the fair as well, though they tended to linger at the area for community colleges, two-year certificate schools, and culinary institutes. South Hill wasn't very far away physically, but it stood at a distance in every other way. If you got expelled from ISM, it was the school on the receiving end, a bucket catching fuckups like rain through a hole in the roof. If you couldn't afford ISM, or your parents' company didn't pay for it, you also went to South Hill. It seemed as if that was why the school existed. I'd never been on its campus, but I'd heard about who ended up there. South Hill had no rules, no guards outside the gates like ISM, no politicians' children. There were also a number of scraggly-haired, guitar-strumming boys who went there. There was something newly appealing about them. Meeting Tyler had changed my opinion.

Application season began the next week. I filled out forms for seven schools, even a few in the Ivy League. I decided it was worth a try, since before coming to Mexico I'd worked hard and gotten good grades. I'd even drafted my essay last year in a class I took after school that was just for writing college-application papers. That felt like a lifetime ago.

When the applications were finished, Maggie priority-mailed them from the Embassy; unlike my letters to Nora, I didn't need to worry about her steaming them open. Now that I'd either be accepted or not, I was officially free to let loose in the excitement of Mexico City. I wanted to explore the *antros*—the city's famously frenzied nightclubs. They stayed open until dawn, and I imagined emerging into the sunrise and smog while the party inside was still going strong. The ground beneath me was already shifting, and there hadn't even been an earthquake yet.

A few weeks after our move, Maggie joined the Lomas Country Club, a private, very fresa oasis and the most expensive country club in the city, which I guessed was an attempt to blend in with our newly *rico* surroundings. She could afford the hefty membership fee because of our lack of expenses and she splurged, even though she didn't even play golf. The men did, though, and she was on the prowl for a handsome, rich one. She still dreamed of the jet-set life, all glamour and international businessmen who would give up their womanizing ways for her. She longed to be whisked off into romance, expensive restaurants, and five-star hotels. Aside from escaping her family, I knew this was secretly the reason she had joined the Foreign Service in the first place. So there we were, lounging by the club's fancy Olympic-size pool on a Sunday afternoon.

"What about him?" asked my mother, pointing across the lawn to a fit blond guy.

I squinted. "Too young for you, too old for me," I said, squeezing more sunscreen out of the tube and into my hand. I rubbed my hands together and applied the cream to my already singed shoulders.

"Him?" Maggie peeked over her sunglasses at a man carrying golf clubs over his shoulder. A skinny woman ran toward him from the snack bar, and they started kissing.

"Something tells me she's not his sister," I said, and we laughed. It was one of those warm, slow days when even my mother and I could find nothing to argue about. I wished she acted this way all the time, joking with me like a friend.

I peeled off my oversized shades to take a cooling dip, and then fell into a deep sleep on my towel. When I woke up my back was sore from the sun and Maggie was sitting at a picnic table a few yards away, talking to a thin, salt-and-pepper-haired man in blue swim trunks. He was smoking a cigarette and had one hand on his hip. His left hand. And it was ringless. This surprised me, since my mother was attracted only to unattainable men. That's what had happened with my father, and it had been the same with every boyfriend she'd had ever since. I saw it as the side effect of my grandfather's affairs, which I'd overheard my mother and grandmother talking about. At first, my mother had thought her father's abandonment was merely a paramour gone— briefly—one step too far.

"Why couldn't you go out and get a fucking Porsche like every other old man in a midlife crisis?" I pictured her shouting the day he loaded his suitcases into the trunk of his frugal Toyota to leave for good. She thought he'd turn around and come back, but he didn't. That's when she found out about the Thai waitress from the lunch place in a strip mall near the hospital where he worked, and she vowed never to speak to her father again. She took off and was settled in her little room on the Mayan Riviera by the time my grandfather married the twenty-three-year-old waitress. His wedding day—March 7, 1976—was the same day my mother met my father on the Playa del Carmen beach. Eight months and a week later, I was born.

My mother and her father were close when she was growing up, but after the blowout fight, where he wrote her out of the will and the Thai waitress in, she made good on her promise. Years later, he called her with an olive branch in his hand, but she refused to see him. I'd laid eyes on my grandfather only once, when I was eight and we were in L.A. visiting my grandmother during the holidays. He had somehow learned that we were there and showed up at the house, banging on the door and demanding to meet his only grandchild. I tried to peer through the kitchen window. He was wearing plaid shorts, but that's all I saw of him before my grandmother pulled me away. She and my mother hurried me into the windowless downstairs bathroom and we stayed in that tiny box, beneath the humming of the fan that turned on with the light switch, until the banging stopped. I still remember those moments of near-silence, the three of us looking tired in the mirror under the unflattering light, huddled and waiting for the man to leave.

"You know, Milagro, I met Armando before that day at the pool," my mother said, squeezing lime into a big bowl of guacamole on the counter of our airy, tiled kitchen. I sat at the round table puzzling out a calculus problem, trying to concentrate on that and on my mother's loud voice at the same time. "He told me he only got up the nerve to ask me out after we ran into each other there. Isn't that adorable? And after the diplomatic conference the other day he walked me to the car, and he put his arm around my shoulder right in front of the other guests," she gloated, stirring vigorously. "Sarita from the office said, 'Wow, he must really like Maggie.' Apparently he never behaves this way. He has a reputation for being reserved and paranoid, but he doesn't seem that way to me."

"Well, I'm happy for you," I said, giving up on the problem and doodling in my math book.

I saw his car pull up from her bedroom window. His bodyguard got out of the front seat and opened the back door for him. He stepped out and the bodyguard rang our doorbell. My mother's heels clack-clacked against the red-tiled floor of the entryway. Armando was tall and handsome, his shock of wavy hair perfectly gelled into place. His tailored suit looked custom-made. He had an electric energy about him that I was drawn to immediately.

I ran down into the foyer to greet him. My mother was already there, waiting as he approached with a bunch of roses under his arm.

"Thank you!" Maggie gushed as he passed her the flowers and pecked her on the lips. "This is my daughter, Milag—"

"Mila," I interrupted. We kissed on the cheek, in the typical Mexican style of saying hello.

"It's a great pleasure to meet you, Mila," he said. "She's beautiful," he said, smiling at Maggie. "Just like her mother."

His formal English was so sweet, it almost verged on nauseating. I don't think I'd ever seen my mom blush before.

It was the first night Armando had come to our house for dinner. As Maggie and I carried her usual man-pleasing appetizers on Mexican ceramic platters from the kitchen to the living-room coffee table, she smiled in a way I rarely saw, a smile that meant she really was happy, not just her usual pretending that everything was fine when it wasn't. We laid out the array of spinach dips, tomato bruschetta, and all the other little dishes that appeared when she thought a man was special. Unfortunately, she'd fed bruschetta to a lot of bastards over the years. I hoped Armando wouldn't turn out to be one of them.

"So what do you do?" I asked as we walked through the dining room. It was the one thing my mother hadn't explained.

We moved into the living room and sat on the huge white couch in front of the impressive appetizer display. I wondered what Armando would think of Maggie's Mexican decorative flourishes: she'd turned cattle-branding irons into candlesticks, and an old wooden trough she bought on the Toluca highway for ten pesos now held a row of indoor plants.

"I'm in charge of Almoloya," said Armando. "Do you know what that is?"

"I've seen it mentioned in newspapers. A prison, right?"

"Not just any prison. It's the tightest maximum-security penitentiary in Mexico. One politician you may have heard of is in there for murder, but mostly we get the major drug traffickers and cartel leaders. And it is also, I am happy to say, the place where I first set eyes on your mother."

I'd already put two and two together. Maggie had had to visit American prisoners who were being held at Almoloya, mostly for selling drugs or being mules—trying to import coke, pot, heroin, and methamphetamines into the United States. Part of my mother's job was to make sure the prisoners were being treated humanely and not abused, though the U.S. government couldn't do a thing about getting them out of there. Mexico's law was the reverse of the American: guilty until proven innocent. My mother brought the prisoners vitamins from the Embassy commissary and magazines in English. Sometimes they requested Doritos, Twinkies, or sugary breakfast cereals, and she got those at the commissary, too. There was U.S. government money allocated especially for that sort of thing: the Count Chocula for the Incarcerated Fund.

"Almoloya is nothing like a U.S. maximum-security prison," said my mother, biting into a piece of bruschetta, tomato juice dribbling down her chin. Armando patted her face with a napkin and kissed her cheek.

"It's more of a small village, a community," said Armando. "Inmates have their own TV sets in their cells, and they are allowed to run little businesses within the prison. One of my favorite guys has a taco stand. Another runs a T-shirt company."

"One imprisoned drug lord lives in a two-bedroom suite with cable TV," Maggie chimed in. "They don't have to wear orange jumpsuits, either. The big drug guys still run their own types of businesses from inside the jail, too."

"Not since I took over," Armando said, poking her gently in the ribs.

Armando had originally studied theater but had switched to law. He became a very successful criminal lawyer who was then appointed to the position of federal chief of police and, now, to Almoloya. His job made him a man admired by many. Others wanted to see him dead. He spent half his days trying to get drug-cartel leaders locked up and the other half making sure they stayed that way.

Armando and I talked while my mother got the seafood paella ready in the kitchen. "Do you want to join the Foreign Service like your mother?" he asked, pouring himself a glass of wine and passing me the bottle. I filled my own glass a quarter full and corked the bottle, pushing it away from my mother's plate. She usually didn't allow alcohol in the house, but Armando didn't know that when he'd stopped at the wine shop.

"No way," I said. "I don't enjoy moving around all the time. I mean, it's amazing to see different countries and have all these experiences, but it's too hard to play out your whole life this way. I know my mother loves it, but it's not for me."

"What do you think you want to do?"

"For a career?"

He nodded. "Or, if you prefer, you can just tell me about the *antros* where you and your friends go dancing."

"We're going to Mekano next weekend for my birthday, but don't tell my mother. That's as far ahead as the rest of *my* life is planned."

"I didn't hear you say that," he said, his warm eyes sparkling. "Did you know that in Mexico you have to choose a *carrera* before you begin college?"

"This guy I just met said he was being forced to study engineering or go straight into medical school," I said.

"Exactly. You have to decide on what you want to do when you're eighteen, and you can't change it without starting over from year one as I did. What would you say right now?"

I thought for a second. "I go through journals so fast I've probably got ten books' worth. Writing, maybe for *Travel & Leisure*." I imagined jetting off to review a new resort in Bali, or spending a month living among weavers, field-workers, and shamans in a town like Angahuan.

"You do already have a good background for a journalist."

"I have an article coming up in the school newspaper," I said, suddenly wanting to impress him.

"Remember to bring me a copy. I can't wait to read it."

I loved his accent. "Thanks." I smiled. "I'm going to Angahuan next week, to work on the piece."

"Where is that?" he asked.

"It's a little town in Michoacán that was totally destroyed by the Paricutín volcano. We're studying it in Mexican-history class."

"See?" he said, lifting his glass of red wine to his lips and taking a sip. "You already have something to teach even an old man like me."

Maybe this was how it felt to have a father, I thought. Not a fresa one but a regular dad. Some guy who eats dinner in your house every night and encourages you to figure out what you want to do with your life.

Maggie came in with a steaming bowl of paella and put some on Armando's plate. They smiled at each other. I wondered if he knew my father, whether their paths had ever crossed. I'd pieced together at school that all the higher-ups in Mexican government ran in the same circles.

I left for the trip to Angahuan in the morning. We walked through the dusty streets and the main square, through an outdoor market where I bought a tiny Michoacán leather flask that came with whiskey in it, and a new journal.

Pulverous black volcanic ash covered the land everywhere. A farmer named Dionisio Pulido noticed one day in 1943 that a giant hole had opened up on his land. The earth started to rumble, and church bells rang all by themselves. The townspeople thought heaven was about to punish them, but it turned out to be the Paricutin volcano.

I tried to take pictures of some of the locals to go along with the article, but they turned and ran; it was the type of place where people believed that photographs steal your soul. The volcano wasn't active anymore, but the town was still desolate, the earth ashen. Rows of shacks had enormous satellite dishes next to them, presumably gifts from relatives who had crossed the border into the United States in search of more prosperous lives. No running water, but hundreds of TV channels. No one spoke much Spanish, either. People conversed in Purepecha, a native ancestral language. Women did traditional weaving, and men rode in on horses and burros from their work in the fields. They didn't have much, but everyone seemed content. It amazed me that the fresas and these indigenous people coexisted in the same country. We had Internet, sushi restaurants, and platform sandals. They had corn, ash-covered roads, and deeply grooved faces. We must have looked like imposters, invaders from the plasticized modern world they saw live only via satellite. Or, like Cortés with the Aztecs, light-skinned heavenly beings who could turn into conquistadores at any given moment.

We rode horses along a trail of deep black soil for three miles up to the summit of the volcano. At one point, my horse sank to its knees in dark volcanic ash. It huffed along, and I looked out over the jarring moonlike charcoal rocks and sparse greenery. It was so stark, a surreal landscape that could have been the surface of another planet. At the top, I peered down into the volcano. Wisps of smoke still drifted skyward, whispering of some eruption yet to come. At night, alone in my hotel room, I scrawled out my article for the newspaper, and it came out the next week.

"Pretty good, Mila," said Mr. Payne at the next newspaper meeting.

"Not too bad for a start. I want you to try a little column for me every week."

"A columnist gig, really?" I thought at best I'd get to write something once in a while, being new and all.

"On one condition," he said. "Never turn in a boring story. As I said, this is a fine start, but I want you to think deeply about things, go beneath the surface, explore your environment, the school, this city. Be controversial, if you will. Don't process, just be yourself and stay in the moment. Know what I mean?"

"But writing *is* how I process the world around me," I told him.

"You self-edit, though. I can tell. You're the type of person who thinks about what you're about to say before you say it. I bet that when you write in that diary I never see you without, you put your perspective down unfiltered."

"But that's private, Mr. Payne."

"I want this to be an exercise that shows you how to be more revealing in your writing. You don't have any reason to hide, or anything to hide from. You have a voice."

"I'm just—new," I said, not entirely sure what I meant.

"This school, this city, these experiences—they're yours for the taking, too, you know. Step up and own it."

"Are you calling me insecure?"

"I know you feel that you'll always be the new one, that you've been moved around a lot and have no control. It's easy to get out of control in your life because of it."

I was shocked that Mr. Payne had called it so perfectly.

"How do you know all this?" I asked.

"I've been there, too. My father was in the British foreign service, and I had the same life growing up as many of my students."

"So you get it."

"Then do we have an agreement? You'll hand in something every week?"

"I can write about anything?"

"Anything."

Moving my most private thoughts into a public forum wouldn't be easy, but, as Mr. Payne insisted, I was going to learn how to stop hiding from the eyes of others. I would reveal more of myself in the only way I knew how: not face-to-face but on paper. And one thing I knew for sure: I was never going to tell Maggie about this. It was perfect. She may have gone digging around my room for anything remotely private, but she would never read the *ISM Observer*.

"So, what are you going to call your column?" Mr. Payne asked.

"Doble Vida," I said, immediately thinking of my double life. I'd always had one, starting from my origins, which were secret even to myself. And with moving around all the time, my only consistent, authentic-feeling existence was internal. Every time I moved, I revised myself for a new culture and new surroundings, becoming more attuned to which aspects of my persona were best suited to the different people and situations I encountered. Mr. Payne was right: I did self-edit, and not just my words. With the column, I would have a chance to reveal myself, exposing my true thoughts to the same people I was tailoring my new outward appearance for.

Mexico City was finally starting to grow on me, just as my mother had promised it would around the three-month mark. I felt as if the plane I was on was finally reaching cruising altitude, that strange, discombobulated feeling lessening. I was getting comfortable on the huge smoggy streets, and in my own little room, which I plastered with black-and-white photography ripped from music magazines. It was the height of grunge in the States, and the fashion, music, and lifestyle had migrated all the way south to ISM. The fresas didn't understand the clothes or the music, and would wonder aloud in class why *los Norteamericanos* dressed like the homeless.

"Se ven como nacos, no?" said Catalina, a popular fresa whose mother was a telenovela star, as she passed us between classes in the hall.

"Que horrible," said her friend Beatriz, wrinkling up her altered nose and looking us up and down.

"What are *nacos*?" I asked Kai.

"It means low-class, like 'white trash' does in America, only it's way more insulting. See, an *indio* is an indigenous person, somebody who's poor. That can be neutral or mean, depending how you say it. A *naco*, on the other hand, is always an insult. Somebody *naco* might even have money, but they have no taste."

"Don't pay attention to those fresas," Naldo interjected. "They're nasty."

"They're beautiful, though," I said.

Kai rolled his eyes. "They're one percent of the population," he said. "And a percentage better off ignored."

I hadn't told him I'd hatched a secret plan in Angahuan to accelerate my Spanish lessons, to get to know the fresas better: fodder for investigative reporting. Maggie already had a tutor coming over after school three days a week, and Armando said he would help, that he'd talk as often as I wanted. I vowed to perfect my past-imperfect tense. *Pasado imperfecto.* It was the hardest part of the Spanish language, but I was going to conjugate if it meant speaking for six hours a day.

ISM OBSERVER
October 18, 1993

Doble Vida: Exploring New Places

—By Mila Márquez

Welcome to my new column. I moved here this year, and this is the place where I'll be telling you about the process of adapting. I'll attempt to be as candid and honest as I possibly can, even at the risk of potential humiliation, in order to reveal something meaningful to you all about being an American girl adjusting to life in Mexico City, and my experiences here may be the best place to start. It's been difficult to adjust; so far I've been surprised by what I've found. I will say only this: My mother expected a beachy culture, as if you'd all be wearing Bermuda shorts and hot-pink leis. Mariachi music, spicy food, eighty-degree weather year-round. But what I've found so far is harsh, stark, striking. Mexico City has a dark underworld, far from the daily existence of the vendors and taxicabs passing by as the haze in the sky brightens, then fades with the setting sun. Even the weather is dramatic, constantly changing. I was freezing at the bus stop this morning, icy dew covering the plants in my yard. Now, as I write this in the afternoon, the sun is scorching the pavement outside in the school yard. At night, I'll need a warm jacket again. It's using up four seasons' worth of clothing in one day.

Lately, I've lived like a failed existentialist, in the past and the future but not the present. I've been doing a lot of thinking about this moving around type of life and the effects it has on someone who's part of it. There's no one I can turn to and say, "Remember when . . ." Not having anyone to share any of your memories with kind of feels like those mindscapes could have been invented. I could be a compulsive liar and no one would even know. Maybe that's why I feel the need to record everything, which might be the real reason for this column's existence. (Sorry, Mr. Payne.)

What really gets me about Mexico City so far is the freedom of movement, and the way the city goes by its own time. When people here make plans, whatever time they say always means an hour later. Clubs and restaurants never seem to close, and everything is so laid-back and yet uber-intense all at once. I still get disoriented sometimes, still don't have the city down as a map in my mind. I hope you'll follow my column as I start the journey toward filling in that map with neighborhoods, street names, parks, and plazas, as I document my year in Mexico City. I hope you'll live it along with me.

FOUR

November

Día de los Muertos, November first and second, was the strangest holiday celebration I'd ever experienced, but also my new favorite. Armando drove my mother and me to a little town that carried out all the rituals of the festive take on death, gathering in the graveyard, decorating the family graves with designs of the Virgen de Guadalupe in yellow, pink, purple, and blue petals. Tiny old ladies with raisin faces and woven shawls lit incense and prayed loudly. Biting into the sugar skull Armando had bought for me, its crunchy sweetness melting on my tongue, I thought of how the one certainty of life was death, and the whole point must be to enjoy it while you're here. As we wandered around, I couldn't stop thinking about Dave and wishing I could undo those first few weeks when I'd felt so lost and confused. We watched the parade of papier-mâché, cartoonlike skeletons, men wearing death masks and women carrying their babies swaddled in bright woven blankets. At dusk, hundreds of candles lit the graveyard in a soft orange, and we got into Armando's Mercedes to head home.

The next day was Sunday, and my seventeenth birthday. I got the best present from my mother: a business-class plane ticket to D.C. for Thanksgiving break and a phone card to call Nora and tell her I'd be coming to visit. In the evening, I gathered my group of friends to go to dinner at Spago, then, unbeknownst to my mother, dancing at Mekano. Spago, the hip California hot spot, had just opened in Polanco, which made sense since the area was known as the Beverly Hills of Mexico City. Nina, Naldo, and Kai rode in a taxi with me, and Tyler and Sisley met us at the restaurant. They'd broken up as soon as Sisley heard about her father's transfer to make it easier when she actually had to leave, but they were still together all the time. I ordered a Splash, the high-school drink of choice and classic Mexico City cocktail. It was a sickeningly sweet blend of Amaretto, orange juice, and grenadine that reminded me of the thinly wrapped Italian cookies my mother kept in a crystal dish in our kitchen. I sucked down my drink, ordered another, and gulped that one down, too.

"I have to go to the bathroom," I said. I stood and felt dizzy.

"Wait, I'll come with you," said Nina. We shuffled through the dimly lit, Deco-style restaurant, past the tables of high-society Mexican ladies and men puffing cigars. In the women's room, I grabbed onto the sink as the room moved in circles, round and round, like an Aztec calendar, which wasn't even really a calendar at all but a gladiatorial sacrificial altar, a *temalacatl*, used in warrior ceremonies.

I struggled to steady myself.

"You're really drunk, aren't you?" said Nina. "Happy birthday." She turned around, her long skirt flowing with the movement of her body. "Come on, our food is probably here."

"I think I'm okay," I said, still clutching the edges of the sink. But Nina had already left the bathroom. Still, when I got back to the table I kept ordering the sticky-sweet orange drinks. It was my birthday, after all.

Mekano was a cheesy club in the Zona Rosa that played a lot of eighties music and had an elevated dance floor. Fake smoke hissed from the ceiling and I breathed in its refreshing, misty scent, the smell of a club heating up. Kai moved along with me to instinctual choreography. "Girl, you dance fierce," he said, snapping his fingers as we laughed. "No, seriously, have you studied professionally?" he asked.

"I used to be a cheerleader," I said, and rolled my eyes.

"You? Really? I don't believe it."

"I'm serious!" I shouted above the bass.

"I always wanted to be a cheerleader," he yelled back. "But you can imagine what would happen to me at school."

"Is it really that bad?"

"However bad you're imagining, it's worse. But I only applied to colleges in the States, where I can take dance classes without being called a *pinche maricón* every five seconds."

Around eleven, Naldo announced that he had to leave—he had to get up at five-thirty for water-polo practice.

"I'm supposed to have breakfast with my dad," said Kai. "It's our Monday-morning ritual." Kai's parents were both psychoanalysts who worked from home, so he was one of the few kids who actually seemed to have a mom and dad, and hadn't been raised by women named Guadalupe or Concepción. His father was Japanese, his mother Mexican. They lived in a Zen sanctuary of a house where even the Mexican maid learned to make shumai. Kai's father taught her to cook Japanese food, sizzling strips of steak prepared on their imported dining-room table, which opened up into a stovetop. Everyone was quiet and respectful at dinner, unlike the way my mother and I usually argued when we ate. The Atsuhikos didn't know that their son dated boys, though.

"I'll stay out with you," said Nina.

"No, you won't," said Naldo. "Mom said you had to come home whenever I did."

"Since when did she start to care?"

"She said she wants to see us before heading to Tokyo tomorrow," Naldo said.

"Why does she want to see us?" Nina asked. "That's, like, a first."

"No idea, sis, but we have to go."

"*I* don't have to wake up tomorrow," said Tyler.

"Aren't you taking me home?" asked Sisley.

"No," he said. "You can go if you want to."

Her mouth dropped into a perfect oval, her eyes narrowing.

"Sisley—" I said, but she grabbed her things and ran toward the exit.

"Seems everyone's bailing except us," said Tyler. We sat back down at our dark corner table.

"What do you want to do?" I asked. "I'm supposed to be home in an hour."

"Actually, I got you a birthday present," he said. "I didn't plan on giving it to you tonight, but what the hell." He pulled a piece of tinfoil out of his pocket. Inside were two tiny white paper balls.

"Microdots," he said. "You up for it? I wasn't sure, but I thought you'd like these."

I had no idea what he was talking about, but I felt up for anything. "Is it fun?" I asked.

"You don't know what fun is until you've tried this. But it's more than that."

I looked up at him as he placed one on the tip of my tongue. His eyes were huge and blue, with big pupils that looked like the center of gravity on Jupiter. I swallowed.

"Let's go for a walk," he said.

We exited out to Reforma, where the cars streamed up and down, a perpetual river of red and white light. The Ángel de la Independencia loomed before us in all her golden glory. I tried to think of what the story behind the angel was. I remembered reading that she was a gift from France, made of solid gold, and that at one point thieves had tried to steal her off her perch. We crossed the avenue and sat on the steps of her base, looking out over the stream of exhaust, cars, and concrete, the palm-lined street, the overwhelming hugeness of it all.

"We could be in Paris," I said, standing up. "Yeah, we're in Paris, and this is the Champs Élysées!"

"Weren't they designed by the same guy?" asked Tyler, a faraway look in his eyes.

"Actually, I think Maximilian, the emperor of Mexico, wanted to do something similar to Baron Haussmann's renovation of Paris. It was to make his wife, Carlota, feel more at home in Mexico City."

"Someone's been paying attention in history class."

"Nah, I'm just lucky. I have a good memory," I said, staring out over the boulevard.

I felt as if I could travel anywhere I wanted without even leaving where I was. I didn't need to be Maggie's patchwork doll. I only needed this, this moment. I started feeling warm, then hot. I took off my sweater. I stared at the moving traffic, the giant palm trees, transfixed. Then I started laughing. It was all so funny and absurd, and I couldn't control it, any of it. "It's a giant outdoor hallway. An oversized bowling alley. How did you figure this out?" I said to Tyler.

"It's hitting you, isn't it?" he said. "You're tripping."

"I'm what? No, it's just really hot out." Then I looked up at the Angel. She was beautiful. Her wings began to move. A little, at first, then with vigor. Soon she lifted straight off her platform and flew, getting smaller and smaller as she escalated higher and higher into the starless, smoggy Mexico City night sky. Then she vanished behind the clouds.

"She flew away," I said.

"What?"

But when I looked back up at the monument she was right where she always was, anchored down, heavy.

"How do you feel?" asked Tyler. He put his hand between my shoulder blades and rubbed my back.

"Mmm. Good," I said. "You know, I really keep too much stuff. I have to start throwing it all away."

I dumped the contents of my purse on the ground between us. There was a crumpled-up article that I'd written about a swimming championship for the high-school newspaper in D.C. A pen from the Radisson in Vienna, a vacation with Maggie. Coins from the Czech Republic, England, and France. An Amstel napkin where this guy who'd given me and Maggie directions to our hotel in Amsterdam had drawn a map. My Istanbul postcard and another from a New York City restaurant, the 21 Club, where my mother had taken me for my sixteenth birthday. An umbrella from the Louvre. The phone number of a guy named Andrew, whom I'd met at a funky L.A. café one summer two years ago while I was there visiting my grandmother. Andrew had taken me up to Malibu on his motorcycle, which led to a camping trip at Joshua Tree. We'd kept in touch for a while after I went back to D.C., and I remembered thinking that he could have turned into a great love if only we'd had the time. Keys to the old condo in Washington. Keys to our current house on Monte Athos. A *New York Times* article I'd clipped about a writer named Joan Didion, whom I wanted to be just like one day. A Polaroid Nora had snapped of me with her beat-up Barbie camera the day I dyed my hair black. In the picture I look happy.

"You come with a lot of baggage, don't you?" said Tyler, staring at all the stuff.

We both started laughing as if it were the funniest thing in the world.

"See those cars?" he said, pointing at the flow of white headlights down on Reforma below, heading in our direction.

"Yeah?"

"All those white lights are on the road to heaven. The red ones"—he pointed at the retreating traffic, going in the direction of Lomas—"are on their way to hell."

"But when you're in the car, it's always red, so—"

"We're all going down," he said. "But hell is only a temporary place to exist until we repent."

"Well, that's comforting," I said, employing my best sarcastic tone.

"The thing is, Mormonism actually makes sense. The basic premise is that if you're here living on earth it means you've accepted God's plan to make you grow. All your experiences get you closer to heaven in the end. That's what I love about this stuff. It's, like, a shortcut."

"I don't know if God would agree with you on that," I said. I'd picked up atheism from my mother, though I realized that if I replaced the "God" in Tyler's statement with "the Universe," I might have agreed entirely. What was that phrase? Two birds by the same name? Something about a different stone? Maybe a rose by any other name or calling a spade a spade. I couldn't remember. All I knew was that if there was a bunch of clichés about something it was usually true.

Tyler started talking about the Mexican Revolution, his idol Che Guevara, about overthrowing the PRI, and about people he called the "real" Mexicans taking back what was rightfully theirs.

"But you're not even Mexican," I said.

"Neither was Che, but this is all the same spirit. You know I'm from Arizona, right? Well, that was Mexico and it still should be. When I lived there, I'd sometimes cross over the border to bring water into the desert, for the people trying to cross over."

"Wasn't that dangerous?"

"My neighbors were part of this radical underground supremacist-type group that would hunt down illegal immigrants on their way over and chase them with shotguns. I felt I had to do something. My English teacher at school there, he turned me on to Che, the great revolutionaries, and activism. We used to go down together, in his jeep. I helped him paint it camo, in the color of sand."

"And here I thought you were just some slacker alt-rock dude."

"I'm lying low for a while, that's all. Making money."

I didn't have to ask what he did. I'd figured it out.

"Mr. Gonzalez was my teacher's name," Tyler went on. "He went to jail for killing one of the fucking militia nazis. That's real, not all the bullshit at ISM."

"What?" I asked, startled. "He *killed* someone?"

"He's getting out next year."

"What?" Tyler's voice sounded like it was coming from inside an echo chamber.

I suddenly realized I'd become so absorbed in the acid trip and in Tyler's stories that I'd completely lost track of time. I had no idea how long I'd been around or awake or alive. I grabbed Tyler's wrist and looked at his watch. It was either 12:30 or 2:30, either of which meant I was late.

"I have to call home," I said, watching his face turn from white to green to a light shade of violet. I looked all around for the flashing neon sign that was tinting his pale skin, but there wasn't one. For the first time all night, I wanted to get away. We left the Angel and I found a pay phone on Reforma.

"Hello?" My mother's voice sounded breathless.

"Mom? It's me."

"Where the hell are you? It's past three in the morning."

"It's twelve-thirty."

"No, it's three. What's the matter with you?"

"I'm just having a good time on my birthday!" I said, and hung up. It seemed more and more absurd to go home the later it got. I was trapped. If I went home, she'd know something was wrong with me, and if I stayed out I'd be in more trouble with her later. It was a—what's that word for a no-win situation? Not faux pas . . . Oh, impasse. Yeah, an impasse, a zero-sum game. I felt fizzled out, like that stupid old eighties drug commercial with the sizzling eggs.

"I have to go," I told Tyler.

"All right, let's get on the subway."

"Subway?"

"Do you have cab fare?"

I looked in my purse.

"I spent all my money at Spago." Spago. It felt like we'd been there days ago.

We descended into the Insurgentes station, bound for Tacubaya, where we'd transfer to the orange line to Auditorio, a round-about trip heading south only to go back up again, but it was the only way. I sat on a bench on the platform and stared at the train flying through the station, and suddenly got the feeling I'd found the meaning of it all.

"The fluorescent lights. The tracks. The tunnels. There's an entire city beneath the city," I said. "It's all layers on layers on layers, like the subconscious, like human interaction. Talking with more meaning beneath the words than what we actually say. The spaces between words—that's what means more than the attempted communication, that's where we say what we really mean. It's all in layers. From underground on up. And everything just goes around in circles."

"Mila," said Tyler. "Shhhhh." He wrapped his arms around me, and I buried my face in his flannel shirt, inhaling deeply.

I saw colors and tasted smells. His scent was the desert after a rainstorm. I wanted to leave the city, go someplace far away with grass and trees and nobody, somewhere I could see the stars. But, right there and then, the sound of the train on the tracks was my mind grinding out thoughts. The noise in my brain met the soprano of the brakes until all I heard was the great colorful illusion of music, the city's drumbeat, subway doors sliding open, rhythmic footfalls as new passengers tramped in and old ones tramped out. We emerged from the Auditorio station near my house and out into the pre-daybreak light. Auditorio was a futuristic structure where all the big concerts were held. I looked up at the marquee: U2, Guns N' Roses, Pavarotti. The trip from the Zona Rosa to Auditorio took half an hour by taxi, but the subway and the drugs had disoriented me. It could have been one hour or nine or twenty-four.

I went into the ground-floor bathroom as soon as I got home. I knew Maggie would be awake in her room at the top of the stairs. I flipped on the bathroom light and stared into my eyes, which were huge and strange. My pupils took up my entire iris. I couldn't stand to look at my own face for too long. It looked distorted, pale, greenish, frightening even. I went to the kitchen and saw a letter with Nora's return address sitting on my place mat, and suddenly remembered that I never wrote her again after my mother opened the last letter. I tore the envelope and squinted to read it in the blue moonlight.

November 10

Dear Mila,

You didn't answer my last letter, or maybe it got lost in the mail. I hope you haven't forgotten about me or our plans to visit each other. Things here are the same as always, but I miss you a lot. We won the cheerleading championship! I figured you'd be excited about that. The homecoming dance was amazing this year, too. Rob got us a hotel room for a party afterward, and Diane brought a bottle of vodka! It was kind of fun, but I couldn't stand the taste of it. It reminded me of when we used to steal my dad's beer, but way more rebellious. Maybe this is the year we really grow up but get to act more like kids than ever at the same time, do you know what I mean? Rob and I might break up, though, if he gets into that Georgetown foreign-service school and I end up moving to Boston. What's new with you? Please call or write—you have to make your travel plans soon.

Love,
Nora

Was this how my life used to be? I wondered. Cheerleading championships and feeling like we were pulling something off by drinking bottom-shelf vodka in some cheap hotel room? She'd hit on something, though, with her line about us growing up but acting more like kids than ever. That was what I loved about Nora; she'd be silly and funny, then hit you with an astute observation.

A silhouette stood on the second-floor overhang: my mother. When I got upstairs, she followed me into my bedroom. She didn't turn on the light, thankfully, or she would have seen my eyes.

"We need to talk," she said, sitting down on the edge of my bed as I climbed in. Her voice was unusually soft. "What on earth is going on with you? Please, tell me what you need."

I needed answers about my father. I needed to get that night with Dave out of my system. I needed the comforts of a stable home I'd never known. I needed to get away from her. I needed to be able to talk to her. But I didn't know where to start.

"Well, you know that little maid house on our property? The one that's empty since Rosa doesn't actually live here?" I said. "I want to make it into an art studio, so I can paint. Or maybe a recording studio, so I can take guitar lessons and make an album."

"We'll get you a guitar if you need an outlet," she said. "At least that's what I think you're saying." Her voice trembled, sounding desperate or as if she were afraid of me.

"It's kind of screwed up, suddenly being here, where my father's from, isn't it?" I said.

"Don't do this, Milagro."

"I don't even understand why you named me that."

"Are you taking drugs?"

"You would know, wouldn't you?" I watched her face turn from a tiger mask into a butterfly and back through colorfully shifting Venetian masquerade illusions.

"What is that supposed to mean?"

"Grandma always says she never knew what to do with you when you were a crazy hippie, hitchhiking around to follow the Dead and running off to live on some beach in Mexico."

"And look where that got me, all the fun I was having drinking piña coladas at the bars that I can't even remember when it turned into something else. What I do remember is how hard I had to fight to get back on track and make things work for us. Don't look to me as an example for how to model your life, Milagro." She stood up and walked across the room. "You don't need to turn into some beatnik with a giant backpack. That's no way to find a rich man to take care of you. And *that* is the answer, not some free-spirit bullshit. I know it all too well. It leads no place you want to go."

"You're the so-called addictive personality, not me," I said.

"You're too young to be able to tell the difference," she said, her voice suddenly softer. "These things are genetic, anyway." The door clicked shut behind her.

I couldn't sleep the rest of the night. I lay in bed with my headphones on, staring out the window up at the sky as the strains of Pink Floyd's "Breathe" on the rock station colored the air. Roger Waters was singing about being home again. *I like to be there when I can . . .*

I'd wanted to get out of my skin after the move to Mexico and the mess I'd found myself in. Just as I was working through it, trying to move past it, Tyler showed me how. I never imagined it could be as easy as popping a tiny piece of paper into my mouth.

I could barely see straight when I pulled myself out of bed two hours later. It was Monday morning and I had to go to school. I hadn't quite returned to my normal state of consciousness.

"You look a wreck," said Maggie when I came down to the kitchen for breakfast. "I'm making you a cappuccino."

The thought of drinking cappuccino made me want to vomit. What I really wanted was to crawl back into bed and sleep the day away.

"Forget about coming to Ixtapa with Armando and me this weekend," she continued. "I know there's more freedom in Mexico City than you're used to, but staying out all night is ridiculous. Don't think I'll let you run wild going to clubs and drinking and throwing away everything you've worked so hard for. I hope your trip back to D.C. reminds you what that was."

"I'll be moving out soon enough," I said. "Why do you care so much if I enjoy everything *my* Mexico has to offer? You jealous?" I knew I'd gone too far.

"You little ingrate," I heard her mutter. I wanted to apologize, but I couldn't get the words out. My whole body ached, and I wanted a cigarette. I put on my sunglasses and left for school.

In first-period art class, I took out my pastels and the still-life sketch assignment from Friday. I'd drawn the exact duplicate of a candle. It looked forced, a class exercise. The other kids got out their candle drawings and everyone's was identical. The teacher placed the candle in the middle of the table where we were seated and put objects around it: a vase, a small plant, a bottle of water. I ignored everything but the vase, which I colored in bright blue. Then I drew in flowers that weren't really there—dead flowers, still in tropical colors but bent over, not straight up and down. Wilted yet vibrant.

Miss Aramba, the art teacher, circled the room looking at everyone's drawing, assessing. When she got to mine, she stopped.

"Mila, this is not still life." She shook her head. "Look at what is there. Look at what is here. It is not the same. What we are trying to do is replicate reality. You've gone and distorted it."

After the bell rang, I went down to the pay phone past the lockers in senior hall. First, I called Nora's line with my mother's AT&T card. I left a long message on her answering machine about the plane-ticket birthday gift and how sorry I was that she never got my previous letter. I told her that it must have gotten lost in the mail. Then I hung up and dropped in some one-peso coins to dial Tyler.

"I'm not feeling so hot," I said when he answered. "I don't know how I'm going to make it through the day."

"So cut out of there, come over," he said.

I paid the guard at the gate fifty pesos and went over to Tyler's. He taught me the bass line of a song he wrote and we played all afternoon. I was barely passing calculus, but I was beginning to master the bass guitar.

"Is Sisley doing any better about the move?" I asked. "She seems so distracted whenever I see her around school."

"I don't know," he said. "We ended it."

"But you didn't want to."

He shrugged. "The move just gave me a good reason. It's not like she and I were never going to date anybody else. Besides, there's a girl I've had my eye on ever since I first saw her."

"Oh yeah? Who?" I asked, though I knew this game perfectly well.

"Well, she's smart, and she's beautiful, and she has long black hair, green eyes, an amazing body . . ." As Tyler kissed me I forgot about ISM, about my mother, and, for a moment, even about Dave, though he always seemed to be lurking somewhere in my mind. Sometimes that night went into hibernation for a while. Those were the times I could relax and look around again, forgetting that night in the blue bedroom, with the skylight. It was a place where Dave didn't exist and I wasn't angry all the time.

"Come on," Tyler said. "Let's go to Coyoacán."

Coyoacán, a neighborhood in the south, was a historic part of town with a famous plaza full of fountains with coyote statues, the area's namesake. We took the subway there. It was a complicated ride: the orange line to the brown line to the lime-green line (because there was a hunter-green line, too). The trip took more than an hour. The Mexico City subway system—at nineteen cents a ride, the world's cheapest—heightened my awareness of the sheer number of people who lived in the megalopolis. As I'd observed that night on the microdots, there was a whole city's worth of people underneath the city at any given moment. They flooded the passageways between train lines, a red sea of humanity all pushing their way toward some figurative shore to wash up on.

When we got there, we hailed a little green Volkswagen Bug taxi to the plaza even though we weren't supposed to, because more and more passengers were being robbed by street taxis. We walked through the artisan market in Plaza Coyoacán. Balloon and cotton-candy vendors wheeled their carts by. "Globos, un peso," they cried out almost in unison. Tyler introduced me to a hippie vendor friend of his, Carmen, a traveler who'd been everywhere, even Prague, one of my favorite cities. Though she didn't have much money, her life's priority was to see the world. She had, and still did. To support herself, Carmen made jewelry out of stones and glass, which reminded me of my mother's life before

I came along, only Carmen seemed so laid-back. Tyler bought me an amber pendant, sold Carmen two hits of acid, and we said good-bye.

"Where now?" I asked.

"We're going to Las Islas."

"What's that?"

"It's a place in the middle of a field on the UNAM campus. Little grassy knolls that look like islands, with palm trees on them. Did you know UNAM's the oldest university in the Western Hemisphere? It makes Harvard seem like it opened its doors yesterday."

"Harvard. I applied there. Crazy, right?"

"Think you'll get in?" he asked.

"Probably don't stand a chance. Isn't this whole area called University City?"

"Yeah, C.U.," he said. "*Ciudad Universitaria.* The government declared it an artistic monument," he explained. "We're walking on top of an ancient, solidified lava bed."

We passed through a huge field where university students sat, smoking and studying. Las Islas, I learned that day, was where you could buy anything—pot, acid, mushrooms, coke. It was a virtual candy store of mind-altering substances. Tyler asked one of the men to restock him, and then I knew for a fact how he always managed to have money without his parents' support.

"Do you ever worry about getting caught?" I asked him as we walked back through the square toward the subway.

"I've been caught a few times by the *poli*," he said. "A little profit-sharing solves that problem, no questions asked."

"Right, I forgot all about that."

"You ever bribed a cop?"

"I don't think I could get up the courage," I said.

"Nonsense, baby. Repeat after me: *No hay otra manera de hacer esto?*"

I repeated the words, which translated as "Isn't there another way to do this?" It was the universal phrase for "May I bribe you now, please?"

"Very good," he said, ruffling my hair.

~   ~   ~

Tyler hugged me good-bye when we got out of the train at Auditorio.

"Next time you skip to hang out with me, I'll take you to La Feria," he said.

"The amusement park over on Insurgentes?"

"In Bosque de Chapultepec. It's awesome. You drop a little acid, you're having the time of your life."

"I heard the place was shut down once because that rickety wooden roller coaster flew off the tracks, right out into the highway."

"I think that's an urban legend," Tyler said, kissing the top of my head. He was a whole foot taller than I was. His lankiness reminded me of that tall, skinny pumpkin-headed character in *Nightmare Before Christmas*. "I like you," he said.

"I like you, too," I said, looking at the ground, the outline of Tyler's Doc Martens against the rippling pavement, still cracked in some places from the '86 earthquake. I suddenly remembered that Maggie and I had been in Guadalajara at the time, eating breakfast, when we felt the rumble and ran outside. It was an 8.1. In Mexico City, which was closer to the epicenter, twenty-five thousand people died.

Tyler and I kissed again, then went our separate directions.

When I got home in the afternoon, my mother was waiting for me.

"How was school today?" she asked.

"What are you doing home from work so early?"

"I got a call from Vice Principal Horney saying you were marked present in first period, then the rest of the day—poof! Vanished."

"So I skipped a few classes, nothing serious."

"Where did you go?"

"A friend's house."

"That dropout boy whose father works in Admin?"

"No."

"If you're going to lie, you should stop writing everything down."

"But I didn't write it. It was just today."

"There. You admitted it. Even if you didn't, I waited down the block outside his house and saw you come out."

Maggie approached parenting the same way she dealt with her job. Stealthily, with investigative skills that would put even the fifth-floor employees to shame. And she was due for a promotion any day.

"Do you think you could talk to me, Mom, instead of stalking me?"

"You make me this way," she said.

"You're that way to begin with." Which came first, I thought, *el pollo* or *el huevo*? "I'm out of here." I pushed past her, out of the room. She tried to grab me, but I ran outside. Then she ran past me, to the gate, locking it from the inside with a key that I didn't have. Enraged, I grabbed the umbrella I carried in my bag and pressed the little silver button. It extended with a pop. I lunged after her, swinging at the air as she backed away.

"Milagro! Calm down. What do you think you're doing?" She was pressed against the gate, shielding her face with her arms. "Stop it!"

"Let—me—out!" I screamed, forcing the keys out of her hand. She ran crying back into the house as I let myself out into the Mexico City evening. The air smelled of sewage.

"Milagro!" my mother shouted out of her bedroom window.

"What?" I yelled back.

"Be home by midnight," she said icily, slamming it shut.

"And it's *Mila*," I called out to no one.

I lingered outside the house for a few minutes, debating whether to go back in. I looked up and saw my mother, who couldn't see me in the dark. She'd collapsed onto her bed. Part of me wanted to go back inside and bury myself in her arms. I longed so hard for them to be arms I could bury myself in.

I grabbed a taxi from the Esplanada *sitio,* the taxi stand. A Virgen de Guadalupe dangled from the rearview mirror.

"Calle Schiller en Polanco, por favor."

"Claro, señorita."

I chatted with the driver for the entire ride in my newly almost-fluent Spanish.

"*Eres de España?*" he asked. "*Tienes un pequeño acento.*" He thought my accent was Spanish, as in from Spain. I was so proud of having picked up the language so quickly that I could fool even a Mexican.

"*Sí, de Barcelona,*" I proudly lied.

Tyler was sitting outside his house, on the hood of Sisley's beat-up gray Chrysler. She leaned against the car, smoking.

"Hi," I said, hesitating as I got out of the taxi, giving Tyler a look: *Does she know?*

"Oh, relax," said Sisley. "I'm leaving in two days. I get it. But couldn't you at least have waited?"

"I'm sorry. I—"

"Right. He slips you some of the good stuff, you think you've found the answer to all your problems, and you fall in love with him."

"We broke up," Tyler said to her. "What am I supposed to do?"

"Not invite that little *slut* over when I come to say good-bye to you!"

The reminding jab stung, but I let it go. Sisley slipped into her car and started the engine. Then she was gone, off to Africa. I would never see her again.

I stayed at Tyler's until late, watching him paint lily pads in a pond in oil on canvas. I tried to keep up on the bass as he played Syd Barrett songs on guitar. When I got home, I was stoned and tired and had to listen to Maggie yelling, "I've created a monster!" I pretended not to hear her. I thought Tyler had the perfect life—no school, no meddling parents, and complete freedom, though apart from his unstructured days, his life wasn't that different from Nina's and Naldo's—or any ISM student's, for that matter.

"We have an appointment to go see your school psychologist," my mother announced before even saying hello after work, as she walked into the foyer of our house. "I called her from work today. She said it would be a good idea if we both went in to see her."

"But you don't believe in therapy," I said. "You think people should overcome their problems on their own."

"It's that Tyler boy you're hanging around with. You're running off who knows where, acting like a lunatic. . . . *My* daughter cared about school and success, and gave me no reason to worry about her. This person"—she pointed at me—"isn't her."

I coughed a few times, as though something were stuck in my throat. There's something about a mother's words that can pierce a daughter like a sewing needle through her heart.

The next day at eleven I picked up a green slip in the office and Mr. Horney signed it, excusing me from second period. I was happy about the appointment, if only because it was the day we were dissecting the pig fetuses and I'd planned on refusing to do it.

Sandie Doone had kind eyes that seemed to give away that she was in a helping profession. She wore a knee-length beige skirt, black flats that matched the rims of her stylish glasses, and a white button-down shirt.

"Come in," she said. I looked around for the couch that I thought I was supposed to lie down on, but there wasn't one. There were two burgundy leather chairs instead, and my mother and I sat on those. Sandie Doone settled in behind her desk, crossed her legs, and picked up a pen.

"Now," she said. "What's been going on with this beautiful mother and daughter?"

"Well, Miss Doone," my mother said, "first of all, she goes out dancing and wants to stay out all night."

"Is that what this is about?" she said. "I see this a lot, and I want to start by saying you do have to realize that that's part of the social norm here. And call me Sandie, please."

I sat in my armchair, not daring to smile. Sandie Doone was on my side.

"Don't you think an eleven o'clock curfew makes more sense?" asked Maggie.

"Mom, the clubs open at eleven."

"Miss Epstein, I'd say a more reasonable time would be two."

"Two *in the morning*?" Maggie asked, shocked.

I liked the psychologist. She understood the reality of life in Mexico City. She also understood the divide between my mom and me.

"I see this a lot with parents and kids who are new," said Sandie, her voice even. "It can seem strange and overwhelming. The best way to handle it is to be more flexible. It seems strange for the kids to have all the freedoms they do here, and it's easy to worry about their safety in such a big place. But the best thing to do is to allow them to do as their Mexican peers are doing."

"But those *peers* have drivers and bodyguards!" yelled Maggie, enraged. "Milagro isn't protected like they are."

Sandie reacted with the type of composure only a mental-health professional could.

"What do you think, Mila?" she asked, her voice soft. "Do you feel safe?"

"As much as I ever did anywhere else. We're always in groups and there are so many people around; it's not like we're lurking in dark alleys or going to bad neighborhoods." I thought of Las Islas but quickly pushed it from my mind.

"So you really think the best way to get back in control of my daughter is to give her more freedom?"

"You should at least try it," said Sandie. "I've seen it work for other American families. I also think Mila would benefit from some type of outlet."

"I learned to play the bass," I volunteered with a sideways glance at Maggie. "My boyfriend taught me."

"Your *boyfriend* is a dropout druggie. And I am absolutely not spending four hundred dollars on a clunky guitar that doesn't even sound good on its own."

"If your daughter is interested in something, you might want to encourage it," said Sandie. "At this stage of life, they're extraordinarily sensitive."

"But she'll sit around and play with it instead of doing homework."

"Well, let's make it into homework," said Sandie.

"What do you mean?" I asked.

"You are signing up for the high-school jazz band," she said to me, making a note on her pad. "I'll discuss it with Mr. Richards, the instructor. Rehearsals take place after school, so you'll be seeing less of this boy your mother seems to think is a bad influence."

Satisfied, Sandie Doone stood up. Maggie and I followed.

"You can call me or come see me anytime," she said. "Mila, that goes especially for you. If you have any trouble or want to talk, drop by."

"Thank you," I said.

My mother didn't seem as content with the outcome of our meeting. I walked her to the gate.

"Do you really think my letting you go around till late is the right thing?" she asked. "It seems totally illogical to me."

"Stop second-guessing everything. You heard the psychologist. If she's seen it work for other people, we shouldn't question it." Of course I was biased, but it felt like a triumph.

I went back to Sandie Doone's office at the end of the school day and rapped lightly on the door.

"Hi, Mila," she said. "I didn't expect to see you again so soon."

"I wanted to thank you for this morning," I said. "You were really good at getting my mom to listen."

"When you go off to college next year and live away from her," she told me, "a whole new side of you is going to come out. I sense that you're a strong person and a lot of the tension between you and your mother is making you repress that. She has such a big personality that you adapt your own persona to accommodate whatever's around you, like a human chameleon. Does that make sense?"

That's it, I thought. I'm telling her everything.

"Do you think we could talk for a while? Just us? I want to ask your advice about something."

"Sure," she said, a look of surprise crossing her calm, moonlike face. "Come on back in."

The next morning the announcements came over the intercom, but Mr. Horney gave them instead of Tomás, the president's son, who was senior-class president. Mr. Horney said the name of a kid in my grade, Pablo Juárez, and that he'd been killed in a motorcycle accident on the Periferico. Later in the day, it spread around school that the boy's body couldn't be found for a week because his wallet, leather jacket, helmet, and crashed-up motorcycle had been stolen from the scene of the accident. Pablo. I got out the student face-book they passed out at orientation and looked him up; I remembered having seen him around campus. He was a popular fresa, always in front of the pool with his friends and Marianna, his girlfriend. She had long, wavy blond hair and was petite but curvy, with huge brown doe's eyes. She acted like a telenovela star—with reason, since she was an actress and had been a recurring character on one. Pablo's parents had to go from morgue to morgue, looking at unidentified bodies, until they found their son.

I made an appointment to see Sandie Doone after school.

"How are you doing, Mila?" she asked after I sat down in one of her big leather chairs.

"I'm upset about Pablo, even though I didn't know him."

"Well, his death is a tragedy for our whole community, so it's natural for you to feel an impact."

"It's got me thinking, you know, about how anything can happen at any moment."

"And where does that leave you?"

"I'm tired of my mother thinking she's protecting me by holding back the truth. I'm doing everything possible to distract myself, but I want to find out who *he* is, even though I'm not supposed to."

Sandie Doone knew the story of my father; I'd told her when I went back after she met with my mother and me, when I realized that she had me pegged in five seconds. I trusted her, which surprised me, since she was, after all, a high-school psychologist.

"What would you say to him if you did find him?" she asked.

"I wouldn't have to talk to him or anything. It would be research, a project, an assignment to find out who he is and what he does."

"That's quite a plan, Mila," said Sandie. "But I don't think it's wise to pursue an endeavor of that scope without speaking to your mother about it."

"Nobody would have to know," I protested.

What *I* didn't know was that, completely at random, the chance would eventually arise.

I sneaked out to see Tyler the night before I left for Thanksgiving break in D.C. One thing I loved about international schools was getting more than one country's worth of holidays off: we got five days for Thanksgiving, another five for spring break, one for Día de los Muertos, and three for Cinco de Mayo. Tyler and I smoked a joint on his roof, crouching behind a water tank so the security guards from the Canadian Embassy wouldn't be able to see us. Afterward, we climbed into bed.

"Do you have a condom?" I asked as he pulled my jeans down around my ankles.

"Right here," he said, fumbling with his wallet.

As I clicked open my gate at four in the morning and tiptoed up the driveway, I couldn't help feeling I'd finally righted things, now that my memory of sex would be good, warm, slow, easy, voluntary—nothing like the first time.

"Mila!" shouted Nora as I rolled my luggage cart through the sliding glass doors of Dulles International Airport.

She looked exactly as I remembered her: cute and petite, with almond skin and a smile that took over her whole face. I ran up to her and we hugged, tight.

"It's so good to be back," I said over her shoulder. Her parents, Kamau—the Kenyan ambassador—and Adele, waited a few feet away. I broke away from Nora to greet them.

"Thanks so much for having me," I said.

"We're so glad you could come visit," said Adele, whose newly grown-in short hair made her look chic, healthy, and like the strong-minded French woman she was. "I know how much Nora has missed you."

The air outside was chilly and crisp, the near-winter smell already present. I pulled my sweater tight around me, no longer used to the cold. We climbed into the old Suburban with Kenyan diplomatic plates. Kamau drove, Adele sat beside him, and Nora and I were in back, already whispering animatedly, as we always had in my formerly regular life. I told her about the night of my birthday and the date with Tyler, leaving out the acid trip.

"And he's really a dropout? What's up with that?"

"He's a former Mormon who thinks his calling from God is to help the 'repressed Mexican peoples.' He's such a mishmash of things, oddly religious to rebel activist," I said, looking out the window at the blur of cars and trees on the road into Maryland.

"Well, he sounds interesting, but I don't know," said Nora.

"What does 'I don't know' mean?"

"Don't get upset, but it doesn't sound like he could be a very good influence."

"He's not an *influence*. Geez, you and my mother." I'd landed barely an hour earlier, and I didn't want to get into a fight. Nora and I rarely argued. "He's really smart and cool is all. And he looks like Kurt Cobain."

Nora wrinkled her nose at the mention of the grunge star. "Those people are all on drugs."

Kamau pulled into the driveway of the family's two-story house in

Bethesda and we hopped out. I grabbed my luggage, brought it up to Nora's room, and flopped on the bed.

"What's the plan for tonight?" I asked.

"I wish we could see a movie with Rob and Karim the way we used to, but I doubt that Karim's new girlfriend would go for that. Maybe you and I could go to the new Starbucks in Georgetown."

"Who's Karim going out with?"

"Diane."

"Really?"

"What's the big deal?" Nora asked, pulling a comb through her thick hair in front of her mirror.

Hearing the name of a formerly good friend linked to my ex-boyfriend's hurt unexpectedly, probably in the same way Sisley had felt about my getting together with Tyler. You couldn't blame people for moving on in your absence, but that didn't make it any easier to accept. After all, you hadn't chosen to break up—you had to. It was a matter of distance. I'd missed Karim at first, but being the one who moved made the separation more tolerable. The person left behind gets stuck with feelings of abandonment, of being haunted by familiar places and the now empty space the person who departed once occupied. The leaver has it somewhat easier: an unfamiliar place to explore and new friends to meet. There was nothing like a change of scenery to help sever an old attachment.

"I guess Starbucks. What is that, a club?"

"No." Nora laughed. "A coffee place. Dance clubs are only twenty-one plus, don't you remember, silly?"

"Right," I said. "Mental slip or culture shock. Probably both. I'm pretty tired."

"Well, maybe we could get Rob's brother to procure some alcohol tomorrow night so we can party," she said.

Getting our hands on alcoholic beverages used to be a night's activity in itself. At that moment, I realized that being a teenager in Mexico City had its privileges.

We ate turkey and stuffing and cranberry sauce, all the typical

Thanksgiving dishes. When the plates were cleared and I'd finished updating Nora's parents on life and school in Mexico, Nora borrowed the keys to her father's Suburban and we headed to the first Starbucks I'd ever seen.

"I'll have a double-tall extra-foam vanilla latte," Nora told the cashier. "What about you, Mila?"

"Um, a coffee?"

Nora balked. "Don't you want to try one of the specialty drinks? They have mocha, caramel, hazelnut—"

"How about *café de olla*?"

"What's that?" Nora asked.

"It's amazing. It has cinnamon and all these other things." I asked the cashier, but she'd never heard of it.

"If you sold it, you'd make a fortune," I told her. "No one outside Mexico seems to know about it."

Nora and I sat down at one of the uniform tables.

"Did I tell you that in Mexico all the clubs serve girls drinks for free?" I asked.

"No, you didn't. Sounds pretty wild," she said. "Seriously, I'm glad you're getting used to living there and all, but it must feel good to be home."

But I knew it wasn't home any longer. I had a new home now. It was here that I was a visitor.

Nora went to the counter to pick up our coffees. I took out my journal and scribbled notes for the beginning of a new story: *Sitting in Starbucks, next to the parking lot, in the first world. . . . Everything has been plastified. All of my circumstances have been exaggeratedly temporary.*

I'd grown used to the colorful chaos of Mexico City, and my former home seemed absurdly sterile by comparison. Everything looked so orderly and calm, one vast chain-shop-dotted Utopia. While the size and the grittiness of Mexico had first intimidated me, I now knew for sure that I'd adapted, and had even come to love it.

The Friday after Thanksgiving, Nora's boyfriend, Rob, came to pick us up for a night out. We went to a pizza restaurant and slid into red vinyl booths beneath fake Tiffany hanging lamps. After ordering, I asked Nora to come outside with me while I had a cigarette.

"You're *smoking* now?" she said, stunned.

"Everyone in Mexico City smokes."

The little bell above the door tinkled as we passed through it into the chilly night air. The parking lot at the pizza place was practically empty. We sat on a bench on the curb. I lit a Marlboro Light.

"What do you do on the weekends there?" Nora asked.

"It's pretty crazy. I tried acid once."

"Mila!"

"Once you try it, you can never go back to how you thought before."

"How could you do that to yourself? You could die!"

"Those are all lies put together by the authorities to keep people away from consciousness-expanding substances," I said matter-of-factly. I knew I was being a bitch, but I didn't care. I suddenly wanted her to see the new, real me.

"I can't believe you'd even say such total nonsense."

I still hadn't said a word about Dave, about how tense things were with my mother, how strange it felt to inhabit the same city as a father I didn't know.

"Nothing happens *to* anyone. Things are just happening, and you can choose to go with the flow or not."

"So, what, now you think your old friends are naïve? That you're so sophisticated? You were the most Goody Two-Shoes of all, Little Miss Mexico City."

"I didn't mean it like that."

"You've changed, I can tell."

"I don't want to fight, Nora. Not on my last night here."

You've changed were the two most poisonous words in a friendship between teenage girls. I watched Nora's pretty face hoping for a forgiving reaction. She would either forgive me or our friendship would be over right then and there, in the cold, late November night outside a box-shaped suburban family restaurant.

"You know why you never got my first letter? I never sent it, Nora.

Actually, that's a lie. I gave it to my mother to mail, and she opened it."
I didn't pause to watch her reaction. "Yes, there's this whole lifestyle of
clubbing and all these glamorous people who have it all. But if I've
changed that isn't why, even though I do all that now. I was raped by
this guy pretty much right when I got to Mexico. If you'd gotten that letter, you would have thought it all happened just like with you and Rob,
on some great, amazing night. That's how screwed up I was right afterward—denial, you know? I think the reason my mother intercepted—I
mean the bigger reason, not that she wasn't suspicious that something
was going on with me—was so that I wouldn't lie to you, so that I could
come here and tell you the truth. I was just scared to, so I acted like a
jerk instead."

There. Nora was silent for a moment, then her eyes welled over
with tears.

"I wish you could have stayed here with me, and that never would
have happened." She wiped her eyes with the backs of her sleeves. "I
can't believe your mother did that. I mean, knowing her, I *can* believe
it—but it makes me so mad!"

"Some screwed-up things have happened," I said. "But I wouldn't
change a thing. I feel clearer now. I know that's weird, but I do."

"Are you okay?" she asked.

"Was it Sartre who said that life begins on the other side of de-
spair?"

"Come on, Mil, put out that disgusting cancer stick and let's go eat
some pizza."

"You'll still come visit me, won't you?" I said.

"I have to see what's so incredible about this place you can't stop
talking about, right?" she said as we walked back inside.

After too many slices of greasy pizza, it was time to commence the
alcohol hunt. Rob's older brother was out of town, at his girlfriend's
house in Connecticut. He was usually the group's direct source, so we
resorted to trying to pay a stranger to buy us beer in the parking lot
of a liquor store. We sat along the curb waiting for a benevolent
passerby.

"This is such a hassle," I said, scuffing my Doc Martens on the concrete.

"Do you have a better idea, Mila?" asked Rob.

"Yeah, you and Nora come visit *me* next time."

I was only joking, but Rob looked angry.

"You think you're better than us now, because you live somewhere you can order a motherfucking Corona and they'll serve it to you with a perfect little lime wedge on top, no questions asked?"

"That's not what I meant, Rob."

"Ease up, babe," Nora said to him. "Seriously, Mila, let's drop this Mexico stuff and focus on the task at hand."

"All right, all right," I said, exasperated. "I have to pee. Come with me, Nora?"

Not ten minutes later, when Nora and I emerged from the bathroom at the adjacent gas station, Rob was gone. We scoured the neighborhood but eventually had to give up and go home. Nora cried the whole subway ride and I tried to calm her, my arm around her shoulder. At 3 A.M. she got a call from him on her private bedroom phone line. It turned out that Rob had asked an off-duty cop to buy some beer, and his dad had to bail him out of jail.

"He's grounded till graduation," Nora said when she hung up the phone. "Months of community service."

Because of *beer*? It sounded like a joke to me. Then I realized how accustomed to Mexico City I'd become.

We passed the last day of my visit quietly, lying around the house in Bethesda, flipping between MTV and the movie channels, waiting for something good to come on.

FIVE

December

As the plane touched down on the tarmac of Benito Juárez International, I felt relieved to be back. Nora might not have understood my connection with Mexico City, or how different life was for high-school kids here, but when she visited in the spring she would see for herself. I passed through customs quickly with my black Diplomatic passport.

"Did you hear about Tyler?" my mother asked when she picked me up. I sat in the passenger seat of the Golf as she zipped out onto Viaducto, the sulfuric smell fading the farther we got from the airport. I shuddered at her question, imagining him dead of an overdose or killed by a drug dealer.

"He's in Arizona," she continued.

"Oh," I said, surprised but relieved.

"Do you know *why* he's in Arizona?"

"Uh, vacation?"

"He was caught by the DEA for possession of drugs and deported to a rehab program. They know about you, too."

"What do you mean, they 'know about me'? What are you talking about?"

"A DEA officer called me into his office today. Tyler was caught selling and taking drugs, and they suspected you were his girlfriend. So they broke the lock on your closet and searched it and found some type of water bottle that you turned into a pipe to smoke *marijuana*." She said the word in a whisper, as if it were a dirty secret.

How could this happen? I thought.

"They sent him to Arizona because of a little pot?" I wasn't sure whether my mother actually knew everything or was trying to extricate information from me, so I downplayed. "That's absurd. Why would they do that?"

"You never know who's watching," she said, never taking her eyes off the road. "Drugs are a big problem in this country."

"How could you let this happen? Can't you undo it? Tell them it's all a mistake? He doesn't need rehab! He's an *artist,* and a good person. He's on a different path in life, and you can't stand that."

"He was disowned. You, young lady, are not and never will be. I'm going to find addiction meetings for you, and you're going. Case closed."

"Addiction? I've barely smoked pot here and there."

"And we need to nip it in the bud before it gets any further than that."

"Oh, such a clever occasion to use that cliché, Mom. This is bullshit."

"Don't curse, Milagro. If I don't save you, no one will."

Maggie didn't say another word the rest of the ride. I felt the devastation creeping up on me at first, then taking over, like a punch to the gut that pains your whole body. I couldn't run outside and hail a cab to Schiller Street. I couldn't go to Coyoacán with him, smell the faint scent of green-apple shampoo on his long blond hair. I couldn't even call him in Arizona. It was as if he'd evaporated, disappeared entirely. I was used to people leaving and to having to give things up, but I'd always known when it was coming. This was like a sudden blow to the head. And there was something strange about Tyler's sudden departure. Was his little business bigger than I knew? The whole trip I'd fantasized about the sex with him, and I couldn't wait to see him again. I was overwhelmed by a feeling of abandonment. I wanted to jump out of the car into speeding traffic.

"Stop crying, Milagro. It's for the best he's gone."

That only made me cry harder.

Back in Lomas, I closed the blinds, lay down in bed, and fell asleep even though it was only seven. I dreamed about Tyler. He'd escaped from the rehab, which in my dream was prisonlike, with loops of barbed wire on top of tall fences, and he had crossed the border in Mexico with bottles of water, showing faceless Mexican families which way was safe to cross. Then *la migra* was chasing him, or so I thought until I realized that it was the separatist militia. A man in a van stuck a rifle out the window, aiming it at Tyler's head. The Mexican families disappeared. The rifle went off with a bang in the orange dust, and I shot up in bed. I looked over at my clock radio. I'd been asleep for less than an hour. I remembered that Sisley's flight had taken off for Africa the night before. I couldn't believe Tyler was suddenly gone now, too. My first days back passed in a blur. I went from class to class in a daze, and when Rodrigo brought Nina and me home in the afternoons I asked to be dropped off at my house.

One such afternoon, I was lying on my bed, waiting for some purple hair dye I'd pilfered from Rosa to set. I'd grown bored with my black mane and wanted something a little more extreme. I took out my journal and started thinking about the jet-set type of life that people who didn't have parents with jobs abroad thought we led. It seemed glamorous and exciting from a certain angle. We could spend weekends in the South of France and winter ski trips in the Italian Dolomites, because the government paid our bills and rent, and we could live close to those places, so the tickets wouldn't be exorbitant. But in reality the only thing I had control over was myself—my grades, school newspaper stories, the color of my hair, and writing in my note-books, which were so close to me that Maggie even read them to find out what was going on inside my head instead of coming out and ask-ing me. Not that I would have told her, anyway. It was our lifelong pat-tern; she didn't trust me to tell her the truth, so she snooped. Once I'd planted a fake diary for her to uncover. In it I was the dream daughter, the perfect girl who wrote about how great my life was, how motivated I was to make my way in the world, to "travel and have adventures."

The phone rang, bringing me back to the moment. I sat up and reached over to my nightstand to grab it.

"*Bueno?*" I answered.

"*Hola guapa.* It's Manuel."

"Rosa *no está.* She comes tomorrow."

"Mila?"

"*Sí?*"

"This is Manuel. You know, from school?"

Manuel Amador, the fresa? We hadn't spoken since that day at his house with Nina. "Oh, hi," I said, startled.

"You didn't remember me," he teased.

"It *has* been over a month since you asked for my number, and you don't say hello to me in chem."

"Well, I called to see what you were doing."

"Writing," I said. "I have a newspaper column due, then I have to finish reading *Nausea* for the Existential Literature paper I should have written before the break."

"How's that class?" he asked.

"It's my favorite," I said. "Next semester Miss Sanchez is letting me do an independent study on the Beat poets."

"The what poets?"

"The Beat Generation . . . I'm obsessed with it. Jack Kerouac and William Burroughs even spent time in Mexico City. Anyway, it was a counterculture movement in the fifties, when everything was at its most traditional, and these guys—"

"Mila, sorry to cut you off. It's really interesting, but I wanted to see if I could persuade you to stop all that working and come see a movie with me. You can tell me about the Rap Generation in person."

I was too surprised to correct him. A fresa was asking *me* for a date.

"Are you there?"

"It's not a date."

"It's a movie, not a marriage proposal, Mila. Come on, it would be good for you to get out if you're depressed about some asshole."

"He wasn't an asshole."

"If he's not with you, he's an asshole."

"It wasn't his fault."

"What happened?"

"He had to move away." No way would I tell Manuel the story.

"I was thinking we can see *The Usual Suspects* at nine-thirty. You do like movies, don't you?"

"Are you kidding? I love movies. They're the expression of man's desire-to-be-God complex, by creating a mini-universe. You know, let there be light! Camera. Action! And the characters are born. That's what writing is, too."

"You're funny," he said. "I'll be there in twenty minutes."

"Mom!" I called out, bounding down the hall. "I have a date with Manuel!" I knew if I acted excited about going out with a fresa she'd let me out of the house.

"Who's Manuel?" she asked. "You're supposed to be grounded."

"He's a fresa! Exactly the kind of boy you wanted me to meet. His father is a big-deal doctor-slash-art collector."

"Then he has to come in and say hello, and you'd better wash that junk off your hair."

I took a quick shower and blow-dried my now purple hair. I wondered whether Manuel would take one look at it and drive straight back to his electric-fenced estate.

~   ~   ~

Manuel picked me up in his Mercedes SUV. His well-bred manner, combined with his sweater-vest and checkered button-down, ensured Maggie's instant approval.

"It is such a pleasure to meet you!" She beamed.

"Nice walls," he said, looking around. "Very . . . cheerful."

"You like them? I painted all this myself. Makes it feel a little more like Mexico in here," she said.

"Mom, it was in Mexico before this atrocity, too."

Manuel started to laugh but quickly stifled the sound with a pretend cough.

"Don't have Milagro back too late," my mother said to him.

"I'll take excellent care of your daughter, Miss Epstein."

Manuel steered his Mercedes up the Toluca highway to Centro Comercial Santa Fe, a brand-new upscale shopping mall half an hour north.

"What do you call this new hair color?" he asked.

"Eggplant," I said. "Fresh out of the box. I needed something to distract me." I almost mentioned Tyler, but didn't.

"It's very purple."

"That's the point."

"I think you're prettier with your natural looks, but if it makes you happy I guess that's all that matters."

"You've never seen my natural looks. The black was a fake color, too. I'm actually blond."

"Really?" He glanced sideways at me. I thought maybe he didn't really believe me. "All dark-haired girls want to be blond. What's your point in dyeing it?"

"It makes me feel more like myself," I said. "I'm so used to change, I think I like to put it on display."

"Well, then maybe I like it, too." He tried to reach for my hand, but I pulled it away.

"Not a date, remember?" I said, but Manuel just smiled. I was secretly excited to be out with him, but I also felt hesitant to do this again so soon after what had happened to Tyler.

We walked down the marble-floored walkways of Santa Fe, stopping at a booth to fill out a form to enter a sweepstakes for an all-expenses-paid vacation to Acapulco.

"I'm taking you if I win," he said. I tried to picture lounging on the beach in front of the Princess hotel with Manuel Amador. The image seemed absurd to me. I missed Tyler's rough edges. Part of me wished I were lounging on his roof while he painted, or helping him come up with lyrics for a new song he was working on. Instead, I was in a fancy shopping mall with one of the most fresa guys in school. He was being kind and gentlemanly to me, though, and I felt happy. Spending the evening with him definitely beat moping around the house and taking shit from Maggie. Besides, it was good research for the column I wanted to write about the subcultures of ISM.

After the movie, Manuel said he was surprised when I told him I'd known it was the Kevin Spacey character all along. It had to be, I said. Always figure on whatever is the least obvious. It's a surefire way of puzzling out the answer to what's going on in a movie, or in life. We headed to a restaurant for margaritas and dinner, then back to his house for a nightcap. But when we got there police cars were lined up around the block, blue and red lights spinning.

"*Papá*," Manuel said under his breath before jumping out of the car, leaving the motor on, and running to the gate. Political assassinations were commonplace in Mexico, and since a lot of the fresas had politician fathers it was usually someone's father who was the victim of an assassination, or helped plot one. But Manuel's father was a plastic surgeon—who would harm a surgeon? I was stiff, frozen, looking around at the flashing lights that had taken over the usually quiet, well-secured block. There were guard shacks on so many corners in Lomas, and the guards had Uzis. Finally, I turned the car off, pocketed the keys, and went into the house.

~   ~   ~

Manuel's father was there, and his mother was crying. My mother and Armando were in the downstairs vestibule, too.

"What the fuck?" I said out loud, then clapped my hand over my mouth, regretting cursing in front of Manuel's parents before I'd even been introduced.

"*Dios mío,*" said Manuel's mother. "Thank God you two are okay."

"I told you it was a hoax," said Armando. "This has been happening lately."

"What?" I said.

"Criminals set up booths outside movie theaters, win-a-free-vacation things. They take all your information, and when you go inside to watch your movie they call your parents and say you've been kidnapped and they want the ransom left within two hours or they'll kill you. They ask for a reasonable amount, something you could withdraw from the bank. The family, of course, cooperates, and then the kid comes home from the movie."

Manuel looked blank.

"The trip to Acapulco," I said.

"See?" Armando said to Manuel's father. "I told you this was going to be the explanation."

"Everything's okay, then," said Maggie. "Do the police usually catch these guys?"

Armando laughed and shook his head.

"We'll have to mention it in a travel warning," said Maggie.

"Mom? Can we go home now?" I said. I suddenly felt self-conscious about my ripped jeans and Doc Martens. Manuel's mother, a chestnut-tressed beauty in pearls and a Chanel shift, was staring at my purple hair.

"Sorry," said Manuel. "Mila, these are my parents, Gustavo and Regina Amador."

"Nice to meet you," said his father. His mother offered a stiff-lipped smile.

"Well, that's enough drama for us today," she said. "Come, Manuelito, let's go upstairs."

I got into the backseat of Armando's car. Of course he'd driven the three blocks from our house to Manuel's. I stared out the back window at the passing palms and the gated mansions. If Manuel ever introduced me to his friends, I would stick out among all the perfectly retouched noses, the skinny girls eating jicama with lime juice and chili, sitting by the pool and gossiping. We were from different worlds, just meeting for a moment in between. It was all as real as winning a free vacation to Acapulco from some clever criminals.

"See, Milagro, it's not safe for you to go out here. Look what happened just going to the movies," said Maggie.

"But *nothing* happened," I insisted. "It was a scam."

"Something could have happened. What if you were really kidnapped? I had such a scare until Armando told me this happened before and wasn't really a kidnapping. Imagine if I hadn't known?"

"I think it's safe for her to go around as long as she's in a group," said Armando.

My mother turned around and looked at me. "Armando seems to think that sending you to substance-abuse meetings isn't necessary. He gives you a lot of credit, Milagro. Don't you, sweetie?"

"She's not a child anymore. I think it's difficult for a mother to see that sometimes."

"Thanks," I said. I loved Armando; he always said the right thing. I wanted Maggie to marry him. He'd be the perfect stepdad, an antidote to my mother's neurotic ways.

"I'll decide about Milagro's rules," she said to him.

"Maggie . . ." he said, taking a hand off the wheel to put an arm around her shoulder.

"But maybe you know better, Mr. Almoloya," she said, stroking his forearm as he drove.

Nothing could influence my mother like the right man. Armando had won her over.

~   ~   ~

I wasn't about to let my mother take away my freedom because of something that turned out to be nothing. I'd never felt I was in danger. I was discovering a new world, a magical place. Living here, I understood why magical realism had its roots in Latin America. Mexico City really did feel mystical. It seemed that anything could happen. Even the bad stuff, like fake kidnappings, was magical bad stuff, surreal, like a movie or one of those dreams where you're watching yourself from someplace outside your body.

Manuel called me on Sunday. We laughed about what had happened at the mall, though we both knew it was actually more appalling than funny. He picked me up early the next morning and we went to the VIPS restaurant up the street from school. It was a chain diner owned by Wal-Mart, but the food was amazing. We slid into the red plastic seats of a booth and ordered *molletes* and coffee. I told Nina I had to be at school early for newspaper meetings so I wouldn't need rides, at least for a while. It became something of a morning ritual, getting up an hour early to drink coffee with Manuel and talk and wonder. I loved our dates, but secretly thought we met this way because our social worlds could never mix. Neither of our groups of friends would understand the relationship between the two of us—the Armani-wearing, Picasso-collecting slick-haired boy whose father had a multimillion-dollar art collection, and the nationless, purple-haired mystery gypsy girl who was fatherless, took acid, wrote confessional columns, and scrawled in her journal, smoking in the bathroom between classes. Washington, D.C., was orderly and composed, and I'd fit in, overachieving in school, running for student government, and getting a Presidential Physical Fitness certificate. Here, I felt myself becoming ever more like Mexico City, chaotic and unruly.

The next morning, I told Maggie I had to work on a science project at Nina's that afternoon and was sleeping over.

"I'm going to call her mother to make sure you're really there," said Maggie.

"Of course," I said. Nina had already made arrangements with Concepción to pretend she was Sonia Rothman when my mom called. I wondered how Concepción could pull off socialite-speak, but Nina had given her lessons in Sonia lines, like "I can get you in to see Luca at Luca Paolo. Your hair may be simply hopeless without him." Of course, Concepción was for hire. She would take a *mordida*.

After school, Nina and I went straight to Charco de las Ranas, a chichi taqueria that was popular with the fresas. Some of them came in and sat at the next table. They didn't say hello. I told Nina the story of my strange date with Manuel, since she seemed to be over her irritation with me, though I didn't mention our regular breakfasts.

"I can't believe it," she said. "I mean I can, because that is *so* something that would happen. No wonder your mom doesn't want you to go out."

"Armando even told my mom that it was fine. She's really taking this whole thing too far. I mean, it was a scam. It wasn't a big deal."

"She is so overdramatic, I can tell."

"She can be controlling. But she gets totally mad and an hour later she's fine, like it never happened. She's always been that way, but now Armando calms her down."

"Then it's lucky for you that she found him."

Reina, Nina's second housekeeper, buzzed the two of us inside after our lunch. Reina had a lazy eye and was good at keeping secrets. If she saw us sneaking out at night through the glass sliding doors right outside her room, she kept quiet about it. And she made killer ham-and-cheese quesadillas. *Sincronizadas,* they were called.

"If you don't let me in right away when I buzz, I'm going to tell my father you're slacking off," said Nina. Nina's sudden shift of moods surprised me every time. She was either energetic, generous, and up for a good time or angry and depressed. She was perfect in so many ways, but I couldn't understand why she had such trouble focusing.

Maybe she had some type of attention deficit disorder or a chemical imbalance, since she sometimes ran the gamut of the emotional spectrum in one day. Either way, there was no in-between with her; it was one extreme or another. Kind of like my mother, I thought.

I felt sorry for Reina, who rambled out apologies, her hands shaking. Mexican racism was rampant. The Mexicans of indigenous descent were subservient to the wealthier, European ones. The strangest part, though, was that the Euro-Mexicans were way more nationalistic, and hated Americans. Maybe this was because they didn't need us, while the poor saw the United States as a place where they could actually earn a living wage.

We went upstairs to do our homework. I pored over Mexican history and Jean-Paul Sartre. Nina tossed her books aside after a few minutes and picked up a paperback romance novel. She burned through them like firewood, which was how I thought of them.

"Why don't you get your homework done so it's over with in time for the senior *coctel* at Medusas tonight?" I asked. There was no science project.

The student council, which never organized school activities but, rather, rampant alcohol-fueled social events, planned weekly *comidas*—Friday after-school "lunch" parties, if you considered Bacardi and Jose Cuervo to be food groups. *Cocteles* were their nighttime counterparts. The student council rented out entire clubs for these big midweek parties. I never quite figured out where the funding came from.

Nina shrugged and turned her attention back to her page in the romance novel. My eyes followed her long shiny black hair down her perfect long legs to the tips of her trendy high-heeled sandals.

"Can I borrow something to wear tonight?" I asked.

"Of course. Check the closet."

I opened the door to her walk-in. Who needed that many clothes? I thought. "Hey, this is my shirt!" I said, noticing the gray cashmere top I'd bought only the week before.

"I borrowed it when you were asleep last week. I knew you wouldn't mind."

"Borrowing usually involves *asking*," I said.

"Relax. I'll give it back tomorrow."

"I'm going to wear this with a white tank top," I said, holding up a skirt.

"That's what I was going to wear," she said.

I shot her a dirty look.

"Oh, fine, honey," she said. "If it *really* matters that much to you."

"You don't have to get all passive-aggressive. It's only a skirt."

"If it's only a skirt, why does it matter who wears it?"

"I don't want to argue about something so dumb, Nina. You said I could borrow something."

"All right then, lend me your leather jacket."

I don't know why I said yes, but somehow I heard the word come out of my mouth. I made a mental note to be sure to find it again when it reached the back bar of her closet.

At ten-thirty we slid out the door next to Reina's room to get a cab from the *sitio*. We headed to Medusas, to revel in a night of dancing at the *coctel*. Medusas was a huge club down in the South, near Coyoacán, that was known for its creative live show, which announced the opening of the dance floor for the night. Sometimes there was a Renaissance theme, or an elegant ballroom dance that ended in murder, or vampires waking from the dead. The show was performed by the cage dancers, who worked at the club and got to wear fun, luxurious-looking costumes with feathers and jewels. I wanted to be one of them. They were gorgeous, like exotic birds. They moved like no one out on the dance floor, their bodies weaving in ways I didn't know were possible.

"Do you think I could be a Medusas dancer?" I asked Nina after my third Splash at the bar.

"Why not?" she said. "You're a great dancer, so why not do it in a cage in a cool outfit where everybody's eyes are on you? And you'd make money. We could buy some more weed and those vinyl boots from that boutique in La Condesa."

Nina was a great encourager. Whenever she upset me, I reminded myself that that was what I loved about our friendship. She could talk me into things I wanted to do but wasn't bold enough to try without words of support, hers in particular.

"I think I'll audition," I said.

I found the club's manager in an office down a long, closed-off hallway behind the dance floor. He looked me up and down and said I could come by the next week to try out, that he'd have his assistant call me. Thank God Nina let me borrow this outfit, I thought. I ran back out and found her chatting with Kai at the bar.

"Guess what? I'm coming in next week," I said.

"What are you doing?" asked Kai.

"Mila's going to be a Medusas dancer," said Nina.

"That is so *fierce!*" Kai shouted, jumping up and down in excitement.

It was perfect: I'd learned to dance while cheerleading, and I missed it. It's not that there wasn't a cheerleading squad at ISM. The problem was the social stigma attached to it. Being a cheerleader at ISM was a sign that you were a loser. The fresa girls wouldn't be caught dead wearing polyester pleated-skirt uniforms. I heard them making fun of the all-American cheerleaders from inside a bathroom stall while they were congregated around the mirror primping, putting on lipstick, and brushing their long, thick hair. Nobody cared about the football team except the American guys who were on it, like Dave, and the cheerleader girls, who were cute and Midwestern with puffy hair. No one went to the games or to homecoming. It was surreal—sometimes everything about the way things worked at ISM seemed reversed.

Nina and I were on our way to the dance floor when two guys stopped us to introduce themselves.

"I'm Jorge, and this is Mauricio," said one of them. He had a shaved head and an orange shirt with a robot logo. "We're DJs here."

"We're having a party at our apartment a few blocks away," Mauricio said. "You girls want to come?"

"When is it?" I yelled above the blaring house music.

"It starts in an hour," he said. I grabbed Nina's wrist and tried to make out the numbers on her watch. I never wore one. It was two-fifteen.

When we got there, the party was raging with Coyoacán hippies and rave kids, different DJs spinning, and free drugs being passed around. Mauricio was in the kitchen making what looked like a miniature statue of a man out of clay.

"What's that?" I asked him.

"A peyote sculpture," he said. "I'll make you one."

"Peyote, as in Castaneda peyote?"

"Pues, claro," he said. "But of course."

"Can you make one for Nina, too?"

"Sure."

Soon we had our own little sculptures. Mine was a gargoyle, hers some kind of dwarf. Mauricio was apparently a visual artist.

"Where did he learn to do that?" I asked Jorge.

"He makes stop-action animation movies when he's not DJ-ing," he said.

"Now you eat them," said Mauricio.

"They look too cute to eat," said Nina. But I knew she was avoiding it because she was nervous. We'd never tried peyote before. Tyler had said you had to take a train twelve hours and ride a burro down a mountain to the Real de Catorce desert just to get the stuff. Nina and I had planned to do that at some point, but here it was, in peculiar little figurines, in front of us on the kitchen table in this strange apartment in Coyoacán.

"I'll go first," I said. The taste made me think of green pepper crossed with cow manure—bitter and dirty yet earthy. It had a sharp aftertaste—vile, nauseating, horrible. I gagged.

"We can make a milkshake if that's too strong for you," said Jorge, who appeared in the doorway.

"Yes, please," I looked up at him and said, coughing.

He dumped the little sculptures into a blender with ice, milk, and chocolate syrup. When the foamy mixture was sufficiently blended, he poured it into a tall glass and handed it to me. "Here, drink half and she can have the rest."

I chugged it and tasted chocolate going down. But when I put the glass down the aftertaste filled my mouth. I felt like throwing up. Mauricio said the only thing to do about that was deal. Nina threw back her half and made a face. I drank some orange juice that I found in the fridge.

"You might not want to do that," said Jorge. "*Jugo de naranja* tastes worst on the way back up."

"Now we wait," said Mauricio. The guys went to the turntables to spin records. They worked the clubs, they told us, but sometimes threw these private after-parties.

I was dancing when it hit me: a vibrant colorful sensation, then everything started pulsating around me. The lights, the dancers— everything took on a psychedelic glow. The universe opened up. I felt spiritual energy flowing through my body. I went to find Nina. She was in the bathroom crouched over the toilet, throwing up.

"Are you okay?" I asked. "Do you need water?"

"You know that girl Cristina from English class? Manuel's ex?"

"Yeah, why?"

"Do you think that when she goes home she changes out of those outfits? I mean, do you think she lounges around the house in them, or does she, like, put on sweatpants?" Nina leaned over the toilet again, clutching its sides.

Cristina always wore classy silk scarves tied perfectly around her neck, button-down shirts tucked into tight designer dress pants with skinny belts, or form-fitting knee-length skirts, like a 1930s movie star, with spike-heeled knee-high boots or sexy stiletto heels.

"I don't know," I said. "Why don't you ask Rafael?"

Nina went over to the sink and rinsed her mouth. "Who's Rafael?" she asked, pressing some toothpaste out of a tube onto her finger and licking it off.

"Her brother. He's a junior."

"That would be too weird."

"You're right. Are you feeling it a lot?"

"Not yet," she said. "Jorge told me that after you throw up the trip really starts."

"Well, don't throw up too much. You're too skinny already."

"Too skinny? No such thing."

I personally didn't want to throw up. I hated vomiting more than anything. And I didn't feel nauseous. So I floated back out to the dance floor.

When the party wound down and people started leaving, Nina, Jorge, Mauricio, and I decided to go to another club, a place near the Zona Rosa called Bulldog, where people Nina and I knew from school who were in a band would be playing a late-night set. It was four in the morning. They were probably about to go on.

Jorge drove down Insurgentes. I watched him carefully, but I couldn't tell whether he was fucked up; his driving seemed normal. Peyote doesn't interfere with motor skills, I noted. It just makes you perceive everything from its core, stripping away all the false layers and leaving the world raw and exposed, everything revealing its true nature. Nina and I watched the people in other cars and made up stories about their lives. I lit a cigarette but immediately threw it out the window.

"That's so toxic," I said. "Cigarettes are so disgusting right now." Then I started to cough. The cough deepened. I couldn't stop. Then peyote bits and muddy milkshake came up all over the floor of the backseat of Jorge's car.

We pulled up outside Bulldog.

"Go get paper towels and water and clean up the mess," Jorge yelled. I was in no state of mind to do that. I was so far outside concrete reality that I didn't understand how I could possibly go into the club, get paper towels from the bathroom, and clean the vomit out of the car. It was everywhere, and being near it made me nauseous all over again.

Nina and I went inside the club, but we never went back out. Guys needed to be with girls for the bouncer to let them in, so Jorge and Mauricio were stuck outside. We left them out there in the night to deal with the mess themselves.

"He had to understand, right?" I said. "How can he know I'm in the state I'm in and think I'd conceivably be able to clean that disaster? He's done this before; he must know I'm in no condition. I feel bad and everything, but there's no way he could seriously expect me to deal with that right now."

"Calm down, sweetie, you're rambling," said Nina. "You didn't give him your number, so it's like you never existed."

"The puke just materialized in the backseat."

"Exactly."

"What is this stuff? Everything is so beautiful and so ugly at the same time."

Red disco lights pulsated on and off, and the band took the stage. The red light filled the club, oozed and leaked over everything, burned into my eyeballs. Nina and I ran out into the cool early-morning air. We hailed a taxi and gave him her address. The cab rumbled forward and got on the Periferico.

"Where'd you get that coat?" I asked. I may have been hallucinating, but I could have sworn Nina had borrowed my leather jacket and hadn't been wearing a khaki trench.

"Coat check," she said, and winked. "I just had to have it." Nina lowered her voice to barely above a whisper. "It's Prada."

"Where's mine?"

"Oh," she said, fumbling in her oversized purse and pulling out my now wrinkled new jacket. "Here."

I wanted to say something, but I suddenly realized that I didn't recognize any of the streets we were passing.

"Is this the way?" I whispered to Nina.

"I don't know," she said. "I don't think so."

"Should we say something?"

The driver was on a cell phone, and his words were scrambled in-

side my brain. I couldn't understand what he was saying. Were we being kidnapped? I wondered. Where was he taking us? Why was he on
the phone at six in the morning? Was he talking to his car of accom-
plices, behind us? I turned around and scanned the other cars on the
road.

Nina knew that I was forbidden to take taxis ever since drivers had
started robbing tourists down in the Zona Rosa. I elbowed her and in-
dicated the driver. She understood.

"Excuse me, sir," she said. "This isn't the way I usually go."

"Don't worry, señorita, I know a shortcut," he said, and grinned.

We clutched each other the whole rest of the ride. I was so grateful
when we finally turned into Lomas from another direction that I gave
the driver a hundred pesos on top of the cab fare.

By the time we came in at daybreak, we'd conveniently stuffed our
gym clothes into the oversized purses and changed out of our club outfits inside the tubular slide in the little corner park on Nina's block.
Sonia was in the kitchen, brewing coffee in her velour tracksuit.

"Where did you girls go so early in the morning?" she asked.

"For a jog," said Nina. "We're trying to get in better shape."

Sonia nodded. "Good thing you're starting now, girls," she said. "As
I always say, there's no worse fate than fat. Try not to be late for school,"
she called after us as we ran upstairs.

"Did you hear that shit?" said Nina, wrapping a towel around her
hair after showering. I'd gone first and was already dressed, waiting.
There's no fate worse than fat," she whined, imitating her mother's Argentine accent. "My mother's been on a thousand-calorie-a-day diet
since she had me and Naldo."

"You have *nothing* to worry about," I said, eyeing the spot where the
towel ended on her skinny thighs.

"Whatever. I hate my parents. They travel all the time, then when
they're here all my mother does is point out my fat spots. And my dad
just ignores it. He thinks she's silly and that I should take it with a grain
of salt."

"Does he tell her to stop?"

"No, she's his queen."

"Why don't you talk to her about it?"

"She'd just get mad and call me fat. Hey, can I borrow those earrings?" She pointed at the dangly feathers I'd hooked into my earlobes not five minutes earlier. I pulled them out and gave them to her, hoping they would cheer her up a little.

"Thanks, honey, you're the best," she said, putting them on. I was beginning to suspect that the way all my stuff migrated to the back of Nina's closet might not have been an accident on her part.

I had my Medusas audition the week after the peyote trip. I choreographed dance moves and practiced. I had to dance in front of the owner, the manager, and the woman who was in charge of putting the shows together. I was nervous when I walked into the room, but soon I closed my eyes and pretended I was back with my cheerleading squad in D.C. instead of with Eduardo, the Medusas manager.

When they called me back, Maggie answered the phone. I didn't even know it was the club until she came into my room in tears.

"Where did I go wrong that my daughter wants to work as a stripper!" she shouted.

"I do *not* want to be a stripper. Where the hell is this coming from?"

"Don't try to wriggle your way out of this one," she yelled. "Some club just called about your 'audition.' " She held up both hands and curved her index and middle fingers into that quotation gesture I hated.

"Medusas called?"

"They wanted to *hire* you. Strippers get murdered in Mexico all the time! Not that that's why you shouldn't do it! What on earth were you thinking?"

"It's not stripping. It's a performance-artist job. Part of a theatrical show, with costumes and stuff, like cheerleading, except it's to encourage people to dance at the club. I worked really hard to get ready for that audition."

"Well, I told them never to call here again."

"I'd better call them back and explain it was a misunderstanding."

The manager told me that in the ten minutes that had passed since his call, he had filled the position with another artist. They couldn't afford to deal with some fresa's crazy mother. How funny, I thought. Me, a fresa.

The curtain fell on my Medusas fantasy, but I wasn't about to let Maggie get away with running interference on my life again.

She was lying on her stomach on the bed, the newspaper spread out in front of her. I flopped down next to her.

"Really, Mom, how could you even think I would audition to be a stripper?" I asked, trying not to raise my voice.

She looked over at me. "I thought it was very obvious what being a dancer in a nightclub would entail."

"That is so deluded."

"What would you think if a club manager called to talk to your daughter about a *job* she auditioned for?"

"I'd think to ask her what it was about."

"You wouldn't tell me the truth," she said.

"Don't you get it? If you'd let go a little, we might be able to talk to each other in the first place."

"Ever since we came here, you've gotten more and more out of control. First with that Dave, then the stringy-blond druggie guy. Maybe you'd take a stripping job for the money to buy those drugs I know you're smoking."

"Why are you doing this?"

"I'm stopping you from hurting yourself. I saw worse when I was in my early twenties in Mexico."

"I'm seventeen."

"Trying to go on thirty."

"Remember how you wanted me to be a model?"

"That's different."

"Why? Putting your body on display for a paycheck."

"So you're admitting you *were* going to be a stripper."

"I'm playing devil's advocate, Mom."

"Milagro—"

I stood up and heard myself raising my voice. I couldn't control it. "You moved us away for my senior year. We live in the same city as the man who's my father, and you won't even tell me who he is, as if I'm going to pick up the phone and call him!"

"That's enough now."

"Why won't you trust me?"

"You hide from me so often I don't know how you think you have the right to ask that question. Anyway, it's not even a matter of trust. It was a contractual agreement. I can't tell you his identity. He could have anything done to us."

"We didn't even need some bullshit hush money! The *U.S. government* covers my upbringing!" I screamed.

I ran out, slamming the door behind me. We always seemed to go around in circles only to end up back in the same place we'd started from.

Mr. Payne called a newspaper meeting on Monday.

"I love your stream-of-consciousness style and how you no longer seem afraid to tell everyone about what's really going on," he told me.

"Is there a 'but' here?" I sensed that he was trying to figure out how to phrase a criticism.

"No, not really. I was only going to say that I do think you could push yourself further. I like it when you show us what's on your mind, but maybe you could find a conflict going on in school, or, you know, something external."

I stared out the window, trying to come up with something that wouldn't be clichéd and snotty, like a rant about the fresas' designer outfits while their countrymen suffered in poverty. I watched students coming out of the music room on the ramp, walking down the winding outdoor stairway down to the palapa for lunch. A kid with a broken leg gripped the handrail with one arm and swung his other arm around his buddy's shoulders. Another friend carried his crutches.

"I got it," I said.

"That was fast," Mr. Payne said over from the computer.

"ISM's campus is totally unfriendly toward the physically challenged."

"Well, do we have any disabled students?"

"No."

"It's a private school. There's no law that says it has to be accessible to people with disabilities."

"Why does there have to be a law for the administration to recognize that there's a need for this? I'm going to spend a day in a wheelchair and report on it."

"Interesting," said Mr. Payne. "Go for it."

"Thanks. I will."

"And, Mila?"

"Yes?"

"You're doing this undercover, which means you can't tell anyone why you're in the wheelchair."

"The catch."

"Not a catch, just a classic guinea-pig story. Never reveal that you're doing something in order to write about it. Do the thing as if it were real, then write about your experience."

"I like that concept." I was already thinking of another way that I could use it.

I arranged to borrow a wheelchair from the nurse's office. The next day I got to school early after breakfast with Manuel, got into the chair, and wheeled around the halls for practice. For the first time since Dave, my fear of being mocked by other people resurfaced. I can handle it, I thought. But since I couldn't tell anyone what I was doing, not even my friends, they were going to think something was wrong with me, or at least wonder why I was pulling such a strange stunt. Had my legs gone paralyzed overnight? Had I twisted an ankle? Or did I have an invisible illness? I didn't want to have to answer the slew of questions that were sure to come my way. "I won't cheat," I told myself. "No matter what happens today, I'm in this chair, and I won't say why."

"What happened to you?" asked Kai in fourth-period chem. I hadn't prepared an answer.

"I can't say right now. But you'll find out."

"What hurt you? Is it contagious?"

"Believe me, I'm going to be all right," I said, and smiled.

I scooted around in my chair and accepted the weird looks from my classmates with an unrevealing smile. There were so many reasons you wouldn't want to be disabled at ISM, I discovered: steps, uneven pavement, unfriendly doorways. It was amazing how we took for granted every day the fact that we could simply get around. But I didn't cheat until band. I was glad I hadn't brought my bass home the night before. Going down the ramp to the band room was a breeze, but to get in there was a step up, a platform there for no apparent reason, and a step down. I had no choice but to get out of the chair and haul it up the step and down the other side. I did it. I cheated. I admitted to it in the article. Exactly one week after it ran, the step was removed and ISM released a new measure to make the school "wheelchair accessible." I won that semester's student-journalism award.

"They're really building ramps all over campus because of my article?" I'd said to Mr. Payne when he told me.

"Now you see the power of the press?" he asked, but it was more of a statement than a question. "Use it wisely."

He had no idea how true I would discover his words to be.

When I got home that evening, Armando and Maggie were in her room with the door closed. I cringed, expecting to hear the sounds of lovemaking, but instead I heard muted voices, the tones of an intense conversation. I ran into the kitchen, grabbed a glass, and put it to the wall of the guest room that bordered Maggie's bedroom to amplify their voices.

"I'm not sure how Milagro is going to react," Maggie was saying.

"She and I got along from the first day we met. I know she's only going to be happy for you—for us."

"About the wedding, sure. It's the adoption part I'm concerned
about. I know you mean the best for her, but . . . she's never really had
a father."

"Don't you see why that doesn't make sense? This is precisely our
chance to give that to her. I know she'll welcome me, Maggie."

"Let's talk to her about it this weekend."

I heard footsteps—they were coming out. I backed away from the
wall, ducking into the closet until they were gone. I would have a stepdad. "Dad," I repeated over and over in my head. *"Papá."* Armando was
mysterious, intellectual, creative, a gentleman—everything Maggie
wanted in a man. Everything, I guessed, my father had been. He made
her laugh and took both of us out to places like traditional Mexican hacienda restaurants that were big and sprawled over acres of manicured
lawns. It made sense to me that it would come to this, and fast. Almost
without my noticing, he'd already slipped into my life as a father figure.
It was strange to see my mother in love; it seemed real this time. Armando was actually single; he'd been divorced for more than ten years,
and he had no children. He was that rare, elusive creature: a middle-
aged guy without hang-ups, issues, or crises. I kept waiting for some
deal-breaking flaw to surface, but he was plain old smart and interesting and together. And I loved him for convincing my mother that it was
safe for me to venture into the side of Mexico City that was so different
from her vision of a guacamole-drenched heaven where mariachi music always played.

Maggie told me over dinner that we were having a special outing with
Armando on Saturday, to Las Mañanitas in Cuernavaca. I was sure they
were going to announce their engagement, and I could hardly wait.

But when Saturday came around Armando didn't show up. At about
the time we were supposed to be in Cuernavaca, sipping margaritas

and celebrating the news, Maggie got a phone call. Armando's bodyguard had been arrested. Someone had paid him to release carbon
monoxide through the ventilation system into the house. Armando
was found unconscious and taken to the hospital, where he was given
oxygen treatments. He'd been slipping in and out of consciousness. My
mother went to be by his side, and I wasn't allowed to go along. She
came home past midnight.

"How is he?" I'd been awake all night. I tried to zone out with telenovelas, but I was sober and not easily distracted. Maggie looked exhausted.

"He's awake, which is a good thing. We're lucky there was no brain
damage. It could have been much, much worse than it was. But still,
he's going to have to be a lot more careful."

"Can he quit his job?"

"I told him he should go into hiding, go to the States or to Europe
for a while. He doesn't want to."

She went to bed, but I knew she wouldn't sleep. Armando was released two days later, and he went straight back to Almoloya. They
didn't get him, not this time.

As though the attempt on Armando's life were an omen, my next *ISM
Observer* assignment was an obituary.

Juan Ramirez was a scholarship student whose GPA had dropped
just below the cutoff for him to keep his grant. He shot himself in the
head in his bathroom the night he found out that the scholarship was
being pulled. Everyone was crying that day. I thought it was hypocritical, the fresas who never spoke to him wiping their red eyes in the
girls' bathroom. They were saying what a great guy he was, that they
wished they'd known so they could have helped him somehow. You
never said a word to that guy, I thought. I never had, either, but at least
my eyes were dry. I felt sad, but I couldn't pretend to be heartbroken
just because Juan Ramirez was dead by his own doing. I didn't know

who he was. His story was quickly pegged as a great ISM tragedy, another loss to our school. I thought of the fresa Pablo Juárez and his motorcycle. Alive, they'd been polar opposites, definitely never said a word to each other. Now they were exactly the same.

When I got to second-period typing class, the entire class was bawling.

"You don't have to stay in the room today if you're too upset," said the teacher. "You can go to the counseling office and Miss Doone will see each of you."

"Did everybody here know him?" I asked Jessica, the girl who sat at the computer next to mine.

"He was in this class," she hissed back. Only then did I notice the empty chair.

Mr. Horney put up a huge photograph of Juan in the hall, where people could write messages and lay flowers. I still could have sworn I'd never seen his face. Maybe I'd been too obsessed with the fresas, the beautiful noticeable ones, with their perfect noses, long legs, and luxurious clothes, to notice anything else that was going on around me, all the others at ISM who didn't fit in. So I volunteered to write an obituary. I met with Juan's family, who lived in a modest house two hours away from school. His mother offered me *pasteles* and reminded me of an older version of Rosa.

ISM OBSERVER
December 2, 1993

Doble Vida: Remembering Juan Ramirez

By Mila Márquez

Juan Ramirez was weeks shy of his eighteenth birthday when he died at home from a single, self-inflicted gunshot wound. His mother, Estrella Ramirez, showed me the note he left when I visited her at home last Friday. She wanted me to read it, she said, so I would understand, so we could understand, why and how this had happened. She never saw it coming—who would have? She never imagined that Juan's stress over losing his scholarship could end like this.

"I thought he would go to the public school," she said. "His education was the most important thing to him. He said he was going to go to university to make me and his father proud, and I can only imagine he knew that not going to the International School meant he could not get into the universities he would have wanted." Mrs. Ramirez, a secretary, said Juan had always been bright and ambitious. "He wanted to do computer science," she said. "Now he won't get to do anything."

The whole school is still in a state of shock over the suicide, but now is the time to think about (and learn something from?) Juan's short life. He was a mostly-A student until this year, when his grades began to slip. His mother won't say if she knows why, but she attributes it to pressure and the standards he had to maintain in order to keep the scholarship. We'll never know exactly what went through Juan's mind, but we should remember his life, and not let his death turn into a symbol for this castelike system in which you are born into your destiny.

Feeling melancholy, I went down to Las Islas by myself on Saturday afternoon, compelled by the aftermath of Juan and the attempt on Armando. Las Islas always reminded me of Tyler, and the dealers there always asked when he was coming back to Mexico. I'd say I wasn't sure, but I'd let them know when I heard. My father slipped into the back of my mind; my plan to uncover his identity no longer seemed exciting or plausible. My mother was staying with Armando and wouldn't let me be with them, which only made me angrier. When Manuel called that evening, I told him to come pick me up. Our breakfasts had gone from daily to once every week or two, and we still hadn't come out as a couple at school. But still, we'd grown closer.

"Do you want to do something a little unusual with me?" I asked

Manuel as I got into the car. He drove south, and I fingered the foil-covered paper in the pocket of my zippered sweatshirt. "I don't know if you'll approve . . ."

"I'm not how you think I am," he said. "Not some tight-ass preppy dude." He imitated an American accent, and we both laughed.

"Sure, but this is acid," I said. "Do you even know what that is?"

"I'm no fool, Mila."

"You've done it before?"

"No, but I would try it once, with you. Is it fun?"

"You don't know what fun is until you've tried this," I said, hearing myself echoing Tyler's words.

We went to El Hijo del Cuervo in Coyoacán and sat outside. He ordered two *micheladas.* It was about eight o'clock.

I unwrapped the tiny piece of foil in my bag and handed him a small square of paper. It was then that I noticed they had tiny snail decals on them.

"Look," I said. *Caracoles.*

"They carry their home with them wherever they go," he said. "Like you."

"Maybe that's why they were so drawn to me that day outside your house."

"How will it feel?" he asked after popping it into his mouth.

"It's impossible to explain," I said. "But it's definitely interesting."

"I hope so," he said. "Because there's no going back now, right?"

"Right. You've committed yourself to the next seven hours."

We walked down the block, turned right toward the Pemex station and the taxi *sitio.* I suddenly felt uneasy about Manuel, about taking such a risk. I felt a wave of panic flood my body; I didn't even know him that well, and we were about to find out each other's insides.

We took a cab to Bar Milan, a small, dark lounge away from the main drag in the Zona Rosa. The bar's décor was mostly shiny black. Green cacti and bright-red flowers stood tall behind the white, amber, green, and clear rows of bottles. Nothing was happening yet. I liked this place, because to buy anything to drink you had to exchange your money at a cash register for Milan dollars, the alcoholic equivalent of Monopoly money, so the bartenders wouldn't have to deal with giving change. Milan dollars came only in amounts equivalent to the cost of drinks and tips. We exchanged two hundred pesos and sat down on the barstools.

"It's called *milagro* money," said Manuel, squinting at the pink bill in his hand. I inspected the colorful rectangular papers that were exchangeable for alcohol instead of little plastic houses. He was right: *5 milagros, 10 milagros.* The second sign of the night: first snails, now miracles.

I ordered a Splash, he a Sol.

"I think we're meant to be here," I said, smiling.

"What is this 'meant to be'? You mean fate?" he said.

"I enjoy believing in fate," I said. "It makes me feel like even when things make no sense, it's all going to turn out to be part of some larger plan."

"That's what I love about you, Mila," said Manuel. "You are hope impersonated."

"Incarnated," I said, and smiled.

"Can I touch your hair?" he asked.

"Um, weird, but—okay."

He scooted his barstool closer to mine and ran both hands through my long plum-colored hair. Then he cupped my chin, leaned over, and kissed my forehead, then my cheek.

"You're so chivalrous," I joked, and giggled nervously.

"Come here," he said. Our first real kiss was slow and gentle, the beginning of something that was *something.* I could feel it right away. All my thoughts about fresas, class, money, chaos, rebellion, and acid fell away around those two barstools. In that moment, it was just me and Manuel, the two of us colliding into something new.

"You don't act like it at school, but you're so open," he said. "I could see that in you from the first time we talked that day at my house. You're inquisitive. It's the best quality someone can have."

"And I could see that you weren't the person I thought you'd be."

"What did you expect?" he asked.

"Fresa," I said, and we laughed.

We were deep into a conversation about Manuel's relationship with his father almost an hour later.

"He's my hero," he said. "I admire him so much, but at the same time he tries to control my life. All I want to do is paint, but I'm supposed to become either a surgeon like him or an engineer like my grandfather was."

"That's so fucked that you don't have a choice."

"I think something's starting to happen." Manuel looked down at his arm, then studied his hand.

"Yeah. This is how it starts." I felt the familiar warm flush, the fever in my stomach.

"Anyway, you said your father was Mexican?" asked Manuel.

"I don't know who he is," I said.

"I wanted to ask you about him, but I wasn't sure if it was—how do you say it—a touchy subject?"

"I've never told anyone the truth before. But yeah, he's Mexican. Yours wasn't in Playa del Carmen in '76, was he?" I was joking, but I was suddenly overcome by the urge just to make sure, since everything was so interconnected in Mexico's beau monde.

"I don't think so. My parents lived in Spain when I was born. They hadn't been back to Mexico in a long time."

"I wonder if they know each other."

"Who?"

"Your father and mine."

I knew that I was talking in circles. I decided to tell Manuel the whole story. Or, at least, the version of the story that I knew. I let everybody else think my father had passed away when I was a baby, or changed the subject and then they knew not to ask, but I wanted Manuel to know.

"My father was a Mexican politician," I began. "He was on vacation with his wife."

"Really? Your mother told you that?"

"Right before we moved to Mexico," I said.

"How did she meet this politico?"

"My mother was a jeweler. The politician's wife saw the *milagros* she was using to make necklaces, bracelets, and earrings, and she had to have some. She ended up buying out the whole collection. Usually tourists picked up a piece or two, but that fresa lady bought everything. The politician paid my mother and praised her craftsmanship."

Manuel nodded, never taking his eyes off mine.

"He asked if she had any more in her showroom. She told him her showroom was in the same little building on Quinta Avenida where she rented a place to stay. She gave him a card. He showed up at her door later. She says she didn't intend what happened next."

I always imagined that the only other thing in the room besides the table where she worked was the bed. That, at twenty-four, Maggie was slim and toned from swimming, her skin perpetually browned by the sun, her thick chestnut hair almost reaching her waist. She had an exuberant energy about her, and talked all the time, even in her sleep.

When the politician left, I imagine she was left questioning why she did it. She was intoxicated by power—powerful people, images, her own power of seduction. And she couldn't resist a well-known, handsome, and important man. She never examined the pattern of her own behavior, but I imagined that she was stepping into the role of the Thai waitress, winning back her father's affections. Repeat rather than remember, not that I believed everything Freud said. But that phrase had stuck with me.

"She never told me his name," I continued. "All I know is this story of the random way I came to be. My mother tracked him down after she found out she was pregnant, and somehow got his secretary to put her through on the telephone. She always had a way of figuring out how to accomplish anything she wanted. She told me my father pretended not to remember her that day on the phone, claiming he'd never met her. He accused her of lying, then she cried and cried until he changed his mind and said that she must have planned it. That she did it to get money out of him. He promised to send her a large amount as long as she stayed out of his life forever. Which meant keeping me out of his life, too. Maggie refused the money at first. She begged him to leave his wife and marry her. As if. Since the payments were all she was going to get, she accepted them instead. My father never spoke to her, just deposited the money in some overseas account at intervals over the course of her pregnancy. After the payout, there was no trace of him. It was as if he'd never existed in the first place, except that my mother suddenly had a baby and a lot of under-the-table cash. I used to look up Mexican politicians in magazines and newspapers in the library, compare my features with theirs, and guess which one might be my father, just for the fun of it. And that, my friend, is the name of that tune."

"You never tried to find him? If there's anything I can do to help . . . I mean, if you're even interested . . ."

"I thought about it. But my mother and Armando are getting married. He's going to be my stepdad and he's the best, so there's no reason to search for a complete stranger and potentially fuck it all up."

"You are not like any girl I've ever met, Mila." He shook his head and craned his neck toward the ceiling. "You amaze me . . . such a wild life, but so . . . together."

"I'm not sure about together. We'll see about that."

"I don't think I can sit here anymore," he said, shifting uncomfortably on the barstool. I looked at his pupils. They were the size of quarters. I had to make sure he didn't freak out.

"Me neither. Where should we go?"

"Somewhere quiet. Where we won't run into anyone we know."

I can't remember how I got the idea that it would be fun to sneak into the Chapultepec graveyard, but I knew we certainly wouldn't run into anybody there, and it would be an adventure. We had to climb through a hole in the fence and run in the dark through weeds and plants that were taller than we were, like cornstalks or wheat or really tall grass. And everywhere there was the sound of dogs barking. Packs of wild dogs. I was terrified that we would run into them and be mauled and I would be the stupid girl who died on an acid trip, and got the son of the most respected surgeon in the country killed, too.

We finally came out of the grass and up toward the graves. We walked around for a while, whispering nervously. We lay down on the grass, and a few raindrops fell. The sky turned red, then deep purple. We walked around some more, and I saw a wedding scene—a ghostly bride standing beside a dark groom, being married by a skeleton. I knew it was a hallucination—I could see that the bride was really a tombstone monument and the groom a tree. The skeleton was a few tombstones and some overgrowth and garbage on the ground. I knew that. But I couldn't stop seeing the apparition of a deathly wedding ceremony. Something's coming, I thought. I rubbed my eyes and looked the other way. I looked back, and there was nothing but tombstones and trees. Then the dogs came. Manuel saw them first—a pack of strays, howling a little, ambling by. They stopped when they saw us. The dogs stared at us. I looked back at them, like a deer in headlights, at their mercy. After a few moments, they continued on their way.

"It's almost five," said Manuel. "As much as I want to sit here and watch the sunrise with you, I should be getting home."

"Are you all right?" I asked.

"I just can't believe this exists," he said, putting an arm around me and pulling me to him. "It's a very strange thing to go through."

"But good strange?"

"I don't know if I like to see so clearly, you know?"

"No."

"Too raw or something." He shrugged. "Let's go."

He left me outside Nina's house and hugged me tightly, just for a moment. I inhaled the smell of his leather jacket and dug my fingers into his back. I climbed the tree next to the wall of the house and tapped on her window until she opened it.

"Just come in," she whispered groggily. "I'm sleeping. We'll talk to-morrow."

I lay in her bed, forcing my eyes shut and still seeing colors dancing.

"What happened last night?" she asked when we woke up, raw sunlight streaming in through the blinds.

"I had a date with Manuel."

"Oh, *really*!"

"I sort of tripped with him."

"What? How did you convince him to do *that*?"

"I didn't have to. He wanted to."

"So he likes you that much," she said, getting out of bed and pulling out her long dark ponytail. She shook out her hair and ran her fingers through it, mussing it up even more. She yawned deeply and stretched. She reminded me of a luxuriating panther.

"What's that supposed to mean?"

"I guess I was worried he'd get hurt," she said, crossing into the bathroom and out of sight. I heard the hiss of the shower turning on, the water pelting her Jacuzzi tub. I jumped out of bed and ran in after her.

"How could you say that? You're supposed to be my best friend."

"But, honey, Manuel is fragile right now. Cristina really got to him."

"You think I'm a rebound girl?"

"I'm just looking out for you both, that's all." She pulled the shower curtain aside, stepped in, and pulled it shut.

"At least I can be myself around him, and he listens," I said, and slammed the bathroom door. Unlike you, I thought.

I walked home, the sidewalk snaking in front of me like a multicolored rainbow river or snail slime. I took a bath, then called my mother at Armando's.

"Mom, can you come home and take me to the pool?" I asked.

"In a few hours, okay?" she said.

"Can't we go now, please?"

"I'll be home by noon, all right?" I heard her yawn through the receiver. She hung up and I started to cry—I missed her. I knew she couldn't tell when I needed her; we'd pushed each other away so much since coming to Mexico, and I couldn't entirely blame her for distancing herself. Armando needs her more than I do right now, I thought. I'm no little girl crying for mommy. I went to my closet and took a tiny hit off my plastic water pipe, just enough to calm myself down.

Armando and Maggie showed up in the early afternoon and we went to Lomas Country Club. Armando was pallid and tired easily, his immune system weakened, but otherwise he'd made a complete recovery.

"Why so quiet, Mila?" he asked.

"I'm just tired," I said. "I need to get in the pool and wake up."

"I'll teach you to dive off the high board."

The Volkswagen rolled to a stop at a red light.

"Guess what?" said my mother, turning to look at me. Here it comes, I thought.

"What?"

"Armando and I are getting married!"

Armando smiled weakly and squeezed my mother's hand.

"We're thinking of a spring wedding in Cuernavaca," he said. He looked at my mother, his expression proud.

"Yay!" I shouted, clapping and feigning surprise.

"I told you she'd be excited," Armando said to Maggie.

At the club, my mother went to save us lounge chairs and Armando bought me a cappuccino at the café.

"You really are quiet today," he said. "How are things going?"

"Good. You know, fine."

"That's not an answer. Your mother says you have a boyfriend? Is he Mexican?"

"Yeah."

"Well, he must be a really nice boy, if you like him." He winked.

"I'm ready to dive now," I said.

I loved Armando, but I was feeling too queasy to talk.

December 5

Dear Nora,

Are you still coming to visit sometime this spring? I hope so. I'd love to see you again and hear how you're doing. I'm sorry we had that argument while I was there, and I hope you haven't changed your mind about continuing our friendship. *Huge* news: my mother is getting married! To that prison director I told you about. I love him. Love, love, love him. He always says the right things at the right times, and he treats me like the adult I am, not the kid my mother thinks of me as. And I'm seeing an amazing new guy, a Mexican named Manuel. You will approve this time, I swear. Things with him and me are simple, but that may be what scares me most about this new relationship. You'd think someone who read histories of philosophy at fifteen would be able to handle simplicity. Anyway, please write and tell me you're still coming. I promise I'll show you everything that's so phenomenal about Mexico City, and you'll understand why I acted the way I did in D.C. Not that it's an excuse if I was rude to you or Rob. Is he still grounded for trying to get that off-duty cop to buy us alcohol?

Love,

Mila

SIX

Ventana Abierta, Puerta Cerrada

What's going on in Mexico today is beyond fiction.

—Peter Lupsha, Professor Emeritus, University of New Mexico

Maggie was finally promoted to Sisley's father's old job. She now reported to a higher-level boss, a guy named Harvey, who was, in fact, the spitting image of Harvey Keitel, her favorite actor. ("He's so handsome," she'd say every time I replayed *Reservoir Dogs*. I didn't get it.) Her new position was Head of Property Recovery, which meant that if Americans had any valuable property stolen south of the border my mother would be on the case to get it back.

She was amazing at it; so far, she'd recovered a helicopter, an airplane, a handful of cars, and a yacht. One day Maggie got a call that a motor home had been stolen from a California man who was vacationing in Baja. The aging California hippie was sitting in a parking lot by the beach when two policemen approached, told him to please step out of his motor home, and took it. No questions, no problems, no arrests. Just drove away in it.

"They're using it for something," Maggie said in the kitchen that evening. She dropped two soon-to-be quesadillas in the frying pan. They crackled and hissed.

"What would two cops need a motor home for?" I asked. "To drive their families around?"

It could have been true. The police in Mexico were corrupt, but not simply because they were greedy. They were poorly paid members of the lower class working for the state to protect the upper class, a group of people who oppressed them and were part of a government they did not vote for or support. They lived on a salary that didn't afford them enough, and taking *mordidas* from the likes of me and my friends was an easy way for them to make more. So was taking a motor home.

"Maybe," my mother said. "I have to look into it more, but my leads tell me it's likely in the hands of government officials. They're pretty sure it's parked at Los Pinos," she said, referring to Mexico's version of the White House, the president's home.

The next day at work, she called the chief of police and said she wanted to recover the motor home from the impoundment lot. The chief refused, saying he wouldn't allow it.

"Why is that?" she asked. "Because it isn't there?"

Without cooperation, she couldn't do her job. Maggie always did her job, so she took it upon herself to get the right people on her side and accomplish near-impossible feats. And whatever Maggie took upon herself she took upon me. I couldn't count the number of times I had been her accomplice, support staff, or assistant. From working at the visa barn to hearing about which big drug dealer would be imprisoned next at Almoloya, I got to see parts of Maggie's life and work that I only wished I could write about in my newspaper columns. As up and down as my mother and I were, those were the moments I admired her most, proud of all she'd accomplished despite the odds.

On Saturday, we were at Los Pinos trying to track down the stolen motor home. The compound is set up like a fortress—high gates, long roads, the house itself way out of sight. That was the only reason I wasn't worried that Tomás, the president's son who went to my school, would see me and Maggie hanging around his house like a pair of wannabe James Bondesses, trying to solve an international mystery. At least I knew I would see him coming first, though, with the entourage of bodyguards that always preceded and followed him wherever he went. Maggie and I peered through the gates into a vast parking lot.

"Do you see anything, Milagro?" she asked.

"Nope," I said, craning to see the farther corners of the lot. "Nothing at all."

"Let's go to the south side."

We walked around the whole border of Los Pinos, looking in through cracks under the gates and through fences. We were at the last entrance, our failure of a mission almost over, when I saw a group of men headed down the driveway to where their armored cars were waiting, right outside the gate my mother and I were standing in front of.

"Look casual," Maggie whispered when she noticed them. "Like we're tourists."

"Except tourists don't come to Los Pinos, Mom. That's the flaw in your plan. It's not the White House." No tours, no outsiders.

"Just try to do what I say, Milagro."

I took the camera I had around my neck and pretended to take a picture of a passing *pesero,* those omnipresent one-peso microbuses. The men were coming closer. They were all dressed in suits even though it was Saturday, and carried briefcases. They were flanked by armed guards. Shit, that's Manuel's father, I thought. Manuel had mentioned that his father was the president's friend and doctor. He'd given the president his excellent, very natural-looking face-lift. Seeing him here like this made me wonder if he was involved in areas other than medicine. I looked away. He wouldn't recognize me anyway, I hoped. Then I looked back and noticed another man. He must have been in his early sixties and looked striking in his blue pin-striped suit. Who is that? I wondered. As he passed in what felt like slow motion, he looked quizzically at my mother and me. Maggie didn't see him; she was gazing at the buildings, playing out her interested-tourist drama. The man kept staring intently, trying to place her, as if he knew her from somewhere but couldn't figure out where. Then his eyes, which even from that distance I could see were deep green, locked with mine.

I had a feeling in the pit of my stomach, the grip of a realization. Though Mexico City was enormous, in certain places it was the smallest of worlds.

"I don't think we're going to find it today," said my mother. "Let's go home."

"Did you see those men?"

"Please tell me you didn't stare."

"Course not, I was just asking. One of them was Manuel's dad."

My mother's dark eyes widened. "He didn't recognize us, did he?"

"I hid behind my Pentax. Who was that guy in the pin-striped suit?"

"Come on, let's go to the car."

"Did you see that other man?"

"I don't know who you're talking about," said Maggie.

A week later, my mother spoke up about the motor home at the Bilateral Meeting, where U.S. and Mexican officials met to discuss relations between the two countries on major issues like immigration and drug trafficking. In the middle of the meeting, while someone was praising how wonderful relations between the countries had been lately, Maggie said, "What kind of relations are they if stolen American vehicles are being used by your government?"

"And what, exactly, do you mean by that, Señorita Epstein?" one of the Mexicans asked.

"There is a motor home belonging to a U.S. citizen that's being held at Los Pinos," she said. "It's being used to transport the military."

My mother's lead had provided her with snapshots of the motor home on the road. The men in the front seat were clearly in military attire. She'd shown them to me the night before, and now she spread them out over the table in front of her questioner.

The official, embarrassed, told her that wasn't possible and invited her to the impoundment lot the next morning to look for the motor home. She went. And there it was.

"The car pound was filled with such nice things," she told me when she got home. "Ferraris, Cadillacs, even a yacht. There was an impound seal around the motor home. Funny thing is, they said it had been sitting there for months, yet the seal was brand-new. When I asked them why, they said the motor home was so nice that they changed the seal on a regular basis. I mean, come on! They expect me to believe that?"

She had solved her case. It would be a while before I solved mine, but I had a feeling I was getting closer.

Armando was assassinated on Tuesday. He was giving a lecture in the UNAM and had lunch in the cafeteria afterward. He was eating a sandwich, probably his favorite, *jamón serrano.* He was reading *El Universal.* He read it at our breakfast table every morning that he stayed over, but that morning he was in a rush, so he took it with him. He never even saw the man coming. One bullet to the head.

It was my first funeral. It was a grand society affair, all prominent government officials and Mexican aristocracy. My mother's relationship with Armando was still new, considering how long everyone else there had known him. Though they were friendly to Maggie, I could tell from the way she held herself around them, stiff and uncomfortable, that they made her feel ill at ease. As we entered the church, people kept coming up to my mother to offer their condolences. She stopped to speak with them in hushed tones. I felt as if I were sleepwalking. Some of the Mexicans from school were there, too. I was surprised whenever they murmured hello as we ran into each other.

"What are you doing here?" asked Catalina, one of the major fresas, as we looked for seats toward the front of the church.

"Uh, my mother was *engaged* to him?" I said, not bothering to take off my dark sunglasses and make eye contact. She clearly didn't read my column.

Catalina didn't say anything. She just looked me up and down as if she couldn't believe it. I went to look for my mother, whom I'd last seen crying and hugging Armando's younger sister, Elena. Elena looked about thirty-four and had the same wavy hair as her brother. I'd never met her, but apparently she and Maggie had become close in the past few months. Elena and her husband were sitting near Armando's closest friend, Raul Aguila, and some other people I didn't recognize. I didn't see my mother. Finally, I found her in the bathroom crying hysterically.

"He was the one, Milagro," she babbled. "He was the one, and now he's gone and I'll never be able to be with a man again." She had killed a whole bottle of Merlot while getting dressed that morning, plus I'd spotted her stealthily nipping at something tiny and portable out of her purse during the service. Maggie stumbled on a black high heel, almost falling and hitting her head on the marble sink. Seeing her like that brought back bad memories of three-bottle evenings nearly ten years earlier, when she constantly burned dinner and vomited in the bathroom. She was what you could have called "functional," always showing up on time for work and overperforming. She got a grip one day when she sat down for eggs and toast with a martini—I grabbed the drink and dumped it over her head. "This water makes you stupid," I'd said. I was nine. A summer in a West L.A. clinic took care of it. I'd stayed at my grandmother's and visited on weekends. I hoped she wasn't going to have a relapse after Armando's sudden death.

"Mom," I said. "You need to calm down. This isn't going to help."

She washed her face and we made our way back. Armando looked so calm in his coffin. They'd done an amazing job of reconstructing his face.

I cried amid the other mourners. I wanted him back, acutely and suddenly. I wanted Armando to open his eyes, sit up and laugh, get up from the coffin, and drive us to Las Mañanitas, as we were supposed to do that day to officially celebrate the engagement. Rage crept up in my throat, but I kept it down inside. I knew it would only end up coming out later. If Maggie hadn't joined that stupid country club, she might never have dated him. He would have been dead and she would have known him only as a business acquaintance. We wouldn't be at this funeral and my mother wouldn't be drunk. Raul Aguila gave a eulogy about the strides Armando had made in the prison system and his immeasurable contribution to Mexican society. Elena talked about growing up with him, how he evolved into the noblest person she'd ever known, and not just because he was her brother. A few others made generic speeches. I realized that Armando didn't have many close relatives, and not even that many friends.

"Mom, are you going to say something?" I whispered. I'd seen her give compelling diplomatic speeches at all the work functions she'd dragged me to over the years.

She just shook her head and wiped her red eyes with tissue.

We went outside to follow the procession to the graveyard. It was late afternoon and the city was darkening. A rare mid-December storm was on the way; I heard thunder rumbling in the distance as we walked to the car. We shut our doors just as the sky opened up.

"Are you okay to drive?" I asked as we pulled out of the parking lot.

"I would *never* do anything to put you in danger," she snapped. We rode in silence for a while. She seemed sober enough now, and I figured we'd get something to eat soon anyway at the private reception Raul Aguila was holding at his sprawling Lomas home after the burial, though the last thing I felt like doing was acting sociable.

"Do you mind if we skip the food part?" my mother asked, as though she'd read my thoughts. "I have no appetite."

"Won't Elena be upset? You'll have to explain to all those people why we're not going," I said. I thought she'd want to spend more time around them, to ease the shock of Armando's violent end.

"I'm just not up for it," she said. "Those people were in my life because I was going to be married to Armando. I don't really feel like standing around talking with a group of strangers about times we didn't have."

"But, Mom, they're your friends, too."

"They remind me of *him.*" She started crying again, and I worried about her driving.

"It's okay—you don't have to explain. Whatever you need."

"They'll understand," she said through her tears.

I was secretly relieved that I wouldn't have to see Catalina again and could go back to ignoring her when Nina and I passed the fresa spot in front of the pool on our way to lunch in the soccer field. We pulled into the driveway of the Chapultepec graveyard. I couldn't believe I had been here, tripping with Manuel, only two weeks before. Things I'd thought were important then seemed like ephemeral nothings now.

As the coffin was lowered into the ground, I silently said good-bye to the man I would have called *Papá.* My mother stood beside me, her expression now blank. Elena's arm was around her; Armando's friends and colleagues surrounded us. They consoled my mother as if she'd been his wife of ten years. It reminded me that their relationship had still been relatively new.

I couldn't sleep that night and stayed up until sunrise scrawling away about funerals, politicians, and drug lords who could shoot you even when they were locked up in prison.

I was too depressed to go to school the next morning, and Maggie didn't try to make me go. I looked around the kitchen for bottles and was relieved to find none. I threw two bagels into the toaster oven as my mother walked in looking haggard, clad in her red bathrobe.

"I'm making us breakfast," I said.

"I'm going to L.A.," she said. "I need to get out of here for a week or two. You can stay with Nina if you want, or she can stay here with you."

"Don't you want me to come with you?"

"I think I need a little time alone, away from everything, so I can get it together."

I read between the lines that she'd probably spend the whole time going to meetings, trying not to drink her way through her grief.

I went downstairs and turned on the TV. The news said that the Popocatépetl volcano was on the verge of erupting, that it was spewing red-hot rocks. I walked outside and looked underneath the leaves in the garden; they were coated in thick black dust. I wondered if Popo would explode all over us, bringing down the city, a modern-day Pompeii. The volcano's name meant "smoking mountain" in Nahuatl, the Aztec language. Evacuating Mexico City would be impossible. With so many people, and the chaos of everyday life, there was no way we could get out. In the end, we didn't need to. But the volcano was active and rumbling, begging to explode and devour the city. There was a joke paralleling the explosion to how corrupt Mexico's president was: "What is that smoke coming out of Popocatépetl? It's President Salinas burning his papers."

The other lead story was the sighting of an apparition of the Virgen de Guadalupe in the Hidalgo subway station. I decided to go look at it, just for something to do with myself. When I got there, hordes of people were gathered around, offerings of flowers and candles strewn about. I pushed my way to the front of the crowd and saw the big, splotchy water stain on the gray cement wall. The Virgen de Guadalupe was a puddle.

That evening I was feeling restless. I dialed Manuel's number, but someone on the family's staff told me that he wasn't home. I hadn't seen him at all during the crowded funeral and wondered why he hadn't called me yet. I had to go somewhere, do something, so I went down to Coyoacán to meet Nina and Kai, who had plans to get drinks at

El Hijo del Cuervo. They were sitting at a table outside when I got there. I ordered a *michelada* and looked around the plaza. A spotlight illuminated the church in a cast of white light. Balloon and cotton-candy vendors wheeled their carts around, and a woman with thick black waist-length hair sold corn on the cob lavished with cheese and chili. A man with a windup music box played on the corner.

A tarot-reading fortune-teller, an old man who was notorious in Coyoacán for being a little bit loco, wandered over to us. He pointed at me. *"Tú. Escritora,"* he said. *"Ven,"* he beckoned to me, then walked away.

"What was that?" I asked.

"He called you a writer," said Kai. "That's weird. Maybe he's not insane and really *is* psychic."

"Mila's not a *writer,"* said Nina.

"Haven't you read our school newspaper?" snapped Kai.

"Excuse me, Kai, I know my own best friend. She's way too much fun to really care about something so boring." As the two of them got into a ridiculous argument, I walked over to where the tarot man sat.

"Puedes leer mi futuro?" I asked. "Can you read my fortune?"

"Are you ready to have your cards read?" he asked.

"Why wouldn't I be?"

"You have to be ready to know your destiny before it finds you. The spirit won't reveal himself to you until you are ready. But when he does, he will reveal himself completely."

"What does that mean?"

He looked at me but didn't answer. He shuffled the cards and spread them one by one before me.

"You are hiding," he said.

"From what?"

"Some things have happened to you recently and since you came here. This is what you should be paying attention to, and exploring the unfamiliar, the world around you. Soon you will meet the most familiar face you've never seen. You see, *niña,* in life everything comes full circle. But not just once. Over and over again."

He spooked me, but I thanked him, dropping an extra ten pesos in his hat before walking away. I found Kai back at Hijo del Cuervo.

"Nina got mad, for no reason, of course," he said. "She left in a huff." We moved inside to the bar and ordered more tequila while Café Tacuba, a popular Mexican alt-rock band, blared over the speakers.

"What's going on with her?" I asked. "She's so hyper these days. She's not her normal self. And she's always looking to pick a fight. Otherwise she's just moody."

"I think she's bipolar," Kai said. "I know way too much about this stuff. It's a common side effect of growing up with psychoanalysts for parents."

"Like manic-depressive?"

"Exactly," he said.

"Would that explain why she always borrows my clothes without asking and never returns them?"

"Kleptomania can go along with a manic episode, but no one knows exactly what causes it."

"I think she does half the things she does for the attention. She loves attention. All she gets from her family is purses, shoes, jewelry, and lectures on keeping her weight down." Now I understood that Sonia Rothman didn't keep her closets locked out of neurosis. She kept them locked out of Nina.

Kai nodded. "You might make a pretty good analyst."

"No thanks," I said, smiling. "Journalist."

"Same difference," he said. "So how are you holding up? I mean with your mom and everything that just happened."

"We're in shock. I still can't believe it. It doesn't feel real. I keep imagining Armando will be at my house when I get home." I started to cry.

Kai hugged me. "I'm really sorry, sweetie."

"What am I supposed to do?" I said, reaching for a napkin to blow my nose.

"Nothing you can do but process it," he said, rubbing my shoulders. "Do what you do best."

ISM OBSERVER
December 11, 1993

Doble Vida: Losing Armando

By Mila Márquez

I locked myself in my room after I heard, an ill feeling passing over me in waves. I have never been close to anyone who was murdered before. They tried to do it before, whoever "they" were—people whose business he was hampering by keeping these types locked up. First they tried gassing him in his home, letting the gas leak in through the pipes, but that time he was lucky. This time, there was no time. I can't even begin to grasp this, to comprehend its enormity. My mother, who was—as I've written here before—his fiancée, is beside herself with grief. It was the first time she'd been in love for as long as I can remember, I mean, really in love, and with a man I loved, too. He and I used to talk. He was available to me and to everyone else in his life. He was someone who actually cared. It's hard to know what to say or do to comfort my mother—maybe I just need too much comforting myself. This is all too big for me. These are the things that make me hate this city. This political, corrupt, evil society and its backward systems.

I would get some backlash for calling the society evil and corrupt, but I didn't care. I was pissed, and I wanted everyone to know it.

I went over to Nina's the next afternoon. I'd stayed home again, still not ready to go back to school.

"Why did you leave that way?" I said. I flopped down on her bed and waited for her to ask me about the funeral, about how I was feeling, about Armando. About anything I was going through. But she didn't.

"You missed the crazy outfit Daniela Sanchez wore today—I think it was Chanel. She looked like Jackie O in the sixties or something. Anyway, so I like this boy. I don't know why I never noticed him before. His name is Gabriel. Who's that novelist I like so much, what's his name?

García Márquez. Oh! Márquez, like you, now you want to be some kind of writer too now, right? Anyway, he's that guy in the back row in English class, the one with the dark-brown eyes and the wavy blondish hair that's almost down to his shoulders. And those adorable glasses. I don't know why I never noticed him before."

She was on hyperspeed—one of her episodes coming on. When she got like this, she was entirely closed to the world around her, as if she were the only one who existed. It scared me, though usually I just let the mania ride out. Now all the anger I'd tried to hold inside at the funeral came pouring out of me.

"Could you at least ask me how I'm feeling?"

"What do you mean?"

"I mean Armando. The funeral. My future stepfather being shot and killed. It's fucked up! And you don't even remember that that's why I wasn't at school today? What the fuck is wrong with you?"

I thought she might apologize, or seem at least slightly embarrassed. Instead, she reacted as though I were the one who'd done something wrong.

"Don't get so mad, Mila," she said. "I'm just trying to tell you what happened."

I was floored. I couldn't say a thing. I got up, went over to her closet, and threw open the doors. Possessed, I began pulling clothes off hangers, tossing them on the bed, digging around in the back of the closet, searching. She stood there dumbfounded as I pulled out what was mine, which was a lot, and started gathering it up in my arms. Then she snapped.

"What do you think you're doing?" she yelled, lunging at me, tackling me down onto the bed.

"Getting my things back," I hissed. She pulled my hair and clawed at me with her perfectly manicured talons. I pushed her off, and she landed on the hardwood floor with a thud. She screamed, and the bedroom door flung open.

"*Qué pasa aquí, chicas?*" Reina had run upstairs to see what was going on. I pushed past her with my armload of clothes, which fell everywhere, leaving a trail of sequined tops and old favorite jeans, while clutching tightly to my favorite leather jacket. I ran down the stairs, through the front door, down the long driveway, and out the gate. I was out of breath by the time I got back home. I knew I'd lost some things along the way, but I didn't care. I had my jacket, some pants, skirts, tops, even a couple of hats, and my long-lost pair of rectangular DKNY sunglasses. Nina had been stealing from me the entire time I'd known her, and I'd never faced it, or wanted to, until now. I swore to myself that I wouldn't go back to her this time.

We ignored each other at school for a week. I was lonely, depressed about Armando, and sad for my mother. I remembered that Nina's mother had forced her to see a psychologist once, but Nina told me she refused to speak the entire time she was there. The shrink gave up and fed her mother the old treatment cliché that she couldn't help Nina until Nina was ready to help herself.

On the ninth day of our not speaking, a note made its way through chemistry class to me:

im sorry for how i acted. please come to acapulco with me and my parents for the break? naldo has a water-polo championship in monterrey so they specifically asked me to invite you. we r staying at the princess hotel. love, nina

I knew she'd been the mirror I'd been reflecting myself through since I came to Mexico, the person I'd confided in, etched words and pictures into my memory with. We face different mirrors and come up with different faces, schizophrenic and confused.

But when Nina was up she was still the most fun girlfriend I'd ever had, even if she wasn't the most stable. I wanted to keep filling my diaries with pages of our adventures, but I stuffed the note into my pocket without a reply.

Manuel called me back the next morning.

"I was away on a sailing trip with my cousins," he explained. "I'm so sorry about Armando Salazar. Is there anything I can do for you or your mother?"

"It's really sweet of you to ask, but I don't think so."

"If the two of you would like to come with me and my family to our Acapulco house for the break, you're invited."

My heart rate shot up, as it did when I'd had too many *cafés de olla*.

"My mother's going to my grandmother's house in Los Angeles," I said. "But I'm going to Acapulco, too, with Nina."

"Can I see you while you're there?" he asked.

"I'd love that."

When I hung up with Manuel, I pressed speed-dial one.

"Didn't you get my note?" Nina asked when she picked up the phone.

"It's just that I feel like you haven't been yourself lately," I said coolly. "If you paid more attention to what's going on in other people's lives, you'd understand why I've been so upset."

"I'll try harder, I swear," she said. "But will you come to the beach? It will be so much fun." In an instant, she was up again.

"My mother said she wants to go to L.A. alone, to try to get over things a little, so, sure, I'm free."

I packed my least favorite clothes, because people never really changed. If there was one thing I'd learned from trying not to be like my mother, it was to love them anyway, flaws and all, not just pick up and leave. Or maybe I was only telling myself that because I secretly wanted to spend some more time with Manuel.

The late-December Friday afternoon that Nina and I left for our Acapulco vacation, I thought I was hallucinating when I saw Tyler standing outside ISM's gates. He looked the same, long blond hair and strung out. I ran over to him.

"Hey," I said, tapping him on the shoulder. He turned around and looked surprised to see me. I could have sworn I saw anger cross his face. "I'm so sorry about the Arizona thing," I said. "I got a lot of shit about everything."

"So you know the story?" he asked icily.

"Yeah, about the DEA? So bizarre."

"Oh, so is *that* what your crazy mother told you?"

"She said they'd been watching us or something."

As soon as Tyler burst into venomous laughter, I realized how ridiculous and untrue it sounded.

"Because the DEA doesn't have a really impossible job to do in this country. They're busting high-school kids now."

"So what—"

"Your mother," he said, cutting me off, "went to pay my father a visit in his office. She had all this photographic evidence of us, smoking weed on the roof, hanging out at my house during the day when you used to cut class—"

"She had *pictures*?"

"She was following us around. Apparently she has a friend at the Canadian Embassy who let her use his office to spy on us on my roof. No offense, but what a psycho. I can't believe I'm even speaking to you. I guess it's not your fault, but still. She ruined my whole fucking setup."

"Oh. My. God." How could she do this to me? I'd never felt so humiliated in my life. Maggie may have been extreme, but I couldn't believe she'd gone so far to get Tyler out of my life.

"I had no fucking idea, but I should have. Are you pissed at me?"

"It's not your fault your mother's a psycho bitch," he said, but his voice was angry. Of course, he would take it out on me. "I need money. I'm moving into an apartment."

"Did you get kicked out of your house?"

"No, I just had to get out. I'm crashing with a friend, but I have to find my own place," he said. "I go to South Hill now, actually."

So Tyler was back in school, at the reject ISM.

"Are you waiting for someone?" I asked.

"No, I'm working to get the money I need for the apartment."

"What kind of job?"

"Same," he said, looking up the street instead of at me. "The least you could do is buy something."

"What do you have?"

"Green Planets today."

"Nina and I are going to Acapulco," I said. "I think I'll surprise her."

"So, two? It's eighty pesos."

I took the tiny pieces of wrapped foil and tucked them into the pocket of my jeans.

"I'm really sorry, Tyler."

"Save it," he said. "I know it wasn't you, but don't expect me to let myself be seen with you."

It hurt, but I understood.

Nina's driver pulled up in the Escalade, and we piled into the backseat with her mother. Her father sat in front.

"Are you excited to go to Acapulco?" Sonia asked.

"I've never been before," I said. "I can't wait to stay at the Princess. What do you want to do tonight?" I asked Nina.

"Go out dancing, what else?" she said. "And I have a surprise for you. Something special."

"I have one for you, too! But you like surprises. I hate them, so tell me now."

"You'll find out tonight," she said. "When we go dancing."

The Princess was a grand hotel, majestic, befitting its name. Nina and I had our own room, and it was nowhere near her parents. After checking in, Sonia and George headed straight for the spa for their pre-booked couples' massage and seaweed wrap.

"Bye, girls, have a great time!" said Sonia as we wheeled our weekend suitcases down the hall. We were free.

"Your parents are awesome that way," I said to Nina.

"No, they're just in love," she said bitterly. "They have the only thing they've ever wanted: each other."

"You have nothing to complain about."

"Oh, but I do," she said.

"I'm going to call Manuel. He wanted to have dinner with us."

Nina and I decided on Carlos and Charlie's, a local chain popular with tourists. The three of us were seated at a table, sipping strawberry daiquiris and looking at menus, when she pulled out three white tablets wrapped in Saran Wrap and dropped them in the middle of the table. They had peace signs etched into their chalky white surfaces.

"I have three because my brother was supposed to be with us," Nina explained. "But then his water-polo team made championship."

"Monterrey, right?" asked Manuel. Nina nodded. "Good for him. They wouldn't have made it without him, that's for sure."

"What *are* these?" I asked, grabbing the pills, which Manuel seemed to be trying to ignore.

"Ecstasy," she said. "It's a new drug." I guessed we wouldn't be needing the Green Planets in my pocket yet.

"*Buenas noches, puedo tomar su orden?*" asked a waiter.

"I'll have the *tacos al pastor,*" said Manuel.

"Mixed salad with no dressing," said Nina.

"I'll take the *pollo con mole* and a salad *with* dressing," I said, looking straight at Nina.

Nina handed me one of the white tablets. "Since Naldo couldn't make it," she said, giving the third one to Manuel. I couldn't tell whether he was feeling resigned or just spontaneous, but he shrugged and popped it into his mouth, followed by a sip of his drink. I did the same. We waited.

I picked up a red crayon. There were a bunch of them in a wooden cup in the middle of the table. The tablecloth was one of those paper ones for kids to draw on. What is the word for this? I thought. "Zen," I wrote.

"What?" asked Nina.

"Zen," I said. "That's what this is. It's everything coming together at once. It's the unity, the beauty of it all. It's Zen."

Nina just laughed.

A dark alien carcass smothered in brown sauce coasted down in front of me on a flying saucer. I can't remember this next part very well, but I think I screamed.

"*Qué pasa?*" asked the waiter.

"What is this *thing*?" I squealed. "Take it away!"

I had lost all sense of decorum.

"It's your *pollo con mole,*" he said, aghast.

"I don't want it anymore!" I yelled.

"We'll just take the check," said Manuel.

There was a stage inside Carlos and Charlie's—a catwalk for drunk girls to dance on. Nina and I hopped up. We swayed our hips to the music, then we started to kiss. As Nina and I made out wildly, the Carlos and Charlie's patrons stared. We just laughed and kissed some more, just two girls on the catwalk, in ecstasy.

I don't remember what, if anything, Manuel said or did. After I don't know how long, Nina and I hopped down, much to the relief of the patrons and the dismay of the waitstaff. A long line had formed outside the bar, clubbers eagerly waiting to see the "hot gringas." The three of us ran outside the restaurant, down the driveway.

"That was interesting," Manuel said, laughing and kissing my ear.

"Look," I said. "A golf cart!" Like a white stallion, a single golf cart glimmered at the end of the driveway among all the cars. "It's here for *us.*" Wanting nothing but adventure, I pressed the On button. I was on, everything was on—the stars were on over my head, the ground was on beneath my feet, beneath the gas pedal of the golf cart. And I stepped on the gas.

We were a sight coming through the Palladium, the most exclusive club in Acapulco, on the golf cart. But I maneuvered proudly between a Ferrari and a Porsche, both driven by fresas, maybe even fresas from our school, though I didn't stop to look. The valet stared at the golf cart.

I pulled up, slicked on some cherry-flavored lip gloss, and left the cart with him as if it were the most normal thing in the world.

"Gracias, señor," I said, slipping out of the driver's seat and strutting into the club. Manuel and I held hands as Nina wobbled on four-inch heels through the entry line.

"I think I'm falling in love with you," Manuel whispered in my ear. A warm flush passed through my entire body.

"Me, too," I said. It hit all my senses at once that he and I had something deeper than what I'd imagined it would be at the outset.

Palladium had a wall of glass that looked out over the whole bay. It was beautiful. The dance floor hadn't opened yet and a Wallflowers song played over the sound system. When it faded, the DJ took to his booth and the crowd shouted as the beat of house tracks upped the energy level.

Manuel and I were dancing an hour later when we spotted some of his clique over at the bar.

"Want to get out of here?" he whispered. I saw Nina over by the bar, deep in conversation with one of the fresa guys.

"I want to walk on the beach," I said to Manuel.

We puttered down the hilly roads to the beach in the golf cart and ran onto the sand, pulling off our shoes, all the way to the water's edge.

"You're so beautiful," he said, pushing my hair behind my ears and kissing me. I gestured toward the water with my head.

"Let's get in."

Wordlessly, we undressed and dived in, past where the waves were breaking on the shore. The moon's reflection split across the undulating water like pieces of shattered glass. We kissed again, and I felt his body press up against mine. I let my feet float up and close around his waist. Then he was inside. The water moved around us, with us. I tasted it on my tongue. "You *are* perfect," he whispered. "I knew I would love you."

"I love you, too," I said. "More than I even know how to explain right now."

"Your body is perfect."

"So is yours."

"So is your mind, your whole personality, your everything."

"So is yours."

The current shifted, and I worried that we might be pulled under. But he held on tight, and we stayed, joined, heads above the waves.

The E was good. It was pure MDMA, though I didn't know that at the time. The bad part was that I was coming down. I was standing on the shore again, using my shirt to dry my wet body before getting dressed, when it started wearing off. It felt as if a truck had hit me. One minute I was enraptured, serotonin escalating, my senses heightened. Then sinking—definite, incessant sinking. Hitting a wall, a big, sturdy, cement wall. Boom! All I could think was *No!* Being on Ecstasy felt like waking from a coma into some sort of divine consciousness. Now I was crashing down to the depressing state formerly known as everyday consciousness.

"I have to get back to the hotel," I said. "Nina will start wondering."

"Come over to my house tomorrow," Manuel said. "I'll take you out on my Jet Ski, to my father's boat. We can have lunch, go scuba diving." He kissed my ear.

"Sounds like heaven," I said.

In the breakfast room the next morning, Nina and I noticed a group of guests staring at us. People from the restaurant who had witnessed our little act. Of course, they were all staying at our hotel, I realized. We quickly grabbed some coffee, yogurts, and spoons and ran out to the beach, slapping on sunglasses.

"Did you fuck Manuel last night?" Nina asked as we spread our towels on the sand.

"I wouldn't call it fucking," I said. "We, you know, but it wasn't—"

"That makes three guys in half a school year," she said. She paused, presumably for the dramatic effect she was so fond of. "I didn't want to say this, but I think you're starting to become a *slut*." She whispered the word under her breath.

"You think so?" I said. "You were the one who was handing out the Ecstasy. You hooked up with that fresa at the club."

"I guess Dave doesn't count, but still, three is too many. I mean, even if you were on drugs."

"Way to look out for me, Nina. I'm sorry if you liked Manuel last year, but whatever happened or didn't happen had nothing to do with me. In fact, you may want to vaguely consider being happy for us. Ever thought of that, Nina? Being happy for someone besides yourself?"

"Don't think you're going to go out with him the rest of the time," she said.

"It's not as though I'd ditch you. You could come."

"You're on this vacation here with *me* and we are *not* seeing him today."

I knew Nina too well. There was no way I could win. I pulled the silver foil out of my beach bag and unfolded it to show her the tiny squares of blotter paper. "Look, Green Planets," I said.

"Where'd you get those?" she said, suddenly excited, her opinions and judgments forgotten for the time being. I handed her one. We took them, lay back on our towels in the sun, and waited. The hot, late, lazy afternoon crept up as slowly as the waves rising and breaking against the shore. I launched into the story of Tyler, my mother, and what had really happened.

An hour later, Nina and I were torpedoing around on Jet Skis, the acid just having hit. I was used to the feeling, but with the cobalt blue of the ocean, salt hitting my lips as we sped on the waves at seventy miles per hour, it was like new again. The water looked cartoonish, as did Nina in her neon life jacket and leopard-print bikini. Everything seemed strange all of a sudden, but strangest of all was the feeling that the girl who had become my best friend had it in for me. Why did I feel so attached to a kleptomaniac who judged me? We'd reached a truce in our drugged haze. But acid wasn't really a haze. It was closer to looking at life through a microscope, the mind latching on to those tiny intricacies that otherwise went unnoticed.

We docked at a white raft within swimming distance of the shore. I lay on the plastic, face pressed into the side, colored waves rising from the white, a vivid illusion, hyperreal, more real than reality. I couldn't stay still. When I did, everything was too much, too vivid, too beautiful. I had to get back on the Jet Ski. Nina wanted to stay out, so I rode in to shore alone and returned the key to the man in the rental booth.

I was on my way to the room when I ran into George and Sonia. We hadn't seen them since we'd arrived, and I'd actually forgotten they were even in Acapulco with us. Suddenly frightened and self-conscious, I put my glasses on to hide my wide-as-quarters pupils from them.

"You girls enjoying yourselves?" asked George.

"Oh, yeah, tons. This is great. Thanks, Mr. Rothman. You, too, Mrs. Rothman."

"Keep having fun!" said George, taking Sonia by the hand and walking toward the pool area.

"Book a purification facial at the spa, they're phenomenal," said Sonia. "See you later, Mila."

They smiled and waved as they strolled away, off in their own world as always. That's it? I thought. I wondered how they could exist in their bubble, all fancy accessories, travel, and material things, thanks to George's high-powered career and Sonia's almost too delicate beauty. It nearly made me appreciate Maggie. Of all the things my mother was, plastic wasn't one of them.

When I asked the receptionist at the front desk for the room key, she handed me a scribbled phone message along with it. "Manuel Amador," it said at the top. And then: "Princess of the Princess, call me. Your oxygen tank awaits."

I could have used an oxygen tank. But I didn't call him back.

SEVEN

January

When I got home from Acapulco, dense jungle rising above endless open road giving way to smog and concrete, Maggie had already returned. I ran straight to her room and threw open the door. Her blue-and-white striped overnight bag was open on her bed and she was folding clothes for what looked like a weekend trip. I was too infuriated to ask what she was doing.

"Have you lost your mind?" I screamed.

"What happened?" asked my mother.

"I should be asking *you* that, and don't try making excuses to cover the truth like you always do. I know about Tyler."

My mother sighed exasperatedly.

"What do you know about Tyler?" she said, her tone flat.

"I knew you'd do this!" I yelled. "Let's just say I know it wasn't the D.E.A. that got him sent to Arizona. I don't understand how you could take that upon yourself. What is *wrong* with you?" I waited for her to fight back, but she remained composed, tersely stacking folded blouses in the overnight bag.

"I was protecting you, and one day you'll thank me for it," she said. "That psychologist did nothing helpful, so I took care of things myself."

"*Took care of things,* you call it? By *spying* on me?"

"I didn't follow you. I explained to Tyler's father that his son was known to be selling drugs, and to *my* daughter."

"I know you held a stakeout at the Canadian Embassy, Mom. I found out because he's back."

"Is he? That wasn't supposed to be allowed, Milagro. If you start hanging around with him again—"

"Don't worry," I said. "He's definitely not going to be calling." I walked out of her room. "You made sure of *that*!" I yelled from down the hall, then slammed my door hard.

I was lying on my bed an hour later, writing in my diary, when she appeared in the doorway.

"What would you have done, in my situation?" she asked, leaning against the dark wood of the door frame. "In the States, we could easily do something about your behavior, but here it has the potential to be so much worse, don't you think? And it's practically accepted! You have easy access to drugs, no enforced drinking age, classmates who go clubbing till all hours every night of the week. . . . You've changed so much since we've been here, Milagro, and so have I. You've adapted your ways, but so have I."

"By becoming a stalker."

"If you think I'm just going to stand passively by while my only child ruins her life, you are sorely mistaken."

"Reading my diaries, opening my letters, and deporting my boyfriend isn't exactly the way to show you *care.* I've always known you go through my shit. I've written some of the stuff in there just to throw you off."

"And I know you've been trying to hide what's really been going on in your life from me. You never confide in me, just to some stupid piece of paper in a notebook, or a letter to Nora. What am I to you, a stranger?"

No, but my father is, I wanted to say.

"I have a right to a private life. Anyway, I'm going away this year, re-member? How are you going to deal with *that*?"

"You may be in college, but you'll actually have less freedom. When you're back in the States, I'll know you can't get away with bribing po-licemen and that you'll get carded if you try to go to a bar. I don't want you to have the same problem I had."

"I'm not you. It's impossible for me to learn anything without mak-ing my own mistakes."

"If you would only listen to me, you wouldn't be making those mis-takes in the first place," she said. "Nobody else is going to save you from yourself."

"Mom, I'm exhausted," I said, tapping my pen on the open page of my notebook. "How are *you* feeling, anyway?" I asked, remembering Armando, and desperate to steer our conversation away from the brick wall it was speeding toward.

"I can't believe he's gone." Her voice cracked. "Getting away helped as much as anything could."

"So then why are you packing when you just got back?" I asked.

She wiped her eyes and cleared her throat, back-to-business Mag-gie. "Work trip, if you can call this idiocy work. This stupid American girl—where do I even start? She's nineteen years old, from Kentucky, runs away to Mexico. Gets an Indio boyfriend and goes with him to this tiny town with no running water, gets pregnant, and has his baby."

"She's nineteen?"

"From a trailer park in Oklahoma. So the boyfriend beats her up and forces her to take care of the farm by herself. I guess she strapped the baby to her body in the middle of the night and, get this, got on a *donkey* because that's all there is in the town, and rode down the mountain and got on a bus to Oaxaca. She called the Embassy, of course, and since I'm on duty now I have to go pick her up, get her and the baby on a plane to the States."

"On duty" meant that my mother could be called anytime, day or night, to deal with emergencies. It was a rotating part of Citizen Services that fell to a different officer every few weeks. Catastrophe always struck when it was her turn. She carried around a pager every day for those two weeks that she was on duty and inhaled sharply whenever it went off.

"Won't it be tough to get the baby out of Mexico?"

"I'm impressed. You've done your homework."

"No, I've just been your daughter for seventeen years."

There was a rule in Mexico that if a baby's father was Mexican the mother could take the baby out of the country only with written approval from the father. Machismo, as usual. I thought of this teenage girl, only two years older than I was, with a baby and an abusive boyfriend in a dusty village.

"Mom, I know things haven't been easy this year. I never meant to scare you or anything, but you need to loosen up a little."

"Something needs to change," she said. "We'll talk when I get back."

"When?" I asked.

"It's just overnight." Her expression turned stern. "And I don't want to hear of any trouble while I'm gone."

"I'll either be home or at Nina's."

"I don't like that Nina," she said. "But, all right, her house only." She kissed me on the cheek and picked up her overnight bag. We'd reached a truce, for the time being.

As soon as she left, I went downstairs and turned on the television to drown out the silence of the house. I was absentmindedly flipping channels when I saw the man, the one from Los Pinos the day with the motor home. He was giving an interview on the street outside a government building, something about NAFTA, which had just come into effect, but I couldn't focus on what he was saying. His face filled the screen. He had dark-green eyes like mine, the same forehead, and large, masculine versions of my nose and lips. *Señor de la Garza,* the reporter kept calling him in the interview. *Señor de la Garza.* I ran to the computer Maggie had just installed in the guest room and logged on to the Internet. Google was still a decade away, but I found a search engine and typed in his last name. A page of results popped up, some related to him. *Eliodoro Márquez de la Garza,* an important Mexican politician and member of the president's close inner circle. He was in a behind-the-scenes position, but one that came with a lot of power. Márquez was a pretty common name, but I wondered if it could be more than just a coincidence. Could my mother have given me the last name not because, as she said, she liked the way it sounded but to create a connection between the man I was never supposed to know and me?

If there's anything I can do, Manuel had said. I picked up the phone and dialed, nervousness churning my stomach. His maid answered and called for him without asking who was on the line. I heard a scuffling, then the familiar voice on the phone. *"Bueno?"*

"Hi. It's Mila."

"Qué milagro."

"What's that supposed to mean?"

"I was just kidding. It's a joke, you know? You're Milagro, and it's a miracle that you called."

"Sorry it took me so long," I said.

"Well, the best things are always worth waiting for, even if I was a little mad at you for not calling me in Acapulco. And I *was,* you know."

"Nina wanted us to spend time alone together," I said. "Sorry."

"I get it. I know she wants you all to herself. Would you care to come over and see my new Picasso? I just brought it home."

"Another one?"

"Yes, and this one is very special. It's a drawing, actually, from his Blue Period. And I've been painting, too. Would you sit for a portrait?"

"I love *The Frugal Repast*—you know that print with the blind man?" I said, ignoring his question. "Blindness was a prominent theme during Picasso's Blue Period. I prefer his Rose one myself." I knew I was showing off, but it's what I did when I felt nervous.

"Mila, please come over? I'd really like to see you."

He didn't have to ask again. I slipped out the gate, the metal clicking softly into place as I gently shut it. I was trembling, but I wasn't sure why. Maybe because I'd let him see who I'd become since moving here, allowed him to join me on that mental vacation that had opened my eyes to perception, or the doors, as Aldous Huxley called them. Or maybe, as I thought of that first night with Tyler, just a trip I could take without my mother. If things really worked out with Manuel, I would be sitting in front of the pool during lunch, going to the weekly *cocteles* with him, and accompanying his family to art auctions on Sundays. And, maybe, I would find out about the man I'd seen on TV.

When I got to Manuel's house he was sitting on the leather couch, staring at the picture on the wall, the drawing he wanted to show me.

"There it is," he said. "My latest acquisition."

He lifted a Corona to his lips and took a sip. The drawing was beautiful, a half-rendered portrait of a woman's back.

"Very nice," I said, pretending to scrutinize the sketch. "It's a lot like the *Blue Nude*."

I sat down on the sofa's wide arm.

"Lapinski's physics class is killing me," he offered, steering our conversation away from the art.

"Then why are you taking it? It's not a requirement."

"I'm going to do engineering in college. I made the decision. I have to get started."

"I thought you wanted to be a painter."

"I'll always paint," he said. "But you need to understand that I'm never going to be able to go to art school. It's either engineering or surgery. I've told you this."

"That's so much pressure, living to carry out someone else's expectations of you. Why don't you go to university in the States, where you can switch majors without starting from scratch? Then your dad wouldn't have a clue whether you were in engineering, art, or becoming a fucking ballerina."

"You're good," said Manuel. "I'll think about it."

He grabbed me around the waist and pulled me down onto the couch with him.

"Do you want to go to the *coctel* with me tonight?" he asked.

"Won't all your friends be there?"

"Of course," he said. "So what?"

"At Palladium in Acapulco, I thought you were avoiding introducing me."

"You thought I wanted to leave to hide you from them?" Manuel laughed.

"What's funny about that?"

"I wanted to be alone with you, silly girl. I didn't want to be stuck hanging around with them all night."

Could he really not care about breaking the social order? I wondered, forgetting the reason I'd called him in the first place.

Manuel pulled me through the jam-packed club to the VIP area, where you had to either buy hundreds of dollars' worth of bottles or bribe the bouncer. All the fresas were there. There was Katia, whose mother was a telenovela and movie star and whose father was a CEO. And Cristina, Manuel's ex-girlfriend, whose father was Katia's father's right-hand man. Beatriz, the one with the perfect nose job who'd won "best looking" in the yearbook, was a senator's daughter, and Tatiana was a descendant of Spanish royalty. Manuel's guy friends were Tomás, the president's son; Jaime, whose father ran GasMex, the country's petroleum giant; his brother Rafael; and Jorge, the son of the head of a huge investment bank. From a distance, life in front of the pool looked plastic, a perfect crowd of beautiful people in designer clothing. Up close, I noticed that there were subdivisions within the fresas—the richest, the rich, and the less rich, who were still ostentatious. Hierarchies within a hierarchy. Manuel brought me into his clique, the first group.

"This is Mila Márquez," he said, introducing me.

"Márquez? I didn't know you were Mexican," said Beatriz.

"Half Mexican," I corrected. "Neither here nor there." I smiled at her.

"But you're so light," she said.

"Beatriz—" Manuel interrupted.

But I cut in. "So are you."

"But you said your father is Mexican. Your mother's American, right? So if they met in the U.S., your dad is surely an Indio. So I was only asking, what kind of Mexican are you?"

I was so shocked at what to me was the perfect illustration of the kind of racism and class consciousness that existed here, and was more often left unsaid.

"Beatriz, don't be stupid," Manuel said.

She rolled her eyes and went back to sit with her friends. Manuel turned to me and lightly kissed my forehead.

"Don't pay her any attention," he said. "I'll talk to her and she'll change her attitude. So, what are you drinking?"

"I'll have a vodka and orange juice, I guess," I said, surveying the VIP room as Manuel mixed the cocktail from the bottles on the table. Beatriz might as well have come out and said she figured my mother had screwed a gardener in L.A. And as much as it stung, and as much as that kind of scenario might have been true had Maggie's life gone differently, I still wanted to get her to see that she was wrong, that I belonged here.

Cristina lounged on a red velvet couch, whispering with Catalina. I didn't know how to negotiate her. Manuel wouldn't say how she had reacted to the news that he was dating me. She couldn't be pleased, but Manuel uninhibitedly walked me over to the group and talked with his friends with his arm around me the entire time, even making an effort to include me in the conversation. After a few hours, though, he seemed restless and bored.

"Let's go someplace else," he said.

I stashed the half-full vodka bottle in my bag and we walked out into the warm air, our arms around each other. We came to a park with long, winding stone stairways and a view of the city below and went down a few steps. Manuel spread out his jacket for me to sit on. We passed the vodka bottle back and forth.

"Where do you want to go next?" he asked.

I thought about it. La Boom was usually good on Wednesdays, but maybe Medusas would be even better. "What time is it?" I asked.

He looked at his Rolex, a birthday present from his mother. "Almost three."

I took a swig of vodka. Then I felt a presence behind me, eyes like invisible lasers over my shoulders. I turned around. "Oh, shit," I silently cursed.

"Buenos días, jovenes," said the cop. He wore a dark uniform, and his badge shone in the lamplight. "Drinking in public, I see?" He took the bottle out of my hand.

"Do you want to come with me?" he continued. "Or . . ."

"Get your wallet out," whispered Manuel. "I spent all my cash in the club."

I had only two hundred pesos, which I handed to the policeman. He looked at the money and laughed. "Looks like you're coming with me."

"Esperen aquí," said Manuel. "Wait here." He jumped up and took the steps two at a time. I guessed he was going to find an ATM. I sat there nervously while the cop stood on the step above me, staring out over the light-speckled view.

"Entonces, pasaste bien la noche?" he asked. "So, did you have a fun night?"

"Sí, muy bien, gracias," I said. "Very much so, thanks."

We sat in awkward silence for a few minutes, which felt like an eternity.

"Va a regresar, tu novio, sí?" "Your boyfriend is coming back, yes?"

I'd begun to wonder myself if he'd return. Then he appeared in the shadows, holding a black box. It took me a moment to recognize the CD player from his car. It was a brand-new ten-disc changer that must have cost several hundred dollars. He came down the steps and handed it over to the cop, who broke into a toothy million-dollar smile.

"*Gracias joven,*" he said, grabbing the proffered player. "*Que la pasen bien.*" "Thanks, young man. Have a good time."

The policeman handed the vodka bottle, but not the two hundred pesos, back to me, and walked away into the night. I was about to try to console Manuel about the expensive new CD player, but then I saw that he was smiling.

"*No hay pedo,*" he said. "I'll just buy another one in the morning."

The next day at lunch, I sat in front of the pool.

Poolfront life was like fodder for a soap opera or one of those teenage TV shows. The fresas were dressed as though they were going to a couture fashion show instead of high school, and they'd all known one another since childhood, so they were full of inside jokes and intrigue. Sitting by the turquoise-tiled Olympic during lunch with Manuel and the other fresas, I nursed my hangover with a diet Coke. Nina walked by with Kai on the way to their usual smoking spot on the soccer field. I waved, and Kai gave me a thumbs-up, but Nina shot me a dirty look. I didn't care what she thought anymore. I was with Manuel, suddenly on the inside, in a world I never imagined I could penetrate. Still, no matter how hard I tried not to, I missed her and thought about her all the time.

"Why don't you come to Santa Fe with me after school today?" Manuel asked.

"I guess a movie sounds good."

"Not for the movies. I want to buy something for you."

"Why?" I asked. I couldn't imagine what he would want to get me or for what occasion.

"You're beautiful, Mila. I want to give you . . . I don't know, something that will accentuate it."

I sipped my cafeteria take-out coffee and looked down at my old jeans and plaid flannel shirt with my pack of Marlboro Lights in the breast pocket. Then I looked at Manuel, in his Armani pants and leather jacket. I wanted to feel excited about the shopping trip, but instead I was flooded with skepticism.

As though he could read my mind, Manuel said, "You know, Mila, we're people, too."

"What do you mean?" I asked.

"Just because my friends and I have the lives we do doesn't mean we think we're better than you."

"Speak for yourself," I said. "None of your friends even make the effort to say hello to me."

"Have you ever made an effort with them?"

I exhaled audibly. "So now what?"

"So now we go to Santa Fe after school."

We sped up the Toluca highway in one of Manuel's cars, a silver BMW.

"What exactly are we shopping for?" I asked, watching a *pesero* speed by. It was so full that people were hanging out the door.

"Your new look."

"Who says I want a new look?"

"Try something on for me, then. If you don't like it, I won't get it for you."

"I'm still not sure I understand why you want to get me clothes in the first place."

"As I've said, Mila, you're beautiful, but sometimes I think you try to hide it on purpose. You don't like to be seen. But you deserve to be seen, and you should let people see you."

"Maybe I'll try on just one thing," I said. "Only for you."

Manuel just smiled, concentrating on the speedway ahead.

We walked the marble-floored hallways of Centro Comercial Santa Fe, past Gucci and Coach, Prada and Via Spiga. Manuel took me from one boutique to another, each one with more beautiful clothes than the last. He knew my taste, or what it would be if I had that kind of money.

I tried on a pair of platform sandals like the ones Catalina had and balked at the four-thousand-peso price tag.

"This would look great with those," he said, handing me a pair of cropped gray vicuña wool pants, a silk peasant blouse, and a tailored tan leather jacket that was light enough for spring. "Try it on."

"Manuel, I *said* just one thing!"

"Just to see, come on."

I loved the outfit. The fabrics were luxurious. I felt ten years older and a thousand times richer.

"That's why they dress this way," said Manuel.

It made sense, I realized. No wonder they appeared to feel beautiful and sexy all the time. Who wouldn't, in these cuts and fabrics?

"Try something else," he said, surveying the racks and picking out more things. The one-outfit try-on soon turned into a full-blown shopping spree.

"I want all of this for you," he said. I let him buy me the clothes, even though my jaw dropped at the register. He acted as if it was no big deal; he may as well have been buying a bag of groceries.

My mother was back when I got home, the smells of *chilaquiles*—tortilla strips—drowning in a meat sauce, wafting into the vestibule.

"Where did you get that outfit?" she asked, a look of shock dancing across her face.

"It was a present," I said, smiling. "And so were these." I held up the bags.

"Designer clothes? Are you sure you didn't take that stripper job?"

I was about to get mad when I saw that she was kidding.

"Manuel thought they'd look good on me," I said.

"Now you see what I mean, don't you?" she asked.

"What?"

"Rich men."

"Mom!" It wasn't like that. Was it? "I don't care about his money. He's really smart and cool. It's just . . . a pleasant side effect."

"Well, I'm very proud of you for coming to your senses, Milagro."

"How's the American girl you rescued?"

"Oh, on a bus to Oklahoma," she said.

Would it be so bad, I thought, if my new diversion made my mother happy, too? It would only mean that my life would get a lot easier. She would trust someone like Manuel; he was exactly the kind of person she dreamed I would end up dating. It was an amazing coincidence that I actually liked him, too. We'd said we loved each other while we were on Ecstasy, but now it seemed it could be happening in real life, that the Ecstasy only served to speed things along in the direction they were headed anyway.

Manuel and I were sitting on one of the picnic tables by the pool the next day, swinging our legs.

"Will you come with me and my parents to Valle de Bravo for the weekend?" he asked.

"You're inviting me to Valle?"

"I invited you six months ago, remember that?"

"I didn't think you were serious."

"I was then, and I am now," he said, leaning in to kiss me.

Manuel's parents owned a huge villa on the lake. He'd described it to me before, and I'd wanted to go ever since.

"Do you think your parents will be okay with that?"

"I already asked. Of course they are," he said. "Do you think your mother will let you?"

"She thinks you're nice. She told me."

"Good."

"I think she trusts you," I said.

"I want to make an appointment for you with my mother's personal hairstylist in Valle. The purple hair doesn't suit you anymore. You're different now. You're starting to show who you really are."

Who I really am, I thought, or who you want me to be? But I would never say something like that out loud. I felt too lucky.

~   ~   ~

The letter was under my gate when I checked for the mail in the late afternoon.

January 19

Dear Mila,

   Yes, I'm still planning to come. We all go through things, so no, I'm not upset with you. I'm excited to meet this Armando guy, and your new boyfriend, too. He sounds way better than the last one. When's your mother's wedding?

Love,
Nora

Oh God, I thought. I was going to have to tell her about Armando. I'd write her back later, after the trip to Valle, so there would hopefully be good news to offset it. I went to my room to pack for the long weekend, or *puente* (bridge), as it was called in Mexico.

After a morning on the yacht and a long afternoon hair-salon visit from which I emerged a born-again blonde, we went to dinner with Manuel's parents. The restaurant was a beautiful old hacienda, high vaulted ceilings with wooden beams, colorful tiled floors, and waitstaff in traditional dress. At our garden table, we were served white wine and the maître d' greeted Manuel's father by name and kept coming over to our table to make sure we had everything we needed.

   His mother, Regina, raised her glass. "Welcome, Mila, we're so glad you were able to come with us. *Salud.*"

   Our glasses clinked. I was still surprised every time the family went out of their way to make me feel at home.

   "Maria did a great job of restoring your natural hair color," said Regina.

"It took long enough to do," added Manuel. "But I like it better, too."

"So, Mila," said his father, Gustavo. "What are you thinking of studying in college?"

"Well, I'm going in the States, so I won't have to decide as soon as I graduate the way Manuel will. But I'm sure I'll major in journalism."

"She writes her own column every week for the student newspaper," said Manuel. "It won last semester's student journalism award for an article she wrote about how ISM wasn't accessible to handicapped people. No one ever read that paper until she came along."

Gustavo's interest was piqued. "What else have you written about?" he asked.

"It's actually mostly a confessional column about being a foreigner here," I said. "But what I'd really like to focus on is politics. I'd love to cover world events someday."

"You sound focused enough that you *could* go to a Mexican university," said Gustavo. "If only Manuel were as passionate about engineering."

Manuel pretended not to hear.

"Where were you again before Mexico?" Regina asked.

I took a deep breath. "Shanghai, Guadalajara, Bolivia, Rome, Oslo, Prague, and Washington, D.C., in that order," I said. Regina held up a finger for each country as I named it.

"Eight countries by eighteen years old!" she said. I felt my face flush red.

"Let me know if there is ever anything I can do to help with your work," Gustavo said. "My son brings an ambitious young woman home for a change, I want her getting everything she goes after."

"For a change?" I raised an eyebrow at Manuel.

"Most of the girls just want to find a husband," said Manuel. "They want to get married right out of high school, to a guy who will take them shopping, buy them spa treatments and diamonds. Then they have babies and want their husbands to buy them breast implants."

I looked at Regina for hints of offense, but I didn't see any.

"I went to ISM, too," she said. "When I told my girlfriends I was going to Harvard Business School, they all thought I was crazy. Why work? they asked me. You're married to a successful man, why would you want to do that to yourself? In the States, you work for the sake of goals, for a sense of purpose. Here, if your husband has money, then you have money and you aren't expected to want to have a career. It's a machismo society, by all means."

"I've noticed," I said. "So, how long have you been running your gallery?"

"Too many years to count." She smiled. "I've been meaning to ask you, with all that moving around is it difficult to identify with any one particular nationality?"

"I guess I've been raised with an American mentality, because my mother is the ultimate American career woman," I explained. "She's always been a single working mom."

"Where is your father?" asked Regina.

On the news, I thought, but went with my well-rehearsed answer. "He died before I was born."

After dinner, Manuel and I went for a walk down to the lakeshore. The water was still and black, pierced only by the lights from the floating barge restaurants in the distance, Pericos and La Balsa. I could vaguely hear the sounds of the music and the revelers inside.

"Should we go get a drink over there?" I asked Manuel, indicating the colorful aquatic hot spots with a slight toss of my head.

"They adore you," he said. "I can tell. More than any of my exes."

"You think so? I'm shocked." I laughed.

"Why?"

"I think we both know I'm not like Cristina, Beatriz, or any of the other girls in your group."

"No, you're not," he said, and kissed me. "That's why you're better. Better for me."

"Even though I'm not part of the world your family belongs to?" I looked distractedly out over the lake.

"You open my eyes to different things," he said. "I've lived the same life since I was little."

"I didn't want to lie to them," I said.

"You could have told the truth. They wouldn't care that you don't know your father."

"Remember that night you said you would help if I wanted to look for him?"

"When I was on that strange drug we tried? I probably thought I knew the meaning of life that night."

"I don't mean *you* could help me," I said. "But your dad could."

"Why? You think he knows him?"

"Yeah."

"But *you* don't even know who he is."

"I think I'm onto an idea, actually. But do you mind if I don't talk about it yet? I'd want to be sure first."

"Come on, Mila, if it's someone my father knows, you should tell me."

"All right. I think it's a guy named Eliodoro Márquez de la Garza."

Manuel didn't speak again for what felt like a very long time.

"You're not sure, though, right?"

I just looked at him.

"Are you?" he asked again.

"It's not proven or anything. But I saw him on the news and I saw him with your dad, and—"

"Strange," said Manuel, shaking his head and looking out across the lake. "My dad's his doctor."

"He had plastic surgery?"

"I think just a chin tuck. But my dad does other stuff, too."

"As in nonmedical stuff?"

"Okay, my beautiful journalist," he said, leaning in and kissing me again. "That will be enough questions." I wondered what he was hiding, but then got lost in the moment.

"So how am I supposed to approach this man?" I asked.

"You'll figure it out," he said. "Things have a way of becoming clear. The answer will come to you when you least expect it."

I had a flash of déjà vu before I realized that Manuel's words were oddly reminiscent of what the Coyoacán tarot reader had said.

"Is that what you think?" I said playfully, standing on my toes to kiss his cheek.

"I am not joking," he said in his perfect, barely-there accent. "Life comes at you from directions you aren't facing."

The trip passed quickly—lazy days on the yacht slowly sipping margaritas with the family, evenings in the hot tub as the sun set in a pinkish dusk and the lights down in Valle came on. Manuel sneaked into my room at night. We made love quietly, then talked until daybreak. So this is intimacy, I thought. He didn't get up and run away, and he didn't hold anything back. Manuel was himself, a genuine quality I hadn't seen in my American boyfriends.

We got back to his house after the three-hour drive on Sunday evening. I started getting my things together to go, thanking Regina and Gustavo, when Gustavo took my weekend bag out of my hand.

"Don't be ridiculous. You'll stay for dinner."

I called Maggie, and it was the first time she was happy that I would be coming home late on a Sunday. We sat down and the cook served us *robalo chileno* and vegetables.

"Gustavo, can you really help me get an interview for my column?" I asked, scooping rice onto my plate and feeling the timing was right.

"Depends on who," he said.

"A politician, Eliodoro Márquez de la Garza. Do you know him?"

"I do," he said. "He's a college friend; we're still quite close."

"I'd love to speak with him about his role in prison reform," I said casually. I'd been carefully following de la Garza's issues in the news.

"You probably wouldn't get much from him, information-wise. But

I'll ask. He went to ISM also, so maybe he'll agree to help you with a school-newspaper article."

Back in el D.F. after the long weekend in Valle, the city looked new and full of promise. Maybe it was because I was finally feeling accepted as a part of something. With my new wardrobe, blond hair, and fresa boyfriend, I was starting to feel a little bit like I belonged. Even Cristina, Manuel's ex-girlfriend, was coming around. She'd started dating the president's son again two weeks earlier, and since she seemed to be over Manuel she even began speaking to me. It was just to say hello, but it was better than the cold shoulder.

I was in my room writing my next newspaper column when Maggie called out that the phone was for me. I picked up the cordless.

"Hello?"

"I just wanted to say congratulations," Nina said icily.

"What are you talking about?"

"You made it in. You and your fresa boyfriend, and your fresa friends, and your new clothes—"

"You're pissed because for once you can't steal them! You stole my stuff, now you wish you could steal my life."

"I'm fine now," she said. "I started medication. You're the one who can't see what you're turning into, *Milagro*."

"Do *not* call me that," I said, and hung up the phone. I was angrier with her than I'd ever been before. She couldn't stand that I was finally happy, that I was moving in a different direction.

I heard Maggie out in the hall.

"Milagro . . ." she called.

"It's Mila," I called back.

She rapped lightly at my door. "Are you all right in there?" she asked.

"Yeah, I'm fine."

"Was that Nina? Are you two having an argument?" She was probably secretly thrilled.

"Just tell her I'm not home if she ever calls again," I said.

"Can I come in?"

"I guess so."

My mother looked stunning in a flowing black skirt and white tank top, eerily reminiscent of the outfit I wore the day I first met Manuel. She was wearing her *milagro* jewelry. It was the first time I'd ever seen it on her; it usually sat in her jewelry drawer, a piece of her past, a relic of another time. Ancient history.

"What's up with the *milagros*?" I asked.

"New beginnings." She smiled, looking like a little kid about to get ice cream. "I have a date."

"With who?" I asked.

"Why does it smell like smoke in here?"

"My clothes. From going out."

"You've got to air them out. I'll put them in the laundry basket. Rosa's coming tomorrow." She started gathering up a pile I'd left on my chair.

"Mom! You didn't answer my question."

"I can't right now, Milagrito. I'm late to meet Harvey." She covered her mouth and her eyes widened like shiny ten-peso coins.

"Your *boss* Harvey?"

Maggie looked distractedly out my bedroom door. "Yes."

"He's *married*."

"His wife lives in Wisconsin."

"With their seven-year-old adopted Vietnamese daughter."

"He says he's divorcing her."

"Jesus, Mom, how many times have you heard *that* line?"

She let that one go. "Aren't you going to tell me how Valle was?"

"It was amazing. Manuel's parents have a beautiful house in the hills, with a hot tub out on the deck, and a view of the whole town and the lake. And a kick-ass yacht."

"I'm so happy you found a nice boy. Finally, after that Dave and the stringy blond thing. And you're not always scribbling away in that diary of yours."

"Maybe I finally learned to hide it better," I said. But I wondered if she was right.

January 29

Dear Nora,

Don't freak out, but Armando was killed—assassinated, actually. Okay, I hope you're not freaking out. Let me explain: Since he ran a prison with all these top drug dealers, they organized a way to have him "removed." Obviously, there's no wedding, no anything anymore. My mom already has a rebound guy, Harvey. Her married boss. I know.

It's crazy, the way these things happen. I miss Armando so much, even though he was in my life for such a short time. When someone's assassinated here for trying to fight the drug trade or organized crime, everyone's kind of, like, "Oh, another day . . ." as if anyone who messes around with that world has it coming. As for me, I'm doing all right. I just got back from a vacation in Valle de Bravo with Manuel, the new boyfriend. (My mother had Tyler sent out of the country. Long story. I'll tell you when you visit.) I think I'm *in* love for the first time in my life, for real, which is helping a lot as far as coping with Armando's being dead. We spent all day on a yacht in the middle of a soothing lake, stream of sails, indescribable light defining the softness of backlit clouds. I sat on the edge with my toes in the water, writing, waiting. The sky is so big there, the lake surrounded by mountains with gorgeous villas on them. It reminds me a tiny bit of the Hollywood Hills, where my grandma would take me for drives when I visited her when I was little. I love Manuel's parents, too. They're so different from how I thought they would be—nice, not snobbish. His father, Gustavo, went to Yale; he's really smart. And his mother, Regina, is the reason he got into collecting art. She's a painter like Manuel, and unlike their home in Lomas, which is full of Manuel's Picassos, his dad's Renoirs, and his mom's Giacometti sculpture collection, this house only has paintings made by Regina and Manuel. Her work reminds me of

Georgia O'Keeffe's—lots of big flowers and allusions to the female form. Manuel's are really abstract, very technical, the way his mind works. It's funny how much his art expresses the engineer in him, even though that's not what he really wants to do. (I'm trying to persuade him to study in the States, so he can be an art major and his father wouldn't have to know, and for selfish reasons, too, of course.) Anyway, I love Manuel, I really do, and for the first time since I moved here I can honestly say that I love my life. I'm just really sad that Armando isn't here to be a part of it. It just felt like he *belonged,* you know? I try not to think about that too much, because nothing will bring him back, but it's as though fate has it out for my mom as far as her relationships go. I almost can't blame her for the bad decision to date her boss. She was, of course, even more traumatized by what happened with Armando than I was, and that's saying a lot.

Talk to you soon, I hope,
Mila

I came home from the newspaper closing the next evening to find my mother and Harvey eating some type of artichoke appetizer and drinking red wine on the couch. Maggie was giggling the way she did when she first started dating a man, when everything he says is funny and everything he does is right. But Harvey was everything wrong. He was attractive, in an unusual way, but by no means classically handsome. Like I said, he was a Harvey Keitel look-alike, which to my mother meant downright sexy. He had blue eyes that reminded me more of shutters than windows. I'd met him before at an ambassador's dinner my mother had dragged me to a few months earlier. For the most part he was quiet, but there was something about him that made me ill at ease, and it wasn't just that he was married.

Soon enough, he was always around. Maggie stopped coming home after work. She usually called but would sometimes forget. She was one of those women who become obsessed with their relationships, which, for me, translated into my spending more time alone, and the rest of the time listening to her talk about the relationship. I noticed it happening and never mentioned it, even when she and Harvey had a fight one Sunday morning and she took me to lunch at her favorite restaurant in Bosques, spending the entire time crying to Elisa, the owner, about Harvey's unpredictable bursts of anger. When I was a little girl and Maggie went out with a boyfriend, I would turn on all the lights and both televisions in our apartment, and even then stay close to the front door, usually reading in the chair in the entryway; sometimes I cried because I was convinced that there were ghosts. Now that I was older, I knew there was nothing lurking in my closet or under the bed, but I still left all the lights on. Maggie seemed to be slowly coming out of the depression she'd been immersed in since Armando's death, though, so at least Harvey was helping her to forget.

A few weeks later, Maggie took me out of school early on Friday for a mother-daughter trip to Villahermosa, to get away from the city and see the Olmec ruins in Palenque. On the plane ride down, she told me she was swearing off dating any Mexicans of high stature, that she couldn't stand to go through what had happened with Armando again.

"And it's better to date a married guy?"

"Milagro, how many times do I have to tell you, he's getting a divorce. They haven't lived together since he joined the Foreign Service."

"How many years ago was that?"

"Oh, I don't know, twenty-five, twenty-six?"

"And he didn't get divorced before because . . . ?"

"Frankly, my relationship isn't your business."

"My life isn't your business."

"Fine."

"Fine." I turned and looked out the window, the tops of green trees spread across the jungle in every direction, blanketing the earth.

Down south in Chiapas—one of Mexico's poorest states—the

weather was damp, the air humid. We took a white van with other travelers down to see the ruins of Palenque. The road wound round a hillside, stones and dirt crackling beneath the tires as the tired engine rumbled. It rained a little in the jungle. We continued on to Agua Azul, an area with a waterfall and a river where some women were washing clothes in the rapids, standing in water almost up to their knees. They stopped scrubbing to watch us, the foreigners, watching them. The jungle was green, the trees tall and covered with vines. We spent the afternoon hiking through the forest, leaves crunching beneath our feet, the air humid and rich, smelling of the flowers and foliage, a sweet dessert.

"Did you know that the Olmec actually might have been the mother culture, not the Mayas?" she said.

"Yeah, I remember it from Mexican history, that the Mayas may have been dependent on Olmec achievements," I said. "I wonder how credit for what they accomplished got passed off on a whole other culture. Kind of like the DEA deporting Tyler when it was really you all along."

"Milagro, aren't you over that yet? If it weren't for me, you wouldn't have Manuel now. It was all for the best."

"I know you were trying to 'save' me. But you really crossed a line. I'm not one of your work cases."

"I'm your mother. I do what I know is best for you."

"Like never telling the truth about my father?"

"For the millionth time, I can't do that. Now, pass me the camera. We're almost at the waterfall."

We flagged down an old bus along a stretch of barren road to get back to our hotel. The riders greeted us warmly, not used to seeing two gringa women traveling on their own, without an organized tour group. A group of men in the back were talking about how the EZLN had just taken over an area of Chiapas. The political situation in this region was soon all over the papers.

The next day, my mother bought a Subcommandante Marcos

muñeca—a little effigy of the black-hooded Zapatista revolutionary—from a local craftswoman.

"This is a piece of history," she said.

"It looks more like a voodoo doll to me," I told her.

The little Marcos was prominently displayed on a shelf in our living room for the rest of the year, a conversation piece in the days before you could order the masked dolls online.

EIGHT

Señor Márquez
de la Garza

When I told Mr. Payne that I would be dropping my regular slice-of-life columns to profile a politician, and that I had an interview lined up with Eliodoro Márquez de la Garza that Saturday afternoon at his office in el Centro, he was more than a little confused.

"I know I've been pushing you to write challenging things, but aren't you going a little over your head here?" he asked.

"This is a great chance for me to see what being a real journalist feels like."

"Everything you've been doing is 'real.' "

"But I'm ready for something different."

"What are you even hoping to get from this guy?"

"I'm not sure yet. But I'm also not sure why you're discouraging me."

"It's just . . . this isn't the United States, Mila. You're not paying a visit to your friendly Massachusetts senator."

"You're acting like I'm setting up a meeting with Subcommandante Marcos. Maybe I should do that instead."

Mr. Payne was silent for a moment, deliberating.

"Fine, do your interview," he said finally. "Just please make sure you have a flattering angle for the story. We don't want to go upsetting anybody around here."

The vast dust bowl of Mexico City was equal parts beauty and hideousness. Sometimes I thought it mirrored exactly how I felt inside. Especially the Centro Historico, with the Zocalo, its main plaza, sinking into inevitable oblivion. It was built in 1524 on top of Tenochtitlán, the ancient Aztec capital, supposedly the spot where the city's founders saw the eagle alight on a cactus—the scene depicted on the Mexican flag. The cactus was believed to be in Lake Texcoco, so the lake was filled in and the city was built on top of it. In the Centro Historico, the rooftops of the buildings are at a slant, one edge pointing toward the earth, the other toward the sky. I wandered around the Zocalo that day feeling that I was sinking, too.

Walking into the Palacio Nacional building felt overwhelming. The long stone Spanish-style structure that housed government offices was *conquista*-era meets modern technology, fiber cables running through the old stone walls. It was home to the enormous Diego Rivera murals; all around a staircase, they depicted the history of Mexico, the Spanish conquest, and Quetzalcoatl, the bird-snake god of the Mayas and the Aztecs. The murals were chaotic, dreamlike, as severe as the world outside, and yet somehow human, full of love for a country, its people, its birth, and its life.

I waited in the politician's bare, enormous lobby while his secretary paged him. Señor de la Garza would be right with me, she'd said.

"You can go in now."

I walked into his office and there he was, the man I saw at Los Pinos with Manuel's father. The man from the interview on TV.

"Are you okay?" he asked. "Your face became very pale."

I must have seemed like an anxious, inexperienced high-school newspaper kid; at least I hoped that was all he'd think.

"Sorry, I . . . I'm just nervous. I've never interviewed a man of your caliber, señor."

"Your boyfriend's father is an old school friend of mine. I'm happy to do this for you. Tell me, do you enjoy living in Mexico?"

"I had some trouble at first . . . for a while, to be honest, Señor de la Garza."

"What happened? And please—call me Elio, sí?"

"Adjusting, I guess. It was different than I expected, though I didn't know *what* to expect. Everyone at my school is so wealthy, so attractive. The rest of the country is different. Most people are so poor, but their spirit feels richer than that of all the fresas combined. No offense if you used to be one. It was just hard, you know, around people who are so exclusive."

"But you seem to have found some friends now. Friends in high places, for you to be here, taking up my time." He laughed.

I looked around the huge office. Marble floors, heavy red velvet drapery, all the markings of top bureaucracy.

"I'm going to get to ask the questions, right?"

Eliodoro smiled. "It's nice to converse a little first, yes? Tell me, how did you come to be in Mexico?"

"My mother works at the U.S. Embassy."

"And your father?"

My stomach caved with apprehension.

"He's not around. My mother was going to marry someone, though. Armando Salazar. Did you know him?"

"He was head of Almoloya."

"Yes."

"I did know him, I believe. Not well, though. I'm so sorry for what you and your mother must be going through."

"Me, too. He was like the father I never had growing up." I looked into his eyes, trying to see if he could recognize any traces of the familiar between us. I couldn't tell. Maybe this was where I got my great poker face, I thought.

"Are you married?" I asked.

"Going on thirty years," he said. "My wife's name is Laura." Eliodoro leaned back in his armchair by the window. "All right, go ahead with your questions. I'll answer as best I can."

"Let's see . . . Can you tell me a few of your goals?"

"The rumors are true—I do plan to run for president eventually, when the time is right. I want to create new opportunities for the people of Mexico." I scrawled attentively in my notebook. I wanted to seem focused, professional.

"Tell me more about your family."

"We have two children, Carlos and Daniela. They're both in university now. My son is studying political science, and my daughter is majoring in journalism, as you will be. She is in the U.S., at Harvard. Carlos goes to the Ibero." He pointed to a picture on the desk. "That's them."

Daniela had green eyes and the same nose. She could have been my sister. I wondered if Elio noticed the resemblance and was choosing to ignore it. I couldn't tell.

I suddenly felt the urge to get out of there. A panic rose in my throat and I got lightheaded and confused.

"I have to go. . . ." I said. "I didn't realize—"

When I came to, Elio and his secretary were standing over me. I sat up, dizzy, and she gave me a cup of water.

"Are you all right?" he asked.

"I'm sorry," I said faintly. "I don't know what happened."

"Have you eaten today?"

"Not very much, no. I should probably go, get some lunch, get home."

"Rosalba, tell Julio to be downstairs with the car to take us home."

"That's okay, you don't have to—"

"What would I tell Gustavo? 'You sent your son's girlfriend to meet with me and I let her walk around starving?' " He winked at me. "You'll have lunch at my house."

~   ~   ~

His driver, Julio, rounded the narrow streets of the Centro Historico and turned on Avenida de Hidalgo to get to Reforma. I stared out the window as we passed Palacio de Bellas Artes, the Taj Mahal of downtown Mexico City, an enormous white-marble opera house with pre-Hispanic motifs along an Art Deco façade. Elio called Laura from his cell phone to tell her that he was having "the young journalist from the ISM newspaper" over for lunch, so Lupe should make extra food.

"Where do you live?" I asked.

"Lomas de Chapultepec."

"That's my neighborhood!"

"Which street?" he asked.

"Monte Athos."

"We're right on Tarahumara."

"Funny. We're practically neighbors."

We made small talk the rest of the way in the car until Julio pulled up to a wall that obscured an entire block. The guard opened the gate for us to pass through, and I found myself on the grounds of Eliodoro Márquez de la Garza's massive mansion. A fountain stood in the center of the *glorieta* at the end of the driveway, and the gardens were filled with lemon trees and tropical flowers.

"Have a seat," said Elio. "Laura!" I perched on the edge of the modern white couch. The whole room felt too big.

"Hola, que tal?" said Laura as she walked in. She was a willowy blonde, tall and slim-waisted in a cinch-belted floral dress. A Stepford type, I thought, but her eyes were kind. She looked at me as though she were trying to place me from somewhere.

"Hi, I'm Mila," I said, attempting to dispel any thoughts she might have been having that we'd met somewhere before. I stood to kiss her cheek.

"Welcome to our home," she said. "Can I offer you coffee? Tea? Have we met somewhere before?"

I shook my head. "Café con leche would be wonderful, thank you."

"*Lupe! Un café con leche, uno negro, y te para mí, porfas.*"

She spoke the way the fresas from school did, down to their slang for *por favor,* but there was a more sensitive quality about Laura. She was demure, feminine. Someone who had been a wife for a very long time. Someone who was Maggie's opposite, I couldn't help thinking.

Then I noticed them. The two dangling silver pairs of eyes—*milagros* that represent spirits or angels watching over their wearer. I felt faint again, and inhaled sharply.

"I love your earrings, señora," I managed to say.

"*Ay, gracias.* They're my favorite pair." Laura ran her perfectly man- icured nails through her blond blowout. She leaned closer so that I could get a better view of the jewelry artisan's handiwork.

"Where did you get them?"

"Oh, it was such a long time ago—about eighteen years or so. Where did I find these, darling, do you remember?" I looked over at Elio. Poker face.

"I think on the beach somewhere?"

Lupe came in with coffee and tea. I sipped slowly, meticulously, my eyes darting from Laura to Elio and back. Laura asked about my school newspaper work, and I told her about my column. She chatted a little about their children. Elio asked about my mother's work for the State Department and I tried not to say too much. Lupe came back with plates and set the dining-room table.

"Let's go sit at the table, ladies," said Elio. "Lunch is served."

Lupe had made *pollo con mole,* enchiladas, and quesadillas with rice and salad. We had flan for dessert.

"I'm glad to see there's color in your face again," said Elio. "A hearty meal was just the solution."

"This was exactly what I needed," I said. I turned to Laura. "Thank you so much."

"Of course, dear. You're welcome in our home anytime." She smiled broadly. "I think your little journalist here is just lovely," she told her husband.

An hour later, I was sitting in the back of the town car again, watching the streets of Lomas fly by, the enormous houses behind tall gates, the palm trees in the *glorietas.*

"Where should I drop you off?" asked Julio.

"Right up here, the house with the guard truck outside."

"Well protected, aren't you?"

"Actually, this is my boyfriend's house."

"Bien hecho! Estás pensando en casarte con el?" said Julio, as if I'd hit the jackpot.

I rolled my eyes. "I'm not thinking of getting married anytime soon," I said. "It's not as typical for an American girl to marry straight out of high school."

"You might want to reconsider, *no?*" he joked.

"Thanks for the ride." I smiled and shut the car door.

"You do know who de la Garza is, don't you?" asked Manuel as we lay side by side on his bed with the TV on the music-video station. I loved the moments after we slept together, how he would just hold me, my head on his shoulder, like there was nowhere else he wanted to be.

"I've been reading that he has presidential potential, and that he's involved in prison-reform measures." I'd been poring through all the information about him that I could get my hands on.

"Mila, you don't understand how it works. Eliodoro de la Garza is involved in drug trafficking between Mexico and the United States, and he rakes in huge profits in *mordidas.* Everybody knows. But no one will touch him. And if they try . . ."

"Yeah, I know what happens."

I wondered if Elio could somehow have been connected to Armando's assassination. It seemed possible, since they both had ties to the administration of Almoloya, but I hoped not.

"Don't you think it's odd that his last name has Márquez in it? Maggie would do something like that on purpose, just to . . . I don't know, just because it's the kind of thing she would do."

"Your mother is eccentric," said Manuel. "Not insane."

"Well, if Elio is so corrupt, why is your father such good friends with him?"

"Old ties," he said.

"I don't know how you cope with being surrounded by this stuff all the time."

"How do you think any of us deal with who our parents are? Everyone at ISM has parents who are linked, powerful, who control the country. We don't talk to each other about it. We have our own lives."

I sat up and swung my feet over the side of the bed, to the floor.

"*Everyone* at ISM?"

"You know what I mean."

"I have to go," I said, picking up my strewn-about clothes off the floor. "I have a column due in the morning." I needed to get away, to be alone to think about what had happened that day.

I walked the two blocks to my house in the dark, past the taxi *sitio*, across from Nina's, and up Monte Athos to my gate.

Downstairs, Rosa was wrapping up her day, eating yellow rice and chicken at the kitchen table.

"Your mother called; she's working late. She said to tell you a tourist jumped off a hotel balcony and she has to clean up the mess," she said, making a face.

I knew she meant the figurative mess of calling the next of kin and arranging the body's flight home; Maggie had developed a dark sense of humor about such things from dealing with them so often. "Sorry you had to hear all the details," I said.

"She said she'd probably be here around midnight. Are you hungry?"

"Maybe I could eat a quesadilla. Don't get up, I'll make it."

I poured some water from the giant bottle delivered weekly by the water truck and sat down at the table.

"Something's wrong?" Rosa asked. "Guy trouble?"

"In a sense," I said, and left it at that.

Rosa picked up the remote for the tiny kitchen television and turned to a telenovela. It was my favorite, too—*La Bruja de Hidalgo.* Guadalupe was about to tell Juan Pablo she was pregnant, and Juan Pablo would accuse her of carrying Jorge's child, and then it would turn out to be an immaculate conception. When telenovelas ended, the network looped them over again from the beginning. It was like going back in time, watching the series all over again knowing what would happen to the characters in the end, the story coming full circle. Sometimes I wished life were that way.

I woke up feeling as if I'd been hit by a truck, and I barely had the energy to dress. I put on my old flannel and ripped jeans and spent my four morning classes in a haze. When the bell rang for lunch, I went to find Manuel in front of the pool, but he wasn't there. Catalina and Katia were gossiping about last night's *coctel* at La Boom, the first one I hadn't gone to. I tried to get in the conversation, but they kept talking to each other. This was how it was when Manuel wasn't around. They were nice to me when I was with him, but without him standing next to me I didn't exist. If he and I broke up, I would be back to having no one, not even Nina. I'd be alone in Mexico City again.

"I'm going to the bathroom," Beatriz whispered to the girls. "Who wants to come with me?"

Katia laughed. "I'm trying to cut back."

Catalina shook her head. Beatriz was gathering her things when she seemed to remember I was there.

"Mila?"

"I guess so," I said. I didn't see what the big deal was.

And so there I was, in the middle of the concrete stretch between the pool and the soccer field, walking toward the school building with

Beatriz Villareal, queen bee of the fresas, the most beautiful and popular girl in school thanks in part to a flattering nose job by an expert plastic surgeon.

Beatriz opened the bathroom stall. I went to the sink and began reapplying makeup.

"Come in with me," she said.

"Why?" I asked. But she just winked and said "Coming or not?" and it was Beatriz, so I followed her in. Then I saw the small bag of pulverous white in her hand. She placed a black notebook on top of the toilet tank and dumped the powder out onto the notebook, moving it into little parallel lines with a razor that she pulled from her compact. Then she rolled up a ten-peso bill, inhaled two of the lines, and passed the bill to me. I never would have guessed, but looking back I should have known. Several things made sense all of a sudden.

"Is this your secret to staying so thin?" I half joked.

"It helps." She shrugged, dipping her finger in the bag and rubbing powder on her gums. "Take some."

I only believed in taking drugs to experiment with altered states, or at least that's how I justified everything I did at the time—with words like *consciousness raising* or *experience*. I knew this was different: hedonistic, pleasure for its own sake. But, standing there in the bathroom stall with Beatriz, all I could do was bend over and inhale a line. It hit right away, and a warm rush of confidence flooded my body, followed by numbness in my nose and a bitter taste coursing down the back of my throat. Beatriz did another one and smiled.

Manuel was in front of the pool when we got back. "Were you in the bathroom with Beatriz?" he asked.

"I was."

He raised his eyebrows and scanned my eyes. "I don't know about the idea of you getting into what they've been doing lately," he said.

"I'm fine."

The bell rang. I headed to English to take a test on *Anna Karenina*. I wrote quickly, my mind racing. I aced the exam.

~   ~   ~

I was working on my Eliodoro profile for the *ISM Observer* that evening when the phone rang. I expected it to be Manuel and was surprised to hear a Spanish-accented female voice on the other end of the line.

"Mila?"

"Yeah?"

"It's Beatriz."

"Oh, hey, Beatriz. *Que onda?*" She didn't take the bait to switch the conversation into Spanish. Even though I spoke almost perfectly now, it was like a class thing, a dividing line between me and them.

"Listen, Catalina and Katia are coming over Saturday night. *Papá* is going to Monterrey for a conference, and we'll have the house to ourselves. We thought you might like to come."

I was surprised, since it was the first time the fresa girls had invited me anywhere without Manuel.

"I don't have other plans, so . . ."

"*Bueno.* We're going to Aguila y Sol and La Malinche, so dress well!"

I called Manuel after she hung up and asked him if he'd set this up, but he swore that he hadn't. Were the girls finally accepting me? I wondered. We had more in common than they would ever have guessed, but I was still nervous about being alone with them.

We met at Beatriz's and got dressed up together at the long vanity in the spacious dressing area between her bedroom and bathroom. We did our makeup and a few lines as a pick-me-up for the long night out. Beatriz's house in Bosques was three stories tall, with large grounds enclosed by a high and high-surveillance gate with a guard shack in front. Her loftlike bedroom looked out over the rolling hills below and was off to the side of the house, like a separate penthouse apartment. Everything in it seemed new—sparse modern furniture, a four-poster bed, and a marble-floored bathroom with a separate shower and Jacuzzi. Her room was even nicer than Nina's.

Beatriz's driver drove us in a giant SUV to the nouveau-Mexican restaurant Aguila y Sol in Polanco. We ordered its famous *tamarindo* margaritas and ceviche appetizers. None of us were hungry enough to stomach a main course. It really was how the fresa girls maintained their model-perfect physiques: cocaine and plastic surgery. For months I'd thought it was effortless, genetic blessings and the effects of high heels. Katia pulled her long dark curly hair into a ponytail and carefully applied some lip gloss.

"Girls, we are going to have a party for spring break," she said. "Carlos's father's jet will fly us up to Acapulco, we're renting out the Palladium, and we're going to have the time of our lives."

"Que padre," said Catalina. "I can't wait."

"Sounds like a fun trip," I said. "I could stay with Manuel at his house."

The three of them exchanged a look.

"What?" I asked.

Catalina took a breath, giving me a look that said she felt sorry for me. "We don't think you'll be coming to Acapulco," she said. "I've been meaning to talk to you for a while, but I didn't know how to tell you."

"Tell me what?" I asked, stunned.

"People are saying that Manuel is using you," said Beatriz.

"Using me? For what? What could I possibly have that he would want?"

"Don't you know what happened with Cristina?" said Katia.

"I don't know, Katia. They broke up so long ago. Manuel asked *me* out."

"And why would he want to ask you out?" asked Beatriz. "When he could have any girl he wants?"

"I don't know," I said, looking into the brown slush of my frozen margarita. It was melting and a tiny puddle was beginning to form on top of the muddy-looking drink.

All my old insecurities rose to the surface. I fidgeted, moving my fork through a jicama salad on my plate. "You're saying he's using me for sex? That doesn't add up."

"Manuel is a guy who gets what he wants," said Beatriz. "It's true."

"Mexican girls stay virgins until marriage," said Katia, stirring her drink with a red straw. "Or at least until a serious, serious relationship. *Respect* from a man is very important to us."

"Manuel and I *are* serious," I said.

"No, he was serious with Cristina," said Katia. "But she wanted to wait. He didn't. He respected her for it, but he's a guy. He'll grow up someday—and she's the one he'll marry. You don't think he heard people talking about you the first few months you were here?"

I remembered what Nina had said to me earlier in the year: "Remember, every guy only cares about getting laid."

"We know Manuel and Cristina will end up back together," Catalina went on. "And what are you going to do? You're going to the States for college anyway, yes?"

"Listen, Mila," said Katia. "We like you. We think you're *padre.*"

"But you can never really be one of us," said Catalina. "Though you make an admirable effort."

Catalina wore a smug smile. Katia sipped her drink. Beatriz was staring at her plate. So Manuel only wanted to mold me into somebody else, someone like the fresas. I looked down at the Armani jeans, silk top, and black blazer, the high-heeled sandals he'd bought me. I looked like a fresa girl. But like a fresa girl he could fuck. What they were saying made sense; it was just what Nina had told me, and I hadn't listened. I'd become someone I didn't recognize. I'd brought it all on myself. *So vapid, Mila,* I thought, remembering the word that won me a plagiarism accusation from my freshman English teacher. I got up and ran to the bathroom.

I was sitting in a stall, my head in my hands, when I heard Beatriz's voice.

"Mila?"

"I'm here," I said.

She tapped on the bathroom door. "Let me in."

I unlocked the door and she stepped into the stall and pulled her little mirror out of her tiny Gucci purse.

"I'm sorry you had to hear that. Have some of this, you'll feel better." She dumped some white powder on the mirror and handed me the littlest spoon I'd ever seen. "I got that in Coyoacán. They make it precisely for this purpose."

I took a few bumps and handed it back to her. "I didn't know you went to Coyoacán."

"The boys go to Las Islas to get this stuff, and we girls shop in that little bohemian market in the plaza. They have great silver rings. And little spoons."

"I used to go down there all the time," I said, remembering Las Islas, Nina, Kai, and Tyler. "With my old group of friends."

"If you talk to Nina, tell her to hang with us more. We miss that girl. She's so much fun."

Beatriz sucked more coke up her flawlessly sculpted little nose. I'd almost forgotten that Nina had hung out mostly with the fresas the year before. She told me about her chameleon tactics, how best-of-both-worlds it was to be able to go to La Boom with Beatriz and Katia on Friday night and smoke weed on Tyler's roof with her brother and Kai on Saturday. Nobody else at school could pull that off, but I wondered how much her manic depression had to do with it. I felt a sharp pang in my stomach; I missed her.

"Come on," said Beatriz, snapping me back to the moment. "Let's go back to the table. It's Catalina and Katia's turn to come in here."

She smiled and bounced out the bathroom door, her platform heels clacking on the earthy-red tiled floor. The fresas may have had everything, materially speaking, but it was all on the surface. For the first time all year, I didn't envy them. Now I could see the competitive undercurrents that permeated their relationships. There was so much pressure on those girls to pull off an image that required constant upkeep. And now I was learning their shortcuts.

After dinner, the driver took us to La Malinche, a huge nightclub in el Centro, in an old Spanish hacienda. Beatriz rolled up the window between us and the driver and passed around her compact again, with its razor blade and white powder. When a random fresa inside the club asked me to dance, I agreed just to avoid the girls. After a while, his arms were around my waist. Then we were kissing in the middle of the dance floor.

A hand on my shoulder pulled me out of the kiss. I turned around.

"What the hell are you doing, Mila?" said Manuel. The guy sensed something was going to go down and quickly pushed his way through the mass of moving bodies on the dance floor.

"The question is, what were *you* trying to do?" I yelled above the music. "*Our* friends told me tonight that there's only one thing you want from me."

He grabbed me by the shoulders and shook me, almost violently. "What are you on?"

"What do you care?"

"I don't know what makes me angrier, that they would say that or that you believed them."

"What am I supposed to think?"

"I made up my mind as soon as I met you. Now I understand that you're so used to leaving that you treat people like they're already gone. You can't stand the idea that you might actually *need* someone. You'll do anything to fight it."

I turned around and pushed away from him, through the crowded dance floor, swallowing against the lump in my throat. I ran outside the club; the walls were caving in and I needed fresh air, if only there were some. Manuel found me crouched down on the cobblestone, lighting a cigarette.

"Maybe my driver should take us to my house."

"I'm sleeping at Beatriz's. All my stuff is there."

"She won't care. Come with me. We'll talk."

"I thought this could work out," I said to him. "I'm so sorry, Manuel." I stood up and headed to the row of taxis waiting along the curb.

"Are you really so afraid of getting close that you need to push me away?" he said, but I slipped inside a cab, slamming the door. The driver sped down the road, away from the club, away from Manuel, away from us.

"Bad night, señorita?" the driver asked.

I nodded and caught my reflection in the rearview mirror. Mascara streaked down both my cheeks. Coked-up raccoon was a new look for me. I was sobering up, but instead of the unsettled panicky anxiety that usually accompanied this transition I felt unnaturally calm. The whole evening seemed ridiculous, from the dinner to the fight with Manuel. I was tired of everybody and glad to be alone, racing through the night in the little green taxicab, bound for the house in Lomas that had become my home. The driver cruised along Parque Lira, past La Feria with its rickety giant old wooden roller coaster, through the roadways of Chapultepec Park. I looked up at Chapultepec Castle on its steep cliff, home of dictators and the martyred Niños Héroes. I felt safe in Mexico City—like the whole place was one big playground just for me. It seemed a strange moment to feel a surge of confidence, but such things always came about at the most unpredictable times. We merged onto Reforma, the traffic a blur of red and white lights. Salvation or damnation, I thought, remembering that first night with Tyler. The taxi wove quickly through the cars, switching lanes over and over to gain speed. My thoughts raced just as fast as we were barreling toward Lomas. I peered into the rearview mirror again; rosary beads dangled from it, clicking along to the movement of the car. As I wiped the black streaks from my face, I realized that I'd been looking for other people to show me who I was at any given moment. Always being a chameleon meant adapting to the colors around me rather than creating any influence or impact of my own. I'd been subjugating myself for no reason. My life of blending had rendered me too eager to fit in; I could see it now. It was time to find my own shade.

~ ~ ~

I was at my locker late Monday morning, taking my books out between first and second bell for third period, when Beatriz came over with my bag of stuff.

"I'm sorry, Mila," she said, dropping the bag at my feet. Then she walked away.

I knew I couldn't sit in front of the pool. I couldn't go to the soccer field with Nina. Suddenly I was nowhere, but for the first time I felt that was all right. I paid Rosa three hundred pesos to dye my blond hair back to eggplant-purple that afternoon. She accepted only on the condition I'd tell my mother that I went out and bought boxed hair dye at the *supermercado* and did it myself.

ISM OBSERVER
March 1, 1994

Doble Vida: How We Relate

By Mila Márquez

I read somewhere recently that people keep records of events in their lives in an attempt to find some sort of theme, an underlying, recurring pattern that helps them to understand. I finally understand what I wanted to say from the beginning: I wish all of us would talk more openly about how things really are here. Everybody knows it, but no one talks about it.

There are three or four different visible worlds at ISM, depending on how you look at it. First are the Mexicans. You're called fresas, but I hear that you don't particularly appreciate the word. You come from important families and wear clothes with name labels, and you're well protected. Then there are the American-Americans. You come straight from the States and haven't lived anywhere else before; you've always held on to a strong American identity. The third group is the Americanized-international people, and if there is a fourth it's the nearly indistinguishable internationalized-American people. Groups three and four tend to blend, but there is a difference. The last sort of person has an anything-goes policy, wearing ripped jeans and steel-toe boots one day and a fresa uniform (though it won't be a label) with a string of pearls the next. You try to blend in wherever you go, and your mind is open to pretty much anything. You crave belonging and understanding and tend not to see people as being from any one place. You believe in a global culture that may or may not really exist. I had a friend who moved like a summertime breeze through every group, which amazed me, because the one thing everyone here has in common is sticking to their cliques. The Mexicans sit in front of the pool, the Americans have a spot on the football field, and the others wander around or go to the small garden behind the library. It always leaves me wondering where someone who is a combination of things fits in. It's as though there were fences between all of us. I'm reminded of that expression "Good fences make good neighbors." My wish is to tear those fences down, if only they weren't so much taller than I.

I started stealing away to the library during breaks, hiding in the second-floor reading room with stacks of Beat Generation books, psychedelic psychology, and novels with names like *Zen and the Art of Motorcycle Maintenance*. By Friday, I was lonely and thought about trying to talk to Nina. I went to the library intending to study for a calculus exam, but I headed to the upstairs section where all the fiction books were instead. As I walked toward a back table, I saw a blue baseball cap in the corner, the face beneath it hidden by a large hardcover. I took a breath. I could either turn around and leave the library or I could confront him. I walked over to where he sat.

"What are you doing here during lunch?" I asked.

Dave looked up at me. He seemed nervous. "Just reading. Hey, your hair's purple again. Nice."

I ignored his comment and looked at the cover of his book: *Walking Backwards, Dealing with Guilt?*

Dave just shrugged his shoulders, not lifting his eyes to meet mine, and nodded.

"And what's that?" I asked, bemused. There was a short stack of books under *Walking Backwards, Dealing with Guilt.* He lifted it up so that I could see: *Dealing with Depression Naturally*; *Life After Loss: A Personal Guide to Dealing with Death, Divorce, Job Change, Relocation*; *Learning to Love Yourself*; *Men Who Hate Women and the Women Who Love Them.*

"Wow. What's going on with *you*?"

"I've been doing a lot of thinking."

"I see."

"I mean, I don't know how you're going to take this, but especially when I drink, I've been feeling like sometimes I lose control."

"And I lost my virginity, right along with my dignity. Now you're looking for inner peace about it?"

"I'm sorry I ruined your first few months here. I really am. I was partying, getting fucked up. A lot."

"Don't use that tired excuse. I've heard that one before. Admit it," I said. "You wanted to make it look as if I'd be the one who was lying if I ever told anyone. So you struck at me first."

"You have every right to think I'm a sociopath, but I've been racked with guilt over you for months. I'm going to tell people the truth."

"Please, don't. The last thing I need is a reminder news flash going around school." The thought of rehashing everything made my heart palpitate and my mouth feel as if it were filled with cotton.

I let Dave drive me home that afternoon in his new jeep. I missed riding with Nina so much that it ached, and I was the only senior who rode the bus, but really I saw it as my chance to right what had haunted me all year.

"Cool car," I said, flipping through radio stations. I found one playing "Smells Like Teen Spirit" and turned up the volume.

"I just inherited it from my dad. He got the new model."

"So is it full of spy equipment?" I joked. We were suddenly on unsteady ground, as if a seismic shift had occurred, tectonic plates settling back into place after a quake.

"Want to come over and smoke?" he asked. "My parents are home, but we can hang in the yard, order a pizza or something."

"Why aren't they at work?"

"They just got back from Colombia."

"Business trip?"

"Top secret," said Dave.

Dave's house was far out in Bosques de la Herradura, which was across the border of el D.F. in Estado de Mexico territory. The houses were newer, the streets quieter and greener. His CIA parents were in the kitchen playing Scrabble.

"Hi, Mr. and Mrs. Johnston," I said. They stood to shake hands. No cheek kissing for the staunchly American Johnstons.

"You used to live in the Embassy building, didn't you?" asked Dave's father, a hardened-looking man who was going bald and had that ex-military vibe.

"Yeah, the apartments from hell," I said.

"Tell me about it," said his mother, fluffing her pouffy, permed brown hair. "They were nah-stee. Eh-nee-way, we were always askin' Dave why he didn't ever invite you over for dinner. I wanted to meet my son's girlfriend!"

All in all, the Johnstons didn't look or act the way CIA agents did in the movies.

"Mila's not my girlfriend, Mom," said Dave, staring at his Nikes.

"Well, either way we're delighted to meet ya," she said in her sweet Southern drawl. "Help yourself to sodas, and there's homemade brownies in the fridge."

"Um, thanks, and nice to meet you, too," I said, wondering how these two friendly, regular-seeming middle-aged people had come to hold jobs as super-spies, and whether they knew anything at all about their son. Or were they just as wrapped up in their own dealings as career-climbing Maggie, socialite Sonia, self-absorbed George, and pretty much all my other classmates' preoccupied parents were, and assumed that their kids were well looked after by the Concepcións and Rodrigos they hired?

Dave and I smoked in his backyard, which sloped down out of view of the kitchen window where the Scrabble game was going strong. We passed the pipe back and forth, eagerly anticipating our pizza delivery. The best part of resolution with Dave was that he felt he owed me, and while I knew that I was being selfish in trying to recoup a debt that was impossible to repay, I didn't mind a bit after what had happened with the fresas.

"What's *pizza al pastor,* anyway?" Dave asked, exhaling a long stream of blue smoke into the hazy air.

"It's like a *taco al pastor,* except it's on a pizza," I explained. "It has meat, cilantro, onions, and pineapple."

"Pineapple's gross."

"So pick it off."

"Why don't you talk to Nina anymore? She's a cool girl."

"How well do you know her?" I cocked an eyebrow.

"Why? What's so bad?"

"Being a guy, you'll probably never experience it. She's a kleptomaniac."

"No way!"

"I'm serious. She stole from me all the time—my clothes, shoes, jewelry."

"Aren't her parents totally loaded?"

"It has nothing to do with *needing* the stuff. It's psychological. I did some research in the library, and I think she's manic-depressive. Sometimes she'd call me in the middle of the night and she was hyper and social, and then she just crashed."

"At least she's pretty as hell."

"So good looks and psychological disorders are mutually exclusive?"

Dave laughed and shook his head. Then he reached over and touched my hair. I flinched.

"You're funny," he said.

"No, I'm not."

"Can I kiss you?"

"No."

"Please?"

"Okay."

I don't know why I did it. As I drew back from that masochistic kiss, his father called out from the balcony that lunch had arrived. We were ravenous, so we devoured the pizza, downing sips from a big two-liter Coke bottle in between. Afterward, we walked to a park and Dave rolled a joint.

"Drugs are just good and cheap in Mexico, aren't they?" he said, licking the paper closed.

"They killed my mom's fiancé."

"He was an addict?"

"No, stupid. He made prisons more secure. The drug lords were having trouble running their businesses from jail, and having even more trouble paying people off to get out of jail. So they had him exe-cuted. The guy who has the job now, the drug lords and their govern-ment friends put him there."

"Why doesn't someone do something?"

"Because they'd end up just like Armando. Besides, everyone's got a hand out."

"How was it meeting that Garza guy? Awesome profile, by the way. It was like you really got inside his skull. My dad says he's supposed to be real crooked. Does he seem it?"

"You actually saw that?" I asked, surprised.

"The column? Yeah, why wouldn't I?"

"I'm sure most of the school doesn't read it. You're the last person I ever expected would look at it."

"I read it every week," he said. "Not just because I feel like an ass and I'm sorry. It's really good, Mila. Look, I know I fucked up. I'm not a bad person."

He tried to kiss me again, but I pushed him away.

"I know you're not with that stick-up-his-ass fresa anymore. Let me make it up to you."

"With more of the same? Fire-with-fire type thing?" I asked.

"I could really love you this time. I want to, if you'll let me. I'm different."

Suddenly what I wanted was to slap him, hard, in the face. But I just didn't have it in me. "First of all, by the way, Manuel was amazing, even though it didn't work out," I said. "He was better to me than you could ever understand. Second of all, how could you even have the nerve? Plowing through the whole self-help section won't make you a good boyfriend."

"Prove you wrong?" he said.

"Dave, I can't. I'm speaking to you, and that's huge. I'm trying to get over things. But I'm also in a totally different place. I shouldn't have kissed you just now—it was screwed up. I don't know what's wrong with me."

"I'm sorry," he said again.

I was lonely, as I'd been when I first moved here. I missed Manuel. It was as if I'd fallen asleep and was suddenly jarred awake again. *Semana santa*—spring break—was right around the corner. Easter was a huge holiday in Mexico, a time for rebirth, that point on the three-hundred-and-sixty-degree voyage where things start anew.

PART II

Spring, Summer

NINE

Real de Catorce

In consciousness dwells the wondrous,
with it man attains the realm beyond the material,
and the Peyote tells us,
where to find it.

—Antonin Artaud, *Les Tarahumaras* (1947)

I read on a plaque in the Museo de Antropologia that the Aztecs built their city on land they felt was holy. It made sense they'd chosen this spot. Mexico's precolonial cultures deeply worshipped nature, and in some places in Mexico today the people still did. In Mexican history, we'd just studied the Huichol tribe of the Sierra Madre, who still practiced the same brand of ancient shamanism that they did in pre-Columbian times; they were said to be the last tribe on the continent to preserve these traditions. The Huichol believed in the healing powers of herbs and plants, and that we're woven from the same fabric as the natural world. The presence of the ancient in Mexico lent a mystical feeling to the landscape outside the polluted, crowded capital city. I'd wished that my first experience with peyote was somewhere other than a nightclub, but I never expected to get the chance to go to Real de Catorce, the rural desert town known for mystical peyote pilgrimages, the place I'd been aching to explore since I first heard about it from Tyler. I read *The Teachings of Don Juan*—there was actually a copy in ISM's library—and daydreamed about the "Yaqui Way of Knowledge." At the English bookstore in the Zocalo, I bought a book called *Plants of the Gods: Their Sacred, Healing and Hallucinogenic Powers* and studied the origin and significance of peyote:

> Ever since the arrival of the first Europeans in the New World, Peyote has provoked controversy, suppression, and persecution. Condemned by the Spanish conquerors for its "satanic trickery," and attacked more recently by local governments and religious groups, the plant has nevertheless continued to play a major sacramental role among the Indians of Mexico, while its use has spread to the North American tribes in the last hundred years. The persistence and growth of the Peyote cult constitute a fascinating chapter in the history of the New World—and a challenge to the anthropologists and psychologists, botanists and pharmacologists who continue to study the plant and its constituents in connection with human affairs.

Peyote was supposed to cause a mystical loss of self, which sounded good to me, since nothing seemed more appealing than getting out of my skin for a while, as long as I had the option of returning. By the time the opportunity to go to the desert came around, my research was bordering on obsession. I even wrote a twenty-page paper on the history and effects of peyote for Mexican History II.

I remembered the conversation Tyler and I had had much earlier in the year, when things between us seemed promising. We were walking around Chapultepec Park in the dark, weaving through mazes of tree-

lined paths, some of the few in Mexico City, and I'd admired the perfect roundness of the full moon.

"You should try to go to Real de Catorce, see the desert sometime,"
he'd said. "It's definitely meant to be experienced in its own setting. It
just won't let you understand it in its entirety if you abuse its power.
The spirit is very particular about place, and its home is there, in the
desert."

Real de Catorce was a twelve-hour train ride from Mexico City, and
famous for being the destination of many a spiritual pilgrimage. Tyler
had been twice. He loved talking about its incredible ability to open
one's mind to dimensions unseen by the everyday eye. It allows for the
possibility of stepping out of ordinary consciousness into something
higher, and we should take advantage of it, he had said.

Spring break finally arrived, Mexico City mist and smog breathing
through scattered morning sunlight, dusk falling later and later over
Chapultepec graveyard. I couldn't believe that my senior year was so
close to ending, that soon I'd be leaving it all behind for college in the
States, my home country yet a place I'd known only briefly, in a life that
seemed to exist only in retrospect. My mother was away on another
business trip, in talks to recover a stolen helicopter in Morelos. I
planned to spend the week in hibernation, trying to get over Manuel.

The sound of the phone ringing jarred me awake. My mind was
hazy. I made out the red lights on the clock radio: 7:13 A.M. "Hello?" I
croaked, my voice coming out weak.

"Hey! So Dave and I were talking on the phone last night and decided that this week is the perfect chance for us to go to the desert."

"Nina?" I said. She was talking as if nothing had happened, as if our
friendship had never been interrupted. It was classic Nina, but I'd
missed her and was glad to hear her voice.

"You talked to Dave?" I said.

"We've become friendly. He's changed a lot, and I'm so impressed you found it in yourself to forgive him. You're a good soul. He really regrets everything that happened. Anyway, it's a sign, as you always say. So start packing."

I wasn't sure what the sign was, but then I thought of Beatriz and the other fresas piling into Carlos's father's private jet. I got angry all over again just remembering that night.

"I'll be ready in an hour," I said to Nina.

"Oh, I'm so glad," she said. "I tried hard not to miss you, but I did."

I called my mother on her cell phone. "I got invited to Beatriz's party in Acapulco," I told her. "We're staying at her parents' beach house. We're flying on a private jet!"

"That's so exciting!" she said. "You'll call me when you get there?"

"Well, see, that's the thing. It's a new house and the only phones installed right now are in the pool cabana and the guard shack, so I'll call you from there if I can."

"Milagro, make sure that you try to—"

Her voice was overtaken by static, and then the line cut out. She must have had poor reception in whatever remote jungle region she was in, for which I was grateful. ("But, Mom, there was no cell reception!")

By ten o'clock that morning, we were loading our bags into the trunk of Dave's black jeep, inspecting a map, figuring out how to navigate the 257 miles north to Real de Catorce. Then we piled in and set off on Mexico City's freeways, desert-bound.

"So why did you and Manuel break up?" asked Nina. "Not because of me, I hope."

"No, not because of you. Don't worry."

"Good, I know I was a bitch to you about dating him. Sorry about that. I really am."

"I'm sorry, too," I said. "I'm sorry it didn't work out. Because I'm fucking in love with him." I thought I saw Dave make a brief expression of disgust.

~   ~   ~

Soon we were well outside Mexico City. Its jarring architecture vanished, the heavy smog lifted, and in front of us only softly rolling hills and an endless stretch of highway remained. After five hours of speeding, we'd almost reached our destination. We turned off the highway onto the cliffside dirt road that would take us into Real de Catorce. The road wound around the cliff, giving us spectacular views of desert and the land far below and off in the distance. The landscape was harsh: jarring cliffs, dry rock, and dirt. It felt as if we had crossed into some sort of vortex, a place with no time or history, an abstract plain. The road kept winding, the jeep kept moving, and everything seemed endless. The smoggy city and its twenty-five million inhabitants were far behind us. We drove down dirt roads, rocks crunching under the tires, with nothing in sight save cacti, wall-like rock formations, and miles of empty sky. The road veered off, curving around a mountain to the deep, vacant valley below. The car was sandwiched between a wall of rock to the left and a steep drop-off to the right. I imagined plummeting off the ledge and shuddered. Just as we thought we had indeed left the earth behind and arrived at some uninhabited alien territory, the road gave way to a downward slope. We circled around a corner, and then there were signs of life. A small town of adobe buildings and thatched roofs appeared in the distance, vague, dreamlike, a mirage. Below us, in all its adobe glory, lay the town of Real de Catorce. The roads changed from dirt to cobblestone, and people turned to look at the city kids in their nice car, the inhabitants of some other world.

When we reached the town's entrance, a little boy ran up to the jeep and flung himself onto the hood. We flailed our arms around, gesturing for him to get off, but he wouldn't.

"I'll tell you where to go for a donation," he said in Spanish. He wanted to point us in the direction of the hotel in exchange for a few pesos. Only later did I learn that this was the standard greeting for strangers arriving in Real, a long-standing tradition.

~   ~   ~

Our hotel was built around an open courtyard. The room was simple, two queen-size beds with natural-fiber white sheets that were a little rough, and a small balcony with a view of the desert. At night, I went out on the balcony. I could see the exact line where the town ended and the unknown began. The tiny points of light from houses, restaurants, and cantinas just stopped. Then blackness, ongoing, limitless. I stayed outside until the town lights began turning off. The stars were brighter than I'd ever seen them in my life, illuminating the mystical Real de Catorce desert.

I left Nina and Dave in the room and went up to the roof, a four-sided balcony atop the rooms. You could peer down into the courtyard or out into the infinity of the desert. Two men sat there in candlelight, bedecked in tribal outfits and seemingly in a trance. One beat steadily on a drum; the other chanted. The night felt hyperreal, and even though I hadn't eaten any peyote yet, I could practically feel the shift in consciousness.

In the morning we stocked up on supplies: oranges, water, jackknives. We went to the spot where the hotel owner told us to catch a jeep down to the train station. Dave wanted to drive, and we had to talk him out of it; there was no marked road and the way down was steep and rocky, so travelers depended on experienced natives to get them out into the desert. Once we got to the station, we would switch to a pickup truck, which would take us forty-five minutes farther, dropping us, finally, at the starting point of our journey.

The jeep lurched forward and I gasped, clutching Nina's bony arm. Even with the driver applying pressure to the brakes, it felt as if the vehicle might give at any moment, sending us careening down the side of the mountain. The driver would slam on the brakes and we would lurch to a stop in the middle of our descent; then he would let up, allowing us to inch, ever so slowly, downward again. After what felt like aeons, we reached the bottom, the train tracks, halfway to our destination. Men with leathery skin passed by, women with babies wrapped papoose-like to their bodies, American hippies who wandered down years ago only to be drawn in and remain, Mexicans from all over the country on peyote pilgrimages. Real de Catorce was a mecca of undefined spirituality, a dream world, the ends of the earth, fields of brain fruit for harvest by curious seekers.

The three of us climbed into the back of the pickup truck with three guys who said they came from Aguascalientes, and four bags of oranges for the vitamin C. There was an urban legend I'd heard at school that vitamin C intensified the visual effects of hallucinogens, but in all my reading I could never find any evidence to support this. I did know that our bodies could definitely use extra antioxidants in the harsh desert climate. We paid the driver and rolled straight into the dust, the train station with its squat buildings receding rapidly behind us.

"Whatever happens, don't lose sight of those trees," said the driver when he stopped to let us off. He pointed at a cluster of trees, the only trees, on the side of the red dirt road. "If you do, you will be lost in the desert and no one will ever find you," he added.

"You can bet your beat-up pickup truck we won't be losing sight of those trees, then," I said, pretending to joke.

"*Muy bien,*" he replied, before driving away. How were we supposed to get back? I wondered. The whole adventure was off to an unstructured start. I'd expected groups led by guides, but we were on our own.

Dave, Nina, and I hopped out of the truck along with the three twenty-something hippies from Aguascalientes, who looked as if they belonged here, with their beaded jewelry, hand-carved walking sticks, and hemp bandannas that held their long dark hair out of their faces. They had deep-brown skin and carried giant backpacks stuffed to the brim with oranges. Everyone got the same advice about desert survival, I guessed. The three hippies, who told us they were university students back in Aguascalientes, were here for the first time, too. Feeling that we were at the beginning of some great adventure, we set out on the walk into the dry, rocky terrain. We were giddy and excited at first, in an undefeatable state of mind. Even after four hours slowly passed and our optimism waned, we stayed the course. When I turned around, the trees were a tiny dark cluster in the distance. We had not found any peyote. I had seen it before, in the city, and knew what it looked like: green "buttons" that formed a circle, with a tiny dollop of fuzz on each one.

"I have to go to the bathroom," I announced. "Where am I supposed to go?"

"On the ground?" Dave said.

"You're a genius," I replied sarcastically.

Everyone had stopped and was staring at me.

"Turn around," I told them. *"Voltéanse."*

It was like a scene out of the theater of the absurd: one girl pulling down her pants in the middle of the desert while her companions looked away, arms folded across their chests. I squatted. The urine felt cold as it escaped between my legs. Then somehow I lost my footing and slipped, falling backward on my bottom. My derrière landed on a squat, round cactus. The tiny spikes pierced my butt and hooked in. If a girl falls bare-assed on a cactus in the desert and she screams, does it make a sound? The only people around to hear were Dave, Nina, and the hippies from Aguascalientes.

"Are you all right?" asked Dave, still looking in the other direction.

"I'm sitting on a fucking cactus."

"Mila? I'm going to turn around, okay?" said Nina. Next thing I knew, all five of them were working on extracting the needles from my behind as I clenched my teeth. The tiny hooks tore my skin, and one of the Aguascalientes boys used his bandanna to wipe blood from the fresh cuts. Someone sprinkled some water over it before someone else screamed that we couldn't stand to waste more than a few drops. When I was sufficiently dusted off, cactus extracted, blood blotted by an old tissue discovered in the pocket of one of the hippies, we continued. We walked until the trees were nearly invisible, all the oranges gone.

"We should go back," said one of the guys. "This doesn't seem to be working."

He was right. Too much time had passed. We were hot, tired, and thirsty, and there was no sign of any peyote.

"Let's go on for five more minutes," I said.

"Five minutes," said Nina, whose perfect bow lips looked parched. "If we don't see anything by then, we're turning back."

Only two minutes into those five, we saw it: fields of green bulbous cacti peeking out at us from the earth like alien pupils. We stopped, in shock. "Do you know the reason this happened?" asked one of the guys.

"What is it?" I asked.

"Ancient native legend has it that when the spirit is not ready to make himself known, you will never find him. But when he is ready, he will appear everywhere." I thought again of the psychic in Coyoacán. ("The spirit won't reveal himself to you until you are ready," he'd said. "But when he does he will reveal himself completely.") Whether there was truth behind that legend or not, whether this was even what he'd been alluding to, the so-called spirit seemed to have revealed himself.

We cut the tops off some of the cacti with the switchblades, as we'd been told to do: cut the tops, not from the roots, as it must grow back for future seekers. We ate quickly. The familiar nauseating green pepper—cow shit taste filled my mouth. I barely choked it down without its coming right back up. After forcing the green bites down our throats, we began walking. It was the only thing to do. We had no choice but to start heading back.

The pickup-truck driver had told us that the natives used peyote not only as a means to another spiritual realm but to walk. Just to walk. They had long distances to travel, and the plant made you light on your feet. So we walked. Through effervescent landscapes, dreamscapes, bright colors in the flat, dusty desert plain, walking, walking the way the natives did. I didn't notice my thirst or tiredness. My senses felt as open as a child's. All was light, the clouds with literal silver lining, sun bright; the desert felt like home. Land. Earth. Belonging. I was a being of the desert and the spirit revealed himself within my mind: the journey within the journey. It felt as if years had passed within those hours, and I wished Manuel were experiencing it alongside me. I wondered what my mother was doing in Morelos at that moment, whether she'd recovered the helicopter yet.

When I first saw the cows, I didn't believe they were real.

A herd of golden Guernseys in our path. Gentle beasts, ambling through the middle of the desert.

"Do you see them?" I asked Dave.

"I think so," he said.

Everyone else saw them, too. Dusty orange and off-white, their pink noses glistening in the weaning sunlight. They made cow sounds, low and peaceful.

"Take a picture," said Dave.

"It makes sense that Hindus think cows are holy," I said. "I mean, just look at them." I could have sworn the animals were smiling.

Nina took out her camera and snapped a photo. A week later, when she had the photos developed, the ones of the sky, of us in the car, the pickup-truck ride, the search, would all be exactly as we remembered. The shot of the cows came out blank.

We got back to the train station well after nightfall, not yet feeling our exhaustion. The trip was spent walking, but the illuminations came afterward.

"No wonder the native people used peyote to help them walk distances," I said to Dave.

"You don't feel any pain. Or much of anything, for that matter, except that weird—"

"That feeling," I said.

"Yeah, it's impossible to explain."

"You just know everything is where it's supposed to be, everything is right with the universe," I kept going. I wanted to walk and talk forever. "Like even the bad things have their purpose; we just can't see why and how until much later." I stopped and opened my bag to write down what would otherwise be a fleeting thought:

There's another way of life here
A life of dreams
Not like American dreams of success
And things
But the dream of life itself

When I looked up, Nina was staring down at the ground, eyes over-cast, arms extended in front of her as if she were trying to steady herself.

"Are you all right?" I asked.

"Huh? Oh, I'm fine. Just having . . . a *vision.*"

I could see in her eyes that it was something else.

"What are *you* thinking?" she asked.

I smiled. "That we are the puppeteers and the marionettes in this grand and wild adventure."

"You're crazy," she said.

A jeep drove us from the train station up the rocky climb back into Real de Catorce. We sat outside on our balcony in silence. I was reflecting on the size of the earth, the cosmos, the nature of consciousness and time. Time in the desert felt boundless, extended. Softly animated undercurrents to the slow rhythm of life in arid places.

When Dave went out to buy beer and water, I confronted Nina.

"What's going on with you?" I asked. "You need to talk about it."

"The meds aren't helping," she said. "I think it's the wrong combination of pills or something. Or else what I'm taking now and the drugs I like to take don't mix. And I'm a, you know, a kleptomaniac?"

"You're admitting it?" I said. "Are we finally getting somewhere?"

"What's the point of this trip otherwise?"

I heard the key turn in the lock.

"I'm going to get help. I think it's just the pills reacting with the mescaline. Can we talk later?" she whispered, and I nodded.

"I got some Coronas, and limes, and a huge jug of water," said Dave. "And I bought some snacks, too, in case we get hungry later."

"I can't even imagine eating right now," I said, clutching my stomach.

Nina just looked at the adobe-tiled floor. I produced a joint from my Marlboro Lights pack. I lit it and passed it to Dave, who passed it to Nina. It brought the hallucinatory effects of the peyote right back. I stubbed out the joint in an ashtray.

Like Alice shrinking, I went inside my head and strange thoughts began coming out. Dave told me later that I talked about my father all night, which I don't remember, that I seemed to have figured out who he was. I was saying it was beyond intuition and that this time I knew. Dave said my voice sounded almost as if it were coming from some other place, somewhere deep inside myself. I said he was probably just tripping himself.

The next morning, everything finally felt clear. As we drove back to the city, trip over, heading toward everyday reality, I noticed that the soft virgin hills of desert land, the rolling, barren terrain, were the same as we entered the outskirts of Mexico City. The same land, but with buildings on it. First a few, then many, then more and more, the concentration so intense that the earth was buried beneath the concrete of what at the time was the largest city in the world.

Dave dropped Nina off first, then turned the corner to my house.

"So, can I come in?" he asked.

I was quiet for a moment, as I considered why I'd let Dave back into my life at all. "This is a huge mistake," I said.

"Where's that coming from? It was going well, patching things up."

"I always want to hang on to the past, because everything's always so fleeting with me. It's as if I could press rewind and fix things, tape over my images of what you did and replace it with something new. But I can't, not with you."

"But what about the trip and everything?"

"It was amazing. Now I can remember you as more than that guy who made my first months here pure torture."

"Is that what this was all about? Staging a new memory so I wouldn't be just some monster in your mind?"

"I wasn't doing it on purpose, but looking at it now, I think so. Isn't that how things go? You don't necessarily understand your motivations until after the fact?"

"I guess," he said.

"There's always more to people," I said. "Sometimes I seem to do irrational things in the name of finding out what."

"Mila?"

"Yeah?"

"You're weird," he said.

"And don't I know it."

I closed the door behind him when he left. After that, Dave and I said hi to each other when we passed in the halls, and occasionally he'd come look for me to compliment me on a newspaper piece he'd found particularly interesting. Still, I avoided the spot on the field where he sat with his friends and kept him at a peaceful distance. Years later, he employed Google to find my e-mail address at work. We exchanged a few casual messages, and I found out he'd become a CIA trainee. Then he dropped back off the map for good.

Maggie came home from her business trip at the end of the week.

"How did it go with the helicopter?" I asked.

"It was being used to fly the governor of Morelos around. The helicopter had been re-registered, illegally changed, and that's why we couldn't find it until now. Amazing, isn't it."

"Yeah. Congratulations, Mom."

"Thanks. Tomorrow I start a new case. Want to hear about it?"

"Sure." Were we actually having a normal conversation, reaching a truce?

"These guys from Texas were selling a private jet to some Mexicans. The Mexicans said they wanted to take it on a test flight—you know, to see if they liked it. It turns out they're part of a drug cartel and they take the plane on a drug run to Colombia. They got caught flying it back in to Cancún, so the plane was confiscated as evidence, and the Americans couldn't get it back."

"How *will* you get it back?"

"My contact at the Ministry of Finance is getting me the information I need. He's this young, energetic guy who's really interested in fighting corruption."

"He should be careful," I said.

"Are you thinking about Armando?"

"I always think of Armando."

"So do I," she mumbled. "Well, at least Embassy guards are stationed outside this guy's house as a favor for helping us. How was Acapulco?"

"Pretty uneventful."

"But you had fun? How was the private jet?"

"It was nice."

"Good," she said.

Maggie hugged me, then we both went to our rooms to unpack from our respective trips.

The next morning, the newspaper headlines announced that the presidential candidate Luis Donaldo Colosio had been assassinated, shot in a rally in Tijuana. No one knew who was responsible, but conspiracy theories abounded. Colosio, a brave, younger man who wanted social and economic equality in his country, was a danger to the PRI dinosaurs who were in bed with the drug cartels. He had dared to speak out against President Salinas, a foolish thing to do to a man so powerful that computers put him into office in 1988 when the opposition candidate clearly carried the vote. There was even a joke about how corrupt he was: "Salinas is meeting with Fidel Castro. Castro asks Salinas, 'What would you like to drink?' Salinas says, 'A Cuba libre,' " the Mexican name for rum and coke, which literally means *a free Cuba*.

" 'What would *you* like to drink?' Salinas asks Castro. 'Un Presidente *derecho*' (up, no ice), Castro says." Presidente is a Mexican brandy. The drink's name translates to "a straight-up president."

A week later, the police chief in charge of investigating the assassination was dead, too. A lone, twenty-something gunman was convicted—yeah, that was likely. Colosio became Mexico's version of JFK, a champion of democracy. His former campaign manager, who was also rumored to be in on the plot, swept up the presidency, keeping the PRI in power.

TEN

When You Steal
from Yourself

Nora arrived the next day. Rodrigo took us to the airport to pick her up. We'd made a giant NORA sign to stick out the window of the Escalade. I kept my eyes peeled for her, and finally saw her rolling a suitcase through the sliding doors, squinting in the blinding morning sunlight, her hair fastened atop her head in a perfect bun. Her half-French, half-African exotic look set her apart from all the passersby. Rodrigo honked the horn, and I waved the sign out the back window. Nora wore a pink and light-gray Argyle sweater over a white button-down shirt with jeans, which reminded me of how I used to dress. Today I looked like something of a combination of my two Mexico City selves, having paired the fresa platform sandals and fitted white jeans Manuel bought for me with a gray Nirvana smile T-shirt and chunky silver chain necklaces fashioned to resemble barbed wire. I'd flat-ironed my long purple hair stick-straight. Nora spotted us, her button face lighting up as she smiled and waved.

"Mila! Love the purple hair on you, it's so interesting," she said as she climbed into the backseat with me.

"Thanks. You haven't seen it before?"

"You're such a change addict. It was still black over Thanksgiving."

"I can hardly keep track anymore," I said. "Nora, this is Nina."

"It's great to finally meet you," said Nina. "I've heard so much about you."

"Same here," Nora said. "Hey, what's that smell, sulfur?" she asked, as the Escalade pulled out of the international arrivals area.

"It fades once you get away from the airport," I said.

"So, when do I get to meet Manuel?"

Nina flashed me a *You didn't tell her?* look and turned around to the front to fiddle with the radio.

"Yeah, I guess it's been a while since my last letter," I said. "Manuel and I broke up."

"Why?" she asked. "He sounded so great."

"It turned out we had less in common than I thought."

Nina turned back around to face us. I could tell she knew I didn't want to talk about Manuel. "What do you girls say we go shopping in La Condesa, then to Polanco for drinks at Aguila y Sol?" She addressed Nora. "We'll give you the perfect little taste of Mexico City."

"Thank you," I mouthed. I hadn't been sure whether to tell Nora about Elio, but right then I decided it would be too much to put out on the table.

The next day, we met Kai in the Coyoacán plaza and ran into Tyler's hippie artisan friend Carmen at her vendor stand. We picked up a few of her hand-carved pipes and some weed from Las Islas before heading back up to Lomas. We were ready to show my old friend what Mexico City was all about. I almost expected her to protest, but she didn't say a word. I couldn't tell whether she'd decided to be cool with it or she felt outnumbered and out of her controllable environment.

It was a sunny day and smog conditions weren't too bad, so Chapultepec Park seemed the ideal place to spend the afternoon. The four of us sat in the sun, smoking and talking.

"Let's smoke some of this pot," said Kai.

"No one's around, but we should still be careful," I said.

"I have just the thing," said Nina. She produced a small contraption that she explained was a joint-rolling machine, and some papers. "See, you put the paper in here, sprinkle in the pot, a little tobacco, and press down on this lever . . . and voilà." A perfectly rolled joint popped out. It looked just like a cigarette. She made one for each of us.

To my surprise, Nora agreed to smoke. "When in Rome . . . or Mexico City," she said before taking the joint. We got stoned and laughed and talked. I was always looking for substitute brothers and sisters, people to fill the void of loneliness that I felt I always carried around somewhere inside me. When I was around people, especially when we were high, drinking, or tripping, I felt camaraderie, like we were all on a team or fighting for the same army in our own little war for social survival. But here, on the grass, in the blaring afternoon sun, sucking on a joint with friends whose lives, in a way, had been just like my own, I felt peaceful. I watched a group of kids playing soccer way in the distance, took a big breath of not-so-fresh air, and stretched out contentedly, watching Nina and Nora chatting and getting along.

"How do you guys deal with seeing all the poverty around you?" asked Nora. She resembled a Japanimation cartoon, so cute it was almost silly.

"What do you mean, exactly?" I asked.

"It's so hard, being here and seeing all the poor people everywhere. It makes me want to give all of them money, but I'd never have enough."

"There are poor people in D.C.," I said.

"Not like this," said Nora.

I glanced over toward the woods, for no apparent reason. Then panic seized me. A cop was walking his motorcycle out of the forest, heading straight for us.

"Guys, look," Nina whispered.

"Put out the joints," I said, stubbing mine out in the grass. Nina, Nora, and Kai followed suit, jamming gum in their mouths, gulping

Coke from a bottle pulled from Kai's backpack. The officer, slowed down by the weight of his motorcycle, approached.

"How does he know?" asked Nora.

"I have no idea," said Nina. "But he has nothing to go on. He just wants some money."

"What?" said Nora.

"We'll explain later," I said. I hadn't told her about the essence of *mordidas*.

The policeman arrived, put down the kickstand of his motorcycle.

"*Qué estan haciendo aquí?*" he asked. "What are you doing here?"

"Just enjoying the afternoon, señor," I said.

He leaned over and picked up the tiny end of one of the roaches from between blades of grass. *La cucaracha . . . porque no tiene . . .*

"*Y esto?*" he demanded. "And this?"

We were all silent.

"I'm taking you in," he said.

Mexican jail. Guilty until proven innocent. We had to come up with some cash, and fast. Between us, we had only what amounted to three hundred pesos. He shook his head. Mexican jail. When you go in, who knows when you'll get out. They can leave you there forever if they want to. Doritos, Twinkies, and back issues of *Newsweek* were the best my mother could do.

"I have money at home," I said.

The cop held Nina and Kai at the park while Nora and I ran to my house. My mother wouldn't be home for several hours. I took the money out of the secret emergency stash. A thousand U.S. dollars, cash.

"What am I going to say happened to this money?" I asked Nora, more rhetorically than in expectation of an actual answer.

"Call your mother?" she said. "Tell her what happened?"

I held an index finger in the air. "The house gets robbed." I was high as a kite. The idea, at the time, seemed ingenious. I turned over furniture and scattered items about as Nora stared on in shock.

"I can't believe you're doing this," she said.

"This is Mexico. Things work differently here."

I left the gate wide open, and we returned to the park. The cop was fine with the thousand bucks. He rode off on his motorcycle singing a little tune. It was a *mordida* the size of which he'd likely never seen before. A very large bite.

When I got home, Maggie's car was already in the driveway.

"Well," she said, right shoe tapping on the tile. "Where's the money?"

I summoned my best inner actress to feign surprise. "What money? Have we been robbed?"

"Yes, we've been robbed. By criminals who didn't touch the TV or stereo or jewelry. In fact, they didn't take anything except the money from the hidden drawer in my desk. What did you do?" she demanded.

I didn't think, just started to talk. "There was this guy. I didn't know him, he was someone our friend Kai had met a couple times. He was giving us a ride home. From the movies. And in the car he suddenly started smoking a joint. We tried to get him to stop, but a cop saw it and pulled us over. We would have been taken to jail if I hadn't paid."

"Why couldn't you have told me? Why did you do something this outrageous? You didn't smoke pot too, did you?"

"No. No way."

"Nora, we're going to have to switch your flight to one that leaves tomorrow. I'm sorry your visit will be cut short, but it's because of Milagro, not you."

"Mom! That's insane."

"So is faking a robbery in your own house!" my mother shouted.

"I think I'm ready to leave anyway," said Nora, flashing me a worried look. "I've seen enough."

After dropping Nora off at the airport the next morning (I wasn't allowed to go along for the ride), my mother sat me down in the living room.

"I don't even know what to do with you," she said.

"I'm so sorry about the robbery thing, Mom. It was totally stupid. I got scared and panicked. Please." I was worried that she was going to suggest addiction meetings again, or worse.

Maggie sighed. An uncomfortable amount of time passed before she spoke. "I'm going to be staying with Harvey for a while. I don't know how to handle you anymore. Maybe when you have to take care of yourself you'll learn responsibility. Maybe then you won't take me for granted."

"That's no punishment, it's the perfect opportunity to get closer to Harvey," I snapped.

"No, Milagro. You kept saying you wanted more freedom? Well, that's exactly what you get. Get it all out of your fucking system, because when I do come back it won't be with any more tolerance for this . . . *shit*!"

"Mom, you're cursing." I'd never heard her utter a swear word before, and whenever I did she always reprimanded me. She strode out of the room, furious, flashing her angry eyes at me one more time before turning and walking up the stairs. I felt horrible. We were finally starting to work our way to better terms, and I had to go and set us further back than we'd ever been before.

Harvey's house was only five minutes away if you drove on Monte Everest across Reforma and over toward Palmas, but it might as well have been five hundred miles. Maggie usually got attached to her boyfriends quickly, but this development surprised me. She was back to her old pattern, married men.

Sunday night before school resumed, I dyed my hair a fiery bright burgundy and tried on my beat-up low-slung jeans with funky midnight-blue platform boots with steel heels. This was how I was supposed to look. It mirrored how I felt. I needed my oldest friend to forgive me. I had trouble sleeping in the house by myself, and at three in the morning I turned my light back on and wrote her a letter.

April 10

Dear Nora,

Everything's going up in smoke, I can see it. It hangs over the city, blanketing everything. I know it's just the smog, but still. I'm sorry for the position I put you in. I can only imagine what you must think of me. What have I become? I wish I hadn't done that (though wouldn't you admit it was just a little exciting?). I don't understand it myself, really, and I can't offer an explanation other than that living here changes you in ways you don't even realize until you're bribing policemen, shrugging over political assassinations that affect your classmates, experimenting with drugs like William Burroughs, and partying in VIP rooms all over the city with the fresas. My mother is staying with her boyfriend now, if you can believe that. He only lives five minutes away, but she says she doesn't know what to do about me so she's giving me the freedom she thinks I wanted all along so I can get it all out of my system, or whatever. Who knows? Does that sound like punishment, abandonment, or a reward? I can't decide. It's just weird and quiet around my house now. How are things back at school—have you heard about college yet? I hope we end up somewhere near each other. Please, please don't be mad at me. I want always to be friends with you. The robbery plan was stupid. I hope you can forget it ever happened.

Love,
Mila

As the bus pulled around Constituyentes and into the gate, I saw the outside smokers in their clusters, the fresas in their Armani jeans, the American grunge crowd with their flannel shirts and steel-toed Doc Martens, the Americanized-international group, and the random scattered kids who didn't really belong to one or another. All of them were smoking—Camel Lights and Marlboros for the fresas, Winstons and Newports for the Americans, purchased by someone's dad at the Embassy commissary. I put on my favorite pair of Kurt Cobain–

imitation giant white sunglasses that hid half my face, darkening the glare seeping through the haze of the muddy, red-flag day sky. After getting back from the desert, I heard that Cobain had killed himself, and I was sad that I would never get to see a Nirvana concert. I lit a Marlboro Light and sat down on a bench outside, exhaling a long stream of smoke. It seemed I'd come some kind of warped full circle that had arrived back at its topsy-turvy beginning.

With Maggie at Harvey's every night, I could pretty much do what I wanted, so I decided to throw a relaxed welcome-back party at my house. I left a message for Manuel and hoped he would come, or at least call me back. I wanted it to be a proper cocktail party, with wine, mixed drinks, and appetizers. I set up the bar on the kitchen table. But the fridge was empty except for string cheese and apples, so I cut them up and dumped them out on the fancy silver serving platters my mother had gotten in Taxco, the famous silver town. The string cheese was from the commissary at the Embassy. The Mexicans who came to my party had never seen it before. Sometimes I was reminded of the fact that I was only seventeen, that my friends and I weren't really as sophisticated beyond our years as we imagined. That we *were* just kids, no Brie or aged English Cheddar, just Polly-O string cheese.

"Where *is* your mother, anyway?" asked Kai. "Out of town?"

"She moved in with her boyfriend, can you believe that shit?"

"No way. Lucky you."

"Seems that way, doesn't it?" I said quietly. I wasn't feeling as lucky as I'd expected once Maggie had left.

I'd called everyone from my past, except Dave, to invite them to the party. Some of them actually showed up. I was drinking tequila on the back patio, still gossiping with Kai, when Nina ran over to us.

"Come here," she said, motioning me away from Kai. I looked at him.

"Go on, sweetie, I'll be fine."

"What's going on?" I said to Nina.

"Manuel is here."

"Oh my God. He came?"

I made my way through the crowd, looking for him.

"Hey," he said when I found him. He kissed me on the cheek. "It's good to see you."

"Same. What are you doing here?"

"Beatriz and I were just saying we missed having you around," he said as she came up next to him and handed him a freshly mixed Cuba libre.

"Mila, such a good idea to have a party to welcome the last three months of school," said Beatriz.

"It's going to be over before we know it," I said. "Do you have any summer plans?"

"I want an engagement ring by August," she whispered in my ear. "I'm turning nineteen and I can't wait forever."

"From Tomás?"

"Who else?"

"We're going to that new club, Pervert Lounge," said Manuel. "I stopped by to see if maybe you'd want to come."

"There's a club called Pervert Lounge?"

"Yes, it opened right by La Llorona. Will you join us?"

La Llorona was a chic club named after the Mexican legend of "the Crier," a vain woman who threw her children into the river in a fit of rage. Her ghost came back to wander by the river, crying, "Where are my children? Where are my children?" Go figure—she throws them away, then when she doesn't have them anymore she wants them back. Parents told their little kids that if they went out alone at night she might snatch them up.

The club was in the Centro Historico. Why the owners dubbed their new locale Pervert Lounge, I will never understand. But I liked the name. I guess that was the point.

"If I can get everybody out of here, I'll go," I told him.

"I hate the way we left things," he said. "I do think about you. We just run in such different circles."

"Circles that aren't round."

"What?"

"Nothing. I'm so glad you came. I wanted to apologize for that night. I know you weren't using me."

"I'm glad you realize that," he said. "Apology accepted."

At three in the morning, we made it to the bar. The décor was futuristic and very seventies at the same time. Rows of funky neon-painted Barbies topped brightly painted disco lamps all along the walls of the long, low space. The chairs were big white plastic curved hands that made me think of the Korova Milk Bar in *A Clockwork Orange.* I ordered a Splash from the bartender, took it, and sat on a hand, watching my friends dance. Manuel came over and sat in the empty hand next to mine. He didn't say anything, just smiled and took a sip of his beer.

"How's your father?" I asked above the throbbing bass.

"Not so good, actually," he shouted back into my ear. "He's receiving threats, so he's not going into the hospital as much."

"Why would anyone threaten a surgeon?"

"It's complicated."

"What do you mean?"

"I can't tell you."

"I promise not to write about it."

"Seriously, Mila, why do you care so much?"

"Because I know what it is not to feel cared for."

"Listen," he said. "Do you want to dance with me?"

I was so thrilled he was asking me to dance, that I'd be able to touch him and be close to him again, that I forgot about my questions and said yes.

At lunchtime on Monday, we walked down by the elementary school so I could snag a forbidden hot dog. Manuel usually never went anywhere other than straight to the front of the pool.

"I don't know how you can eat those," he said. "They're so gross." He crinkled up his nose and made a gagging sound. I ignored him. In ten months in Mexico, country of bottled water and vegetables that needed to be soaked in disinfectant, I'd never once gotten food poisoning. Drugs weren't the only contraband making their way around the ISM campus; there were also the hot dogs.

Kai always stood guard, watching out for Mr. Horney while I shoved my three pesos through the hole in the fence, which someone had cut with some kind of wire-cutting tool. The hot dogs were wrapped in bacon and made out of who knows what—maybe the street dogs we regularly felt sorry for as they limped by on Bondojito, or the cats or rats. I got mine smothered in jalapeños, onions, *queso blanco,* and mustard, feeling the pleasant effect of getting full again after hunger as the hot chewed-up mixture filled my mouth with a spicy-sweet delicious taste. The hot dogs, to us, represented freedom from the oppression of the Horney regime in a place where we might as well have been institutionalized, since we were locked in during the day and forbidden to stroll through the neighborhood streets unless we bribed somebody. Mr. Horney threatened to wire shut our hot-dog holes forever, but as soon as he did another was cut and he'd have to find that one, too. Mr. Horney took such delight in seeing our faces freeze as our food was confiscated, and in yelling at the poor man behind the cart. The fresas didn't eat the hot dogs. They thought street food was the most disgusting, repulsive thing. Other food I ate off the street: *tacos al pastor* from little carts in the Zocalo, corn on a stick dipped in creamy mayonnaise and sprinkled with *queso fresco* and chili, fresh *agua de Jamaica* in Coyoacán, tamales, and sweet potatoes from the whistle-cart man.

The last place I expected to catch a bug, then, was from the melons that came with the beautiful fruit platter for the chocolate fondue at the upscale Lugar de la Mancha, where the fresas and their parents went for high tea, and where Manuel had asked me to lunch with him after school, to talk things over and decide if we were going to be friends or get back together.

Lugar was a beautiful café and restaurant with a metal sculpture of Don Quixote in the outdoor garden area. Patrons could dine on an upstairs balcony overlooking Lomas, or in picturesque breakfast and dining rooms. A little gift shop sold eclectic international items like Florentine paper and Dalí prints. We ordered cappuccinos and the chocolate fondue.

Manuel was sick, too; we couldn't keep anything down. We both knew it was the melons. That's how it is with food poisoning: you just know exactly what it was that got you. And that was how Manuel and I decided to give it another try, while lying green-faced on his bed, staring at the ceiling, and taking turns running to the bathroom. We just knew. We felt it in our stomachs.

"If we die, you must know I do love you, more than I could say," he said.

"We're going to be fine," I said, hopping up and running to the toilet. "And I feel the same!" I called out before vomiting into the porcelain bowl.

Until we got sick, the afternoon at Lugar had felt magical. Something was in the air, the smell of sweet bougainvillea and new beginnings. Giddiness surged inside me, and I could see that he felt it, too. Maybe it was the freedom of spring semester, senior year, or the fact that we'd been away from each other for a while. All the old feelings came flooding back and there we were, suddenly us again.

Manuel walked me home after our sickness passed and we'd managed to hold down a few saltines. We found Maggie and Harvey cuddling on the couch in the living room. It occurred to me that she was somebody's mistress again. I introduced Manuel to Harvey, and could tell that he hated my mother's boyfriend immediately.

"There's something strange about him," he said when we got to the kitchen. I poured us two glasses of water from the jug.

"You mean the fact that he's married and dating my mom?"

"Married people have affairs all the time," he said. "It's something else. The guy's just weird."

"Kids!" Maggie called to us. "Come into the living room, I have news."

"What's up, Mom?"

"I got my next Foreign Service assignment: Athens."

"Congratulations," said Manuel.

"So you're moving this summer." I said. I knew the Foreign Service rotation schedule as if making assignments for the State Department were my job.

"End of June," she said. "You could come for a couple of months, though it'll be hectic with the move and all."

"I'd rather try to enroll in a college summer session. It doesn't make much sense for me to go with you when everything's all unsettled."

"When have things been any other way in our life?" she said light-heartedly.

"Good point."

It was the first time I wouldn't be following my mother. I wondered where I'd be moving at the end of the school year. Decisions from colleges weren't due to arrive for another month.

"Don't you think it's funny that our street here is called Monte Athos?" I said. "It's a sign."

"Oh, Milagro. You think everything is a sign."

"I know them when I see them. It's the universe reminding you that you're on the right path."

"She's funny," Harvey said to Maggie as if I weren't standing right there. Manuel shot me a sympathetic glance, as if he could read my thoughts. I wondered how things would have turned out if Armando were still alive, how my life would be different were my mother married to him instead of trying to get her boss to leave his wife.

On Thursday morning, the news reported that a *brujo*—some psychic witch man who was hired by the federal prosecutor—found the bones of a murdered politician on a ranch belonging to another politician, the uncle of a guy from ISM. The body had turned out not to be who the psychic said it was. The corpse belonged, in fact, to a relative of the psychic. The *brujo* and the prosecutor were subsequently arrested for trying to frame my classmate's uncle. Another odd moment in the surreal history of the city. I had a strange premonition as I listened to the bizarre newscast. I dressed (jean miniskirt, black-and-purple-striped tights, and my platform boots, with a gray cashmere V-neck I borrowed from Maggie), skipped first period, and got to school in time for second, English. The teacher was talking (*Moby-Dick*) when Mr. Horney interrupted, telling Manuel to go to the office immediately. We exchanged glances as he grabbed his jacket and followed the vice principal out of the classroom.

He wasn't back on Friday. At lunch, I went over to the pool to look for his friends. I never went by there anymore, and I didn't talk to any of the fresa girls except Beatriz, in passing, if we ran into each other in the bathroom. I found her sitting with Katia at one of the poolside picnic tables.

"What happened?" I asked. "Where is he?"

Beatriz jumped up and tried to lead me away from Katia, but not fast enough for me to miss the dirty look she gave me.

"You haven't heard?" Beatriz asked.

"Heard what?"

"Manuel's father got killed. That's why he had to leave."

"Gustavo?"

"No, his other father, you idiot," sneered Katia.

"Go to hell, Katia," I said. I ran toward the school's main gate, reaching in my pocket for money to pay the guard to let me off campus.

Manuel's housekeeper let me in, her eyes downcast. She was dressed all in black. Manuel was in his bedroom, sitting at his desk doing physics homework.

"Why didn't you tell me where the funeral was? I would have been there."

"It was closed. Family only." He didn't lift his head from the textbook.

"I'm so sorry. I don't know what to say. Has anyone been arrested?"

Manuel laughed. "What do you think?" He produced a small bag of coke from his pocket, dumping it out on the book. He wasn't doing homework at all.

"Want some?"

I shrugged. He sucked in two of the lines with a rolled-up ten-peso bill. I grabbed it from his hand and vacuumed the other two.

"Will you at least tell me what happened?" I asked.

"He was in the car, on his way to a meeting. They were driving through Chapultepec Park, the driver stopped at a red light, some men ran up to the car—" His voice broke. "They had to break his body out of a cement block."

"Why would anyone do that to a surgeon? I just don't get it."

Manuel put his head on the desk and started to cry, quietly. I came up behind him and wrapped my arms around his shoulders, kissing him gently on the cheek.

"I have no idea what to say," I said. "I'm just . . . I'm so sorry," I said again.

When he stopped crying, he told me the story. "Amado Carillo-Fuentes," he said. "Do you know that name?"

"He was that huge drug guy who just died."

"Yeah, the Lord of the Skies, the number-one man in the cartels. Did you read *how* he died?"

"Wasn't he having plastic . . ." my voice trailed off.

"Surgery," finished Manuel. "He was getting his face changed, so he could, you know, get on with it. In the operating room, he was over-dosed. My father's body was found in a cement-packed barrel on a highway down in Guerrero. They got him and two other doctors from his team."

"Your dad actually performed the operation?"

"He was in charge of it. He didn't just do nose jobs for rich girls. Someone got him into a side business, something he never talked about. I think I know who it was."

He cocked an eyebrow at me, but I didn't flinch.

"So you didn't know anything about it?"

"Please. You think he sat around the dinner table talking about these things? I've known my entire life that this was a possibility. But you can never be prepared for how it feels."

I looked at the math textbook and the razor, with its dusty white edge.

"Your father was killed by drug dealers and you're doing coke?"

"They're not this powerful for no reason," said Manuel. Then he started crying again and I couldn't stand to see him that way, so I left.

I went home and called Eliodoro de la Garza at work.

"What is this regarding?" asked his secretary.

"Please tell him it's the student journalist from ISM, that I would like to see him again if he's willing."

She put me on hold, then got back on and said she would set up an early-morning coffee at a place he liked near his office.

"So this is a series of articles?" he asked, settling into the booth and loosening his tie. It was early, before school, even. A fan spun slowly overhead. The air-conditioning was broken and the heat was unbearable.

"It's turning into a longer piece. I want to maybe follow you around for a while."

"That would be quite boring for you," he said. I couldn't tell from his tone whether he was joking.

"I'm writing a profile. It's important for me to study my subject carefully."

"It's too hot here. Let's go to another place," he said. His bodyguard walked beside us.

He took me to the rooftop of the Holiday Inn in the Zocalo, and we sat outdoors high above the plaza. I looked out over the sinking buildings, rooftops at a slant, the hustle and bustle of the plaza below. I ordered a *limonada* and Elio took black coffee. After the necessary pleasantries, I asked him about Manuel's father.

"I can't believe even surgeons get roped into this sort of thing," I said. "Who could have done something like this?"

He ignored my question. "What you need to understand about the system here, and this is off the record—I didn't say this, even though everybody knows it—is that the drug cartels are intimately intertwined with the very highest levels of government. Pepe Sanchez-Rivera is in your class, right?"

"He's Emilio Sanchez-Rivera's son, that top political guy who was assassinated."

"You know they're trying to arrest the ex-president's brother on charges that he was behind all that."

"His nephew was close friends with Pepe."

"Look closely at the little things going on around you, Mila. That's the best advice I can give. You've got Mexico City's next generation of leaders right in front of you, not because they're really trying but because they're born into it. If you want to know how our system works, all you have to do is get to know your peers."

"It's pretty incestuous in the upper ranks of this city. Even with murders."

"Unfortunately, it's a big part of reality here," he said.

"Like a bunch of bandidos."

Elio laughed. "There is very little difference between our political leaders and bandidos. But I never said any of this to you."

"Of course not. I don't even know you." I smiled.

"I like you. You're a smart girl. You remind me a little of my own daughter."

"That's funny," I said. "You remind me of somebody, too."

When I got home from school that afternoon, I called Maggie at work.

"Citizen Services, Maggie Epstein."

"I need to know if it's him."

"If who is *who*? Are you taking drugs again?"

"Is Eliodoro de la Garza him?"

There was silence on the other end.

"Whatever gave you that idea?" she whispered into the phone.

"When I met him—"

"You *met* him?"

"For the school newspaper column I write. I didn't tell you about it, okay?"

"Don't do any more interviews with that man," she said.

"I'm through with your secrets," I said, and hung up the phone. My mother didn't come home that night, not that I'd expected her now that she was staying at Harvey's. Freedom, rather than feeling like the fulfillment of my ultimate wish, was my punishment.

ELEVEN

Earthquakes

"Guillermo is having a party this weekend at his house in Valle. Do you want to go?" Nina asked in the Escalade on the way to school in the morning.

Naldo sat in the front next to Rodrigo, wearing headphones that didn't confine the pounding sound of Café Tacuba to his ears alone.

"Guillermo invited you to his party?" I asked. I'd heard about Guillermo's parties. His father was huge in the ruling political party, but rumors around school had it that he was involved with big drug money. And Guillermo had a reputation for getting together with as many girls as possible, and not just those from school, either. He organized mass trips to whorehouses for the guys at ISM. A bunch of them went to lose their virginity that way, and Guillermo's father paid for it. Manuel told me the father even went along.

"So you went?" I'd asked Manuel.

"I did go, but when I got there I couldn't do it," he'd said. "Those women are diseased and disgusting." I believed him.

"Mila? Are you in or what?" Nina asked.

"I'm not sure. Manuel isn't going, obviously. How much do you know about Guillermo?"

"I've heard it all. He has a huge house, and all the fresas are going for the weekend. I'm in love with Gabriel, and this is the perfect chance for us to get to know each other."

"You're always 'in love' with a different boy, but you never have a boyfriend."

"Thanks for pointing that out, *Milagro.*"

"I'm definitely not letting you go alone, so I guess that means I'm coming with you," I said.

I didn't have a good feeling about Guillermo's party, but I was probably being paranoid, having smoked half a joint in the shower not twenty minutes earlier. And I was worried about Nina, who was now running every day after school, shrinking in her designer clothes, and skipping so many classes that she was in danger of failing the semester. One night I had dinner at her house with her parents and all she did was move her rice and vegetables around on the plate, making little holes in the small piles of food to trick them into thinking she'd been taking bites.

I tried to get her to talk about what was wrong, but she wouldn't even acknowledge that anything was; the door that had cracked open a tiny bit in Real de Catorce was now locked. "I think Mexico City is getting to me" was all she would say.

"Why's that?"

"There's just too much," she said.

"Too much of what?"

"Too much everything. You know it as well as I do."

"A city can't make you stop eating."

"I'm on a diet."

"But you're too skinny in the first place."

"My brother said I was looking a little chubby."

"I don't believe you."

"When I was twelve, I put on a bikini for the first time, in Argentina, and he said that to me. I never forgot it."

"Okay, well, you're eighteen now and you're taking this too far."

Nina ate one sandwich per day, a bagel shell with the bread scooped out, with mustard and tomato. That was all. And since it was impossible to find a bagel in Mexico City, she insisted that I get them for her from the freezer section of the Embassy commissary. Desperate to see her eat something, I obliged.

"Unless you want to waste away, you're going to need to eat more than those bagels," I told her.

"Mila, it's a *bagel*. It's *so* high in calories," she'd say, throwing the inside of it into the trash.

In the medicine cabinet in her bathroom, I'd seen three different types of pills where before there had been only one. It was hard to know what was ever going on with Nina at any given time. Still, I was drawn to her for some reason that I couldn't comprehend. Maybe it was that people who needed me made me feel more secure in relationships. I knew they wouldn't be going anywhere, so I clung back for dear life.

On Friday we skipped seventh period, slipped the guard fifty pesos, and giggled excitedly as we got into the back of Gabriel's Jetta. Somehow Nina had manipulated him into driving us, deliberately sitting next to him in second-period honors English and whispering something about the big party in Valle. Before the bell rang, she'd gotten him to offer us a ride.

Nina flirted with Gabriel the whole drive. She talked incessantly, laughing too loud and too long. I knew Nina better, but I could see why people at school thought she was a ditz. If she would only be herself, instead of this exaggerated characterization of herself, she'd be much better off. I couldn't quite figure out how to tell her that. My desire to save her from hurt was stronger than any effect I believed could be had by telling her the truth.

We got to Valle after sundown, the sun burning out, the last strip of pink fading across a purple sky. Guillermo's house was far above Lake Avandaro, which I learned in Mexican history meant "a dream place" in the Purepecha language, and was one of the largest I'd seen in Valle, at least twice the size of Manuel's. The house spoke of money, far too much of it. We got our bags out of the trunk and went inside. All the fresas were already there and Gabriel headed over to meet his friends, leaving Nina and me standing awkwardly in the middle of the room. Guillermo noticed us a few minutes later.

"Hey, Nina," he called out. "I'm glad you made it."

"This is Mila," Nina said, introducing me, and Guillermo, who went by the nickname Memo, kissed me on the cheek.

"I remember," he said. "Come, I'll show you to your room."

Memo led us into a huge room with a balcony overlooking the lake. There was an adjoining bathroom sauna, a steam room, and a Jacuzzi. And this was just one small corner of the house.

After dropping our bags and flopping for a moment on the king-size bed, looking at each other like we couldn't believe where we were, we headed out to the balcony and looked down at the pool, where the boys were drinking beer and tequila, and at the tennis courts beyond. Even Nina, who had a very rich daddy, was nowhere near this level of wealth at the ambiguous top of Mexico City society. I could even sense the difference between Memo and Manuel. Manuel's family was ridiculously wealthy, and Memo's was at the level you might think existed only in movies and fantasies. Though Memo was always surrounded by large groups, nobody seemed to know him well.

Nina and I changed into our bikinis and went down to the pool. It was one of those infinity pools that gave the illusion of disappearing off the edge of a cliff, over the horizon, to someplace once thought to be the end of the earth. We sat on the side and dangled our legs in the water. Gabriel and Bernardo were doing tequila shots at the swim-up bar, sitting on two of the six barstools that were built into the pool, submerged in the water. Jorge, Jaime, and Rafael were engaged in a game of water polo. Tomás and another Jorge floated on inflatable rafts, sipping Coronas with lime.

Guillermo swam over to where Nina and I were sitting.

"Hey, *nenas*," he said, smiling. "Are you getting in the water sometime this year?"

"What time are the other girls getting here?" I asked, surveying the testosterone-soaked scene at the pool.

"*Oye,* Memo," shouted Tomás. "Didn't you tell Mila she's crashing a guys' weekend?"

"Guys?" I repeated.

"*Pues, sí,*" he said, slipping into the water and swimming away.

"Did you know?" I asked Nina.

"He's kidding," she said, and giggled.

Memo and Gabriel looked at each other, their eyebrows arched.

"I don't think so," I said. "I think we stumbled into a boys' vacation."

"Don't worry," said Memo. "I'll take good care of you girls."

He got out and headed toward the bar. I didn't trust him, and I was growing increasingly skeptical about Nina's invitation to the two-day party. She plopped into the pool and I followed. We started swimming toward the other end.

"How did you say you got invited to this?" I asked her.

"I *told* you, Gabriel asked me."

"Really."

"He was talking about it with Tomás during sixth period and I told them I thought it sounded like a good time, and they asked me to come."

I was silent, watching Nina pull through the water.

"Fine, I asked if you and I could go."

"And what did they say?"

"That we would be the only girls they would ever allow on one of their guys-only weekend trips."

I mentally noted another good reason to become an investigative journalist: I wasn't sure why, but people eventually told me the truth. It wasn't a special talent or anything; I think a more likely reason was that I'd be pretty quiet until the truth told itself.

"And why do you think that is?"

"Because they'd rather have us around than Beatriz and Cristina and all those fresa girls. We're so much more easygoing."

"And easier."

"Gabriel doesn't think that."

"You don't even know him. They respect the girls in their *grupito*. When those girls are here, things are probably a lot more . . . moderate." I looked over toward the bar, where Memo had joined Gabriel and Bernardo at the tequila bottle. I swam away from Nina, angry that she'd gotten us into this situation, that she'd lied to me again, in her manipulative, haven't-a-clue-but-really-do way. Her mind was probably warped from all the nutrient deprivation. I wondered if her parents would ever wake up and do something about her. They didn't seem to notice how much weight she had lost; or that Naldo seemed to be the water-polo champion of the universe. I pulled myself out of the pool, walked over to the glass edge of the cliff where the area ended, and gazed below to the tennis courts, the rooftops, the lake. One of the Jorges materialized by my side.

"*Qué onda,* Mila?" he asked. "What are you doing all by yourself?"

"Just admiring the view."

"You always look like you're having deep thoughts."

"It's the way my face looks when I'm actually not thinking at all." I smiled.

"Come over to the bar?"

"Sure."

We sat on the submerged barstools and rested our elbows on the dark wooden bar that jutted out of the pool, a veritable island of alcohol.

"I have something you'll like," said Jorge, winking at me.

These guys are such macho clichés, I thought. Then Jorge surprised me. He grabbed his backpack from where it had been sitting on the bar, unzipped a small pocket, and produced a Ziploc baggie of weed and some rolling papers.

"I've never rolled before," he said. "Teach me?"

"How would you know that I know how?" I asked.

"You think we don't go to the same school or something?" he said. "Your reputation, as Miss Olivarez always says in history class, 'su-

persedes you.' " I thought the word was *precedes*, but I didn't try to correct him. So people did talk about me. Maybe I wasn't as invisible as I
had always suspected. I hoped he hadn't heard the rumors Dave had
spread earlier in the year.

Jorge Uno dragged me back to the moment.

"Are you going to start?"

"All right," I said, pulling apart the sticky marijuana and preparing
it for joint-rolling.

"Why is this weed red?" I asked.

"That's what it's called," he said. "Red. It's supposed to send you to
the moon."

I showed him how to roll it, licking the end and pasting it perfectly,
a sweet-smelling cylindrical treat.

"Now you try," I said. Jorge rolled a sloppy but functionally sound
joint, then tried again and made a tighter one. We kept rolling and
rolling until no pot was left, just many joints all lined up on the bar like
skinny white cousins.

"What are we going to do with all these?" I asked him.

Memo got behind the bar, taking more beers out of the fridge, the
bottles clinking together as he pulled them out two by two. "We're going to smoke them," he said.

"Not all of them," said Jorge Uno. "That would take a month."

"It's a contest," said Memo, grabbing two of the joints off the coun-
tertop and holding his lighter to them.

"Are you sure you want to do that?" said Jorge Uno. "It's supposed
to be really strong; something else is in it."

"Here," said Memo, handing one to Jorge Uno. Jorge Dos, Gabriel,
Nina, and the other guys gathered around. Everyone plucked one from
the pile, and Memo passed the lit flame of his Zippo from mouth to
waiting mouth.

I took a drag from Nina's. It was stronger than I was used to. Or
maybe it was just the environment—the huge house, the sprawling
grounds, the overwhelming storybook view of Valle.

It was late afternoon and we played volleyball with a giant beach ball in the pool for a few hours, laughing and clumsily flopping into the water like a group of deranged dolphins. I felt someone swim up behind me, his arms closing around my waist. I craned my neck around: it was Gabriel.

"Don't do that," I whispered, scanning the water to make sure Nina hadn't noticed. But she was listening intently to something Memo was saying as they hit the beach ball back and forth to each other.

"Sorry," Gabriel said into my ear. "Why do you think I said it was okay for you guys to come to Valle when your bony friend over there begged me for an invitation?"

"She was begging?"

"She used to be so cool, but now she seems so messed up and desperate. You're the string holding her together."

"You don't know anything about her," I snapped.

"Will you come into town with me? We can have dinner at this great little place, have some margaritas, and meet the others to go out to Pachanga later."

"I'm back together with Manuel," I said.

"Really? I didn't know."

"We're taking it slow. Why don't you ask Nina to go with you?"

"Because I think she's already taken," he said, motioning with his head at a spot behind me. When I turned around, I saw Nina and Memo kissing against the edge of the pool. His hands moved aggressively through her hair and down over her body, and she was kissing him back, hard.

"Well, I guess I'll go get changed," I said to Gabriel. There was a point at which I could not be responsible for the girl.

We walked through the cobblestoned streets, by clay-red and white buildings with half-cylindrical tiled rooftops, and arrived at Pachanga, the most popular of a handful of exclusive clubs in Valle. Gabriel called Memo's cell phone and told him to round everyone up to come out.

"They're on their way," he said after he hung up.

Everyone else showed up not long after. As we drank and danced at Pachanga, I was surprised to see Memo and Nina huddled in a corner at our table, talking and kissing. Whatever he was saying was making her laugh, and she looked genuinely happy for the first time in months. Maybe I'd been wrong about Memo, I thought. At one in the morning, we decided to abandon Pachanga for Lexia, Valle's other fresa club. Nina and I lagged behind the rest of the group on the sidewalk.

"So, what's going on with Memo?" I asked.

"It's strange, but I think I really like him," she said.

"Looks that way."

"People think he's so mysterious and stuck-up, but he's just shy."

"Are you sure?"

"I just get from talking to him that he tries to play down who he is and the family he comes from. It makes him come across as cocky when he's actually not."

"If that's true, then I'm glad you're hitting it off."

"Me, too." Nina smiled. "See? It was *such* a good idea to come here."

"Just be careful. Make sure you know exactly what his intentions are."

We arrived at Lexia and the doorman waved to Memo, unhooking the rope for us even though there was a line outside. After we put our jackets and bags in the coat check, the cocktail waitress led us to our table, which was already set up with the requisite top-shelf vodka bottles, champagne, ice, and jugs of orange and cranberry juices. Memo poured Nina a glass of champagne and sat with his arm around her shoulders. They kept talking and whispering, like a couple reunited after a long absence rather than the virtual strangers they'd been until earlier that day. I thought I could read people, and Memo's gestures and behavior toward her looked genuine. I sipped my vodka cranberry and danced with Gabriel. The night, like all the others, wore on.

At around three-thirty, everyone was more than a little bit drunk, and an after-hours crowd had started filling up the club. Another group was ushered onto the banquettes next to ours. A fresa in a leather jacket and belted jeans came over to Memo.

"*Guey,*" he shouted. "Haven't seen you around in a while." There was something menacing about his tone. Even above the house music, I could hear it.

"Why don't you and your friends find another place, Javier?" Memo yelled back.

"Because this is *my* spot," Javier replied. "You're the ones who have to leave."

"Who is that?" I whispered to Gabriel.

"Those kids go to the Gates Institute," he said.

"That British school?"

"Please. That school is as British as ours is international."

"It's mostly Mexicans there, too?"

"Rivals, mainly."

"What do you mean?" I asked.

"Different families form alliances for different reasons," he said vaguely. "They don't want their kids going to the same school."

The conversation between Memo and Javier was growing heated, and I heard Memo tell Nina to wait for him at the table. I hoped they weren't going outside to start a fight.

"What's the situation between those two?" I asked Gabriel.

"Javier's father directed antidrug operations in Mexico. Recently, he was killed. Some people think Memo's father is involved in a drug cartel that might've been behind it, which is *mierda.*"

"That the cartel was behind it, or that Memo's father is involved with them?"

"Both," he said. He glanced around the club before gesturing toward my now empty glass. "Want another?"

"Sure," I said.

He poured the drink.

"I'll be right back," he said, and disappeared into the crowd.

Nina leaned toward me across the table.

"I'm bored," she said. "Let's walk around."

"All right." I shrugged.

We wove our way through the circles of people, looking for nothing in particular. When we passed the coat check, Nina stopped short. The closet-size room was unattended, and rows of designer coats hung from the rack.

"What are you doing?" I asked.

"I think I forgot some money in my coat, I want to go grab it."

"We don't need any, though. Everything's on Memo's tab."

"Look, I'm just going to go get it, okay?" she said, sounding agitated.

"Whatever," I said, knowing she'd reemerge with an expensive new jacket. "I'll see you back at the table." It wasn't worth arguing over. Her compulsions would always win.

The Gates kids who had been sitting adjacent to us were gone. As I watched the other guys flirting with girls out on the dance floor, drinks in hand, I realized that my life, had I gone to the Gates Institute, would not have been much different. I might have come into Lexia on this very night, with Javier's *parea*—group of friends—instead of Memo's. I wondered whether I would still have ended up stumbling across Elio.

I finished the vodka cranberry and decided to go see what was happening with Nina and Memo, who hadn't reappeared at the table. After passing through the dance floor several times, I couldn't find Nina anywhere inside, so I went out front. It was four and the club was officially closed, though whoever was still inside was free to stay until he was kicked out in the morning. Outside, the doorman and the line were gone. I paced up and down the short, quiet block. The stone walls in Valle were so thick you couldn't hear any of the revelry that was going on inside. Then I heard a faint sound of shouting from somewhere farther away. I kept walking and turned a corner. I spotted Memo and Gabriel with Javier and a few other guys I didn't recognize.

"Hey!" I screamed, running toward them. "Stop it!"

They were in a small, nearly empty parking lot, in a full-blown fight. Memo and Gabriel were outnumbered, and it showed. They were already on the ground, looking defeated.

The Gates guys just laughed. "I guess we're about done here anyway," I heard Javier say in Spanish. He pressed a button on his key chain and the headlights flashed on the silver Mercedes near him as he switched off the alarm. I stood staring from several yards away, afraid to approach any closer while Javier and his three friends were still there. They got into the car. As they drove out onto the road, I ran toward Memo and Gabriel. When I reached them, the Mercedes pulled back around through the parking lot. I hoped they wouldn't get out and start up again. But the engine kept running. The window on the driver's side rolled down.

"Oh, and your girlfriend was looking for you," Javier yelled to Memo. "She's in the coat check. She wanted to show my friends a good time." He laughed, then took off down the road again. The car rounded a corner and the road went dark.

"Was he talking about Nina?" I asked.

Memo had a black eye, and Gabriel's lip was bleeding. They were bruised, scraped, and stunned, but not seriously injured. Javier and his friends were probably careful to do just enough damage.

"Fuck, we have to go find her," said Memo.

"Mila, go to the club and look for her," said Gabriel. "We'll be behind you. I think my knee is messed up."

I'd started to run before he finished the sentence. I flew down the street and back into Lexia. The rest of Memo's friends were gone. They must have thought we'd gone back to the house. I headed straight toward the coat check. It was a narrow but deep closet, and the attendant was nowhere to be found. I saw a crumpled heap in the corner. I pushed past the rows of bags and jackets and pulled away the ones that were blocking Nina, who was lying on the floor in a white leather jacket that wasn't hers.

She was trembling and crying. She looked worse than Memo or Gabriel. I felt frozen and nauseous as I helped her onto her feet. Memo came into the closet.

"I can't believe they'd do this to her to get at me," he mumbled, putting his arms around Nina.

"We have to get you to the hospital," I said to her.

"No," she whispered.

As Memo helped her up, I saw that her skirt was bunched around her tiny hips. Her underwear was down around her platform shoes. I rushed to pull the skirt down, but it was just long enough for me to see the cuts and bruises on her legs.

"What did they do to you?" I asked. "You need to tell us exactly what happened."

She started to cry. Gabriel appeared in the doorway and helped us bring Nina out.

"We need to tell the manager," I said.

"Let's just go," Memo protested. "We definitely don't want to be noticed right now."

"But look what they did to her!"

"Mila, trust us," said Gabriel. "No attention is much better. Let's get out of here."

I realized they were probably terrified of this turning up in the papers and shaming their families. When we got back to Memo's house, the rest of the guys were lying around the living room with the girls they'd met at the club, smoking more of the Red. Beer bottles were everywhere, and the ashtrays were overflowing. Everyone sat upright when we came in, and expressions of shock passed over their faces at the exact same moment.

"What the hell happened to you?" Tomás was first to ask. "We thought you'd left."

"Javier showed up," said Memo. "And we're leaving, so pack up and go as soon as you can. Lock the house and give me the keys at school. And make sure you clean up your mess."

He left the room without waiting for anyone to answer. Nina and I went down the hall to get our bags.

"I don't want to go to the hospital," she said.

"Did one of those guys rape you?" I had trouble getting the words out.

She nodded, her beautiful face contorting as more tears ran down her cheeks. "I think more than one," she said, sounding ashamed.

"You *have* to go. When this happened to me, my hugest regret was that afterward I did nothing. I can't let that happen to you."

"I have to shower first," she said.

"No! You'll clean everything off!"

"That's the point!" she yelled.

"That's the evidence!"

Memo hugged Nina and kissed her forehead when we met back down at the entryway of the house.

"We'll drive you to the hospital," he said as we walked out to the driveway. "But we can't stay. We need to get back to the city and handle things."

I wondered what "handling things" entailed, but I didn't want to ask. I got into the car with Gabriel, and Nina went with Memo. After they dropped us off, Nina sat next to me on a plastic emergency-room chair, her face frozen, eyes staring blankly straight ahead. I'd pretended nothing happened after Dave. Nina wasn't capable of faking anything when it came to things that mattered. She faked it so well in regular everyday life.

We waited for hours before Nina was seen. We hadn't slept at all. The bruises on her legs had turned from yellow to bluish, and the blood from the cuts on her face had dried. She was wearing the white leather jacket, a trophy from an otherwise disastrous night.

Suddenly, Nina gasped. "What is *she* doing here?" she said.

"Nina, believe me, I didn't want to call her. But this is her job. We need her." *I* needed her. "Technically, as a U.S. citizen, you're her case right now."

"She'll tell my parents."

"She promised she wouldn't. And we have no other way of getting home." I stroked Nina's back and waited for my mother to reach us.

As she approached, I could see that her eyes were bleary from the early-morning drive, her face streaked with tears. I knew that they were tears of relief that this time it wasn't about me.

"Milagro," she said, and hugged me. Her nails dug into my back.

"Ow, Mom. I'm not the one who needs attention here."

My mother spoke to the doctors, then they took Nina to be photographed, every body part from every angle. They would examine her and clean her up. While Nina was in with the doctors, my mother turned to me. We were both slumped uncomfortably in the hard waiting-room seats.

"Milagro."

"What?"

"If anything happened to you, I don't know what I'd do."

It already did, I thought. I wished I had told her then. Too much time had gone by, and I knew I'd never mention it. I didn't want Nina to make the same mistake.

"It won't do any good, both of us like this," I said, wiping tears off my face. "Let's focus on Nina for now. She needs us."

"Milagro."

"What?"

"Yes."

"Yes what?"

"Your question on the phone that day. The answer is yes."

It hit me, a wave I hadn't known was swelling behind me. Like saltwater filling my nose and mouth, a surprise burn.

"Eliodoro?" I said.

"If you ever say anything about this, you and I will be in so much trouble."

"Oh my God, Mom, finally. Thank you."

I scooted over and wrapped my arms tightly around her shoulders, both our sets of eyes tearing up now.

"You knew already. How?" she asked.

"Duh," I said. "I saw him with my own eyes. How could I *not* know."

"You do have his eyes. And his nose and chin."

"I don't know how you thought I wouldn't find out when he is who he is."

Maggie just shrugged. "You'll make a good journalist, Milagro."

"Mom. Mila. Please."

Nina came out of the examining room. "Are you two crying because of me? I already feel bad," she said, sitting down beside me. My mother and I hugged tighter for a second longer before breaking apart.

"You need to find out who these boys are and press charges," Maggie said to Nina. "And I know I promised not to tell your parents, so I won't—but you're going to."

Nina stared at me, her eyes panicked.

"Just say yes," I said. I ran my fingers through her long hair, pulling it behind her ear on one side. "You need to do it for yourself—trust me on this one."

On the ride back to Mexico City, Nina agreed to take action against the boys. But before she even got up the courage to tell her parents after school on Monday, my mother got a phone call at the Embassy from the doctor who examined her. It seemed that the photographs and the medical evidence had somehow disappeared en route to Mexico City. Maggie called me at three on the dot, the minute I walked in the door, to tell me what the doctor had said.

"How could they have *lost* it," I yelled into the phone. "I know they're not always efficient in this country but come on!"

"Milagro," Maggie said, her voice even. "Do you really think this was an accident?"

"I should have guessed."

"Maybe the doctor was paid off. Maybe the photos were taken in transit. All we know is they're gone, and without them we have no case. That boy comes from a very powerful family, and with power comes corruption."

My mother always tried to stay professional, but her voice cracked at the end of her words. I hung up the phone and stared at the ceiling.

Memo never told us what happened when they got back to Mexico City that day, but soon there were rumors around school that Javier from the Gates Institute had been found by the Toluca highway at daybreak with both his legs fractured. He'd been abducted by thugs while leaving a club late at night. They'd beaten him, stolen all his money, and left him there. There was no way to prove that it wasn't just a random mugging, but I knew it was no coincidence.

I met Elio for coffee after school on Friday. I'd told his secretary it was one more follow-up interview, but Elio never asked what was going on with the *ISM Observer* profile. Now, when we got together, all we did was talk. He'd taken me under his wing a little, and I could tell that he saw me as a foreign girl who could use a little help understanding the inner workings of the world she'd found herself in. Our "swimming lessons," I'd nicknamed these marathon caffeinated sessions.

"Javier is lucky that's all that happened to him," he said after I told him what had happened to Nina. "Memo comes from a family that can pull any string they want. His father keeps the lowest profile of anyone powerful in Mexico. There are so many reasons. He had also been very close to Amado Carillo-Fuentes, and what happened to Gustavo Amador? It might have been his personalized touch." Some people think it's yours, I thought. I wondered if the two of them had been friends only in appearance, a case of Elio having kept an enemy closer, or whether the speculation of his involvement in Gustavo's assassination was wrong. Or maybe it was a case where business interests and political pressures outweighed friendship. Elio didn't seem like a sociopath; I wanted to believe he had nothing to do with Manuel's father's murder, but I could never know for sure. I thought of how the fresas coped with assassinations and corruption that their parents might or might not be responsible for. They went to nightclubs, spent money, and looked the other way.

Elio always swore me to secrecy whenever he told me things that we both knew I really shouldn't know, but he'd come to trust me. Something grew between us, an unspoken bond, a friendship. It may have been unusual for a seventeen-year-old girl and a man in his sixties to have lunch or coffee, just chat and catch up, but talking with Elio felt natural. He seemed happy taking a fatherly place in my life, having a stand-in daughter figure, since his kids had moved out of the house years ago. "You have so much potential" was his favorite thing to say to me. It was a tired phrase, but it felt good coming from him.

The next week was Model United Nations. The mock U.N. was an ISM tradition, designed to teach us negotiation, diplomacy, and an appreciation for international relations. Student-council members handed out the forms on which we were to circle our preferred country and delegation. Big ones like "USA" and "Mexico" were typically reserved for seniors, along with the big issues—immigration policy and drug trafficking—the ones that tended to win the Model U.N. honors awards, but the old-timers at school got the good countries. I was Malta for Law of the Sea. Malta was a tiny country that I thought had little global significance, but then I found out that Law of the Sea was its number-one issue, so I had a ton of work to do for nothing. Arguments, position papers, articulation, and dress were all criteria for Model United Nations success, and I could forget about the dress part, since the Maltese didn't do burqas or sombreros. Everything would rest on my arguments, and it was the most complicated school project I'd encountered during my time at the otherwise academically breezy ISM. The future leaders of Mexico had to get good grades, after all, and the school basically handed those out to them. Fresa parents paid a hefty tuition to ensure their children's high achievement.

Nina wasn't in school the last day of Model U.N. week. In his orientation speech, Mr. Horney announced that missing closing debates would be punished with suspension, so I called her house during break. Lupe, the family's newer housekeeper, answered and said she wasn't sure where Nina was but the whole family had left in a rush and hadn't explained anything to her.

"You have no idea where they went?"

"*Ninguna idea, señorita,*" she repeated.

Thoughts on what could have happened flooded my head all through closing arguments. What if someone had threatened them and they had to leave the country? Could something have happened to Nina's father? I didn't hear my name when it was called, and Kai, representing Japan for the Security Council, told me later that he had to pinch me three times before I snapped out of my paranoid imaginings and noticed that Mr. Horney was calling me to the podium. I fumbled through a reiteration of my position paper's conclusion. I was maundering out of worry, and I could tell Mr. Horney wasn't impressed with my speech. I suspected that I wouldn't be winning any M.U.N. awards—Mr. Horney wouldn't care what the reasons for my imperfect articulation were. When I finished, I sneaked to the back of the room, and as the delegate from Panama stood to walk up to the podium, I ducked out. I didn't have to look far. Mr. Rothman's secretary told me that Nina was hurt and that the family was in the hospital across the street from ISM. The price for the school guards' *mordidas* had gone up as the value of the peso had gone down, and I spent a cool four hundred and fifty pesos—about forty-five dollars—to get out the gate. It was an entire week's allowance.

"Nina Rothman," I said to the receptionist at the Hospital Inglés. She scanned a computer screen. "I think she checked in this morning," I said.

"*Aquí está,*" she said. "*Recámara 401.*"

I paced while waiting for the elevator, pressing the button again and again. "That won't make it come any faster," I suddenly recalled saying to Sisley ten months earlier. I wished I had been wrong, that the elevator could sense my urgency. After what felt like ages, the double doors finally slid open and I jammed my finger on four and watched the numbers above the doors illuminate and go dark again with every passing floor: 1—2—3—*ding.*

"Are you family?" asked the nurse behind the desk. To lie or not to lie? "Because you must be family in order for me to grant you access to the psychiatric ward."

"I'm her sister."

The nurse glanced through a file. "She has only one sibling—and you do not look like *Reynaldo* Rothman," she said. "Unless young Naldo has visited plastic surgery in the two hours that have passed since I last saw him."

"Look, I'm her best friend. We're practically sisters. Please," I begged. "I have to see Nina." I dug around in the front pouch of my backpack and fished out the two hundred pesos I was supposed to use to pay Señor Flores, the gardener, that afternoon. I pressed them into the nurse's palm. But instead of the look of acceptance I anticipated, she got angry.

"I'm not taking your money, *chica*," she said. "Please leave."

"I'm sorry," I said, taken aback. No one I'd ever tried to bribe had refused. "Please, please, please let me see her. I'll do anything. Please."

The nurse's expression softened. She looked around the ward's reception area. No one else was around. "I'm giving you ten minutes," she whispered. "Go. And don't tell anybody. I was never here. I was in the bathroom."

"Thank you," I said. "Thank you so much."

I found the room down the hall to the left. Nina's parents were sitting on either side of her bed.

"How did you get in here?" her father asked.

"No one was at the nurse's station," I lied. "I just came in and heard your voices from the hallway."

"Only family is supposed to be allowed into the room," said Sonia.

Nina smiled weakly. "Hey you," she said.

"She wants me here, see?" I said to George and Sonia. "What happened, are you sick?"

"This isn't really a good time," said her father.

"No, Dad, let Mila stay. Can you guys go outside for a second?"

The parents looked at each other as if to say, "What can we do?"

"I'm going to the rest room," said Sonia.

"I guess I'll go get us some sodas," said George, and they walked out of the room.

"Looks like he's finally noticed there are some things Fendi bags can't fix, huh?" said Nina when they were out of earshot.

She didn't wait for me to answer. "I've been dying to get them out of here. All day they've been fussing, fussing, fussing. I don't think they're going to let me go back to ISM."

"Wait. Slow down. What happened to you?"

"I took some pills."

Even for Nina, this was over the top.

"What pills?"

"Tylenol. A whole bottle." She said it as if it were something she was proud of.

"Why would you want to kill yourself? When did you stop telling me what was going on?" I suddenly felt that my face was hot and wet and I realized I was crying.

"I wasn't trying to kill myself, silly."

"Right, because there's another reason to take a whole bottle of Tylenol."

"I wasn't. My dad made me eat a steak. He practically force-fed me, wouldn't let me leave the room until every last bite was down my throat. Then I had to go to the bathroom and he wouldn't let me because he was afraid I was going to throw it all up. There was a bottle of aspirin on the kitchen counter. I got a glass of water and turned around and downed them."

"That makes no sense."

"Let me finish. I handed the empty bottle to my father. We came here right away and got my stomach pumped. *That* was why. Of course I'd never try to kill myself. Fucking steak."

I said nothing for what felt like a very long time.

"But you *are* killing yourself."

"You know I'm a vegetarian, Mila," she snapped.

I would never know which the lie was, but it didn't matter anymore. Nina had gone over some edge I couldn't help bring her back from. Her psychological tailspin had led to either a suicide attempt or an eating disorder that was completely out of control. She couldn't talk about anything real, keeping her life to boys and clothes, and she'd never gotten help for manic-depression or kleptomania, or whatever what she had was named. When Nina got out of the hospital, she was sent to a psychiatrist and then directly to a strict boarding school with a treatment center in a tiny New England town.

I asked Manuel to meet me for coffee at Lugar de la Mancha the afternoon I said good-bye to Nina. I was almost surprised when he said he'd see me there at three-thirty. He'd become distant since his father died, and since I'd told him that Eliodoro Márquez de la Garza might be my father.

"Are you sad?" he asked.

"She was my best friend. Then again, she became a completely different person, or maybe it's who she was all along and I was too charmed by her to notice."

"She fell apart," he said. "Last year she was happy all the time, so energetic and funny."

"Sounds like a manic stage," I said, having done a lot of research on the subject since Kai first mentioned it. "It has an equally intense downside."

"Mila, I've missed you these past few weeks," he said.

"We keep coming back around, though."

"Like one of these days, *mi milagro,* you and I will get it right." He smiled at me, and I knew for sure that the person standing in front of me was my first real love.

~ ~ ~

I thought my mother might move back home, but she was still staying at Harvey's. She would wander in and out of the house, spending a few hours there at a time, and that was all. Manuel stayed over more often than she did. It didn't feel punishing anymore. It was more of a routine that we had fallen into: she'd drop off money for the week, pick up some clothes from her closet, or have a quick conversation about how I should make sure to pay Rosa and tip the water-delivery man. I had a feeling she was afraid that coming back would disturb our newfound balance.

"Things are getting very serious with Harvey," she said, explaining that it was a crucial moment in getting him to go through with the divorce.

"When he gets divorced, then will you move back in?" I asked.

"The next time I live in this house, Harvey will be joining us," she said. "You'll really like him, you'll see." I was nauseated by the thought.

"I think you're jumping into this too fast," I said.

"I'm the one who gives the advice, Milagro," she said.

At school, the fresas were preparing for the senior spring fashion show. The fashion show was a big deal at ISM, since whoever looked the best was likely to win Most Attractive in the yearbook and go down in history as the hottest person in the senior class and the best-looking in the whole student body by default. Catalina was spearheading the fashion-show committee this year, and at break one day all the seniors lined up to be runway models for a day, showing off the latest designer looks. For Catalina, Beatriz, and Katia, it wasn't much of a stretch. Betty and Andrea, the less attractive fresas, were talking about the rehearsals and what they would get to wear. Each pair of seniors, one girl and one boy, would represent a specific designer women's and men's spring collection. Kai scooped up Dolce & Gabbana right away, but the competition for Prada, Gucci, and Armani was ridiculous. For a second, I considered going to the back of the line and trying to get the brand-new Marc Jacobs samples, but I thought better of it and went out to the field for a cigarette. I searched the poolside for Manuel, but he wasn't there. The pool was deserted; every fresa was working on fashion-show administration. I couldn't imagine Manuel as a model. Despite his good looks, he'd never been a show-off, unlike most of his clique. Then I spotted him, behind the long picnic table in the courtyard, signing up members of the senior class for the first rehearsal.

"Why aren't you over there registering for the show?" someone behind me asked. I turned around and saw Alana, a petite blonde with long, thick, wavy hair, large, round blue eyes with heavy lids, and a beautiful wide smile, plump lips always painted a sultry red that not many girls our age could get away with. She was new to our class, recently transferred from France because her father was a French diplomat whose reassignment couldn't have come at a more inconvenient time for his daughter, forcing her to graduate at a new school in a different country. At least I'd arrived at the beginning of the year, I thought. Alana was refreshing, as she wasn't in the least intimidated by the fresas. She made fun of them, openly, calling them silly snobs and daddy's little girls.

"I have no desire to be in the fashion show," I said.

"You're not signing up for *the* event of the century?" she said, and winked.

Alana had been at ISM for only a couple of months, but she already had a reputation for being bold, contradicting teachers in classes, arguing. She had a fiery, outspoken attitude, which was unexpected, given her diminutive size. Her hair was tousled around her small features, accentuating her large eyes. Something about Alana said Trouble, and I was intrigued. Even though she was mouthy in class, unlike most aggressive teenagers she always had a good point, an angle no one had thought of about a book, another way around a partial-differential equation. Her looks and attitude made her a force for even the fresas to reckon with, though they called her a little Parisian princess and imitated her challenging demeanor in the bathroom between classes. It was the only time I'd ever seen Beatriz, Catalina, and Katia jealous of anybody.

"The fashion show isn't really my thing," I said. "I don't think I want to parade down the catwalk with Catalina and her friends."

"Do you want to come to the auditorium steps? I'm meeting Gabi up there for a smoke."

I looked over toward Manuel, who still had at least twenty people in his line. "Sure," I said. Gabi was in our English class, too, and a budding writer. I did my newspaper thing, but I couldn't hold a candle to her when it came to elegant prose and tightly woven stories. At nineteen, she'd finished her first short-story collection and our English teacher was helping her find a publisher for it. Gabi was a brilliant girl, but shy. She'd been a senior the previous school year, and hung out on the periphery of the popular fresas until she disappeared halfway through the year. She had arrived back at school to finish her final semester and graduate. I'd wondered why, since in international schools people who leave don't come back; you might see them years later, walking in the opposite direction from you while changing planes at the Frankfurt airport, but that's about it. One night, while trying to fall asleep, I remembered Nina's story about the pink-and-white hotel in Acapulco that rented pink-and-white jeeps and it occurred to me that she was the Gabi from the story, the one who had been assaulted. Though she still wore her leather Prada backpack and platform sandals, she didn't seem like a fresa anymore; she'd sat alone on the soccer field during lunch reading, until she and Alana discovered each other and became inseparable. Within a matter of days, we became Alana, Mila, and Gabi.

Since Nina left for boarding school, I realized that I didn't have any real girlfriends. The last few months of high school were marked by finding out the difference between real friends and those who had been faking it all along. I wished I'd found Gabi and Alana sooner, but the best things always seemed to come along at the most inconvenient of times.

I watched the fashion show with the two of them. Even though we were averse to the thought of it, we couldn't stand to miss witnessing the big event. We stood in back, drinking too much champagne and analyzing the fresas as they paraded their outfits and professionally done hair and makeup. They did look good up there; Manuel, especially, in a charcoal-gray Armani suit and silk paisley tie. The event was held in a real venue, complete with a catwalk, and the music and lighting were designed by a group that worked on Fashion Week in New York City and Paris. For a second, I regretted not joining in. Then I reconsidered and went back to the champagne bar with Gabi and Alana to grab another glass.

We were standing in line with our empty flutes when the ground began to shake. The champagne bottles clinked together on the table as they danced like the balloon boys at my familiar Reforma intersection. "Earthquake!" someone shouted, and I turned around to see Catalina fall off the runway. The organization of earthquake drills went out the window as everybody ran, pushing and shoving, to get outside.

It was a 5.7. When the rumbling ended, everybody filed back inside and the fashion show went on as if nothing had happened to interrupt it. Except for Catalina, who went across the street to the hospital for a badly twisted ankle. The earthquake, when it finally came, was far from the big one I'd always anticipated. It was a shock, a rumble, undulation, a fall, and then it was over, the earth steadying itself again, repositioned.

I went to find Manuel afterward. He was in line at the bar, looking a little sweaty in a black suit after five outfit changes.

"You were the hottest," I said, coming up behind him and wrapping my arms around his waist.

"Thanks. I wish you'd been in the show," he said.

"I don't." I wrinkled up my nose and smiled. "Hey, do you want to come swimming at Lomas Country Club with me tomorrow afternoon? My mom wants to go."

"Of course," he said. Manuel kissed me and went off to join his friends for the after-party.

I went out with Gabi and Alana, to El Hijo del Cuervo in Coyoacán. The three of us sat around a tiny round table and crossed our legs on the barstools. Alana ordered three tequila shots with *sangrita* and we quickly licked salt, threw back the shots, sucked lime, and sipped the spicy tomato liquid that eased the liquor burn.

"My boyfriend is so controlling," said Alana. "He wants to meet me later, and I'm going to have to make up a story to stay out. Maybe I'll say I'm staying at my grandmother's house." Alana had one pair of Mexican grandparents, on her mother's side. Her mother had moved to France to study as a teenager and then stayed, meeting her father, becoming a French citizen, and settling down. Alana spoke Spanish fluently, but she always said that she felt a hundred percent French.

"How did you meet that guy, anyway?" asked Gabi.

"He's the son of family friends. We've been together on and off for five years."

"So you traveled a lot between here and France?" I asked.

"I spent summers at my *abuelita*'s house. And winter breaks, too. I was living here half the time anyway, so Federico and I were dating as much as we weren't."

"And he's controlling?" I asked.

She nodded. I couldn't picture the fiery Alana listening to what some guy told her to do. Everyone has a weak spot someplace, I thought.

We ordered another round of shots, and then tequila sunrises. I craved a Splash, but I'd learned my lesson about mixing different types of liquors at my first *comida* earlier in the year, when I drank rum, tequila, and vodka and threw up in a garbage can at the fancy after-school lunch party that didn't serve any lunch and was a veiled excuse for getting drunk in the afternoon.

"Where did you go when you left ISM last year, Gabi?" I asked. It was a casual question on my part, but she shrank into her shoulders, her eyes diving toward the floor.

"I was in a psychiatric hospital," she finally said. "It was pretty awful there. One girl pulled out all her hair strand by strand. Another put vegetables in all the pillowcases in the dormitory. I spent every second just trying to get out."

"Why were you there?" Alana asked.

"I cut my wrists in the bathtub one night. I just lost it."

"But you're so smart, Gabi," I said. "I can't imagine—"

"That could have been part of the problem," she said. "But what set it off was this vacation I took last year with Tomás, Nina, and some of the other fresas."

"What happened?" Alana asked.

I said nothing, pretending that I didn't already know.

"I got assaulted by a gang while I was driving one of those stupid pink-and-white jeeps in Acapulco," said Gabi. "I should have known better. I might as well have been wearing a sign around my neck that said 'Tourist.' I've always been a nervous person, and that whole thing just put me over the edge."

I didn't press her for the rest of the story. I understood why she didn't want to talk about it. Gabi seemed wholesome, intelligent, the kind of girl Maggie would want to be my best friend. When I thought about it, though, all of the stories she wrote were dark. I remembered one about a house burning down and the main character's sister going mad, turning into an apparition of smoke that rose from the chimney and took flight. The teacher pointed out Gabi's brilliant religious symbolism. Her parents were devout Catholics and she was raised in the church. I wondered if that had played into her desire to kill herself after what happened.

"How are you doing now?" Alana asked.

"I'm better. I'd never try anything like that again."

"Promise," I said.

"I'm on such strong antidepressants, I've never been so productive in my life," she said, and smiled. I wondered how Nina was faring at boarding school. In my mental image of her, she was still emaciated, her stomach slightly puffy from anorexia and bulimia. I wondered if she was being medicated at the boarding school, and why Maggie had never thought of that as an option for me earlier in the year, instead of keeping me here after my rebelliousness with Tyler and psychedelic drugs. Everything I'd done, it occurred to me, was possibly as much an expression of depression stemming from the move, followed by what happened with Dave, as it was typical teenage angst and the freedom that came with living in Mexico City.

After the bar, Alana went to call Federico to tell him that she was staying at her grandmother's. She returned in a panic.

"He said he stopped by my grandmother's earlier and she said I was out with you," she told us. "He's pissed. I told him to meet me at the VIPS by my house."

"So you have to go?" I said.

"Well, he refused to meet me, but I said I was going to sit there until he came. It's open twenty-four hours."

"What if he doesn't show up?" said Gabi.

"He will," she said. Alana kissed us both on the cheek, and I smelled her crisp Eternity perfume. She spun around, her red overcoat flipping up on the bottom as she moved, stalking across the plaza like a cat that you couldn't pick up no matter how many treats you had in your hand.

"Isn't it strange how Alana is so outspoken but this boyfriend controls her life?" said Gabi.

"Everyone has an Achilles' heel," I said. "He's obviously hers."

"Depression is definitely mine," said Gabi. "So what's yours?"

"My greatest weakness is"—I stopped to think—"perpetual curiosity."

"Like?"

"I developed a weakness for hallucinogens. And I was never supposed to know who my father is, but I tracked him down under the pretense of working on my newspaper column, which was very vindictive. Now we're sort of friends, but I still haven't brought it up with him, and I'm not sure if I ever can."

"He doesn't know who you are?" she asked. I told her the story, in bits and pieces, right up to my mother's confession.

"No wonder you have the urge to escape reality," she said.

"You think that's why?"

"After tons of therapy, I think I can say, clearly. That's a really screwed-up life story, Mila."

Was it? Through everything, I'd never thought of it that way. It was just how things had turned out.

"I think there are other reasons, too," I said. "I've been following my mother around the world my whole life, constantly in a state of up-rootedness." We were quiet for a minute, watching people stumble out of Hijo del Cuervo.

"So he's here in Mexico, your father?" she asked.

I nodded.

"Would I recognize his name?"

"You can't tell anyone," I said. When I told her, she looked surprised and changed the subject.

When the mail arrived the next day, there was a thick envelope from Harvard University. Maggie was home that afternoon, having lunch with me. She screamed and jumped up and down in the kitchen, where I'd sat down to open the package.

"This must be a mistake," I said.

"Milagro! You did this. You deserve it."

"But I didn't work that hard."

"You didn't notice because you're always too wrapped up in every-thing. You've done amazingly in high school—well, until we came here, but still. Your grades, and your activities—"

"Maybe it was my essay." I'd written about trekking through the pyramids of Egypt with Maggie on one of our trips. It was mostly de-scriptive, but I'd tried to carry a story line filled with the symbolism of women traveling alone.

"Whatever it was, that admissions committee saw what I see in you. I wish you could see it in yourself," she said, putting her arm around me. "I'm so proud of you."

April 27

Dear Nora,

I know you never replied to my last letter because you probably never want to speak to me again. But I wanted to let you know that I'm going to Harvard next year. Guess I made it after all! Let me know what's happening with you?

Mila

Maggie and I picked Manuel up in our rickety red Volkswagen and drove to the Lomas Country Club. He and I were both hungover. We spread our beach towels out on the lawn by the pool and watched little kids taking diving lessons. They propelled themselves like baby rockets off the high board, fearless in the way only young children are before they learn to be afraid. I squinted in the sun and saw my mother's head bobbing up and down as she swam laps.

"I got into Harvard," I said. I suddenly wondered if I'd see Elio's daughter, Daniela, there. I knew I would recognize her if I did.

"Congratulations." Manuel rolled onto my towel, grabbed me, and held me in a tight hug.

"Did you decide where you're going?" I asked.

"I got into the Ibero. But I also got into the engineering program at MIT."

"I thought you would. You want to go there, right?" I prodded.

"Everyone who doesn't stay in Mexico to study goes to Boston. MIT would be amazing, but I can't leave my mother alone after what's happened." I was stunned silent. We could end up being neighbors and it wouldn't have to be good-bye after all, but Manuel seemed to have other plans.

"I'll miss you very much," he said.

"What?"

"I'm staying in Mexico."

I chose to ignore this, almost believing that if I didn't hear it, it wasn't happening.

"How was the after-party?" I asked instead.

"Fun. I wish you'd been there. Did you have a nice time with Gabi and Alana?"

"Yeah. Did you know Gabi left school last year for a mental hospital?"

"Something happened to her in Acapulco. Everybody knows."

"I should have guessed as much." At ISM, everyone eventually found out everyone else's secrets.

We ordered Agua de Jamaica, a burgundy punch that tasted of flowers, and swam a few lazy laps before lying out on our towels, exhausted.

We were leaving the club when Manuel realized he'd forgotten his gym bag inside a locker.

"Can we drive back?" he asked my mom. "I'll just run in and get it."

"Of course," said Maggie.

When we parked the car, all the lights at the club were out. It looked as if it had shut down in the few moments since we'd left.

"What, did they close in the last five minutes?" I wondered aloud as we approached the entrance.

A man dressed in black came over to us.

"Excuse me, señor," said Maggie. "We need to go back in—my daughter's boyfriend forgot his—"

She stopped short and her face went white. The man was holding a long black machine gun. He used it to point past the reception area.

"Get inside," he commanded. Time stalled. I felt like I was in a movie, a slow-motion scene. This isn't real, I thought. This isn't happening, and it definitely isn't happening to *me.*

Beyond him, everyone who had been in the club was lying on the floor, hands on their heads.

"*Mierda,*" whispered Manuel.

"Give me your wallet, jewelry, watches, and car keys," the man said. He held out a bag and we dropped everything in.

The three of us walked over to where he pointed and got down on the floor.

"You," he said to Manuel. "Stay here. You two, come with me."

My mother squeezed my hand. We went to him.

"Please don't hurt us," my mother said. "We gave you what you asked for."

"I want to see where your car is," he said.

I prayed that he wasn't going to kidnap us. This could be it, I thought. And if it was, what would be the meaning of *that*? That all signs lead to an impractical death?

"You're not going to want it," said Maggie. "It's a piece of junk."

"It was a smart idea to get that car," I mumbled as we followed him out.

"Shh!" she hissed.

"There it is," said Maggie. "See? It's worth nothing. You can have it if you want it, of course."

"Get inside," the man commanded. "I want you to undress. And maybe your daughter, too."

I would have gagged, but he was holding a machine gun. This wasn't even comparable to what I'd experienced with Dave.

"Get in the car," he repeated. Then Maggie shocked me.

"No," she said. "I will not."

"Mom—"

She waved her hand at me in a gesture of "Shush."

"That boy in there, the one who was with us, well, his father is the chief of police," she lied. "And he's on his way to pick the boy up. I just wanted to let you know before you tried anything."

The man looked hesitant. I just wanted to be somewhere else, anywhere. I thought things were going to get ugly, but then he lowered the gun.

"Get back inside and get on the floor," he said. The '89 Volkswagen Golf was too shitty for even a bandido to steal.

The club was held hostage for an hour longer, then the bandidos left and people gradually trickled out, some in shock, others more exasperated than anything, as though they'd been standing in a really long line at the bank.

And so ended another day in the Lomas Country Club, Mexico, D.F. I had nightmares for weeks, which, Sandie Doone explained to me, was a symptom of post-traumatic stress disorder.

"You were very, very lucky," she said. "Your mother could have gotten you all shot behaving that way."

"She's so used to being outspoken and in control. I guess she had the fight response."

"That's right, fight or flight," said Sandie, looking pleased. "You've been doing your psych homework."

"When it came to me and my mother, though, it was always flight."

"I noticed the avoidance tactics between the two of you. How is that going now?"

"Better, actually," I said. "Much better lately."

Sandie nodded slowly. "I knew it would happen sometime. You two have only had each other. Funny how mutual dependence often drives people apart."

Maggie and I went back to the country club the next day to ask if the police had arrested anyone in connection with the robbery and, undeterred by the holdup, to take a swim. The woman at the front desk just looked my mother up and down blankly.

"Señora, I have no idea what you are talking about," she said, as if it had never even happened. Typical Mexico City.

TWELVE

Senior Trip

May was the month the seniors counted down the days to all year, because right after the Cinco de Mayo festivities came Senior Trip Week. Each year the student council organized a weeklong, alcohol-fueled party that resembled a super-upscale version of spring break. Senior trip was in Ixtapa, and the entire Sheraton was rented out to our school. It was, like everything else, unsupervised, and the last opportunity to party with the class before we'd all go off on our respective paths and possibly never see one another again; that is, except for the tightly woven fresa clique, who would all go to the same Mexican universities and end up as colleagues at the highest echelons of business, government, and industry one not-too-far-off day.

"Do you guys want to be roommates on the trip?" I asked Gabi and Alana as we sat on the pool steps the day we had to fill out our hotel registration forms. They looked at each other uncomfortably.

"We're not going," said Alana.

"Why not?" I asked.

"We just don't feel connected to this class," said Gabi. "It's like a spirit thing, and we were saying how we can't wait to finish the year and get the hell out of here."

"But we could hang out," I said. "It doesn't have to be as a group with the whole class."

"You have Manuel," said Gabi. "It's going to be all romantic for you. We'd just end up in the clubs and on the beach surrounded by fresas."

"And Federico doesn't want me to go," said Alana. Gabi and I rolled our eyes at each other.

I turned in my hotel registration with the roommate selection lines left blank. Whatever they do with me is fine, I thought. I'll be spending all my time on the trip with Manuel anyway.

The evening before we left, Manuel asked me to meet him at Lugar de la Mancha.

The night was a gorgeous one, with a scattering of stars shining through the smog. Manuel looked incredible in all black and his glasses instead of contacts.

"You look like an avant-garde painter," I told him.

"Listen to me," he said. "I think we need to break up."

"Okay, fine, you don't look like an avant-garde painter. I thought you'd take it as a compliment."

"I'm not joking, Mila. We're moving away from each other," he said. "What else are we supposed to do?"

"You're serious?" My heart was up in my throat. "You could go to MIT. We could still be in the same city."

"That's what I tried to tell you. After my father's death, the odds are I'm staying in Mexico. I wish you could stay here with me, but you can't give up Harvard, and we need to do this now so it's not as painful to move on," he said, as though he were approaching the situation logically. I thought back to that night when Tyler dumped Sisley after finding out that she was moving to Africa, and how Karim and I broke up when I learned that I was moving to Mexico. But I wanted Manuel to be more than the past.

"Can't we at least wait and see how things pan out?" I said, feeling more desperate than I ever had in my entire life.

"I don't want you to leave sad. You should say good-bye to Mexico with a smile on your face, not crying because of me."

"Why don't we make the most of the time we have, then? Things are so good, why take a wrecking ball to it now?"

"You're going to meet so many people in Cambridge," he said, cupping my chin in his hands. Saltwater moistened my eyes. "I'd only be holding you back."

"And what about spending senior trip together?"

"I wish we could," he said. "But it would only make it harder to separate."

I was still crying, but now I was getting angry, too. I wondered if he had ulterior motives for choosing this moment to break up with me.

"You don't know when something's worth fighting for even if it's right in fucking front of you." I stood up and walked away from the outdoor table.

"You may be mad now, but you'll thank me when you're getting on the plane," he called to my receding back.

I spun around and yelled, "A plane you could be getting on, too."

I ran the four blocks to my house fighting back the tears. When I turned the corner onto Esplanada off Reforma, I got a strange feeling that I couldn't shake. Something was wrong, something else. I had a weird, fleeting premonition that my mother's car was going to be in the driveway. I thought she was at Harvey's; she was never home at night. I turned the key in the gate, and there it was: the little red Volkswagen.

"What the fuck?" I said out loud.

I unbolted the door and ran up the stairs. I heard a wailing sound coming from Maggie's room, and rushed in to find her sprawled on the down comforter, still wearing her clothes. A suitcase was on the floor next to the bed. She was crying like an abandoned kitten.

"Mom," I said.

"Milagro, he told me to leave. I don't know why. We were having a regular evening and he just lost it and told me I had to pack my things and go." She let out another sob.

"You didn't have a fight?"

"No, nothing. We were going to bed. It was in the middle of the night."

"Manuel just broke up with me."

"Just now?" she sobbed.

"Ten minutes ago." I felt strangely peaceful for reasons I couldn't quite explain. "We're both without men now, huh? So let me guess, you're going to move back in?"

She kept bawling. I imagined the scene that would have occurred if Manuel hadn't broken up with me, if he were waiting for me outside instead:

"What happened?" he would ask when I got back downstairs.

"She's hysterical. Harvey broke up with her in the middle of the night and told her to pack all her stuff and leave."

"I knew I didn't like that guy," he would say.

"Neither did I. I guess you can't sleep over tonight."

"That's okay. There will be plenty of other nights." Then he'd kiss me. I would smell the spicy cologne on his neck. "You're my miracle," he would say.

I lay down next to my mother in the dark. She turned toward me and reached her arm around my shoulders. I nestled into her warm body, returning the hug. Boyfriends had driven us apart. Now, for once, they had forced us together.

"Mom," I said. "Look at us, we're pathetic!" For a second, we laughed through our tears.

After Harvey kicked my mother out, he disappeared, just stopped showing up for work. Maggie made me go with her to his house to look in the windows to see if we could see him or any of his stuff. It was so creepy, spying on him. I was a little scared he might have killed himself and we would find a body, see it lying on the floor or hanging from the ceiling. But we didn't. Instead, we saw that his house was basically empty. As if he'd fled. Later, back at work, my mother found out that he'd gone back to Wisconsin to live with his wife and daughter. Harvey had quit the Foreign Service, just like that, and disappeared without a trace. My mother moved back into our house and my long days of uninterrupted freedom came to an end. I would never admit it to her, but I was relieved.

Senior trip couldn't have come at a worse time, but I already had my plane ticket. The entire class gathered at Benito Juárez International Airport for our chartered flight to Ixtapa-Zihuatanejo. Only Memo and my two girlfriends were missing. At the last minute, Memo couldn't come; his father's body had been found in the trunk of a car. When I heard the news, I realized exactly how accustomed I had grown to Mexico City over the past year. I reacted more with a feeling of sadness for Memo than with the shock I used to feel on hearing that a classmate's father had been assassinated. I hadn't seen Memo around much after Valle and wondered whether he and Nina exchanged letters or phone calls.

"Mexicana vuelo 408 a Ixtapa-Zihuatanejo" came the announcement over the PA system. The gate was full of ISM seniors, ready for a week of nonstop partying, sunning, dancing and drinking on the beach, and world-class clubbing.

We landed an hour later and piled into vans headed for the Sheraton Ixtapa. I stood in line to get my key from the reception desk and wondered who my roommates would be.

"Recámara mil quinientos veinte y cinco," said the pretty dark-eyed receptionist. "Room 1525." I hit fifteen in the elevator, which faced out of a glass wall toward the ocean. The surf pounded the shore and the dark sky was filled with a bulbous moon, its light eclipsed by wispy gray-black night clouds. I turned the key in the lock and pushed open the heavy door. There they were: my roommates.

Mirela and Dani were seniors I'd never spoken with before. They were also a couple. Mirela was from Brazil and a star photographer, her art perpetually hanging in hallway display cases at school. Her girlfriend, Dani, was a shy, quiet Swedish girl with boy-short blond hair who was a computer genius. She had a part-time job doing IT for ISM's administration. I'd never heard her speak before.

"Oh, did they give you the key to our room by mistake?" asked Mirela.

"No, I'm supposed to be the third roommate."

"But we requested a double," whispered Dani. Of course they did. I was an intruder on somebody else's romantic getaway. Then I noticed that the room had only one queen-size bed.

"Fuck," I said out loud.

"Well, yeah, we kind of wanted to," said Mirela, laughing at her own joke as Dani blushed.

I went back down to reception, but they wouldn't move me to another room. There was no space left and the hotel had run out of cots.

"I guess we'll all share the bed together," said Mirela when I got back and told them I'd had no luck.

"I'll try to sleep somewhere else if I can."

"We all got ripped off," said Dani.

"I'm going out," I said. "I'll be back late."

I went to the hotel bar, but no one was there. I ordered a *daiquiri de fresa* and wished it were some potion that would magically turn me into Alice in Wonderland, and I'd prance away in Prada heels and join my fabulous friends. I sipped slowly through the straw.

"All your friends went to the club on the beach," the bartender said when he came to take my glass.

"Thanks," I said. I got up and walked through the pool area, out onto the sand. I walked down the beach alone until I heard the throbbing bass of electronic music. Colorful, spinning lights came into view and the sound became more complex as its other elements came within hearing range. I entered the club from the beach and looked around for familiar faces.

Manuel was dancing with Katia, and Beatriz came out of the bath-room with Cristina. Tomás, the two Jorges, and Gabriel were trying to get girls to dance on the table. They were up in the roped-off VIP area surrounded by bottles of top-shelf vodka and champagne chilling in silver buckets. I went over to the rope and waved at Gabriel.

"*Hola,* Mila!" he shouted, drunk. "Good to see you." He led me in and gave me a glass of cranberry vodka. I danced a little, but no one really seemed to care much that I was there. Manuel smiled and gave a slight wave in my direction, but then Cristina came over to him, put her arms around his neck, and whispered something in his ear that made him laugh. Maybe Beatriz, Catalina, and Katia had been right that night at Aguila y Sol, and I was too absorbed in Manuel to pay atten-tion. Gabriel noticed me noticing and walked over.

"I want you to meet somebody," he shouted above the music. He led me to an adjacent table.

"Mila, this is my brother Alejandro."

"Nice to meet you," he said.

"You, too."

Alejandro was about to graduate from Princeton and had come back to relive senior trip with his brother. He was attractive, but I was an-noyed that Gabriel had pawned me off on him this way.

"I love being back here," he shouted. "It's like being on my own se-nior trip all over again."

"Yeah, I'm having a good time, except the hotel messed up my roommate situation and I'm in a room with one bed and two other girls."

"That doesn't sound so bad," he said, winking.

"They're lesbians," I said. "A couple. It's pretty awkward, because I know they want to be alone."

"I'm staying at a friend's vacation house," he said. "There's an extra room there if you'd prefer."

"And you really think I'm supposed to believe you about my staying in the extra bedroom?"

"Gabriel is my little brother," he said, as though that explained something.

"I'll stick with the lesbian couple, but thanks."

"Suit yourself." He shrugged. "But at least have dinner with me tomorrow. I'll take you to the lighthouse restaurant."

"No funny stuff?" I said.

"Not unless you find something funny about a good meal and a nice view."

I knocked before entering the hotel room, and Mirela shouted, "It's okay, come on in." They were in pajamas watching a movie in bed. I scooted in next to Dani so I was on one edge, she was in the middle, and Mirela was on the other side. I fell asleep and woke up at some point during the night to the sound of stifled moans, but I didn't open my eyes.

On the beach the next day, the fresa girls tanned in a line, sipping from bottles of Corona Light and spritzing each other with spray-on oil that smelled of coconuts. There was a party on the beach all afternoon, with stages set up for pop-star performances and drinking contests sponsored by a big rum company. I saw Manuel and Gabriel playing beach volleyball with a bunch of guys and moved my towel to a spot out of sight. I bobbed around in the ocean for a long time before heading over to the big party to see what the fuss was about.

I felt a tap on my shoulder. I turned around and saw Alejandro, his swim trunks showing off a toned abdomen. "Let's get a Coco Loco," he said.

We sipped a rum drink straight from the coconut shell and listened to a Colombian pop star who had specifically arranged a stop on her Latin America tour for this occasion, her long curly hair falling loosely down to her waist. We stayed on the beach until late afternoon.

"Come on, let's go get ready so we can catch the sunset from the restaurant," said Alejandro.

The dining room was at the top of an old lighthouse on a point where the view was straight out over the ocean, the blue horizon visible in every direction.

"I'm getting us a nice bottle of white wine," he said.

"I drink red."

"I can't believe I'm back here."

"Why's that?" I asked.

"I feel like it was only last week that I was with my own class, that we were the seniors. And now my little brother is graduating from ISM and I've been married and divorced."

"Really? To who?"

"Beatriz's older sister Martina. We married right out of high school and I went to work for her father, buying and selling real estate."

"I thought you went to Princeton?"

"That was actually seven years later. I'm twenty-five. I know it's old to be finishing university, but I had a much different life before now. Believe me, it all goes by so fast."

"I think time passes too slowly."

"I want to hear you say that in five years," he said.

The *mesero* came and Alejandro ordered a bottle of Chianti and a shrimp cocktail.

"*Y para la señorita?*"

"I'll do the ceviche," I told him in Spanish. I took a nervous sip of my ice water and reached over for the bread basket.

"My brother said you date Manuel," said Alejandro.

"Dated. Past tense, unfortunately."

"I knew him when he was a little baby. He's going places, that boy."

"What are you, his grandfather?" I joked.

"Why did you break up?"

"He broke up with me. It's simple, really. He's staying in Mexico and I'm going to Boston."

"I thought he got into MIT."

"He did. He's not going."

"Well, it's his loss." Alejandro leaned into his palms, his elbows jutting out in my direction on the table. "Tell me all about *your* life."

"How long've you got?" I smiled, and the room around me exhaled.

Afterward, we went to Christine's, the best club in Ixtapa, to dance with everyone else. After being there for a while, I was bored.

"Let's go swim in the ocean," I said to Alejandro.

We left the club and ran down to the shore. He stopped where the waves slapped the sand, but I kept going, running, pushing against the tide. Then I dived under, headfirst. When I came up, he was swimming beside me.

"This is really cooling me off," he said.

The water was black, with splashes of moonlight, like the negative of an Impressionist painting. We bobbed in the waves, sometimes swallowing saltwater, and laughing, the sea lapping our ears like an attention-hungry puppy.

"I want to kiss you right now," he said.

I remembered that first time in the Acapulco bay, with Manuel.

"I'm getting cold," I said.

"You want to get out?"

I nodded.

"All right, then. Let's go get changed."

We stopped at my room first. Dani and Mirela were out. I dried off and changed quickly in the bathroom. Then we went to Alejandro's house down the strip, where he put on fresh clothes. We walked back down the beach, the pounding music growing louder as we neared the club.

When we got back, people were whispering and Manuel was giving me dirty looks. I went over to him and asked why.

"Everyone knows why," he said. "You left with Alejandro hours ago; now you're back and both showered and changed."

"Oh my God," I said. "No, we didn't . . ."

He looked angrier than I'd ever seen him. "Save it, Mila," he said, and walked back to his friends at the table. I followed.

"But we're not even together," I said. "You broke up with me."

"I did it so we wouldn't be hurt later," he said. "You had to go and hurt me now."

"And you're not involved with anyone on this trip."

"I'm just having a good time with my friends. Even if I were, I wouldn't go rubbing it in your face."

"I'm having a good time with Alejandro because he's a nice guy. It's not as if there's anyone else here for me to hang out with. All we did was swim in the ocean with our clothes on, and we had to go change."

"Right, like the reason you were kissing another guy in that club that time was because *I* was only using you for sex. You don't have to become your mother, Mila. It's your choice."

"Fuck you, Manuel. I can't believe you'd even say that to me."

I left the club without telling Alejandro. I went back to the room and fell into a restless sleep. I never should have come here, I thought. I avoided everyone for the rest of the week, which ended up as a blur of tequila sunrises, loud music, and fresas in the sun. I slept from the time the plane lifted into the clouds until the only evidence of senior trip was a dark tan and lighter streaks in my burgundy hair.

When I got back, there was a note from my mother on the kitchen counter. She had to go to Cancún to help a lawyer from Texas figure out how to get money back for some investors who'd bought a brand-new condo building that was destroyed by a hurricane and she would be back in four days. I called Gabi and Alana and invited them over. The three of us were in a partying mood. It was late spring, we'd all gotten into schools we never dreamed we would be accepted to—Gabi was going to Stanford, Alana to Yale—it was a week until prom and graduation, and there was nothing left to do but celebrate and enjoy Mexico City's freedoms before we found ourselves in a country where we would be able to drink and dance only at house parties, probably frat parties, and all we'd get was foamy keg beer that tasted like piss. I wanted to squeeze all the excitement I could out of the next two weeks. Two weeks. It was all I had left in Mexico City. Before the girls came over, I colored my hair a rich shade of chestnut brown; it would match the New England fall and my new academic world.

I took the bottle of Absolut I'd bought that afternoon out of my bag and brought it down to the kitchen to mix with juice. I carried the three cocktails back to my room and we sat Indian style on the brown carpet, the dark wail of Portishead playing on the stereo.

"Let's go to Pervert Lounge," said Alana.

"That sounds fun," said Gabi. She produced some pills from the pocket of her jean jacket.

"What's that?" I asked.

"Prozac," she said, cracking them open and pouring the white powder on a hand mirror.

"We can get coke if you want," I said.

"No, you have to try this. It's great." She looked up at us. "What? It's fine. It's my prescription."

And I could use it, I thought. I'd been depressed enough over Manuel, I rationalized. Seeing him snorting coke after his father's death was disconcerting; I realized I hadn't done any drugs since Valle de Bravo and was losing my taste for the mind-altering substances I'd briefly become enamored with. Tonight, though, I was feeling restless. The lines burned intensely going up, and the Prozac made me feel buzzy and edgy. I couldn't sit still.

"Let's go," I said. Dancing would give me something to focus on, something to do until the unpleasantness wore off. We got into Alana's car. I suggested that we stop and buy some pot. I wanted to relax. Alana followed my direction to a dealer's house, a higher-up-the-food-chain dealer who supplied the ones at Las Islas.

"He prefers that I come alone, so drive to the VIPS on the corner and I'll meet you there," I told them.

I'd only been here once before, with Tyler. I remembered it was the only time I'd ever seen him looking nervous on the job; he didn't usually go straight to the source. The dealer's house had two doorbells: a regular one on the gate, and the one you were supposed to press if you were there to make a purchase. A thin cable ran up a tree from behind some bushes, and the electronic doorbell was attached to the back of the tree. It was still there. I pressed it, and he buzzed me in.

The guy looked different from the way I remembered him, taller or something. There was a fat man sitting at a table. They'd been playing dominoes.

"What are you getting?" the dealer asked me.

"I'll take *dos cientos.* Do you have mescaline or anything?"

"I have cocaine."

"I guess I'll get some for later, for my friends."

"Resell?"

"I don't do that. I just give it to them. I'm not really feeling it tonight, you know? But people sometimes ask, so I'll get a gram." There goes my whole week's allowance, I thought. Oh well, it'll be worth it.

He took out the goods, and I took out the cash. But then something went horribly wrong. The man pulled out handcuffs.

"You're under arrest."

Before I realized what was happening, my hands were behind my back.

"What did I do?" I uttered the subtle bribery-request line Tyler had made me rehearse earlier in the year: *"No hay otra manera de hacerlo?"* "Isn't there another way to do this?"

"You're under arrest for buying with the intent to distribute," the large man said as he rose to his feet.

"Wait. I have money. I can get lots of money."

"We're not cops, *chica. Somos los Federales."*

No wonder I thought the drug dealer looked different. It wasn't him at all. They'd arrested him and they were trying to get the people who worked for him in distribution.

"You don't understand, I don't do this. My mother works at the American Embassy."

"How embarrassing for her," the thin officer said to the fat one.

Mexican jail. Guilty until proven innocent.

"I'm supposed to move to Boston in a week," I said. "I'm going to Harvard."

"Tell the judge that," the fat cop said.

I was shaking, tears streaming silently down my face. I wondered what Gabi and Alana would do. They would have to do something when I didn't come back—report me missing, wait there all night, try to call my mother. . . .

"Do you have ID on you?" the thin cop asked.

I shook my head.

"What are you doing going around Mexico City without an ID?" Without waiting for an answer, he said, "Come on," and led me out to the car, the other officer following.

Drip . . . drip . . . drip . . .

In the cell there was a watermark on the ceiling. Maybe if I said it was a Virgen de Guadalupe apparition they would let me go. But it didn't look like Guadalupe. It looked like asbestos.

I couldn't tell what time it was because there were no windows and the fluorescent light in the room was always on: an exercise in sleep deprivation. It was a small lit box with a bench and a steel toilet in the corner. The door had no window.

When I woke up, I had no idea how much time had passed. I'd never owned a watch, and if I had they would have taken it away. I was trapped, alone in a cage. Everything I had, everything in store for me, was vanishing under the harsh fluorescent light. Everything looked raw and ugly beneath it. I picked at a bit of chipped black nail polish on my thumb. I thought about Manuel. I thought about my mother, about time and how fleeting it was. After a while, my thoughts started turning bizarre: I am a chameleon. I am fluid. I change. I run.

I realized how it was that people in solitary confinement went insane. I'd barely even been in there. I tried to imagine how it would feel after years and years. I couldn't.

Then a real *milagro* happened. Someone unlocked the door. A prison peon in a brown uniform with a badge.

"*Puedes ir,*" he said. "You can go."

"Where?"

"I don't know, home. Wherever it is you came from."

"What about the judge?"

His voice grew exasperated. "Look, *niña*. Don't you understand that go means go? You don't question it. *Entiendes?*"

They gave me back my wallet and keys, and I left. It was very early in the morning, the sun just creeping up, the sky that deep shade of purple I knew only from acid trips when I'd been up all night. I walked down the street with no idea where I was or what neighborhood I was in, but I didn't care, and after the little room I wasn't scared. They'd let me go. I picked up a newspaper and looked at the date; I had been locked up less than two nights, which meant that Maggie was still—I thanked the universe—away. I found a taxi *sitio* when the sun was already bright and cutting through the smog and picked up a cab. It couldn't have been my mother who'd gotten me out of there. Even if she weren't in Cancún, the most she could have done was bring me Doritos and Twinkies and magazines. It was somebody else who found the right person to pay or ask for a favor.

I called Elio as soon as it was a decent hour in the morning.

"Thank you," I said when he came on the line.

"For what?" he asked.

"I don't know why else they would have opened the door and let me walk out. How did you know I was in trouble?"

"Your friend Gabi seemed to know somehow that we were familiar. Her father's a friend of mine."

No wonder Gabi had gotten all quiet when I'd told her about Eliodoro.

"I was so stupid. I almost ruined my whole . . . everything," I said.

"Someone has to make sure you don't."

"Do you know I'm supposed to be leaving for Harvard at the end of the month?"

"You picked an ideal time to get into trouble," he joked. Then his voice turned serious. "I would say something about the fact that you were trying to buy drugs, but that's not really my place, is it?"

"Elio, I want to ask you something."

"Yes, Mila?"

"Where did your wife get those earrings, the ones with the *milagros*?"

There was silence on the other end of the line.

"What kind of a strange question is that?"

"One I'd like you to answer."

More silence.

"Let me think," he said. "I was appointed to the cabinet, and then Laura and I went to the beach—"

"Playa del Carmen?"

I heard him sigh heavily. "The first time you contacted me, I thought nothing of it. Every time since that, I've wondered, Why is this girl so interested in who I am and what I do? Why me? I knew I was not an obvious choice for someone you would write about in the *colegio internacional* newspaper."

"Elio, I—"

"I suspected the past would come around to me again sometime in my life, and the more time I spent with you the more I began to imagine it was this. I felt some connection with you when we met, but I couldn't pinpoint it. Now I understand. It makes sense that I would immediately like my own daughter, even if I'd never met her before. But what is it that you want, exactly? I have a family. As you know."

"Please, just come to the graduation breakfast with me," I said. I had no idea I was going to ask him. The words just popped out of my mouth, and I immediately wondered whether I had made a huge mistake. I went with it anyway. "I'll never ask anything of you again. I'm leaving Mexico anyway. You have nothing to lose."

"I could not do that," he said, taking the deepest breath I'd ever heard. I was about to say that I understood, I wasn't thinking, and should never have suggested such a thing.

"Unless your mother agreed."

I told her the minute she lugged her suitcase through the door. Not about my arrest; that's a secret to this day. We were standing in the living room, she by the door, I on the other side of the coffee table, in case I needed to make a run for it out the door, were she to completely blow up.

"You *told* him? Do you have any idea how much trouble we're in? I could not have been more clear that you weren't to mention it!"

"Mom, he was suspicious. And he thinks I figured it out on my own."

"Which you did. Against what I told you."

"Come on. He agreed. He said he thought it would come back around to him sometime. As long as I don't tell anyone how, he'll do me this favor of letting me be around my parents, *my parents,* just once in my life. This is the only opportunity that I'll ever have, and I deserve it."

My mother started to walk over to where I stood, and I moved around the coffee table, hoping she wouldn't slap me. But she didn't come close. She went over to the big bay window that looked out over our garden, the two palm trees linked together by the hammock tied to each end.

"It's going to be strange," she said when she finally spoke. "I only met him once."

I sat down on the couch.

"He can come to the breakfast, then?"

"All right, Milagro." She came over and sat down next to me. "So," she said. "Was he surprised?"

"No, and that surprised *me* at first. But then again, he seems like a man who's seen it all. I doubt anything could shock him."

~ ~ ~

The morning of the breakfast, my mother and I got up much earlier than we needed to and sat in the kitchen reading the newspaper.

"Are you nervous?" I asked her.

"That's a silly question," she said. "Of course I'm nervous. No, not nervous. Try terrified."

"He's perfectly nice."

"You don't know him." Maggie turned a page of her newspaper. "Oh my God, Milagro." I looked over at my mother. Her hands were shaking.

"What? Are you having a panic attack? It's going to be all right!"

She shook her head violently and handed me the newspaper page she'd just flipped to.

"Did you know about this?" she asked, her voice trembling.

I looked at the headline.

"Oh. My. Fucking. God."

EXCLUSIVE: DE LA GARZA ADMITS PATERNITY, it read, above some stock photo of Elio in a tux. "Top Official Acknowledges He Is Father of Seventeen-Year-Old American Girl." The photo and caption were followed by an article full of quotes from Elio about my mother and me. He'd painted what I found to be an overly flattering picture of me, telling the reporter he was happy that I'd found him, and how smart I was in tracking him down. "I welcome her into my family," he'd said. "I'm not proud of my affair, but I fully accept Mila. What father wouldn't? She is an intelligent, pretty, and talented young woman who is going places in the world."

Then the gate buzzer rang. I looked at the kitchen clock. It was eight. It was him. I ran to the door.

"Why on earth would you do this?" I demanded.

"I couldn't take the chance that people would find out on their own," he said. "And you know they would have." He was very calm, dressed formally in a black jacket, white shirt, and burgundy tie.

"What about Laura?"

"Of course I told her before calling my friend at the paper," he said. "She may leave, or look the other way. We aren't sure yet. But she agreed that coming out with this was the right thing to do. I couldn't carry around such a large secret anymore, especially now that you've found me anyway."

"Aren't you going to invite Señor de la Garza inside?" my mother asked, coming up behind me.

I watched their movements carefully. For a moment, they looked at each other without saying a word. Then Elio leaned over and kissed Maggie on the cheek. She clutched his forearm a second longer.

"I'd have thought you would be too humiliated to show up after this," my mother said to him, holding up the paper. "What a surprise."

We all stood there for a moment, each taking in the other two. We all looked as if we thought we were dreaming and expected to wake up at any moment.

"He can't come in because we have to go," I finally said. "We're going to be late."

"Wait," said my mother. "There's something I want to give you for your graduation present."

She went to her room and came back with a palm-size wrapped box.

"Go on, open it now," she said.

I untied the ribbon and gently ripped open the wrapping paper. Inside the padded box was a silver necklace.

"Your *milagro* neckace?" I said, my eyes widening in surprise. There were so many *milagros* on it, but two in particular immediately caught my eye: the hen and the little girl.

"I want you to have it," she said.

"I remember that necklace," said Elio. He reached for it, and I handed it to him. He opened it and clasped it around my neck. "There," he said, turning me around, hands on my shoulders. "Beautiful."

"Full fucking circle," I mumbled, running my fingers over the charms. The *milagros,* whether they held some kind of mystical power or not, had been responsible for my existence. They had brought my mother and Elio together, however briefly. As I watched my parents standing beside each other, I realized that maybe I did believe in miracles after all. Maybe I'd even created one.

My mother whipped around in the doorway, the ends of her hair, which she was wearing loose, fanning my face.

"Don't curse, Milagro," she said, and we were on our way.

Everybody stared when we walked into the banquet room of the fancy hotel in Polanco. From the shock on all their faces, I could see that most of them had read the morning paper, and those who hadn't had heard about it. They seemed a little unsettled, as if contemplating their own family secrets. My situation must have reminded them that things were usually not just as they seemed, that complicated ripples interrupted the still waters in all our lives. We could be sucked down by the undertow when we least expected it, or we would find a way through it. Suddenly, the Coyoacán psychic's words sprang to mind once again: "You have to be ready to know your destiny before it finds you. The spirit won't reveal himself to you until you are ready. But when he does, he will reveal himself completely."

"When did your mother date him?" Catalina whispered to me in the bathroom. "I thought he was married."

"He is," I said. "And they never dated." Catalina looked unsettled, and opened her mouth presumably to ask more questions, but I just smiled and walked out, back to the table where my parents were waiting.

After we sat down to eat our fruit plates and pastries, Mr. Horney made a speech about the senior class, a group of people who'd grown up together, who had all been friends for so many years. I looked around the room. People had tears in their eyes. Most of them *had* known one another since childhood. Horney ran a video that projected onto a large pull-down screen. It showed the fresas in montage: as children, at first-grade parties, in middle-school scenes where even Manuel looked awkward and Beatriz had a bad perm, braces, and a big nose. The group grew up in fast motion, a mélange of shots of them smiling, laughing, their arms around one another. It was then that I realized that even if Elio *were* my father in a regular sort of way, if it turned out that I could have been one of them after all, it didn't matter anymore. I hadn't been around for all the memories, and for the first time in my life I didn't mind that.

After breakfast, when people were sitting around talking, not wanting to leave for the graduation ceremony quite yet, Manuel came over to where I was sitting with my mother and Elio.

"Will you take a walk with me?" he asked.

"Why?"

"I want to tell you something."

"It's okay," said my mother. "You can go." She'd been sharing Foreign Service adventure stories with Elio, who listened with interest. I stood up and followed Manuel out of the banquet room.

We went out into the garden and walked on the path. The sun was bright in the middle of the morning sky, the dewy haze beginning to lift.

"How are you?" he asked.

"Is that what you want, to get the details straight from the source?"

"I'm not talking about the article. I wanted to tell you I know what really happened that night on senior trip, when you disappeared with—"

"I already told you what happened."

"Well, that's what Alejandro said, too. I'm sorry I didn't believe you."

"You asked Alejandro?"

"I had to know for sure. By the way, everybody's talking about you," he said.

"I figured as much."

Manuel looked so handsome in his suit and tie. He put his arms around my waist and looked me straight in the eyes.

"I *have* missed you," I said.

"There's good news. You won't have to, if you don't want. This is what I wanted to say."

"What is it?"

"I'm going to MIT."

"You are? What about your mother?"

"She was the one who convinced me to go," he said. "She said I had to go live my life. I decided I want to do that with you, if you'll allow it."

I looked into his blue eyes and saw that he meant this. So matter could come back out from a black hole, after all. I'd buried a father figure, but found a father. Manuel pulled me in and kissed me. It felt certain again.

"There is one good thing in everything that's happened," he said.

"Really, what?"

"I don't have to major in engineering or go to medical school anymore if I don't want to. I'll give MIT a year, since I'm already in, then switch to an art school, study painting. I heard there's a great program at Massachusetts College of Art."

I felt a smile steal over my face.

"I'm so proud of you," I said.

"We're still going to be neighbors."

We sat down on the lawn, holding hands and watching some peacocks strut about, and I felt hopeful. Could I, a girl who had never lived in one country longer than a few years, really end up with a guy I met in high school?

The one U.S. tradition that had actually caught on at ISM was the senior prom. But it would be the Mexican version—no parties in motel rooms, no school gym or cheap party-room rental. The student council rented out the Hacienda de los Morales in Polanco, a sprawling estate with rolling grassy lawn, complete with peacocks and swans, that was known as the banquet hall for upscale weddings. The building was in the traditional hacienda style—long wooden beams across the ceiling and clay-tile floors. Prom was BYOB. By that point, everyone was presumed to be eighteen, though teachers looked the other way when senior boys brought their underclass girlfriends. Teachers and Mr. Horney were in attendance, but not as chaperones. It was the one night that any bad feelings were set aside and everyone got drunk and danced together.

We got our yearbooks the day of the prom, which was also the last day of school. It had come so fast. I flipped to my senior page to see my picture next to the quotes I'd submitted. The deadline for turning the pages in had been the middle of September, so I had no one to publicly write to, no inside jokes or tongue-in-cheek comments to put after friends' boldfaced names.

Milagro Márquez

"Time doesn't wait, the circle isn't round."

—Antes de la Lluvia

"The road to the Western Lands is devious, unpredictable. Today's easy passage may be tomorrow's death trap. The obvious road is almost always a fool's road, and beware the Middle Roads, the roads of moderation, common sense, and careful planning. However, there is a time for planning, moderation, and common sense."

—William S. Burroughs, who came here, too

Nina flew back from boarding school to go to the prom. Memo was taking her; she told me they'd kept in touch, after all. She was still skinny but less drawn and hollow than before. Boarding school, with its reassuring structure, may have been exactly what she needed. She would be doing a thirteenth year of high school to get her grades and test scores up.

We got ready at her house before Manuel and Memo picked us up. In the bathroom adjoining her room, Nina's makeup supplies were strewn all over the long marble counter. I plucked extra-black eyeliner out of the pile.

"Since you're moving to Boston, it will be just like old times again," said Nina, layering on burgundy lip gloss. "I go into the city every weekend."

"Maybe," I said. "But I'm going to have to work really hard in the fall. My mother's moving to Greece, and I'm going up early for summer classes." I dabbed pressed powder on my nose. "Did I tell you I'm double-majoring in journalism and psychology?"

"Sounds intense," Nina said. "Then how about I visit you over Thanksgiving break?"

I shrugged. "Let's play it by ear."

The doorbell rang with a hollow *clang-clang*. I heard Concepción letting the guys in.

"They're here!" said Nina. "I'm so excited Memo's my date. I couldn't believe it when he said yes on the phone when I asked him last month. . . . I mean, I was so messed up that time in Valle. I guess he really missed me after I left. How do I look?" she asked.

"More beautiful than ever," I said, and hugged her. "Come on, they're waiting."

"You know, Mila, you seem so much happier."

"I think I might be," I said. "I'm going to the best school I could have gotten accepted to, Manuel's going to practically live next door, and my mother and I are on better terms. And there's the Elio thing, of course."

"Not having that be this big question hanging over your head must be a relief."

"Wow, Nina. I'm impressed."

"Impressed?"

"You're actually listening."

"It's all that talking therapy they make us do," she said. "I'm all talked out. Want to go?" Nina smiled, and I realized that she looked happier, too. It could have been our excited anticipation of the end of high school, but I hoped it would last.

I made my way down the long, spiraling staircase carefully clutching the banister so that I wouldn't trip over the hem of my dress.

"You look amazing, but no way did it take that long for you to get this hot," said Manuel, taking my hand as we walked down the long driveway to the waiting car.

The fresa girls were arriving in stretch limos and thousand-dollar dresses, their dates, with slicked-back hair and tuxedos, in tow. My table was an interesting combination of the friends I'd made during the course of the year: Kai and his date, a cute boy who didn't go to ISM; Nina and Memo; Naldo, Gabriel, Gabi, Alana and her boyfriend, who was tall and fiercely handsome, with black hair, equally dark eyes, and olive skin, and whose commanding presence made her usually fiery disposition turn demure. Manuel and Memo's fresa friends were all at the next table. I spotted Dave across the room, wearing his baseball cap with his tux, reminding me of the way he wore it with a suit when we worked in the visa barn. It was the last time that all of these people would be in a room together, and the first time they'd all been at the same party.

"So what did you guys decide about school?" I asked Naldo and Kai, who were sitting near me at our round table. "I feel like I haven't seen either of you in so long."

"With good reason, between your boyfriend and your father," said Kai. "I'm going to San Francisco State. I'm thinking biology and premed, then I'll try to get into UCSF for med school."

"Wow, a budding doctor," I said. "That's a new ambition, isn't it?"

"Pretty much," he said, and shrugged. "As much as I love dancing, I've always been good at science, and I want to help people. Plus, moving to San Francisco is basically gaining entry into paradise."

"Or at least the hottest gay clubs. And how about you?" I asked Naldo.

"USC," he said. "I got a water-polo scholarship. They have one of the top teams in the States. Hopefully, I'll go pro."

"Hopefully?" Nina chimed in. "If you don't, you'll be screwed for life," she joked.

"I have other interests," Naldo protested.

"Oh, yeah? Such as?" she insisted.

"Hey, Mila, let's go dance," Kai said to me, and we left the twins bickering at the table.

"So that thing with the article was pretty crazy," he said as we made our way onto the hardwood dance floor, which took up half the room.

"Yeah, talk about coming clean," I said.

"Are you doing okay?"

"Great, actually. My father is like, well, my father."

"You seem to be hitting it off."

"We have things in common, aside from our DNA."

"How's that?" he asked.

"His personality—he seems laid-back, but you can tell there are all kinds of things going on in his mind. He's genuine but secretive."

"That does sound like you. I think it's great that you found him. Everyone thinks so."

"I don't know if the fresas do."

"They're just worried you're going to out-fresa all of them now that he's claimed you as his. And I'm sure they're wondering what secrets their own parents are hiding. Everyone's a little freaked out by the whole thing."

"I figured as much."

"Can I cut in?" I heard Manuel say behind me. I turned around.

"Go on, steal her away," Kai said lightheartedly. He headed back toward the table.

"How's it going?" asked Manuel.

"So far? I've had two cocktails and one conversation about my father."

"Only one? People are dying to hear all about it—they just don't have the courage to come over and ask."

"I guess you're right—they *are* talking about me."

"And what's the saying about that?"

"Better to be talked about than not?"

"Exactly, *princesa*. You've caused quite the dramatic end to our year."

After eating, drinking, and dancing for a few hours, Manuel and I decided to leave. We went down to Coyoacán so I could see the plaza one last time. The man with the oversized windup music box lent his hat to the earth, welcoming donations of spare pesos as clamorous laughter and conversation rose from nighttime revelers at outdoor cafés. We picked up corn on the cob slathered in mayo, cheese, and chili from the woman who was always there, with her thick black braid down to her waist and her gold front tooth. Her eyes crinkled up when she smiled.

"I'm going to miss this," I said, looking around the plaza. "I'm just glad I'm not going to have to miss *you*."

We went to Hijo del Cuervo, then to Medusas. Manuel's driver waited for us outside almost until dawn, when we asked him to drive us to Chapultepec Park. We watched the sun rise through the mist, illuminating the horizon in a coral-pink haze as we walked around the lake.

"I wonder when I'll see another Mexico City sunrise," I said.

"You've seen so many," said Manuel.

"I'll never forget the one in Real de Catorce. It was magical, the silence of the desert, the way it was all orange, like it was on fire. . . ."

"I want to go there with you. How about next year—what's your schedule like in the summer?"

I smiled. "Remember when we first met?"

"Yeah." He laughed. "I thought you were a little bit crazy with those *caracoles* on your skirt and that purple hair. Beautiful and intriguing, but crazy."

"So why did you ask me out, then?"

"Because you were so different from all the girls I usually dated. I liked you from the first time I saw you in chemistry class. Remember? I smiled at you and you looked down at your book. I could see you were having a hard time here, and I knew I could make you happy."

"That's presumptuous. But . . . you were right," I said. "And how about now? Still think I'm crazy?"

"Now I know it's more like mad-scientist eccentricity, something between intelligence and living on another planet." He wrapped his arms around my shoulders. "But in a good way, a way that made me forget all the superficial things I thought were important. You made me realize for the first time in my life that it doesn't matter what other people think; you just have to go with what you feel. And I was right about you. I had a good feeling about those snails."

I smiled and looked out across the lake. We were silent for a while. The sun blazed through the smog, and workers at the pedal-boat stand were already putting the boats into the water. They'd be open soon.

"It's daylight," I said. "I have to get home."

My flight was the day after next and I hadn't even begun to pack up my room. The Embassy movers would be back in a few hours, bubble-wrapping our furniture, carrying out those familiar boxes labeled "Fragile" and "This Side Up." Then the painters would come, covering over the hideous bright walls I'd grown used to, redoing them in fresh white for the next Foreign Service tenants. I wondered who they would be.

My mother was due in Athens for language training in a week, so I was taking my first journalism class at Harvard during summer session, which was the only way they'd let me move into my dorm early. I could have gone to Greece with Maggie, but the idea of heading straight to another enormous, smoggy city where I didn't know a soul or speak the language wasn't something I was all that eager to jump right into. I was ready to be on my own, in a place that would become familiar. Somewhere I could stay for as long as I wanted.

After a restless sleep, I rose to pack up my life yet again. With my suitcase in the middle of the bedroom floor, I finally started figuring out what to throw away and what was worth keeping. In the end, the "keep" pile was smaller than I'd expected. I dumped my desk drawers into the trash. I kept my diaries, and my clear-sleeved binder full of newspaper clippings. I will use all this one day, I thought, rereading old entries and piecing the year together in my mind.

When I picked up the mail from under the gate that afternoon, there was a purple envelope addressed to me. I recognized the handwriting immediately. I tore it open: a card that read "Congratulations!" in cursive, girly script.

June 1

Dear Mila,

I'm so happy for you. Now maybe you'll get back on track—you better if you're gonna make it there! I'm going to Tufts, so, yes, we'll be in the same city again. Call my parents for my number when you get there. Since you're not going to be insane anymore (I hope!), we should patch things up. Just, please, no more fake robberies.

Always,
Nora

PS: Do you have e-mail yet? I just got it. My address is *nora94@earthlink.net*

E-mail, e-mail. I could have sworn we had that somewhere, I thought, sitting in front of the computer, clicking around on different programs. Correspondence was starting to go electronic. Outlook? This must be it.

To: "Nora" *nora94@earthlink.net*
From: "Epstein, Maggie" *mageps@compuserve.com*
Re: I figured this out!!
Nora,
I got your card, thank you! I'm so excited we're both going to live near Boston. It will be like old times in D.C., only we'll be older and wiser, right? I have *so* much to tell you, I can't even get into it anywhere but in person. You are not going to believe it. Stay tuned.
xoxo,
milagro

I met Elio at Lugar de la Mancha the day before I left.

"Don't order the fondue," I said. He gave me a quizzical look. "The melons aren't good," I whispered.

"Ah, okay then. How about *queso fundido* and coffee afterward?"

"Great," I said, smiling. He gave our order to the waitress.

"So, *Milagro*. I never knew that was your name. It's so funny."

"Don't remind me," I said. Then something occurred to me. "You don't know why that's my name, do you?" I asked.

"Because Maggie is a, how do you say, *hippie*?"

"Besides that, there's a reason."

"That you're a beautiful miracle?"

"You know the other meaning, too. I was a huge surprise."

"Really?" he asked. "How is that?"

"What, you didn't know she couldn't get pregnant?"

"Maybe it wasn't me. Maybe it was *concepción inmaculada*."

I laughed. "I don't think so, Señor Marquez de la Garza."

"Do you know the story of Coatlicue, the mother of Aztec gods?"

"No, what?"

"She was impregnated by a ball of feathers."

I laughed. "That is singularly the most ridiculous story I've ever heard. Not that I don't admire the Aztecs. The universe only knows that in my constant search for meaning I've adapted part of their belief system."

"Oh, have you?" he said, his voice light with skepticism.

"You know, that time goes in circles and all. It makes sense. Everything else does—the seasons, the earth on its axis, the cars in the *glorietas*, our lives."

"That's very creative, Mila," he said. "So is the Coatlicue story. She was the predecessor of the Virgen de Guadalupe, by a long time." Then his smile faded. "You look so much like my child. You always seemed familiar, but I think this is the first time I'm noticing how truly alike we are."

I pulled my pocket mirror out of my purse. I got up out of my chair and walked over to his side of the table, crouching down next to him. I held the mirror up. It was large enough to show only half of my face and half of his. Our eyes were the same shade of forest green. You could have put one of each on one face and there would be little distinction. I held the mirror up as though it were a camera taking our picture.

"DNA is amazing, isn't it?" I said.

He took his wallet from his pocket and pulled out a picture of his family.

"My daughter is twenty-three," he said. "In this photo, she is your age."

I looked at the photo. I could have been her. She could have been me.

"You have very dominant genes," I said to Elio.

"Strong ones," he said. "Do you want to meet her up in Cambridge? She's graduating this coming year."

"You think she'd even want to meet me?"

"I already told her about you, before that story went to press. Daniela is very kind. There's no denying you're going to be a part of my life from now on. I'll give her your number when you're settled and have her call you up for lunch."

"It feels so strange to suddenly have a half sister. And a half brother, too. What about your son, Carlos? Will I meet him, too?"

"Yes, Mila," said Elio. "We have all the time in the world now."

"What does your name mean, anyway?" I asked. "I've never heard anything like it before."

"It comes from *helio*," he said. "The Greek word for *sun*."

"Center of the solar system, huh?"

"It all revolves around me," he said, and laughed.

"What did Freud say about jokes?" I said, teasing him back.

"I thought it was accidents."

"Either way."

We ate our *queso fundido*, then we drank our coffee. Years later, I would lightheartedly compare my father to Prince Albert II of Monaco, when I read in the newspapers that the prince had admitted to fathering a fourteen-year-old who lived in California with her mother. She was a regular girl one day, a princess the next. I clipped the article and sent it to my father, who also found the parallels amusing.

I will never know whether Elio was the one who helped Gustavo Amador become Amado Carillo-Fuentes's plastic surgeon, whether he was on the drug cartels' books, whether he was a corrupt politician or not, good cop or bad cop. What could I do about it, anyway? I finally understood how the fresas dealt with who their parents were; they just did, they had to. You didn't choose your family. Sometimes you didn't even choose your friends. Elio was a part of my life now, and he'd grown to occupy that place naturally, by virtue of our deepening friendship. I was glad he'd filled that blank space I'd always carried around inside me—a particular, peculiar void in a daughter, a space reserved for a father, a space that only a father can fill.

THIRTEEN

Adios, Mexico

Thunderclouds gathered in the afternoon. The rainy season came again.

I stood in the crowded international terminal of Benito Juárez Airport. I might return to Mexico someday, but I couldn't know if I would ever live here again. I recalled the Aztec dancers in Plaza Coyoacán with the bronze-tinged bells on their ankles, beating drums, chanting, forever dancing in circles.

Manuel and my mother stood with me in front of Gate 43, Benito Juárez to Logan, one simulacrum of my life to another.

"Are you sure you don't want to stay the summer and work in the visa barn?" my mother joked. "It's not too late to change your mind."

"I'd love to, but we don't live here anymore." I smiled. She was spending four days with me in Boston, helping me move and get settled, since she was the expert. Then she'd catch her connecting flight to Athens.

I picked up my carry-on. "I can't wait to visit you over Christmas break," I said. "Island-hopping in December."

My mother looked at Manuel. "You should come, too."

"Thanks, Maggie. I might take you up on it, if my mother can join me."

"Of course, she's welcome anytime," she said.

I hugged Manuel, who would arrive at MIT in early August.

"I'll see you when we get there," he said.

"Don't forget," I said, passing him a note I'd written in the car: "Caracoles bring their homes everywhere they go. They move slowly, the way we came back to each other." I waved to him as I walked down the mobile hallway to the plane.

"I miss you already, Milagro," my mother said as we settled into 14A and B, I in the window seat as usual.

"Mom, it's Mila," I was about to say, when I realized that for once, for a change, I didn't feel embarrassed about the name. She buried her head in her newspaper. I took out my journal and pen.

I have always loved how runways have their own specific language, their secret pilot street signs: 16L-34R, 1-19, A ← B →. Waiting for takeoff, I thought of the elsewhere phenomenon, how when you're in one place you can't wait to get someplace else, then when you finally get there you long for what is past. I felt nostalgic and the plane hadn't even left the ground.

There is nothing like a flight to get you started thinking about where you came from and where you're headed. As I lifted off toward a new life in Cambridge, I looked down at the dust bowl, the volcano a dark mass in the night, the rolling-pin spread of twenty-five million now reduced to tiny points of light down below. I watched the receding patterns of the city as we ascended farther skyward. The city I hated at landing. The city I loved on takeoff. I'd been home, found home, and now I was off to the next one. I wanted to hold on to this moment somehow, wrap my arms around the entire urban sprawl, which extended out to all four horizons, for as far as I could see, even at this high altitude. The night sky above Mexico City was filled with stars.

They had been there all along, hidden from view, definitely present but out of sight. And I'd been there, down there, a minute swatch on the patchwork quilt, with its tiny fringes of wealth, its giant squares of poverty. They say this was a year of *revolución, devaluación, corrupción y erupción* in Mexico—referring to the EZLN in Chiapas, the devaluating peso, Colosio's assassination, and Popocatépetl's near-explosion. It was chaotic for me, too. How could I keep such a large external force inside me, forever, no matter how far I went? As usual, I picked up my pen and began to write.

What if life isn't a circle but is shaped more like a snail's shell, spiraling in one direction toward a particular point?

I wrote about that moment with the snails on my skirt and thought of how it stood for the slow beginnings of what my life in Mexico City became. It resembled that model Nora and I had made of the DNA strains: just a representation of something far more complex. Maybe life also unraveled according to a code as predetermined as the spiraling strands of genetic instructions that program us to be who we are.

I'll never forgive my mother for naming me Milagro. Especially because she would never call me by a shortened version of it, as I'd told everyone to from the age of six. Though the milagros might be responsible for my entire existence.

When I came here, I didn't know who my father was, just that I must have resembled him. After all, my mother is the one who looks Mexican, not I. My green eyes were often mistaken for the effects of colored contact lenses.

We were high above now. I looked down at the pinpoints of light glowing below, mapping out the city, which I could see stretching endlessly in every direction, as though the smog had evaporated into the night. It was the clearest sky I had ever seen.

ACKNOWLEDGMENTS

I am immensely indebted to Jennifer Lyons, the most brilliant agent to ever serendipitously appear before an author in a UPS store. She ushered this book into the world with the utmost thoughtfulness, knowledge, and care. Thank you, Jennifer, the Harlem mailbox place, and good timing. I also must thank her brother, Charlie Lyons, who, after hearing five pages of the manuscript, said, "You should send this to my sister." Thanks to Charlie and the synchronicity that makes these things happen.

During the writing of *Mexican High*, I'd taped an article about Spiegel & Grau over my computer. Fortuitously, some months later, Cindy Spiegel acquired the novel and went from dream editor to real one. I'm deeply grateful to her for her tireless work on and enthusiasm for this book.

Others whose energy and drive were crucial in making the book happen—thanks to Meghan Walker, Gretchen Koss, Mike Cendejas, Ruth Mirsky, Hana Landes, Lucy Silag, Kelsey Nencheck, and Rowan Riley.

Gratitude to my mother, who knew I would do this before I had any idea, and who is not like Maggie at all, except for the tropical colors bit. Thanks, Grandma, for always being there for me. Thanks, Uncle Walt, my father, Tom & Bonnie Scheinman, Amy, Vika, and the rest of my wonderful family. Thank you, Grandpa. I miss you.

Thank you, Alex, who joked: "You should become a writer of avant-garde books," at some point during long e-mail exchanges in college.

Thank you to dear friends and earliest readers Eric Lupfer, Georgina Gatsiopoulos, Emre Ozpirincci, Jennifer Cacicio, Josie McGee, Abby Sher, and Anna Marrian for their encouragement, wise commentary, and enduring friendship.

Thanks to Sue Shapiro for sharing her contagious passion, drive, and dedication to the art and craft of writing. Thank you, Sue, and thanks to Alice Feiring, Kate Walter, Rich Prior, and Tony Powell.

I am infinitely grateful to the Jack Kerouac Project of Orlando writers-in-residence program for the beautiful house, the time and space, and the magical summer.

Thanks to Emerson College, Andie Avila, Carmen Scheidel and the team at Mediabistro, Paula Derrow, Daniel Jones, John Glassie, Nick Flynn, Daphne Merkin, Esther Haynes, Virginia Barber, Andy Cohen, Glenn Gordon, Helaine Olen, Kathy Ebel, Kate Greene, Joel Keller, Ana Dahlman, Kathleen O'Connell, Ethan J. Hon, and Laura Primis.

Thanks to Jay Mandel for hiring me into my first real job and for sharing your knowledge of the publishing industry. It would surely have been a much longer, winding road otherwise.

Muchísimas gracias a la Ciudad de México.